Courage

Makilien Trilogy - Book 2

Courage

Molly Evangeline

Living Sword Publishing

www.livingswordpublishing.com

Courage
Makilien Trilogy – Book 2
Copyright © 2012 by Molly Evangeline

Published by Living Sword Publishing

www.makilien.com
www.mollyevangeline.com

Cover Design and Map
© Molly Evangeline

Cover Images
© Molly Evangeline
© mike_experto - Fotolia.com

All Scriptures are taken from the New American Standard Bible, Copyright © 1960, 1962, 1963, 1968, 1971, 1972, 1973, 1975, 1977, 1995 by The Lockman Foundation. Used by permission. www.Lockman.org

ISBN 13: 978-0983774013
ISBN 10: 0983774013

Contents

DOLENNAR MAP

PRONUNCIATION GUIDE

CHARACTER GUIDE

BOOKS BY MOLLY EVANGELINE

To the One who is my courage through tough decisions, spiritual battles, and hard times. You hold me up and lead me on even when I think I can no longer stand.

To my mom and dad for all their love, support, encouragement, and for providing me with a home where I am encouraged to pursue my dreams. And to my little brother, Sam, for so enthusiastically helping me with anything I ask from supplying all kinds of ideas in the creation process of Tanzim to being my photographer. We've had some fun times.

Be strong and let your
heart take COURAGE, All you
who hope in the Lord.
- Psalms 31:24

:Chapter One:

Consequences

Makilien bit down hard, squeezing her eyes shut. Tears leaked from beneath her eyelids, but she brushed them away. Pulling her knees up closer to her chest, she clutched the front of her dress against her throat and tried to block out the pain that snatched her breath away.

"Sorry." Aedan's voice was low with sympathy. "I'm almost done."

He rinsed a bloodied cloth in a basin of warm water and carefully finished cleaning one of several long, deep cuts across Makilien's back. Once the blood had been wiped away and no other wounds bled freshly, he laid the cloth aside.

"There. I'm finished."

Makilien exhaled deeply and took a moment to collect herself. Then she pushed to her feet, holding her torn dress against her shoulders. She turned to her friend, eyes full of gratitude. "Thank you, Aedan."

He nodded but his own gaze expressed concern as he asked, "Are you sure you don't want to go to your mother for help with the bandages?"

Makilien had to shake her head despite her longing to do just that. Contact with her family would only risk their safety.

"No, I'll manage," she answered quietly.

She turned and ducked into her small tent where she knelt down and reached for a roll of bandages. Steeling herself, she began the tedious and painful process of bandaging herself as best she could. It took time, but when she finished, she sighed heavily and wiped perspiration from her forehead.

Laying her torn dress aside to mend, she changed into a new one and left the tent. Outside, she straightened, grimacing, and scanned the small riverside camp at the edge of Reylaun. There were two tents—hers and Aedan's—and a fire built between them. Except for a short line tied between two trees where Makilien dried clothes, the camp was bare.

Aedan sat by the fire, and Makilien sank down across from him. They looked at each other.

"So it was a trap," Aedan said. "Reece acted as bait."

"Yes," Makilien murmured, vivid memories from that morning quick to replay in her mind. She'd secretly met Reece in the old barn nearby to talk to him about Elohim only to have armed guards appear as soon as she was finished. It was now the second time she'd had to endure the agony of being whipped.

"I don't think he meant to see me hurt," Makilien said after a moment of silent thought. "I think he was overcome by fear and felt he had to go to Vayzar."

Aedan quietly stared at the fire. He didn't want to speak or think badly of Reece, but it bothered him deeply that the man had given Makilien up to Vayzar, frightened or not. Having endured his share of beatings, he hated to see Makilien face such punishment.

At her sigh, he looked up.

"My father was there this morning, in the square. I felt terrible for him. I know he wanted to do something, but was powerless." Makilien paused thoughtfully. "But I always hope that maybe seeing how strongly I believe will open his eyes to the truth."

The greatest disappointment Makilien had faced since returning home from her adventures was her parents' unwillingness to believe and accept the truth she shared with them. She knew it was largely out of fear, but it was something that weighed heavily on her every day, especially when others overcame their fear to believe.

Aedan understood just how she felt. His own mother and sister, and his mother's new husband, would not believe either. His parents had wanted nothing to do with Makilien once she began sharing her stories, afraid of the trouble it might bring them. They'd tried everything to get Aedan to stay away from her, but the two of them were in this together. Of everyone, he had been the very first to believe what Makilien shared with him and trust Elohim.

"Do you ever consider leaving?" Aedan asked suddenly.

"I think about it," she confessed. "There are times, like this morning, when I desperately want to, but I know it's not time for that . . . not yet." She stared at him for a moment. "But you can go. You don't have to stay for me."

Though it was one of Aedan's greatest desires to leave Reylaun, to see and experience all Makilien had, she and her mission were more important than his dreams of leaving.

"I won't leave until you do."

"That may never happen," Makilien warned.

"Then it never happens."

Makilien smiled in deep gratitude, immensely thankful for Aedan and his unwavering loyalty, which had helped see her through many tough times.

"Well." Aedan rose. "I should head over to the butcher. Cal promised me pay if I helped him butcher one of his cows today. Maybe I can even bring back some meat for supper."

"That would be wonderful. I don't want to sound ungrateful for what we have, but you can only eat so much fish and rabbits before you start to tire of them."

Aedan chuckled and agreed. "Is there anything you need me to do before I go?"

"No, I'll be all right. Actually, I was hoping I could find work too. I don't expect to though, not after news of this morning gets around."

"Be careful," Aedan cautioned. The guards would keep an especially close watch on Makilien for the next couple days.

"I will."

Alone at camp, Makilien sat in silence for a while, watching the small fire burn down and thinking, as she so often did, of the events and the people who had changed her life. At times she missed her friends so desperately it was painful, and even times when she found herself fearful of the future. Today was a day her fortitude wobbled a little. But to combat it, she turned to prayer. Meniah had promised her she would never be alone and to take courage in that.

"I don't feel as strong today as I do other days," she murmured, "but I know Your strength will prevail in my weakness. The enemy is always trying to fill me with fear and doubt and make me abandon this mission. Help me ignore the lies and have courage to go on each day."

Being reminded of the presence she knew was there, she was ready to face the rest of the day, whatever may come of it. She rose, forced to move more slowly than normal, and left camp.

The sun shone high above the treetops by now, and the village was fully awake and bustling with those going about their daily business. As Makilien passed her first group of villagers, she smiled, but she knew the news of her punishment had already reached them when they did not smile in return. They stared blankly and hurried on as if they had not seen her. Others ignored her entirely. A young child pointed in her direction, but the girl's mother grabbed her hand and hurried her along.

Makilien had grown used to these reactions, but they stung nonetheless. More than half the people in the village looked upon her as an outcast. Many she once called friends avoided her, and most of those who still cared deep down were too fearful to associate with her. They wondered why she insisted on alienating herself, but all Makilien had to do was remember what had brought her back here to know she was doing right.

For most of the morning, she wandered around Reylaun, asking anyone she could for jobs. She and Aedan needed money for supplies, but finding work had become difficult. For anyone to give them aid was not looked kindly upon. Their closest friends offered them odd jobs and errands when they could, but today Makilien could find no such work.

At last, she stopped and glanced up at the sun. Midday was nearly upon her. With a sigh she headed toward camp, hot and tired. Along the way, someone called her name. She turned. Her little sister Leiya ran toward her. Though Makilien tried to have as little contact with her family as possible, denying her sister a chance to speak with her was a difficult thing to do.

When Leiya reached her, Makilien knelt at her level. The seven-year-old's face was drawn in distress.

Makilien rested her hands on her sister's shoulders. "Leiya, what's wrong?"

Leiya's lip trembled. "I heard you were punished again."

"Oh, Leiya. I'm all right. Really."

But the little girl was not comforted. "I don't like it when you're hurt. I want you to go back to Eldor so you won't be hurt anymore."

Her sister's concern touched Makilien's heart. "I am fulfilling a purpose here. This is where Elohim wants me. But, if He tells me it is time for me to leave, I'm taking you, Mother and Father, and Aedan with me."

"I've been praying every day for Elohim to take care of you and make it so you can leave," Leiya told her, careful to keep her voice low.

Makilien smiled widely, amazed by her little sister's faith when she herself had struggled for so long for the same kind of faith. "Thank you, Leiya. Keep praying. Elohim is always listening. Now, you should go. It's not safe for you to be here with me."

"I miss you, and I miss hearing your stories," Leiya murmured. "I wish you could come home."

"I know. So do I." But Makilien couldn't offer any more comfort than a hug. "I love you so much."

"I love you too."

Knowing the danger of being together, Makilien gently urged Leiya to go. With one last longing look at her sister, the little girl hurried away. Makilien stood and watched, her eyes prickling with tears. This was the hardest part of her mission.

Before Makilien could make herself move on, a voice spoke behind her, low and oozing with mock sympathy.

"Oh, how sad."

Makilien bit down hard to keep from retorting and getting herself into more trouble. She turned, coming face to face with the owner of the voice—Vayzar, the most hated man in Reylaun. They stood perfectly eye to eye, the two of them. However, though Vayzar was shorter than most men, he commanded complete respect and obedience. He held the position of Reylaun's governor, appointed by Zirtan to maintain order in the village. He was the greatest reason the people shunned Makilien. They blamed her for his presence. Before she had begun sharing the truth about Elohim, the people had been left alone to govern themselves aside from the guards, but now they had to endure Vayzar's strict rule.

Vayzar's cold, dark eyes speared into Makilien's as he stepped close. "It would not have to be this way, you know. Having to live in that little camp at the edge of the village, shunned by the people, and separated from your family. All you'd have to do is show some loyalty."

His persuasive, almost caring tone might fool some, but not Makilien. "My loyalties lie elsewhere. You know that as well as I do."

Vayzar narrowed his eyes. "One of these days, Lord Zirtan will tire of your rebellion. I would be very frightened if I were you."

Makilien held her tongue. At times, the thought of what might happen did frighten her, but she had faith in Elohim and His protection.

When she would not reply, Vayzar grew impatient with his failed attempts to goad her into foolish action. He motioned to his two bodyguards. They turned to walk on by, but Vayzar stopped before he had passed Makilien and put a heavy hand on her shoulder. In a hard voice, he warned, "I'm watching you closely."

He squeezed her shoulder tightly where one of her wounds was. Excruciating pain shot through her nerves, but Makilien tried not to give him the satisfaction of seeing her react. Finally, he released her and stalked off. Makilien glared after him. When he was out of sight, she grimaced and gingerly touched her throbbing shoulder, blinking at the tears in her eyes. She drew in a deep breath to calm herself and went on her way.

She was glad to reach camp. Though disappointed not to have found work, she now wanted time to herself. Meeting her sister and her confrontation with Vayzar had wreaked havoc on her emotions. She retrieved her torn dress and sewing kit from her tent and walked down to the river. She once hated its trickling sound, but now it soothed her. Sitting in the soft grass along the bank, she set to work mending her dress. This quiet task offered her the perfect opportunity to pray and collect herself again.

The bubbling of the river and the sweet singing of the birds in the trees above reminded Makilien peacefully of Elimar, turning her thoughts once more to the adventures she'd had and her friends. For a long time her thoughts focused on them.

At the sudden snap of a twig, Makilien jumped up and instinctively touched her hip where a sword would have hung.

Upon seeing who it was, she slowly released her breath, allowing herself to relax as she faced the tall, lean young man.

"Derrin, you startled me."

"Sorry," he replied, his eyes dropping apologetically before returning to her face. "I thought you heard me."

It was true. Makilien was usually far more alert.

"I guess I was quite deep in thought."

"I didn't mean to disturb you."

"That's all right."

Awkward silence hung between them for a moment.

"Did you want something?" Makilien watched his expression fall from delight in seeing her, to concern.

"I heard about this morning," Derrin explained, regret lowering his voice. "I came to see if you were all right."

Makilien carefully bent to gather up her sewing. "I'll be fine."

"How did it happen?"

"Reece seemed to want to know more about Elohim so I met him this morning in the old barn. He must have become too fearful and told Vayzar. He had guards hidden there. They heard me tell Reece everything."

Makilien turned away from the river and walked back into camp. Derrin followed. When she stooped to gather wood to build up the fire again, he quickly came to her side. "I can do that for you."

At first, she wanted to say no, but she allowed him to help. She stood aside to watch him collect an armful of wood and carry it to the fire. He laid a couple pieces on the glowing embers. As he coaxed it along, he glanced up at Makilien, his dark blue eyes unsure, yet earnest.

"I hope this is the last time this happens to you."

"I don't think it will be," Makilien replied, fully resigned to that fact.

Derrin stood, brushing his hands against his pants. "Why not?"

"Because Vayzar is growing ever more wary of me, and I'm bound to get caught again."

This answer frustrated Derrin, and he couldn't help but show it as his voice rose a fraction. "Why are you doing this, Makilien? You've been put in the stocks more times than I can remember, and now you've been beaten twice. When is it going to be enough?"

"People need to know the truth," Makilien replied with quiet firmness, knowing full well he had no faith or interest in Elohim. "As long as I'm here, I won't stop trying to share it with them."

Derrin shook his head. "You've come back so changed. Changed . . . and scarred."

The regretful tone in which he said *scarred* bothered Makilien. She touched the scar on her cheek. Clearly he wished she did not have it, but Makilien had always been glad Meniah had left it when he'd healed her wound. It was a reminder, signifying how Elohim had used her.

"But you're back now," Derrin went on matter-of-factly. "Why won't you just live your life instead of always putting yourself at risk?" His tone was now pleading. "This is your home. Why do you refuse to make something of it?"

She watched him closely when he paused. He met her eyes and held them while Makilien mentally urged him not to take this conversation where she suspected he might.

"You know how I have always felt about you, Makilien. What is wrong with me that you feel nothing in return?"

Makilien looked away, suppressing a groan. "It's not that, Derrin. It's just that you and I are so different." Her gaze returned to him. "You were right about me, I am changed. I have seen and experienced things no one here could imagine. And my faith, it's everything to me, but we don't share that faith."

"There must be some way we can work things out," Derrin pressed.

Makilien shook her head with adamant resolve. "It's not that simple . . . I'm sorry."

With a quiet nod, Derrin hung his head and turned his back to her. Compassion squeezed Makilien's heart, and she wished she could say something to encourage him as he walked out of camp, but he was the one who would not give up his pursuit. Sighing, she took her eyes away and turned back to her work.

After putting her lunch over the fire to cook, she carried a pile of dirty laundry to the river and scrubbed one of her dresses on a rough stone along the edge. Channeling her frustration with the day into her action, she scrubbed hard, ignoring the pain it caused her back. It seemed everything had gone wrong today. A twinge of guilt pricked her for causing Derrin to feel such disappointment, but at the same time, she had no other choice.

Perhaps, if they had believed the same about Elohim and other circumstances had been different, she possibly could have found herself caring for him that way. After all, they'd been friends all their lives, and Derrin was not unattractive.

11

Over the years he'd grown from a rather awkward boy into the fine young man he was now, his once sandy-brown hair darkening to compliment his indigo eyes. But circumstances were not different, and Makilien felt nothing for him beyond friendship.

"If you scrub that dress any harder, you'll put a hole in it."

Makilien jumped, startled yet again. This time Aedan stood over her. Amusement played on his face, and Makilien glanced back to the dress.

"I guess I was overdoing it a little."

"You must be particularly annoyed about something."

Makilien stood and wrung out the dress. "Not really annoyed, just frustrated."

"About?"

"This day." Makilien sighed again, wiping her damp forehead and brushing back wisps of hair. All at once, weariness descended on her. "It's barely half over and already it feels long." She put her hands on her hips. "Derrin came to see me. I'm sure you can guess how that went. I also saw Leiya while I was looking for work. It's always so hard to see her when I can't spend time or go home with her. Then I had a little confrontation with Vayzar."

"You really should be resting," Aedan told her. "I'll help you hang up the clothes and then you can sit down."

Makilien exhaled loudly. "You're right." She gave him a little smile. "Thank you. I don't know how I'd do this without you."

:Chapter Two:

Found Out

"Thank you, Nita. Aedan and I are always grateful for your generosity."

The rounded, middle-aged woman smiled kindly at Makilien. "I only wish I could do more for you. I sure do appreciate your help."

"I enjoy helping out," Makilien told her. The other woman certainly needed it from time to time. With seven children and number eight on the way, her work was never done, and Makilien was glad the woman wasn't afraid to let her help.

"You enjoy this bread now, and come back for more if you need it." Nita handed Makilien a basket of two fresh loaves of bread.

"We certainly will. We haven't had bread in some time. Goodbye, Nita."

"Goodbye, Makilien."

Smiling to herself, Makilien left the little farm and walked down the street. She had not made much today, but it had been a good day. She loved working with Nita, and it was the first work she had found since her punishment four days ago. Makilien looked forward to telling Aedan once he came back from helping out at a nearby farm in an hour or so. With more of the meat he had brought back from the butcher and the bread Makilien had received, they would have one of the finest suppers they'd had in a long time.

She had just about reached camp when she froze. Two guards roamed the camp, tearing it apart and scattering what little Makilien and Aedan owned.

Before they could spot her, she dashed over to a nearby building. Setting down the basket of bread, she crept closer, using the trees for cover. Her heart beat hard. Something was not right. Guards had never come to their camp before. She came within hearing distance just as a third guard joined them.

"There's no sign of either of them along the river," he reported.

One of the guards, who had been rummaging through Makilien's belongings, stood. "No matter. Once Lord Vayzar has the girl's family, she'll show herself, and the boy won't be far behind."

Makilien gasped and clamped her hand over her mouth. Never had Vayzar outwardly threatened her family. Something had changed. Turning, she crept away from camp and rushed through the village, dread churning her stomach.

Once within sight of her home, she crouched behind the corner of a neighbor's house and surveyed the area. Four guards stood outside the front of her house. She glanced at the stable in back, seeing no one. Creeping around, she came to the tree she had always used to sneak in and out of her bedroom.

She climbed quietly and peaked through her bedroom window. The room was empty. She eased the window open and climbed through as voices drifted up from downstairs. Tiptoeing across the floor, she knelt in the middle of the room and lifted a loose floorboard. She reached down, her fingers grasping a long metal object wrapped in a piece of leather. She pulled it out and unwrapped her sword, her gift from Lord Darand.

Rising, Makilien buckled the sword's belt around her waist. With all caution she tiptoed to her door and eased it open so she could better hear the voices in the kitchen below.

"...my family has done nothing wrong."

Her father's voice was firm, but desperate.

"You should have better controlled your daughter," Vayzar retorted.

"We tried."

"You should have tried harder!"

"If you must take someone, take me," Néthyn insisted, "but leave my wife and daughter. They are not to blame for any of this."

"Forget it," Vayzar snapped. "Makilien's actions are far too serious for that, and she will learn so. Take them out!"

At the sound of footsteps and her parents' protests as they were dragged outside, Makilien's heart crashed against her ribs. She jumped up and ran back to the window. Climbing down the tree, she raced around the house and pulled her sword from its scabbard, sunlight dancing across the sharp steel blade. She came around the front of the house just as Vayzar and a large group of guards moved to take her family away.

"Stop!"

The men halted at the sound of her voice and spun around. Vayzar pushed his way to the head, followed by a group of men Makilien realized were not guards of Reylaun. Their clothes, though mostly black, were not the same, and none wore armor. The man leading this group, a tall, black-haired, dark eyed man caught Makilien's attention. Something about him seemed strangely familiar.

But she had more urgent matters to deal with. "I'm right here, Vayzar." She locked eyes with the wicked man. "Release my family."

Vayzar scoffed. "Release your family? I think not. You see, I've just learned the details of your escapades last summer. The details of how *you* are the one who killed General Zendon and are responsible for our defeat in Eldor, a most unfortunate setback."

Makilien's mouth dropped open. How did he know? Her friends had promised to keep her secret. She glanced at her family. They stared at her, confusion and questions in their eyes. She never had told them of her part in Eldor's victory, believing the information too dangerous. Grimacing over having kept it from them, she turned back to Vayzar and spoke with quiet confidence.

"You are right. I did meet Zendon in battle and mortally wound him, but my family had nothing to do with it. Let them go."

"Why don't *you* drop your sword and surrender?"

Makilien took her sword in both hands, holding it defensively. "Not until you release my family."

Scowling, Vayzar shoved one of his guards forward. "Disarm her and bring her here."

The guard pulled out his sword and strode toward her. Makilien carefully watched his every move. It had been over a year since she'd engaged in a life and death battle, but she was ready. The guard raised his blade. Makilien brought hers up and swung hard, batting the guard's sword away with a force that surprised him. Again, he raised his sword to attack, more determinedly this time, but Makilien's movements were much more fluid and practiced.

The fight was brief. After easily dodging an attack, Makilien maneuvered her sword around and cut into the guard's side. Though not a fatal wound, the guard stumbled away moaning. By now, another guard had rushed in to help. Just before he reached her, Makilien glanced at Vayzar. He scowled, his face darkening with disgust and rage.

Makilien found her next foe to be more experienced, yet still not a match for her. As hard as he tried, he could find no way to break through her defense. In the middle of the fight, a voice growled out, "Incompetent fools!"

Before Makilien knew it, the guard she fought was shoved aside, and the dark man took his place. He was much taller than her, one of the tallest men she had met. At once everything changed. His skill was far superior to that of the guards, and Makilien realized it instantly. Now she truly was in a fight for her life. Never before had she battled such a skilled opponent. His attacks came swift and unpredictably, eliminating any chance for Makilien to retaliate. She could barely react fast enough to defend herself.

She fought with desperation, but sensed the fight was already lost. At last, the man's superior skill and strength won out. In a flash of movement, his sword slashed down across her arm. Makilien groaned and retreated, but the strength of her opponent's next attack loosened her grip on her sword. Her left hand, tingling from the pain of her wound, slipped as her sword was knocked sideways. The next thing she knew, the razor sharpness of the man's blade pricked the sensitive skin of her throat. She swallowed, thinking in a moment she would be dead. However, the man did not kill her, though the loathing in his eyes told her he wanted to.

"Drop your sword."

Breathing heavily from pain and exertion, Makilien's eyes darted to her family, and she hung her head in defeat. She had done everything possible to defend them, but still had failed. She let her sword slip out of her hand, and it fell with a clatter to the ground.

The man slid his sword back into the scabbard and grabbed Makilien by the arm, careless of her wound. Her breath was snatched away by the sudden, sharp pain as he dragged her into the midst of the group. There, Vayzar gave two of his guards, the wounded one and the other who had attempted to disarm Makilien, a fiery glare.

"I'll be having words with you two later," he spat. He then turned his attention to Makilien's captor. "There, Jorin, you've got Makilien. Is there anything else?"

Jorin's expression was like stone. "Just make sure her family suffers."

Makilien looked up at him, horror gripping her heart, and her eyes went to Vayzar who sneered, "Oh, I will. They will be put on display in the square for all to see, and then, at dawn, they will burn."

"No!" Makilien cried. She struggled to pull away. "They have nothing to do with this!"

Jorin jerked her around to face him. "Maybe you should have considered the consequences before you killed my brother."

Makilien's eyes flew to his, realization crashing in. He was Zendon's brother. She could see that now.

"I killed him in the midst of battle," she argued, adrenaline pulsing through her body. "Do whatever you want to me because of it, but my family is innocent. They weren't there. They had no idea what I did."

But the cruelty in Jorin's eyes told Makilien her pleas were wasted. He looked at Vayzar again and repeated, "Make sure they suffer."

"No!" Makilien screamed. She tried with all her might to pull away, but Jorin squeezed her arm and the pain weakened her attempts. Throwing her at his men, he ordered, "Bind her hands."

Makilien had no chance of escape before her hands were tied securely behind her back. Tears coursed down her cheeks.

"Oh, Elohim," she whispered in desperation. "Please don't let this happen to my family because of the things I have done!"

Makilien's heart broke at the sound of Leiya's sobbing. She gazed at her family, and their fearful, hopeless expressions were seared into her mind.

"Come," Jorin commanded his men. "Let's be on our way."

Fighting against being taken, Makilien looked back at her family with deep remorse. "I'm sorry. So sorry." She wanted to tell them she'd find a way to stop this, but how could she?

The men yanked her along, and though she continued to struggle, it was useless.

"Have mercy, Vayzar, please!" Makilien cried, but he did not even look at her.

19

His men escorted her family in one direction, and Jorin and his men dragged Makilien in the other. She tried to keep her eyes on her family, but they were soon out of sight. Heavy sobs racked Makilien's body as she was forced along, and her heart cried out to Elohim.

Aedan stood aside as Ray and his two teenage sons backed their oxen team and full wagon of hay up to the barn, the last of the day. When it was in place, he picked up a pitchfork and climbed up into the wagon where he pitched the hay into the loft of the barn. Ray and the boys joined him.

For several minutes they worked undisturbed until Ray's wife rushed from the house.

"What's wrong, Elarie?" Ray asked.

"It's terrible!" Elarie exclaimed. "I just heard Vayzar has Makilien's family tied up in the square. He's going to have them burned at dawn!"

Aedan's heart leapt into his throat, and he jumped down from the wagon. "Where is Makilien?"

"A group of men came and took her away."

"Out of the village?"

Elarie gave a sad nod.

"When?"

"I don't know. A half an hour ago, maybe more."

Aedan looked off in the direction of the gate and started moving. "I have to find a way to help her."

Elarie grabbed his arm. "Wait, Aedan. Vayzar is after you now. He has guards combing the village. They will reach here any minute. You must hide until they move on."

Aedan clenched his fists. He didn't want to hide. He needed to go after Makilien. The farther her captors took her, the harder it would be for him to find them. But he had no choice. If he was caught, there would be no hope for either of them or for Makilien's family.

"Here, Aedan, climb back up in the wagon," Ray said. "You can hide in the hay."

Aedan groaned in frustration, but crawled into the wagon. Ray and his sons helped him burrow down into the hay and covered him completely, making sure no part of him could be seen. Just as they finished, Elarie warned in a sharp whisper, "Guards are coming!"

"Quickly, boys, start working," Ray instructed.

They picked up their pitchforks and pitched hay again. Aedan held his breath. A moment later, footsteps approached, and he remained absolutely still. Leaning against the edge of the wagon, Ray asked, "Can I help you?"

"We're searching for the young man who is always stirring up trouble with Makilien," the leader of the group said. "We heard he was here."

"Well, you can look around if you want, but you won't find him here."

"Check all the buildings," the guard ordered.

As his men hurried off, he peered up at Ray. "Do you know where he is?"

"Have you checked their camp?" Ray asked.

"Of course we have," the guard snapped.

Ray shrugged. "I can't say more than that."

The man squinted suspiciously before turning away to wait for the others to return. They searched all around the yard, in the barn, and even in the house, obviously coming back with nothing. Without a word, the whole group moved on.

Ray sighed in relief. "They're gone, Aedan, but don't come out just yet. They are still checking the neighbors."

Aedan waited for what seemed like forever. He hated it. He needed to go and figure out how to rescue Makilien. Both she and her family depended on him. On his own, he didn't think he'd be much help to her family, but together they stood a much better chance of success. Aedan considered asking Ray for help, but the farmer could not fight. None of their friends could. It was all up to Aedan.

More than twenty minutes passed before Ray gave the okay to come out. At last, the guards had moved on to another area of the village.

"What are you going to do?" Ray asked as Aedan crawled out and brushed hay from his dark hair and clothing.

"I have to get out of the village and try to rescue Makilien so together we can rescue her family." Aedan turned to Elarie. "Do you know if Vayzar has done anything with my family?"

Elarie shook her head. "I don't think so."

Aedan was relieved by this, but his thoughts focused on Makilien.

"How will you get out of the village?" Ray asked.

"I'm not sure. There is a loose stake in the palisade where Makilien and I sneak out sometimes, but I don't know if I can get there. First I have to get to Makilien's house. She has weapons hidden there that I need if I'm going to be able to save her."

"Aedan, if there is anything we can do to help, just ask," Ray told him.

"Thank you, Ray. Right now, I don't think there is anything you can do. But, if I can rescue Makilien and we successfully make it back into the village, we may call on you to help us free her family."

"We'll do whatever we can," Ray promised.

Aedan turned to go. Time was against him.

"Aedan," Ray said. "You have our prayers."

Aedan looked back at the whole family gratefully. "Thank you."

He then went on, determined to get to Makilien's house and arm himself. The going, however, was slow. Guards patrolled everywhere. Too many times they nearly spotted him before he had a chance to duck for cover. Heart pounding, he pushed on. Finally, after more close calls than he believed he should have escaped, Aedan snuck along the stable behind Makilien's house. When he reached the back door, he eased it open and slipped inside.

He let out his breath to find the house quiet and empty, and rushed up to Makilien's bedroom. When he walked in, he discovered the floorboard already lifted. Dropping to his knees, he reached into the open space and pulled out an Elven bow and a quiver of blue-fletched arrows. He reached in again, feeling for Makilien's sword, but found it gone. *She must have taken it.*

Aedan rose and strapped the quiver over his shoulder. A bow would be far better than no protection at all. While not as proficient as Makilien, he still had confidence in his skill with the weapon.

Hurrying downstairs, he went to a front window, searching for any nearby guards. Something near the road caught the light and his attention. Makilien's sword! He looked both ways.

The road was empty. His gaze returned to the sword. Going out into the open to get it would be a huge risk, but to have a sword would be worth it.

With utmost caution, he pulled open the front door and stepped out onto the porch. Still, no guards were within view. Praying not to be seen, Aedan dashed out to the road and snatched up the sword before he turned and sprinted back to the house.

Once inside, he closed the door and leaned back against it, heart racing. He flexed his fingers around the hilt of the sword and stared at the blade. He'd held it often enough when Makilien had taught him how to handle the weapon, but this was the first time he would have to use one in defense of his life.

Aedan walked through the house and back out the rear door. He needed to reach the palisade. Getting there proved just as difficult and dangerous as getting to Makilien's house, and he never quite made it before realizing it was impossible. He would be caught for sure if he tried. He sighed heavily. His only other choice was to try to make his escape through the gate.

:Chapter Three:

Unexpected Aid

Aedan peeked around a corner and down the alley between two buildings situated on the main street. If he could sneak down the alley without being detected, he would be able to see how many guards were at the gate. With no one in sight, he inched his way toward the far end of the alley. He had barely made it halfway when someone spoke behind him. He spun around, Makilien's sword extended.

"Whoa, Aedan! It's me!"

Aedan exhaled loudly. "Derrin, what are you doing here?" But he didn't give the other young man a chance to speak. He took him by the arm and dragged him around to the backside of the building.

"What in Dolennar is going on?" Derrin asked.

"The guards are after me," Aedan answered, looking around the corner to make sure no one had seen them.

"I know, I heard. I saw Makilien's family tied up in the square. What happened?"

"Makilien has been taken, and Vayzar is going to kill her family. Apparently he wants me too."

"What do you mean she was taken?" Derrin demanded. "Who took her?"

Aedan shook his head. "I don't know. Men who work for Zirtan, obviously."

"Why would they do this?"

"I'm not sure, but I think I have an idea." Taking Makilien and killing her family on top of it seemed to Aedan to be going awfully far just because Makilien had defied Vayzar. There had to be another reason, and he was willing to bet someone knew what Makilien had done in Eldor.

"What are you going to do?" Derrin asked.

"I need to get out of the village and rescue Makilien so we can save her family."

Aedan did not wait for Derrin to respond. He walked back into the alley. Derrin followed, but did not speak. When he reached the end, Aedan peered around the corner toward the gate a hundred yards away. He scanned the area, and his attention focused on one guard and another man coming up the street. The other man was dressed unlike anyone Aedan had seen in Reylaun and appeared entirely out of place. Aedan found his face familiar. Then it dawned on him.

"It can't be," he murmured, but he'd seen the drawings in Makilien's sketchbook too many times to be mistaken.

"What?" Derrin whispered.

Aedan glanced at him, but did not answer. His mind worked too quickly in an attempt to form a plan. He looked around the alley and spotted a broken axe handle laying a few feet away.

"Hold this." He handed Makilien's sword to Derrin whose eyes went wide at holding such a forbidden object. Aedan retrieved the axe handle and tested it in his hand. It still had adequate weight to it. He pushed Derrin back against the wall of the building. "Stay there and keep quiet."

Aedan returned to the corner and peeked around again. The two men were only a couple yards away. Pressing himself up against the building, he drew in long, deep breaths and prayed for success. In a moment, the guard and other man passed by the alley. Before they could get far, Aedan stepped out and swung the axe handle. It crashed into the guard's helmet. The man stumbled forward and fell face first to the ground.

Aedan glanced toward the gate. None of the other guards had noticed, but they would if he didn't get the unconscious guard off the street. His eyes swung around to the young man. He appeared to be around Aedan's age with dark brown hair cut chin length and deep brown eyes. Now Aedan had no doubt. This was Sirion.

The Half-Elf stared at Aedan, his expression one of shock and confusion over what had just taken place, but there wasn't time quite yet for explanation.

"Help me hide him, quickly."

Aedan took one of the guard's arms and waited for Sirion to take the other.

Together, they dragged the man into the alley. He moaned once, but did not come to. Straightening, Aedan glanced briefly at Derrin who stood in silence, his mouth hanging open, but his attention returned to the other man.

"You're Sirion, right?"

"Yes," he answered, his brows lowered in question. "Do I know you?"

"I am Makilien's friend, Aedan. I recognized you from Makilien's sketches."

Recognition of the name dawned on Sirion's face. "Where is Makilien?" he asked, concern edging his voice.

"She was taken by a group of men," Aedan told him, "and Vayzar, Zirtan's appointed ruler here, has Makilien's family held captive. He's going to execute them in the morning."

"How long ago was Makilien taken?"

"At least an hour. I've been trying to get out of the village to rescue her, but the guards are after me too."

Sirion stood quiet for a moment as he processed the information.

"Is there only one gate in and out of the village?"

"Yes."

"All right, there are at least four guards there right now, but only one is right at the gate. I will distract him long enough for you to run out. I'll follow. We'll make our way along behind the buildings until we're closer."

Aedan nodded, and Sirion picked up the fallen guard's sword. Turning to Derrin who just gawked at them, Aedan took Makilien's sword back. Without further words, Sirion and Aedan jogged down the alley and behind the buildings.

When they reached the last one closest to the gate, the two of them stopped, peering around the corner. The guard stationed at the gate stared off out of the village and would not see them coming. The other three also faced away from them.

"Follow close behind me and try to be as quiet as possible," Sirion instructed. "As soon as I've taken care of the guard at the gate, run straight into the forest. I did not come alone. The others are waiting in the trees, and they will make sure you get there safely."

Aedan squeezed Makilien's sword and followed just behind Sirion as he walked out. All went well until they had just about reached the lone guard at the gate. He must have heard them coming and turned. His eyes widened when he saw Aedan, and even more when he realized they were armed. He reached for his sword and opened his mouth to shout a warning, but in a swift move, Sirion smashed the hilt of his sword into the side of the guard's helmet.

Aedan bolted, straight for the forest. The other guards shouted and ran after him. He glanced back. Sirion was right behind him, but so were the guards. Just before he reached the bushes, something swished past his head. A guard cried out. Aedan looked again over his shoulder. One of the guards lay on the ground with an arrow piercing his chest. The other guards retreated back to the safety of the village.

A moment later, Aedan and Sirion crashed through the brush and stumbled to a halt in a small clearing. Working to slow his breathing and heart rate, Aedan's eyes swept over the group gathered around him. Everyone was familiar from Makilien's sketches, but to see them in person was the culmination of a year of dreaming about it. Halandor, Torick, Loron, and Gilhir all stood before him.

"Aedan."

"Hello, Torick," he replied breathlessly.

The man looked pleased to see him and asked, "Are you all right?"

Aedan nodded. Makilien's friends looked between the two of them, and Halandor asked, "Where's Makilien?"

Sirion turned to Aedan who relayed everything he knew of Makilien's capture and the fate of her family.

"They must be taking her north to Zirtan," Halandor said. "They did not come south or we would have met them on the road. Aedan, do you know if they are traveling by foot or by horse?"

"I don't know," Aedan answered. "I didn't see anything for myself, I only heard what happened."

"Do you know how many there were?"

Aedan shook his head.

"We need to go after them before they get too far ahead," Sirion said as he took his own weapons from Gilhir and armed himself after giving them up to get inside Reylaun.

Halandor agreed. "Let's get the horses."

Everyone followed him deeper into the forest.

As they made their way, Aedan asked, "Did you come here for Makilien?"

Halandor glanced back and nodded. "We came as soon as we realized word was spreading all over Dolennar that she is the one who killed Zendon."

After walking a distance of half a mile, they came upon another clearing where six horses were tied. Everyone went to their own horses, but before Halandor untied his buckskin, he led a tall black horse to Aedan.

"This is Makilien's horse, Antiro. You can ride him."

Aedan took the magnificent horse's reins and looked him in the eyes. "Antiro," he murmured. "Makilien has told me all about you. She will be delighted to see you after we rescue her."

Antiro tossed his head and gave an eager nicker. Aedan stepped back and slipped Makilien's sword into his belt before pulling himself up into Antiro's saddle. He'd never before ridden a horse, but since Antiro could understand his words and would not do anything unpredictable, he was not concerned.

As the others rode out, Aedan gently squeezed Antiro's sides, and the horse followed.

Sweat glistened on the sides of Makilien's face and trickled down her back, dampening her bandages and making them rub uncomfortably. Her arm throbbed deeply, and her head pounded. She did not know how the men kept up such a grueling pace with no sign of slowing.

She had ceased crying, knowing it would do no good and would only make her look weak to her captors. But her heart wept. Nothing was more painful than the thought of her family being burned to death, especially her parents. Without believing in the truth, they were not ready to die. *Oh, Elohim,* Makilien pleaded, *whatever happens to me, please do not let my parents die without knowing You!*

Losing herself in her thoughts and prayers, she unknowingly slowed her pace, but a strong hand shoved her forward. She stumbled, tried to regain her balance, but failed. Landing hard on her knees, she dragged in deep, ragged breaths.

Before she could get back up, Jorin took her by her injured arm and hauled her to her feet. Stabbing pain burned through her nerves, and she could not stifle a whimper.

Leaning close, Jorin said in a low, steely voice, "Get moving."

Makilien locked eyes with him. His expression seemed to be daring her to try something. Summoning every last ounce of determination, she pushed on. She could not let herself be defeated. No matter what happened, she had to trust Elohim was in control.

A couple hours after leaving Reylaun, the sun sank low and the forest dimmed, yet they continued on for another hour.

Makilien's weary muscles burned, but at last, the group stopped to set up their nighttime camp. They sat Makilien at the base of a tree and tied her securely. From this position, she watched Jorin command the tasks of each of his men. She wondered at how enemy leaders treated their men and the way men remained loyal in spite of this hard treatment. Jorin's wish to avenge his brother was the only small indication of care she had ever witnessed within enemy ranks. Otherwise they seemed to have no love for each other, united only by their hatred of those opposed to Zirtan.

In a short time, a fire burned and a meal was set cooking. Makilien wondered if any of this food would reach her stomach, but she doubted it.

Now that everything was settled for the night, Jorin came and stood before her, peering down at her. She studied him, finding him not quite as frightening as his brother had been, but intimidating nonetheless.

Finally, she grew uncomfortable under his intense and silent gaze. "Whatever you are thinking, you may as well speak it."

Jorin was more than happy to do just that. "When I came to Reylaun for you, I was expecting more. The people of Eldor speak of you as some sort of great hero."

Though he meant for his words to hurt, Makilien was not affected. "Stories are often full of exaggeration, especially where heroes are concerned."

Frustration flashed in Jorin's eyes as they narrowed just slightly. But in a moment, he had a comeback. "It's a pity. They were even hoping for you to bring them another victory."

Makilien's brows drew together. "*Another* victory?"

Cruel amusement played on Jorin's face. "Yes, against Lord Zirtan's new and vastly larger army. You didn't believe in your pathetic victory in Eldor that you had truly defeated Lord Zirtan, did you? That was merely an unforeseen setback, but this time there will be no chance of defeat. Lord Zirtan himself will lead this army, and we will crush Eldor and anyone who stands in our way."

Makilien stared at him. She didn't want to believe it, but there was no lie in his expression.

"And news of your death will be the first blow." Jorin's voice lowered with hatred for her. "It will be a slow, painful death for what you did to my brother."

For a moment she said nothing, considering the torture that awaited her, but then she spoke with quiet surety, "You may take my life, but you will never have my soul."

She watched his jaw shift and tighten, and his eyes become shadowed with rage. Without warning, he reached down and slapped her hard. Makilien's cheek stung, and she squeezed her eyes shut, but otherwise she did not react. Looking back up at Jorin, she held his still furious gaze with a calm confidence building in her heart.

Infuriated by the strength in her eyes, Jorin finally turned on his heel and stalked off to the fire. Makilien let out a deep sigh and leaned her head back against the tree. It was going to be a long night.

:Chapter Four:

Rescue

Makilien tugged against the rope and twisted her wrists, desperate to create slack. She kept watchful eyes on the men, careful not to alert them to her escape attempts. It was easier now that it had grown dark, and all the men but one on watch were asleep. The evening march had exhausted her, but sleep could not be afforded. Now was her only chance to escape in time to rescue her family.

With a frustrated sigh, she paused. The thick ropes had not given at all. Her fingers tingled and were going numb from lack of circulation to her hands.

The break did little to restore Makilien's energy, so she resumed her efforts to free herself. If only she could find something with a sharp edge to fray the rope, but she had already felt around the base of the tree and found nothing. She tried to slip one of her hands out, but it was just too tight.

She ceased fidgeting when the man on watch glanced at her. It was a passing but cruel glance before he returned his attention to poking at the fire, bored with his duty. Makilien remained still for a moment to make sure he was completely occupied. She was about to work on the rope again, when something touched her arm. She started a little and looked over her shoulder. Her eyes grew huge when they locked on a face—a face she had longed every day to see again. *Sirion!* Her heart leapt.

Sirion took hold of the ropes that bound her and cut through them. Makilien focused on the guard at the fire, praying he would not be alerted to the rescue. Little by little the rope gave way, and, finally, all the tightness around her wrists released.

Leaning around the tree, Sirion whispered in her ear, "Follow me."

Slow and quiet, Makilien rose to her feet, eyes still on the guard. She had just about risen to her full height, when the guard glanced her way again.

"Hey!" he shouted, scrambling to his feet as he yanked out his sword.

Jorin and the others woke in an instant and jumped up, reaching for their weapons. Sirion grabbed Makilien's hand, and they fled into the darkened forest without looking back. One of the men behind them cried out in pain. The commotion of panicked shouting followed. After a few more cries, it all died away.

By this time, they had reached a clearing where horses were silhouetted by the moonlight. They stopped here, looking over their shoulders, and then their gaze turned to each other. The moon was just bright enough to illuminate their faces. Makilien drew in a shaky breath, her eyes welling up with tears at finally seeing Sirion again. She laughed in relief and put her arms around him. With a smile, he embraced her in return.

When they parted, Sirion asked, "Are you all right?"

Makilien nodded. "I am now."

One of the horses snorted and nickered with great eagerness. Makilien looked toward them, and a smile spread across her face.

"Antiro," she said in delight. She ran over to him and lovingly stroked his cheek. "It's so good to see you, boy."

She kissed him on the nose and turned back to Sirion who smiled at the reunion. Before Makilien could speak, Sirion looked off into the trees. Someone was coming, but he did not appear alarmed.

A moment later, a handful of people poured into the clearing. Makilien's heart filled with joy at seeing her friends.

"Aedan!" she exclaimed. "You escaped! I was afraid Vayzar would catch you too."

"I had some help." Aedan nodded toward Sirion.

Makilien's joy abated in an instant. "What about my family? Do you know if they are all right?"

"I think they are," Aedan told her. "But I didn't get to see them before I left."

Makilien turned her worried gaze to the others. "We must go back to Reylaun and rescue my family before dawn or they will be killed."

"Don't worry. We'll rescue them," Halandor assured her. "But we should go immediately. I don't think anyone will come after us, but we can't take chances."

"Are they dead?" Makilien asked concerning Jorin and his men.

"No, not all of them. Most are only wounded."

Makilien wondered if Jorin had survived, but she would have to wait to ask further questions. They turned to the horses. Before they mounted, Aedan handed Makilien her sword.

"I saw it lying in the street and picked it up in case I needed it."

Makilien smiled and slid it into her empty scabbard. "Thank you." She would have hated to lose such a sentimental item.

She mounted Antiro, and Aedan crawled up behind her. With a sense of urgency, they rode with all speed through the dark forest. Plenty of night hours lay ahead of them before dawn, but no one knew for sure what or how long it might take to rescue Makilien's family.

On horseback, it took them only a couple of hours to arrive back at the village, even in the dark. They stopped at the gate, always closed at sundown. Dismounting, they gathered in a group to discuss a plan.

"Is there another way inside?" Halandor asked.

"We could go through the gap where Aedan and I always sneak in and out," Makilien suggested.

"How many men does Zirtan have inside?" Torick wanted to know.

Makilien looked at Aedan who answered, "It's hard to tell them all apart, but I'd say about twenty."

Torick nodded and asked him, "Can you fight?"

"Yes."

Torick's eyes turned to Sirion. "You came out of the village with an extra sword, didn't you?"

"Yes, I left it in the clearing."

"I'll get it," Loron offered. He hurried away, but was only gone a short time before he returned to give Aedan the guard's sword.

"That makes the odds about three to one," Torick said. "We can do that."

Makilien agreed. "Most of the guards are not well trained, and I wounded one earlier."

"And I gave one quite a headache," Aedan added.

With their odds looking better still, they made their way around the palisade and found the loose stake. After creating the gap by pulling it outward, Makilien peeked through.

"I don't see anyone. Everything seems quiet."

She crawled through, and the rest followed one at a time.

The village was silent and dark except for the faint, far-off glow of torchlight from the town square. Makilien turned to her friends and waited until all were through to whisper, "I'm sure there will be a couple guards in the square guarding my family and a handful patrolling the village. If we're careful we should be able to avoid most of them."

They nodded, and Makilien and Aedan led the way. Navigating was easy for them as they had done it many times in the dark. Tonight the village streets were shrouded with a low layer of fog. Everything seemed unusually silent—eerily silent. All the houses were dark, and not a single person stirred. A feeling of doom hung heavy with the fog in anticipation of the morning's planned execution, the first in the village's history.

Using the shadows and the fog for cover, they came to the edge of the town square. A torch in each corner lit the open area with a flickering, orange glow. Makilien sucked in her breath upon seeing her family. They were tied to a large stake, and already wood had been stacked around them. The only thing that stopped Makilien from rushing out to free them were the four guards who patrolled the square.

Taking charge of the situation, Halandor whispered, "Loron, you and Torick work your way around and take care of the two guards at the far end. Sirion and Gilhir, you can take the other two. As soon as it's clear, we'll come out and free Makilien's family."

The four of them agreed and moved off, disappearing into the darkness. A couple of minutes passed as Makilien, Halandor, and Aedan remained crouched in the shadows, waiting. Then, Loron and Torick appeared across the square and silently made their way up behind the guards, grabbing them from behind. One tried to shout, but was quickly stifled. The other two guards barely saw their comrades fall to the ground unconscious before they too were grabbed by Sirion and Gilhir. Makilien rushed out, followed by Halandor and Aedan. The expressions of relief on the faces of her family as she ran toward them would stay in Makilien's mind forever.

"Makilien!" they exclaimed.

She grinned. "Don't worry. Everything is going to be fine. We're going to get you out of here."

Using her sword, Makilien cut through the ropes binding her family. First Leiya pulled away from the stake and then their mother. But when Makilien reached her father, she found something that jeopardized everything. Not only was her father tied to the stake, his hands were also chained to it. She took a desperate look at the lock.

"Halandor." Makilien had barely called his name when the sound of a bell rang out in the square and echoed throughout the village. They looked up in dismay. A fifth guard rang the alarm bell at the far end. Loron whipped out an arrow and shot the guard, but the damage had already been done. In minutes, every guard in the village would be on them.

Makilien turned back to her father, her eyes wide and desperate. "We must get these chains unlocked!"

Halandor came to her side to inspect them.

"Do we have anything we can use to pick the lock?" Makilien asked, realizing it would take time even if they did. Time they did not have.

"Makilien."

She looked up at the resigned tone of her father's voice.

"Get your mother and sister out of here," he instructed.

Makilien adamantly shook her head. "I won't leave you."

They could say no more. The clattering of guards rushing toward the square caught their attention. Makilien turned to her mother and sister, her voice dire, but calm. "Stay behind us."

Stealth escape no longer an option, Makilien and her friends formed a protective circle around her family. *Please, Elohim, give us victory so I can get my family out of here safely,* Makilien prayed.

A moment later, guards poured into the square. They halted at first, surprised by the group they faced. Before they charged, Vayzar stormed out of their midst, dressed only in his nightclothes, but holding a sword nonetheless.

"You escaped," he muttered with contempt. "Well, just because Jorin was obviously too incompetent to see you get what you deserve, doesn't mean I will be."

"We'll see about that, Vayzar," Makilien shot back. "I know one thing. I'll die before I let you harm my family."

Vayzar scoffed. "And die you will." Pointing his sword at her, he ordered, "Kill them!"

The guards all rushed forward at once. Makilien and her friends stood their ground. As soon as a guard came close enough, Makilien swung her sword. With a clang, it met with the guard's blade, and she did not wait before attacking again.

Chaos ensued. First and foremost in her mind was to protect her unarmed family. At times that meant fighting two guards at once. It took several minutes, but the guards' numbers dwindled, and a quick glance around the square told Makilien all her friends still stood and her family remained unharmed.

Successfully ridding herself of another foe, Makilien saw Vayzar making his way toward her. Their eyes locked, feeling mutual contempt for each other. Makilien raised her sword to block as Vayzar tried to bring his blade down on top of her. They traded a couple more blows. Though Vayzar was better trained than most of his guards, he was not as brutal an opponent as Jorin had been. They seemed almost evenly matched, but Makilien's youth made her faster. After a few more blows, she whipped her sword around and sliced through the top of Vayzar's leg. He doubled over, howling in pain, and she smashed the hilt of her sword down on his shoulders, knocking him to the ground. His sword fell from his hand. He scrambled to reach it, but Makilien stepped on the blade and pointed her own in his face.

"Get up slowly," she commanded.

Eyes flaming, he obeyed. Keeping the point of her sword at Vayzar's chest, Makilien looked around the square to find all the guards lay either dead or injured. Now, instead, villagers gathered cautiously around the perimeter, their eyes wide at the sight before them. None dared to approach, but murmurs and whispers passed through them.

Ignoring their audience, Makilien took a hold of Vayzar's arm and pushed him forward. "Move."

"You won't get away with this!" he snarled, limping along. "I swear, I'm going to see that you die, and it will be slow and painful."

"Funny," Makilien replied dryly. "Jorin said the same thing."

As Vayzar's face turned a shade of deep red, Makilien halted him near the stake where her father was still chained. Looking at Halandor, she said, "Watch him for me."

She reached down and unclipped a ring of keys from the belt Vayzar had buckled over his nightclothes, sure one of them would unlock her father's chains. Makilien turned to her father and, after trying a couple keys, found the one that fit. Néthyn's chains fell away and he smiled proudly, looking upon his daughter with new eyes.

A deep sense of pleasure rose up in Makilien, and she turned to Halandor. "Bring Vayzar here."

He pushed Vayzar up to the stake and helped Makilien chain him with the same chains that had secured her father.

"You will never get away with this!" Vayzar hissed. "When Lord Zirtan finds out, he will hunt you down and kill you all, and I'll be right there to enjoy it."

Makilien put her hands on her hips and looked him straight in the eyes. "Never underestimate the power of Elohim. And no matter what your master, Zirtan, may try to tell you, he is not in control and never will be."

With a satisfied smile, she turned away from him. To her friends, she said, "Let's get out of here."

They turned and left the center of the square while Vayzar shouted curses and threats at them. Before leaving the square behind, someone called out Makilien's name. She turned as Derrin broke through the crowd of villagers. The young man stopped, his mouth opening as he beheld the scene. But he recovered quickly and hurried to Makilien and her friends.

"Take me with you."

Makilien stared at him. "What?"

"You're leaving the village, aren't you? I want to go with you."

"Derrin . . ." Makilien paused. She could hardly deny him a chance to escape, but she could not believe he actually wanted to leave. She glanced at her friends and then asked him, "Are you sure that's what you want?"

"Yes," Derrin insisted.

With one last glance to confirm it with her friends, Makilien nodded. "All right." Her eyes went to the other villagers. By now it seemed the whole village was in attendance. "I encourage anyone else who wants to leave to do it now as well while you have the chance."

A hum of murmurs followed.

"Aedan!" a call came from nearby.

"Mother." Aedan left the group and met his family as they stepped from the crowd.

"Aedan, what has happened?" his mother asked. "Guards came looking for you. We've been so worried."

"I'm fine," Aedan assured her. "I had to go out and help Makilien." He gently took his mother's arms. "I need to leave. It's not safe for me here."

His mother nodded, tears filling her eyes. "I know."

"Come with us," Aedan begged. "Life is better out there than here."

But his mother now shook her head, a sad smile on her face. "This is our home, Aedan. We are happy here. But you must go. I can't bear to see anything happen to you, and I know this is what you've always wanted." She reached up to cup his face in her hands. "You took good care of me and Rommia all these years. We would never have survived without you . . .

I never would have survived. I'd tell you how proud your father would be, but I don't know if that would be true. But I am proud, very proud."

Aedan breathed hard, his chest heavy with emotion. His mother had never spoken to him in this way before.

"Thank you, Mother."

With the tears shining in her eyes, his mother pulled him into her embrace. "Take care of yourself, Aedan. I love you."

"I love you too," Aedan replied hoarsely.

They smiled at each other, and Aedan said, "Someday, I will come back to see that you are well."

His mother nodded, and Aedan turned to Rommia. "I'm going to miss you, little sister."

Rommia smiled and gave him a hug. "Thanks for taking care of me and Mother."

They murmured goodbyes, and Aedan finally faced his stepfather who said, "I will take good care of them, Aedan, I promise."

"Thank you," Aedan replied with deep gratitude. Looking once more to his mother, he said, "I know you have always been afraid, but please, think about all I have told you. It is the truth."

"We will," his mother murmured, trying not to cry.

Though it was more difficult than he ever imagined it would be, Aedan turned away from his family and joined Makilien and the others. They turned their backs on the square and left Vayzar and the villagers behind.

Chapter Five

Flight to Andin

The stars had disappeared some time ago, and the forest had taken on a grayish look in the light of dawn, but traveling at a fast pace, no one really noticed. When the forest finally took on color with the brightening of the morning sun, they stopped for the first time since riding away from Reylaun. The horses panted, carrying more weight since the group had been forced to ride double.

Makilien was as glad for the rest as their mounts. Wearily, she followed the example of the others as they dismounted. She had taken Leiya with her on Antiro. Before she helped her sister down, she touched her aching arm. When she pulled her hand away, it was smeared with fresh blood.

Leiya gasped. "You're bleeding."

All gazes turned in Makilien's direction.

"I'm all right. My wound just opened again," she told them. "I'll be fine."

"We should get it tended to," Halandor said. He had noticed it earlier in the village, but there had been no time to look after it. Turning to Torick, he said, "I think it would be safe to build a fire here."

Torick nodded, and he and the Elves went to work.

Makilien returned her attention to helping her sister down from her horse, but Sirion came to their aid first.

"You should go sit down," he told Makilien with concern.

"Thank you," Makilien murmured.

She walked around the horses and sat down near where Torick would soon have a nice fire going. Her mother knelt next to her with her father and sister looking on.

"Let me see your wound," Hanna said.

Makilien held her arm up. Her mother rolled up her sleeve revealing the long cut near her elbow, which bled slowly but freely. Kneeling next to Hanna, Halandor reached into his pack and pulled out a clean cloth.

"Use this to stop the bleeding."

Hanna took it and pressed it to Makilien's arm. While the others worked around the fire, Sirion came from the horses and offered Makilien a waterskin. She smiled her thanks to him. Water was just what she needed. She had become light-headed from the lack of it after her ordeal. Uncapping the container, she took a long drink of the cool liquid and sighed. She was worn out but had not been so happy in a long time.

While waiting for water to heat to clean her arm, Makilien found it a good time to make introductions between her family and her friends. They were introductions she'd prayed for a long time to be able to make. Once everyone had greeted each other, Makilien looked to her friends and asked, "Does anyone know how Zirtan found out I killed Zendon?"

Halandor shook his head. "That is what we have been wondering. It was not one of us. Someone else must have seen you."

"Is that why you were taken from Reylaun?" Torick asked her.

"Yes," Makilien answered. "One of the men was Zendon's brother."

"His brother?" Torick repeated. "We didn't know he had one."

"Neither did I until he told me." Makilien frowned. "I would like to know if he was killed when you rescued me. He was very tall, taller than the rest of the men, and dark haired like Zendon."

The group looked at each other, but no one could say whether or not Jorin had been killed in their surprise attack. The uncertainty left uneasiness in Makilien's mind. "If he did survive, he is going to come after me."

"We'll make sure to stay well ahead of him or the others until we've reached the safety of Elimar," Halandor assured her.

That gave Makilien another question. "Is it true Zirtan is attacking again?"

Halandor nodded. "I'm afraid it is."

"Jorin, Zendon's brother, told me that we have no hope of victory . . ." Makilien searched Halandor's face to see if that was true and was not comforted by the uncertainty in his eyes.

"He is gathering a much larger force this time . . . but whether we can defeat him or not is in the hands of Elohim," Halandor said.

Makilien agreed. "How much time do we have to prepare, and what has been done already?" she asked.

"I believe we have quite a bit of time, but there is no way to know for sure. As for preparations, Lord Glorlad and Lord Andron have already gathered their armies in Minarald. Lord Elnauhir is still in Elimar, but he is ready to march whenever he needs to."

Makilien fell silent for a few moments as she watched Halandor bring a small pot of heated water from the fire. Her mother moved back letting him take over since she had never had to tend such an injury before. Looking at Halandor as he cleaned her arm, Makilien said, "Jorin told me something else. He told me the people of Eldor are talking about me as a hero and are hoping I will bring another victory."

"That's true," Halandor acknowledged.

"But do they know it was never my intention to kill him, that I was only protecting you? I mean, if you had not been in danger, I never would have gone anywhere near him."

"Some know the details. Lord Darand has addressed the people at Minarald, but word of this has spread so quickly, we don't know what all is being said."

"I'm certainly no great hero who can guarantee another victory."

"Still, that is how they view you, and it would have been a blow to a great many had you been killed," Halandor told her.

"Why are they placing so much hope in me and not Elohim?"

"Not all have the same faith we do."

Makilien glanced at her parents, but nothing in their expressions could tell her what they thought.

"Well, I'll do all I can to help, but it will be Elohim who brings us victory or not," she said.

Once Halandor had finished cleaning and bandaging her arm, he and her friends offered everyone food.

While they ate, he said, "We will rest here a little while longer before going on. We're only a couple hours from Andin. I think we can safely stay there tonight if we're cautious. We'll replenish supplies and buy a couple more horses for the journey to Elimar."

Makilien was glad they would be making this journey on horseback. Whoever was left of Jorin and his men would surely catch up to them if they had to travel by foot.

Less than an hour passed before they rode again, sharing a sense of urgency. They wouldn't be completely safe until they reached Elimar. Even if they stayed ahead of Jorin's surviving men, they needed to be mindful of other enemies along the way. Others could be looking for Makilien with word of her actions spreading so rapidly.

By early afternoon they came upon the open gate of Andin and rode inside. Little had changed since Makilien had first come upon the village. Considering what she had seen in her past journey, this small village seemed insignificant, but her family looked around with great interest.

"There are so many houses and shops," Leiya said in awe.

Makilien smiled. "Yes. Many travelers from all over Do-lennar come through here."

Urging Antiro ahead, Makilien came alongside Halandor as they navigated the village streets. "Will we stay at the Black Stag?"

Halandor nodded. "It's the only decent inn within the village. I'd prefer not to stay there, but there are only a few people here I trust. None of them can accommodate all of us. We'll try to draw as little attention as possible and stay inside until we leave tomorrow. Tonight we'll post watches to be sure."

"Will we need more than one room?"

"I will ask Rindal for his largest room. It will be a tight fit for us all, but it will be safer."

Makilien agreed. Splitting up did not seem wise.

As they rode farther into the village, she kept a wary eye on the villagers they passed. She felt as though she and her group of friends stood out amongst them, but she reminded herself travelers were common. The villagers probably thought nothing of their arrival, so she prayed for peace of mind and for protection in case someone did notice them and mean them harm.

At last, they came to the Black Stag Inn and brought the horses to a stop. Everyone dismounted. Remembering what had happened the first time she had stayed here, Makilien gathered her family together and said, "Stay close to us."

Halandor and Torick took the lead and opened the door. Makilien, her family, and Aedan and Derrin followed while Sirion, Loron, and Gilhir brought up the rear. Not a lot of people were gathered inside the dim common room this time of day. At the counter, Makilien spotted Rindal. He looked just the same as she remembered. She had to smile wryly at the recollection of their first meeting and how instantly annoyed he had been with her.

With business slow, Rindal noticed them immediately. "Ah, Halandor," he said. "What can I do for you?"

"We'd like your largest room if it's available," Halandor told him.

Rindal eyed the group. "For all of you?"

Halandor nodded.

"Well, it's available, but I don't know that you'll be comfortable all together, but if that's what you want . . ."

"It is," Halandor assured him.

The innkeeper turned to grab a key and tipped his head toward a doorway to his right. "Follow me."

They left the common room and entered the hall where the majority of the inn's rooms were located; however, they did not stop at any of these doors. At the end of the hall, they came to a staircase and climbed to the second floor and another hallway. When they came to one of the last doors, Rindal paused to unlock it.

"Here you are," he said, handing Halandor the key.

"Thank you," Halandor replied.

He opened the door and motioned for everyone to enter. Makilien and her family stepped inside first, and took stock. It was actually two rooms. The main room was little more than twice the size of the room she had occupied in the past, and the bedroom was half that size with two beds. Walking across the room, she looked out the window.

"You can see down to the front door from here," she told her friends.

Halandor joined her at the window. "Someone can keep watch from here and out in the hall."

"I will watch the window for a while," Torick offered.

"And I'll watch the hall," Gilhir told them.

As the two of them moved to their places, Halandor turned to Makilien and her family. "We'll stay here until morning. If anyone is hungry, we still have food in our packs and we can get more from downstairs later. Makilien, you and your family are welcome to the bedroom."

"Thank you," Makilien replied.

She looked down at her sister. Leiya was about ready to collapse on the spot.

Directing her into the bedroom, she said, "You need rest. Why don't you lie down for a while?"

Leiya crawled into bed without protest, and their parents entered the room and closed the door. Sitting down on the edge of the bed next to Leiya, Makilien smiled at her sister.

"Are we safe here?" the little girl asked.

"Yes," Makilien assured her. "My friends and I won't let anything happen."

As Leiya's eyelids drooped, she said, "I like your friends."

Makilien's smile grew, and she looked at her parents who had sat down across from her. Seeing how drained and exhausted they were, however, caused her smile to fade as guilt filled her heart. Not only had they suddenly been thrust into this dangerous adventure, but only hours ago they had faced death and all because of her.

"I'm sorry," she murmured. "I'm so sorry for everything I caused you to have to face." Tears filled her eyes.

"Oh, Makilien," her mother said. "Come here."

Makilien rose and sat down between her parents. She shook her head. "I don't know how I would have been able to bear it if you had all been killed. I tried so hard to keep you from being affected by my actions." A tear dripped down her cheek. "I always prayed that one day I could get you all away from Reylaun, but I never meant for it to be like this."

Hanna put her arm around her daughter, holding her close. "We know that, Makilien. We do not blame you. The most important thing to us is that you and your sister are safe. And now, finally, we can all be together."

Makilien wiped her cheeks and smiled a little. "Yes, finally. I don't know what will happen when we reach Eldor with war coming, but I hope we'll be able to stay together, for a while at least."

"I'm sure everything will be fine," Hanna said, giving her daughter an optimistic smile.

Makilien nodded and then rose again "I'll leave now so you two can rest if you want."

"Don't you need to rest?" Hanna asked.

Makilien shrugged. "I've learned how to cope without it when I need to. I'll get the sleep I need tonight."

With a last smile, she left her family and entered the other room. Torick was at the window, and Sirion sat at the table with Aedan and Derrin. She walked to the table, and Sirion pulled out a chair for her.

"Is your family comfortable?" he asked.

Makilien sat next to him and nodded. "Yes. I'm sure Leiya is probably just about asleep already. They are all exhausted." She glanced toward the door. "Are Halandor and Loron caring for the horses?"

Sirion gave her a nod.

When the two of them returned, Makilien spent the remainder of the afternoon recounting her life in Reylaun in the last year and asking of the events in Eldor since her departure.

:Chapter Six:

Pursued

A voice drifted through Makilien's semi-conscious mind, but it was the subtle creak of the door that woke her instantly. Sitting up, she reached instinctively for her sword, but stopped when, in the dim light of dawn, she recognized Halandor in the doorway.

"What's wrong?" she asked.

"Guards from Reylaun are here," Halandor told her, his tone rushed.

"What?" Makilien gasped.

"Vayzar is with them."

Makilien turned to Leiya and shook her. "Leiya, wake up," she said urgently. She scrambled out of bed and woke her parents.

"How many are there?" Makilien asked, turning back to Halandor as her father picked up sleepy Leiya and they left the bedroom.

"We counted six plus Vayzar," Halandor answered. "That isn't many and some looked injured, but they may be able to rally more help here in the village. We have to get out quickly."

Makilien took stock of her friends. Sirion stood at the window watching the street, and Aedan and Derrin were at the table, but no one else was in the room.

"Have any more entered the inn?" Halandor asked.

Sirion glanced away from the window, eyes pausing on Makilien for a moment, and shook his head. "No. There are still two outside."

"How are we going to get out?" Makilien asked.

"We'll try the back door," Halandor answered.

A moment later, their door opened showing the rest of the group standing in the hall. Loron stepped into the room. "They are still in the common room questioning Rindal. We must hurry. Is everyone ready?"

Halandor nodded and dropped a handful of coins on the table. Turning to Makilien and her family, he said, "We must be quick and silent."

Makilien gave a nod and led the way. Her family and Aedan and Derrin followed with Halandor and Sirion behind. In the hall, Torick, Loron, and Gilhir took the lead. Makilien noticed each one had a hand on their swords. *Please, Elohim, bring us safely away from here,* she prayed.

Downstairs, angry shouts came from the common room. A scowl crossed Makilien's face, wishing she could have done more to slow Vayzar down. She had not expected him to come after her like this.

They were halfway down the hall when Vayzar's shouting ceased and footsteps drew near. With all haste, they hurried around a corner to the back door. How Makilien prayed there would be no one standing guard outside. Torick stepped to the door and eased it open. Peering out into the fog-wrapped streets, he motioned for everyone to follow.

Creeping between the inn and another building, they came to a narrow side street and followed it away from the inn, not stopping until they came to an alley several buildings away. Makilien breathed a sigh of relief, thankful they had at least escaped the inn.

"What are we going to do now?" she asked.

"We cannot leave the village without extra horses and supplies," Halandor said. "We need to get to Laena's. She can hide you and your family while the rest of us gather what we need. Torick, continue leading," Halandor instructed. "Sirion and I will guard the back."

With the utmost caution, the group made their way through the village, staying clear of the heavily used streets whenever possible. It was slow going, having to carefully check around every corner before moving on. At last, their stressful maneuvering came to an end for the moment when they reached the familiar shop Makilien remembered buying supplies from with Halandor.

Stepping to the door, Halandor tried the knob. When he found it locked, he knocked gently. A moment later, the door opened, and Makilien recognized the same woman she had met last time.

"Halandor!" Laena exclaimed, clearly delighted to see him. "I haven't opened quite yet, but please come on in."

She pulled the door open wider and beckoned them inside.

"You have quite a group with you this time," she said. "What can I do for you?"

"We all need supplies to get to Eldor, but we also need you to hide Makilien and her family until we're ready to leave if that is all right with you." Halandor gestured to them and explained, "We're being pursued by Zirtan's men."

Laena frowned deeply at the news. "Of course it's all right. I can hide everyone in the back. Come on with me."

She led them into the large storeroom. "What do you need for supplies?"

"Food for everyone and whatever clothing and supplies are needed for Makilien's family."

Laena nodded.

Halandor turned to Makilien. "Some of us will need to get our horses from the livery stable and buy extras for the journey. How many horses do you think we need?"

"Leiya can continue riding with me," Makilien answered. "I think one will be all right for my parents and then two more for Aedan and Derrin."

"You can hide them in the alley around back," Laena told him.

"Will you have enough to pay for everything?" Makilien asked Halandor, feeling a little guilty. "I don't have anything I can help pay with this time."

"Don't worry," Halandor assured her. "Lord Darand gave us more than enough. He knew you would be coming with your family."

Makilien smiled, thankful for the king's generosity.

Turning to the others, Halandor said, "Loron, Gilhir, you two stay with Makilien in case Vayzar figures out we came here. And, being Elves, you would draw more attention from the villagers."

The two Elves agreed, and Halandor, Torick, and Sirion prepared to leave.

"Be careful," Makilien cautioned them. She did not like the thought of only the three of them meeting up with Vayzar and his men. But she also knew they were seasoned warriors.

"How long should we give you before Gilhir and I come looking?" Loron asked.

The men looked at each other before Halandor answered, "If we're not back within an hour, you'll know something happened."

Loron and Gilhir both nodded.

When the men had gone, Makilien named off a list of supplies her family would need. When Laena pointed out a wall of shelves piled with clothing, Makilien, her family, and Aedan and Derrin looked through them. Experienced in what was suitable, Makilien helped her mother and sister outfit themselves with clothing similar to her own. For her father, she found a brown, sleeveless suede jerkin such as the one Halandor wore and suggested a few pants and shirts she knew were sturdy enough the last the journey. Aedan and Derrin paid attention to her advice and were able to outfit themselves.

Once everyone had found the appropriate clothing, cloaks, and footwear, they took turns changing behind the curtain in the corner. Makilien changed from her ripped, bloodstained dress into a new sage green, linen dress.

After lacing her overdress, she stepped out and examined the others. She smiled in satisfaction. Her family no longer appeared as poor village farmers. The deep colors of the dresses her mother and sister wore were far different from the drab clothing they had worn all their lives, and her father, in his jerkin and slate blue shirt, now fit right in with Makilien's group of friends. So did Aedan and Derrin. Aedan had changed into a pair of black pants and a green shirt with a dark brown leather jerkin over it, clasped near the side. Derrin's outfit was much the same as Néthyn's, though his jerkin was black and his shirt a dark, rusty red.

With a nod of approval, Makilien joined them and helped pack their extra clothing and supplies into the leather packs Laena provided. By this time, Halandor and the others had been gone for over half an hour. Now that the supplies were packed, all they could do was wait.

Trying not to worry that something might have happened to her friends, Makilien dug through her old pack. It had been a long time since she looked at the items inside. Her royal blue ceremony dress and black vest and skirt were still there, as was her full sketchbook. Coming to the bottom of the pack, she found a small leather pouch she had sewn together. She pulled it out and loosened the drawstrings. Tipping the pouch, the ring Darand had gifted her with for her service to Eldor fell into the palm of her hand. With memories of that day playing in her mind, she slipped it onto her finger.

Across the room, Aedan browsed a shelf full of weaponry. He had never seen so many different weapons. His eyes snagged on a long, two-handed broadsword. He picked it up and slid it out of the scabbard, admiring the sharp blade. Setting the scabbard aside, he weighed the sword in both hands. It was much heavier and larger than Makilien's sword, but it felt just right, almost as if it had been made for him.

"You like that sword?" Laena asked, coming to his side.

Aedan flashed a smile at the woman. "Yes, I do." He slid it back into the scabbard and stared at the brown, leather-wrapped hilt in contemplation "How much do you want for it?" He knew he had nothing to offer, but maybe, somehow, he could pay Makilien's friends back.

"Well," Laena said a smile coming to her face, "I gave your friend Makilien a sword once because I thought she could put it to good use. I think you could too, so you can just take it."

"I couldn't do that," Aedan replied, setting the sword back on the shelf.

Laena shook her head and picked up the sword. "Sure you could," she insisted, handing it back to him. "You want it, don't you, if you meet up with those guards Halandor mentioned?"

Aedan smiled gratefully and nodded. "Thank you."

He buckled the thick strap of the back-scabbard across his chest so he could easily reach over his right shoulder for the hilt of the sword. The weight of the weapon and knowing it was there and he could use it felt good. While he didn't wish for the violence or conflict, he had a deep desire to be a part of the upcoming battle as Makilien had in the past.

Thoughts of the future vanished as Aedan's attention returned to Laena who felt a particular desire to help their group.

To Derrin and Makilien's father, she said, "You two don't have swords either."

Derrin glanced at Néthyn and shrugged. "We don't know how to use them."

"Well, you can't learn if you don't have one." Laena turned to the shelf and chose two well-balanced swords. "I wouldn't feel right sending you out of here without some sort of weapon knowing the danger you're facing." She gave one sword to Derrin and the other to Makilien's father. "I'm sure your friends will take care of the training part."

They both thanked her, and Makilien too gave the woman a smile for her generosity. She could see just how grateful her father was. The night before he had told her how helpless he'd felt not being able to stop Vayzar, and he wanted to learn how to defend himself and his family. Now he could learn just as soon as they were out of danger.

63

Seeing Aedan armed with his new sword, which suited him well, Makilien walked over to him with something she had taken from her pack.

"Now that you have your own sword and we are out of Reylaun, you should have this back too." She extended the mahogany handle of the dagger that had once belonged to Aedan's father.

"You're the one used to carrying it," Aedan replied. "Are you sure you don't still want it?"

Makilien shook her head. "It belongs to you."

Aedan smiled and attached it to his belt. "Hopefully I'll be able to put it to as good a use as you have."

"I'm sure you will."

Their wait dragged on in silence, for the most part, as everyone stood anxiously wondering when the three missing members of their group would arrive. At last, as the hour was drawing to a close, there came a light knock at the back door. With one hand grasping his sword, Gilhir unlocked it and opened the door a crack to peer out. He then opened it more fully to let Halandor, Torick, and Sirion inside.

"Were you able to get the horses?" the Elf asked.

"Yes," Halandor answered.

"What about Vayzar and the guards?" Makilien wondered. "Did you see any of them?"

Halandor nodded. "Yes, but they did not see us. It seemed they were sweeping the village north of here. If we hurry, I think we can reach the southern gate without being seen."

Knowing time was short, everyone gathered up their share of the supplies. Before leaving, Halandor turned to Laena. Reaching into his pack, he pulled out a large pouch and gave it to her. "This should cover everything."

Laena's eyes widened when she opened the pouch and found it full of gold coins. "I think this is far more than you owe."

"It's for the supplies and for all you've done to help us," Halandor told her. "You're really the only person in the village I know I can trust."

Laena's hazel eyes sparkled as she smiled. "I'm always glad when I can help."

Halandor returned her smile.

Though Makilien didn't mean to be watching the two of them, she couldn't help but notice the way their gaze lingered on each other for more than a moment. Unless she was dead wrong, there seemed to be something between Halandor and Andin's lovely shopkeeper. But whether it was just a slight attraction or something more, she could not tell. She glanced at the others, but everyone seemed too busy preparing to leave to take notice. Suppressing a smile, she bent to pick up her pack. By this time, Halandor had joined them and was once again focused on their escape from the village.

"I think everyone should wear cloaks and keep their hoods up," he suggested. "That way we can try to avoid recognition."

Those not already wearing them donned their cloaks and pulled up the hoods.

"I also don't think we should travel through the village as one group. Splitting up is risky, but fewer numbers would draw less attention."

Everyone could see the wisdom in this, and Makilien asked, "How are we going to split up?"

"Loron and I will guide and protect your family," Halandor said. "Torick and Gilhir will take Aedan and Derrin. Makilien, I think you and Sirion should go on first. The rest of us will be a little behind. Just the two of you will be the least noticeable and if you see any of the guards, two people will be able to more easily get away and hide than a larger group."

Makilien hated needing to be singled out for protection almost as much as she hated separating from her family, but it seemed this was just the way things would have to be. Nodding without protest, she followed everyone out of the shop through the back door. Moving quickly, they attached their supplies to their horses, and Makilien mounted Antiro. Beside her, Sirion mounted Falene, and they prepared to ride away.

"We'll be only a couple of minutes behind you," Halandor assured her.

Makilien nodded, and she and Sirion nudged their horses forward. Riding through the narrow alley behind the shop, Makilien pulled her hood forward as far as she could. She was thankful the fog had not all disappeared yet. It would provide them with some bit of cover and, hopefully, mask their identity.

Still anxious about leaving her family, she prayed in her heart for Elohim's protection over them and their safe escape from the village.

Neither she nor Sirion spoke at first. They traveled at a walk so as not to appear in a hurry. Makilien's eyes scanned everyone on the streets, searching for Vayzar or his guards and, at the same time, praying she would not spot them. As they neared the gate, she glanced over her shoulder, hoping she would be able to catch a glimpse of Halandor and Loron coming along with her family, but she saw nothing yet.

"Don't worry," Sirion murmured. Makilien looked at him. "Halandor and Loron won't let anything happen to your family.

If they do meet up with any of the guards, Torick and Gilhir won't be far behind to help them."

Makilien let a smile come to her face at the comfort of Sirion's words.

Soon the two of them arrived at the gate. Keeping out of sight on the other side, they turned the horses to watch for the others. In the quiet surrounding them, Sirion looked at Makilien though he could only see part of her face because of her hood. He realized now how much he'd missed her in the past months. There were not many people he held so dear in his heart. He had always believed she would be back, though he had never been able to be completely sure. But she was here with them now, thanks be to Elohim, and Sirion was determined to keep her safe from the enemy's clutches. Thinking this, he was reminded of what she had told them the night before.

"I'm sorry you had to endure such pain and difficulty for so long in Reylaun."

Makilien turned her head to look into Sirion's face. In his eyes, she could see the pain and sympathy as he thought of what she had gone through. After what he had endured in Beldon, he was one of the few people who truly did understand the pain she had faced. Smiling at his concern, Makilien replied, "But it never was in vain. I think close to half the village now believes the truth. Many believed right away when I first told them about what I'd seen and learned, but many more changed their minds after I started being punished for sharing the truth. I think when they saw I was willing to continue even then, they knew it was real."

"I admire your courage," Sirion said.

Makilien blushed a little. Compared to Sirion and her friends, she didn't feel that courageous.

"It was never easy for me. Really, it was quite difficult. Most days I had times where I really didn't think I could continue with the constant threats and fear of being caught. More times than I would like to admit I wanted to give up, to leave and return to Eldor. I almost did a couple of times, but then I always remembered Meniah and what he told me. He gave me strength to continue other-wise I never would have been able to go on."

"I prayed for you daily."

This touched Makilien deeply. "Thank you, Sirion."

Aedan stood waiting for Torick to give the word to leave. In the meantime, he decided to try to get to know the horse he had been given, a handsome buttermilk buckskin gelding.

"Hey, boy," he murmured, rubbing the gelding's forehead. The only interaction he'd ever had with horses was in the last day and a half. He had a lot to learn about riding and care along the way, but he looked forward to forming a bond with the gelding.

"His name is Lokye." Torick came up beside them and patted the horse on the neck.

"Lokye," Aedan repeated.

The horse nickered softly in recognition of his name, and Aedan smiled.

A moment later, Torick said, "I think we've waited long enough. Let's mount up."

Aedan stepped around to Lokye's left side and mounted. He glanced over his shoulder to see if Derrin had any difficulty. The other young man had mounted all right, but looked more unsure of his horse than Aedan was. Confidence, however, would have to be gained quickly if they were going to get away from Andin without being caught.

Taking the lead, Torick moved his horse down the alley. Aedan waited for Derrin to come up beside him before signaling Lokye to move, but neither one spoke. With Gilhir just behind them, they entered the streets.

Relief rushed through Makilien to see Halandor and Loron appear from the gate with her family. Though it had really only taken a few minutes, it seemed much longer. She smiled as they joined her and Sirion. Halandor, who had Leiya riding with him, moved his horse up next to Makilien.

"You can ride with your sister now," he said.

He helped Leiya climb onto Antiro.

"Thank you for keeping us safe," Leiya told Halandor.

He gave the precious little girl a smile. "You're welcome."

Makilien smiled too and gave her sister a quick hug. "Are you comfortable?"

Leiya nodded. "Yup."

Giving Antiro a light nudge with her heels, Makilien rode over to her parents who were riding a pretty, sweet looking chestnut mare. "Will you be all right riding on your own?"

She remembered learning to ride Antiro and how hard it was at first.

Her parents smiled.

"I think we'll be all right," her father answered.

"It's going to be a long day, so don't hesitate to ask to stop if you need to," Makilien told them.

Now that everything was situated, they had only to wait for the rest of the group. Makilien turned Antiro again to watch the gate. Time ticked by slowly. Several minutes seemed to pass. She wondered if it was only her, but then she noticed Halandor and Loron look worriedly at each other, and Loron said in a low voice, "They should have reached here by now."

Makilien breathed in deeply to calm herself. She could see on Halandor's face that he was contemplating riding back in, but before he could make that move, their missing friends rode out of the village. Everyone sighed in relief as the four of them joined the group.

"What happened?" Halandor asked.

"We spotted a couple guards and had to take a more roundabout way," Torick explained. "We need to leave here now. It won't take them long to get this far."

Halandor nodded and glanced over the group to be sure they were all ready. Without further words, they all moved out, urging the horses into a fast pace. Andin disappeared in the fog behind them.

:Chapter Seven:

Lessons

The setting sun turned the forest a deep shade of gold by the time they stopped for the evening. Already they were well within the border of Eldinorieth. They had ridden nearly nonstop to remain far ahead of any pursuers. Neither Loron nor Gilhir had been able to pick up any sign that Vayzar and his guards were following closely, if at all. But, to be safe, as soon as they were within the forest's boundaries, they left the road, making their way farther into the trees until they had gone a safe enough distance to set up a camp and build a fire.

In a small clearing, the group dismounted and picketed the horses between the trees around the perimeter. Aedan's body protested being subjected to the amount of riding he had done in the last two days, but every ache and pain was worth it. He could not have counted the number of times he'd prayed to be free of the prison he had been born into, and in his heart he thanked Elohim for the escape.

Paying close attention to what the others were doing, Aedan soon had Lokye unsaddled and joined everyone around the fire Torick worked on. Supper was made and then passed around.

As they were eating, Hanna asked, "How far do we have to travel?"

"Another three days if there are no delays," Halandor answered.

"I can show you on a map when we're finished eating," Makilien said.

Aedan thought of Makilien's map. It had been a while since he had seen it, but it was committed to his memory. He remembered the clear path through Eldinorieth following the river, which would lead them straight to their destination. Thinking of the Elven city Makilien so often spoke of, he asked, "How long will we remain in Elimar?"

"It depends on what may have happened in our absence," Halandor told him. "If all is well, then we'll stay to rest for a couple of days at least."

"I can hardly wait for you to meet Lord Elnauhir and his family," Makilien said, looking at her own family and Aedan. "You'll love Elandir and Elmorhirian. Won't they, Torick?" She gave him a grin across the fire.

"If they can abide their shenanigans," Torick responded dryly.

The group chuckled, and Makilien happily told more about the Elven brothers. Though she had shared these stories with Aedan and her family before, they were anxious to hear them again. The remainder of their meal passed with the enter-taining images of these stories in their minds. Soon, the forest grew dark with only the fire providing light when they were finished.

As she packed away the bowl she had eaten from, Makilien noticed her father looking over the sword Laena had given him. Standing, she walked over to Halandor who was also packing away supplies from their meal.

"Will you teach my father how to use his sword?"

Halandor smiled. "Of course."

"Thank you," Makilien said. "I will ask him if he's up to starting tonight."

She returned to her family and knelt next to her father. "Halandor said he would teach you how to use your sword. Do you feel up to beginning the training tonight?"

Néthyn nodded, and though Makilien knew he must be tired, he was eager to begin. Picking up his sword, he stood and met Halandor on the other side of the fire. Makilien watched and heard her father say to Halandor, "Thank you. I appreciate this."

Halandor smiled kindly, but before Makilien could hear his reply, Derrin caught her attention.

"I want to learn too."

Makilien turned to him. She found herself often surprised by his eagerness to become more like her and her friends. He had never shown any interest before, so his sudden change of mind was unexpected. What she did not see in his expression was how he hoped she would offer to oversee his training as she had trained Aedan. Disappointment shadowed his eyes when Torick spoke.

"Halandor can teach two people, and I can be your sparring partner," the older man offered.

Still watching Makilien, it took a moment for Derrin to nod and stand with his sword.

As he and Torick joined Halandor and Néthyn, Makilien sat near her mother and sister. She smiled at Leiya who tiredly rested her head in their mother's lap, but was not yet asleep, and then watched Halandor begin the lesson with her father and Derrin. A smile lingered on her face as she remembered her own nights of learning from him.

A few minutes later, Makilien said to no one of her friends in particular, "I need more practice." She looked to her right where Sirion sat just on the other side of Aedan. "I didn't have a chance when I fought Jorin. I don't want that to happen again."

"I need the practice too," Aedan said.

"I'd be happy to help you both," Sirion offered.

"Maybe you can teach me a few Elven techniques that will give me an advantage next time I face someone like Jorin," Makilien said, getting to her feet.

"I'll see what I can do," Sirion replied with a smile, "but are you sure you want to start tonight with your injuries?"

She flexed her arm. It was still sore, as was her back, but not severely. "I'll be all right to practice for a little while."

Satisfied, Sirion stood, and Makilien followed him to a gap in the trees opposite of where the others were training so they would not interfere. Makilien pulled her sword from its scabbard and they began sparring, careful not to harm each other. She was glad Sirion had offered to help. With his fighting style more Elven than Halandor's, she could learn little things from him that could do much to aid her in the future.

While the two of them sparred, Aedan sat back, sometimes watching them and other times watching the lesson Halandor gave, hoping to learn more from both. As time progressed, he came to realize Derrin did not seem to be very focused on what Halandor was teaching. More often, Aedan caught the young man's eyes on Makilien and Sirion. His gaze intense, he clearly disliked the obvious closeness between the two. Knowing Derrin as well as he did and how he felt about Makilien, Aedan had little doubt Derrin was jealous about this bond, and that troubled Aedan. He hoped Derrin could look past his own disappointment and respect Makilien's feelings, but some nagging doubt told him that just would not be.

Deep in his contemplations, Aedan did not notice when Makilien and Sirion had finished sparring some time later until Sirion asked him, "Do you want to get in some practice tonight?"

"Sure." Aedan rose and joined Sirion at the edge of camp. Pulling out his new sword, he refocused his thoughts, knowing it would be dangerous not have his full attention on the match.

For over half an hour they practiced. The heavier weapon took some time to become accustomed to, and Aedan's arm muscles strained, but he was pleased with his choice of the sword. He did, however, see how his skills were painfully lacking compared to Sirion's and determined to spend as much time in practice as he could before finding himself on a battlefield.

"Once we reach Elimar, we can spar with wooden practice swords," Sirion said as the two of them returned their blades to their scabbards for the night. "Depending on who you spar with, you can come out with some painful bumps and bruises to be sure, but it's far less dangerous than this, and you can learn a lot more."

Halandor and the others had just ended their lesson and all took seats around the fire. Hearing Torick chuckle, everyone's eyes turned to him. Looking wryly at Halandor, he asked, "Remember our initial training?"

Halandor laughed quietly. "Yes, quite well."

Turning to those eager to hear more, Torick said, "The two of us were trained together by a retired captain. Once we had learned the basics and began sparring, he did not hold back. His belief was the more pain we found ourselves in, the harder we would try and the quicker we would learn. Those first couple of weeks, I thought for sure I was going to die."

"Aw," Makilien replied in sympathy, but she couldn't help chuckling a little.

"He taught us well, though," Torick said, and Halandor nodded in agreement.

Sirion grinned. "But we'll be easier on our students, won't we?"

"Oh, we'll see," Torick replied, cocking an eyebrow. The teasing glint in his eyes just made everyone laugh.

Despite the pleasant mood around camp, Aedan looked to Derrin who sat silent and found no humor in his face. In fact, he didn't appear to be paying any attention at all to what was being said. His eyes were locked on the flames of the fire as whatever deep thoughts he had played through his mind.

But Aedan was too weary to worry about it now. After a full day of riding and their evening activities, all were ready for sleep. As soon as the order of watch was decided—Loron, Halandor, and Torick the first night and Sirion, Makilien, and Gilhir the next—they rolled out their bedrolls and lay down, hoping for a restful, as well as uneventful, night sleep.

When Makilien awoke and opened her eyes to see the dark silhouettes of the trees against a pink-tinted dawn sky, she was relieved. If Vayzar and his guards were going to catch up and attack them, everyone assumed it would have been during their first night, but nothing was amiss and everyone but Torick was still asleep. Warm and comfortable, snuggled up next to Leiya, she let her eyes slide shut again for a few final minutes of rest.

She finally rose and rolled up her bedroll when she heard Halandor get up. Everyone else followed shortly. They ate a cold breakfast and soon packed up camp. Carrying her share of supplies, Makilien walked over to Antiro.

"Good morning," she said to him, running her hand down the length of his face.

Making a soft sigh-like noise, Antiro nuzzled her face, and Makilien smiled as she made her way around to saddle him. Once she had secured the saddle, she turned to pick up the supply packs and found Derrin there.

"Let me help you," he offered, already having the packs in hand. Makilien didn't have time to respond before he attached them to the saddle. Glancing at her, he went on, "You shouldn't have to do all this work alone when you're injured."

"Thank you for your consideration," she replied, "but really, I'm all right. The wound to my arm is not serious and my back is well on its way to being healed."

But Derrin did not give her a response. He kept working until all the supplies were secured to Antiro's saddle. Makilien stood by watching him, not entirely pleased with his intrusion and the way he ignored whether or not she actually wanted any help.

Soon they were ready to go and mounted up. Still standing near, Derrin was quick to lend a hand when it came time for Makilien and Leiya to mount. Again without asking if Makilien needed the assistance, he lifted Leiya up into the saddle. Holding back a sigh, Makilien mounted.

"Thank you," she murmured, but it held no feeling.

As soon as all were mounted, they left the campsite behind, once again coming to the road and following it south at a steady pace. For most of the day, the weather remained good for travel, warm and sunny, but around mid afternoon, dark clouds gathered overhead. The air cooled and the breeze picked up, rustling the leaves and tugging at everyone's clothing. The forest dimmed under the thick cloud cover, and the dampness in the air warned of rain. Before long, low rumbles of thunder echoed in the distance.

Earlier than usual, Halandor and Torick brought the group to a halt.

"I think we should stop and find somewhere to camp for the night," Halandor said. "We'll try to put together some sort of shelter before it rains."

They dismounted and searched for a suitable place to set up camp. Just ahead, they found a stand of pine trees where the ground was slightly raised and would not collect rainwater. Making use of the tree branches and a couple lengths of rope, they created the roof of their shelter, which they covered in pine boughs they cut from other trees. Once it was covered over, they built a quick wall on the side where the wind was blowing. With everyone working together, it did not take long for them to have a nice shelter built that would hopefully keep them dry during the night.

After a satisfied look at their work, Torick turned back toward the horses to get something from his pack. "I'm going to see if I can catch a few fish for supper."

"Sirion, why don't you get a fire going and I'll go with Torick," Halandor said.

"I'll look after your horses," Gilhir offered.

Halandor nodded and he and Torick, and Loron as well, walked off toward the river. Everyone else cared for their horses, and Sirion went to gather firewood. Makilien followed to help him. As she collected dead branches, she asked, "Has there been any trouble with mountain wolves lately?" They were drawing near to the place where she, Halandor, and Torick had been attacked during her first journey through the forest.

Sirion shook his head. "No, not that we have heard of, and we had no trouble coming through here."

This relieved Makilien, though with such a large group, including two Elves, she didn't think they would have had trouble warding off an attack anyway.

As they continued to talk and gather wood, chuckling every once in a while at each other's comments, Aedan helped Makilien's family arrange their supplies inside the shelter. Walking out again, he spotted Derrin standing near the horses. Following his line of sight, Aedan realized he was watching Makilien and Sirion. With a sigh, Aedan walked over to him. He didn't even have a chance to say anything before Derrin remarked, "She spends a lot of time with him."

Aedan could practically feel the other man bristle with envy.

Slowly, Aedan answered, "Yeah, they are good friends."

Derrin's jaw shifted a little, but he spoke coolly. "What is he? An Elf?"

"No, he's Half-Elf. His father was an Elf and his mother was Human," Aedan explained.

Derrin didn't end up saying more, and Aedan prayed he would be able to get over Makilien. What made it worse was Aedan suspected Makilien was the only reason Derrin had left Reylaun.

These thoughts were broken by Makilien calling to Leiya.

The little girl left camp and ran to her sister several yards away. Makilien grinned at her. "Look what Sirion and I found."

"What?" Leiya asked curiously.

"Look up into this tree."

Leiya's head tipped back. Among the branches of the tall, thickly leafed tree above her hung many pale blue fruits.

"Jents," Makilien said excitedly. "Remember I told you about them."

Delight lit Leiya's face. "Can I try one?"

"Of course," Makilien answered.

Leiya looked back to the fruits that hung high above her reach. But in a moment, Sirion scooped her up and set her on his shoulder.

"There, now you can reach them," he said with smile.

Leiya giggled and reached up to pluck a large jent from the tree.

"Try it," Makilien coaxed.

Her little sister bit into the juicy flesh of the fruit, her eyes widening. "It's delicious!" she exclaimed, a little of the juice running down her chin.

Makilien laughed, and she and Sirion grinned at each other. As soon as Leiya finished with her jent, Sirion instructed her to pick a few more and toss them down to Makilien. With an armful, they brought them and the firewood back to camp, and let the others try the candy-like fruit.

In less than an hour, Halandor, Torick, and Loron returned with a string of fat trout, which they cooked over the fire Sirion built. Makilien couldn't wait to eat, remembering how deliciously Halandor cooked the fish. As hard as she had tried back home in Reylaun, she'd never been able to do it like him.

When at last it was served, everyone savored the taste, enjoying a hot meal that warmed them from the inside against the chilly breeze that preceded the storm.

Once nearly everyone had finished eating, Halandor rose and looked to Makilien's father and Derrin. "I think if we are going to have another lesson tonight, we should do it right away before the rain starts."

They agreed and stood, as did Torick. Makilien and Sirion also rose for their practice session. Again, Aedan sat back and observed. Tonight he noticed a difference in Derrin. Though he did glance toward Makilien and Sirion at times, he seemed focused on the lesson. He put a huge amount of effort into it and though this was only Derrin's second lesson, Aedan was surprised and impressed at how well he did and how quickly he learned. Wielding a blade seemed to come naturally to him, which Aedan found the most surprising.

Halfway through the lesson, a flash of lightning lit up camp followed by a deep crack of thunder. In a moment, rain began pattering on the leaves, rapidly growing in intensity. Before they could get wet, everyone hurried into the shelter.

"I guess that's the end of tonight's lesson," Torick said.

With nothing else to do, most of the group put on their cloaks in case the shelter leaked and crawled into their bedrolls to get some sleep.

The muffling sound of a downpour greeted Makilien when she awakened sometime after midnight. In the dark was a person's silhouette, and she barely heard Sirion's voice over the rain.

"It's your turn for watch," he said.

Yawning, Makilien sat up. Careful not to wake Leiya who slept next to her, she made her way toward the front of the shelter.

"Would you like me to take your watch for you?" Sirion asked. "I don't mind."

"No, that's all right. It's only a couple of hours, but thank you," Makilien replied, smiling gratefully.

"Wake me if you need anything," Sirion said, and he went to his bedroll across the shelter.

Sitting, Makilien wrapped her cloak tightly around herself. Her clothes felt a little damp all over and her sleeve was wet from a leak, but overall, the shelter seemed to keep everyone dry. Taking a deep breath of the earthy air made fresh by the rain to clear her mind, she sat back against the tree at the corner of the shelter. She glanced at those still sleeping comfortably and then stared out into the inky darkness. She couldn't imagine anyone or anything that might mean them harm prowling around in this weather, but no one wanted to risk it, so she tuned her ears to any sound that might be heard over the rain to signal an enemy presence.

Not quite an hour had passed when Makilien realized someone else was awake. She had not heard them get up and did not know who it was until they knelt down in front of her.

"Derrin, what are you doing up?" she asked.

"Woke up and couldn't sleep so I thought maybe you'd like company."

Makilien just looked at him. Company would be nice, but not necessarily his. Things seemed especially awkward between them lately.

"You really should be getting rest while you can," she tried.

But he shrugged, "I can rest when we reach the city."

Makilien let out a small sigh, which was masked by the rain, and looked back out into the darkness. Silence fell between them, but Derrin broke it a few moments later.

"Why don't you tell me about your adventures last summer. I'm sorry I didn't really pay much attention to them before."

Makilien was reluctant, but there would only be awkward silence if she didn't speak. Quietly, she told her story, hoping her lowered voice wouldn't be enough to wake anyone. Under normal circumstances, she loved to tell of what she had experienced, but tonight she did not feel that eagerness. Instead, she was apprehensive, as if she had to be careful what she said and her voice carried no joy.

This rather painful recounting lasted for twenty minutes before Derrin cut in with a question.

"How did you meet Sirion?"

So that's what this is about. Makilien bit down hard and stared at him for a moment. Though she could barely see him in the dark, he stared back, awaiting her answer.

"We met in Beldon when the others and I went down there to convince Lord Andron to join us in battle," she finally answered rather coldly. "Sirion was being held prisoner."

"Why was that?" Derrin asked.

"Because Beldon saw Althilion as an enemy at the time, and Lord Andron wanted to withdraw information from Sirion to aid him in an attack on the Elves." Makilien stopped here for a moment and then said flatly, "I'm sorry, Derrin, but now is really not a good time for me to tell you of my adventures. I need to listen for anyone who might decide to brave this weather and attack us."

Derrin said no more, for which Makilien was glad, but it took another several minutes before he stood and returned to his bedroll. Again Makilien breathed a sigh. Putting her head back against the tree trunk, she prayed within herself, *Please, Elohim, show me how to deal with this situation. I just want Derrin to accept how I feel and that my feelings will never be for him.*

:Chapter Eight:

Elven Hospitality

M akilien brushed back the damp straggles of her hair before pulling up her hood and looking over their travel-weary group. They had just spent their third night on the trail, wet and cold. The evening before, they had attempted to build another shelter, but everything was already soaked after the rain, which had persisted all day, and still it rained. Makilien wasn't the only one thankful they would not spend another night on the trail, but in Elimar. The thought of warmth, dry clothes, and warm food helped lift her dampened spirits as she followed the others to their horses who looked as miserable as their riders.

"How are you doing, Antiro?" she asked, stroking his cheek.

The horse shook his head, sending a spray of water droplets into the air.

"I know," Makilien said sympathetically. "But by tonight you'll be warm and comfortable in a dry stall with all the hay you can eat. I promise."

Antiro gave her a pleasurable nicker, and she smiled as she brought her saddle around to his side. She had become so accustomed to this routine she worked almost without

85

thinking. As she turned for the supplies, she found Derrin approaching to assist her. This was the third morning in a row. She was wearied by his persistence, and, with this weather, not in the most charitable mood. Just before he reached her, she picked up one of the packs and attached it herself.

"I can help you with that," he quickly offered.

Makilien shook her head. "Thank you, but no. I'm perfectly capable of doing my work, injured or not."

"I would really like to help you," Derrin pressed.

"I'd rather do it myself," Makilien replied firmly.

Derrin's face pinched in frustration. Finally he said, "You wouldn't decline Sirion's help if he offered it."

Makilien stopped and looked hard at him. She opened her mouth to speak, but realized she could not deny his accusation. Snapping it shut, she turned back to her work; however, Derrin was not finished.

"You hardly know him, Makilien."

She peered at him again. "Whatever you're trying to get at, Sirion and I are close friends whether you think I know him well or not. Yes, I probably wouldn't decline his help, but at least he'd respect my feelings if I did."

She may have gone on to say more, but there was a timely interruption by none other than Sirion.

"Is there a problem?" He looked between them, his eyes expressing concern when they rested on Makilien, but hardening when they switched to Derrin.

A long pause hung between them. Finally, Derrin shook his head.

"No," he muttered, walking away.

With an exasperated sigh, Makilien looked up at Sirion.

"What happened?" he asked.

"He's in love with me," Makilien answered in frustration. Sirion's brows rose a fraction, and she went on, "He has been for years. I keep telling him I have no feelings like that, but he just won't accept it, and now he's jealous."

"Of?"

"You."

Sirion frowned. "Me?"

"Yes. I'm sure he notices every little bit of time we spend together and wishes it were him instead."

"Is there anything I can do?"

Makilien shook her head. "I don't think so. Somehow, I have to make him understand without any doubt that nothing will happen between us, but even then I don't know if his jealousy will go away, at least not for a while."

"Do you think he may try to cause you harm if you keep refusing him?" Sirion asked. He wasn't about to see something like that happen.

She shrugged. "I can't imagine it, but I will be cautious."

Sirion's eyes sought the other man for a moment, eyeing him critically. Finally, he said, "Well, if you do need any help, don't hesitate to come to me or one of the others."

Makilien smiled. "I won't."

With things settled for now, they started on their way. In only an hour, they had left the forest, coming upon Eldor. The rain lessened to a gentle mist, making travel a little more bearable. When midday came around, they did not stop as long as usual, anxious to reach Elimar as soon as possible.

Finally, as late afternoon crept into evening, the road made a turn to the east, bringing them to the river. On the other side lay Elimar looking as if it were glowing in the rainy gloom from the warm light inside the houses. Pausing for a moment at the riverbank, Makilien turned her head to look at Aedan who smiled widely.

Riding on, they entered the water. The typically shallow river was much higher from the rains and came well up around the horses' legs, but they had no trouble crossing. On the other side they entered into the forest city. The surrounding trees were dark with moisture. Everything lay in peaceful quiet, but for the pattering of raindrops on the foliage and the running of nearby streams.

Despite the rain, Aedan pushed back his hood so he could better take in the beautiful city. Patches of vibrant flowers with water dripping from their petals grew along the soft paths winding their way here and there. Studying the buildings they passed, Aedan admired their graceful architecture and creamy white exteriors.

In a few minutes, they came to the largest building in the city and halted. Aedan was more than ready to have a good long break from riding and suspected everyone else felt the same. Tiredly, he dismounted.

Glancing over Lokye's back, he watched Derrin dismount. As the young man slid from the saddle, he bumped into Sirion who had just dismounted. Looking over their shoulders, they traded fiery glances. Aedan shook his head. Things seemed to be escalating. Whatever had happened that morning between Makilien, Derrin, and Sirion had left Derrin in a particularly bad mood where Sirion was concerned. Aedan had seen him glaring at Sirion during their brief lunch break, and his contempt obviously hadn't dissipated. But perhaps once they were all dry, fed, and well rested, things would be different.

After removing their supplies from the saddles, they left the horses at the hitching post and walked up to the large, slate-blue doors of the building, which Aedan guessed was Lord Elnauhir's house. When they reached it, Halandor pushed the doors open and led everyone into a grand foyer. Those who had never before seen it stared in amazement at the smooth, light marble floors and tall, ornately carved pillars supporting the high ceiling.

A moment later, Aedan's eyes were drawn down from the pillars by the sound of a rich, deep voice. A tall Elf approached them, and Aedan knew at once he was Lord Elnauhir.

"You've returned," the dark-haired Elf lord said with a smile, expressing his joy. The smile widened when his brown eyes focused on one particular member of the group. "Makilien, how good it is to see you safe and once again in our city."

With a joyful smile of her own, Makilien replied, "I am so happy to finally be here again, my lord."

Introductions followed. Elnauhir had warm greetings for Makilien's family, and when he turned to Aedan, he said, "I am very pleased to meet you, Aedan. Makilien told us much about you and your desire to have come with her. Welcome to Elimar."

"Thank you, my lord," Aedan replied.

Before much more could be said, an exclamation of, "Makilien!" drew everyone's attention across the room where Lord Elnauhir's family had just appeared.

"Vonawyn!" Makilien responded, and they met near the center of the foyer, giving each other a tight hug.

"I'm so glad you're back and safe!" Vonawyn exclaimed. "I missed you so much."

"And I missed you!" Makilien replied.

They parted and smiled happily at each other.

In the background, Aedan found himself mesmerized by Makilien's Elf friend. The moment he saw her, his heart had slammed itself against his ribs. He'd thought her quite beautiful when he'd seen her in Makilien's sketches, but to see her in person was altogether different. She was without a doubt the most beautiful thing he'd ever laid eyes on.

His gaze followed her as she joined the group, but he only faintly heard Makilien introduce her to her family. The next thing he knew, she was standing right in front of him and Makilien was saying, "This is my friend, Aedan."

"Aedan, it's so nice to meet you." Vonawyn gave him a sparkling smile, her rich brown eyes aglow with kindness.

Almost forgetting himself, Aedan managed, "And it's a pleasure to meet you as well." He felt it was a rather weak attempt on his part, but anything else would have come out awkwardly.

As Vonawyn turned to greet Derrin, Aedan was given a moment to re-gather his thoughts and get a hold of himself, but the beautiful Elf maiden's smile was forever implanted in his mind.

Elnauhir's wife and sons were next introduced. Aedan greeted Elandir and Elmorhirian, mindful of the stories Makilien had told of the two. He knew immediately he liked them both and that they'd be great fun to be around.

"You're just in time for supper," Elnauhir told the group after introductions.

"Excellent," Torick said, with more enthusiasm than usual. "We haven't had a warm meal in days."

Turning to his children, Elnauhir instructed, "Vonawyn, show Makilien and her family to their rooms and see they have dry clothes. Elandir, please do the same for Aedan and Derrin."

To the group, he said, "When you have settled in and changed, you can come to the dining room."

"Just make sure Elmorhirian stays out of the food until we get there," Elandir said, giving his brother a teasing nudge.

Elmorhirian gave him a familiar impish look that made Makilien laugh and brought smiles to others in the group as they followed Elandir and Vonawyn from the room.

Somewhere deep in the house's interior, the group split. Elandir took Aedan and Derrin, along with the other men down one hall while Makilien and her family followed Vonawyn to another. Several doors down, Vonawyn stopped and opened one, leading them inside.

"This room is connected to the one right next to it," she explained. Pointing across the spacious room, she said, "The door is there. You can use both rooms." She smiled as she turned to face them. "While you get comfortable, I will find dry clothes for you."

Makilien gave her friend a grateful smile.

When Vonawyn had left the room, Makilien turned to face her family. She grinned at the way they stared, not quite sure what they should do in such a large room unlike any they'd ever before seen or imagined.

"It's beautiful here, isn't it?" she asked.

"It's breathtaking," her mother replied.

"And big," Leiya added.

Makilien chuckled. "Yes, it is." To her parents, she said, "You can have the next room and Leiya and I will share this one."

They nodded and entered the other room to look around. Makilien walked across the room to take in the view from the windows. It was a lovely view into one of the gardens. A contented smile came to her face. She felt at home here and thanked Elohim for giving them a safe journey.

A moment later, Leiya came to Makilien's side. "How long do you think we'll be here?"

"Probably a few days. We'll have to see what information Lord Elnauhir gives us on what the enemy has been doing."

"I like it here. I hope we can stay a while."

Makilien put her arm around her little sister. "Well, when this war is over . . . if we are successful, then maybe we will live here."

"Do you think we can?"

Makilien smiled down at her. It had been on her mind for the last couple of days. Now that she had left Reylaun again, she would not go back, and that meant getting to live in Eldor as she'd dreamed of for the year she'd been away. If she were going to choose anywhere, it would be right here in Elimar.

"I think we can, if this is where mother and father want to live."

"I hope so," Leiya said with a big smile. But her smile soon faded. "What if we lose the battle?"

Makilien sobered as well, but said confidently, "Then it will part of Elohim's plan, and we must trust Him. He knows what He is doing. In the meantime, we'll enjoy our time here."

They continued to stand at the window until a knock came at the door. When Makilien opened it, she found Vonawyn with a bundle of clothes in her arms.

"These are for you and your family." She stepped inside and set the clothing on the bed. Picking out one of the dresses, she turned to Makilien. "This one is for you."

Makilien took the pretty lavender gown in her hands, running her fingers along the silky fabric.

Vonawyn then picked up another dress and walked over to Leiya. "And this one is for you," she said with a smile.

Leiya's brown eyes lit up as she touched the smooth, light pink satin dress, small enough to be just her size. "It's so pretty!" she exclaimed excitedly. "Thank you."

Vonawyn grinned. "You're welcome." Turning back to Makilien, she said, "I will gather more clothes for you later. I can also have the clothing from your packs washed."

On her way out of the room, she asked, "Do you remember your way to the dining room?"

Makilien smiled. "I think I do."

"All right. I will see you there."

Makilien nodded and closed the door. After bringing the other clothes to her parents, Makilien and Leiya changed. Makilien helped Leiya into her new dress and pointed to a full length mirror at the other end of the room. Dashing over to it, the little girl grinned at her reflection. She turned sideways and then held out her arms to admire the long flowing sleeves. Makilien could tell her sister wasn't quite sure what to do in such finery.

Walking up behind her, Makilien smiled at her in the mirror.

"I feel like a princess," Leiya said.

"You look like a princess."

Positively beaming, Leiya grinned into the mirror. Brushing her hand across her sister's hair, Makilien realized both of them needed to do something about their damp, matted tangles.

"Do you want me to braid your hair for you?" Makilien asked.

"Yes, please," Leiya answered.

Dividing Leiya's hair, Makilien braided it into two cute braids and then braided her own hair into one long braid. By this time, their parents came from their own room, and Makilien led them all to the dining room. Everyone was there when they arrived, and a large meal had been laid out on the long table.

They now took their seats, but before the food was passed around, heads bowed for prayer. Elnauhir gave thanks for their food and company, and especially for giving Makilien and her friends a safe journey. He asked for Elohim's guidance and protection in the days ahead. After a round of "amen," food dishes were passed before Elandir and Elmorhirian could become too impatient.

As soon as everyone had settled into eating, Halandor looked to Elnauhir at the head of the table. "Have you received any new information since we left?"

Lord Elnauhir stopped eating, and sat back in his chair.

"Yes, actually, we have." He paused, giving everyone the feeling the news would be disturbing. "Lord Darand's spies have reported there is an Elf in Zirtan's service."

A shocked silence blanketed the table. Glances were exchanged at the news, but it was Makilien who spoke first.

"An Elf?" she repeated, hardly able to believe such a thing.

Elnauhir nodded grimly. "They are calling him the Dark Elf."

"Are they sure?" Torick asked.

"Yes. Zirtan is making no secret of it. He wants everyone to know so it will disgrace the reputation of Elves."

Once again came silence. Never before had an Elf been in allegiance to Zirtan. It was almost unthinkable.

"Do you know why or how this Elf has turned on his people?" Halandor asked.

Elnauhir shook his head. "No. We have no details. But we must not let it discourage us. Elves are imperfect, just as all races are, and though we believed none of us would ever be swayed to join the forces of evil, it was never impossible. We will continue to prepare for Zirtan's attack and pray that no more join his service."

This sobering news colored the rest of the evening. However, Elnauhir and his family went out of their way to make sure Makilien's family was comfortable. It pleased Makilien greatly to see they truly did seem to enjoy it here.

After supper, the entire group gathered in the main sitting room to visit, but they did not stay there late. Soft beds beckoned to the travelers and prompted them to say their goodnights earlier than they may have otherwise.

In their bedroom, Makilien and Leiya found soft nightgowns laid out for them. Once they had changed, they both crawled into the large canopy bed and pulled the covers up around themselves.

"The bed is so soft," Leiya commented, having never slept on a feather mattress before.

"Yes, it is," Makilien agreed, also relishing the comfort.

Though Makilien knew Leiya must be very tired after the long journey, the little girl's eyes were especially bright as she suddenly asked, "Do you think now Mama and Papa will believe in Elohim?"

"I don't know, Leiya. We will just have to wait and see."

"What if something happens to them before they believe?"

The question put a seed of worry in Makilien's heart. Even though they were as safe as they could be here in Elimar, danger was never far away. Anything could happen to any one of them.

"We just have to trust Elohim will protect them until they do," she said after a contemplative moment.

Leiya nodded trustingly, and her eyes closed. Before long she had fallen into a deep sleep. However, Makilien found herself not so easily able to dispel her worries. Instead of falling immediately into the sleep her body craved, she lay awake in the dark silence and prayed.

:Chapter Nine:

Sparring

Pulling on a soft, green, linen shirt, Aedan stepped across the room to one of five windows, arched elegantly at the top and much taller than he was. There, he was bathed in the dazzling morning sunlight. The heat radiated on his face and even through his clothes, and it felt good. After days of rain, a time of sunshine was greatly appreciated. Especially on their first full day in Elimar where there was much he wanted to do and see outdoors.

Aedan was just in the process of silent thanks and gratitude to Elohim when he heard Derrin get out of his bed across the room. Turning halfway, Aedan greeted him. "Good morning."

"Morning," Derrin responded half-heartedly.

"The sun's shining," Aedan said, hoping it might brighten his mood.

"So it is."

Derrin began changing, and Aedan just shrugged to himself at his failed attempts to cheer him. Finally, he asked, "Are you hungry?"

This elicited a more enthusiastic response from Derrin.

"Starving."

With a smile, Aedan walked over to a chair where his jerkin lay and slipped it on. "Good. Let's go find out if breakfast is ready yet. After the meal last night, I'm anxious to see what is served this morning."

Aedan leading the way, they left the room. After a series of turns and halls, and a flight a steps, they came to the doorway of the dining room. A delighted giggle came from Leiya as they walked in. Aedan saw her sitting at the table between Elandir and Elmorhirian who were clearly having a marvelous time making the little girl laugh. Everyone else seemed to be present except for Makilien and her parents.

Approaching the table, Aedan and Derrin met Vonawyn. With a most lovely smile she said, "Good morning."

"Good morning," Aedan echoed, doing his best not to stare. Whenever he found himself near her it was as though a butterfly had taken up residence in his chest.

"Breakfast is ready," Vonawyn told them. "Makilien went to see if her parents are up. As soon as they get here, we can eat. You may have a seat if you wish."

"Thank you," Aedan replied.

Vonawyn moved off down the table. Aedan's eyes lingered on her, but only briefly as Derrin moved past him to find a seat. He followed, and they both sat. It turned out Vonawyn sat down just across from Aedan next to one of her brothers.

A few moments later, Makilien and her parents walked in. Now that everyone was present and seated, they began their meal after Lord Elnauhir's prayer. Spirits were much brighter than they had been after the news the night before, and much laughter rang out around the table. After some time, they discussed their plans for the day. Makilien wanted to show everyone around Elimar since the weather was so beautiful.

Elandir and Elmorhirian volunteered to head up the tour, which Makilien happily agreed to since they'd been such entertaining guides in the past. When those plans had been made, Aedan said, "I'd like to get in some sparring."

"Yes," Torick agreed, "we should get back at it. Halandor wasn't able to get very far with Néthyn and Derrin's training."

"We can help you practice," Elandir offered, looking specifically at Aedan, and Elmorhirian nodded in agreement.

Vonawyn raised an eyebrow. "You better ask him if he really wants to practice with you." She turned her eyes to Aedan across the table. "When you get the two of them into a sparring match, things can get rough."

"Only between the two of us," Elandir defended himself.

"Or when we spar with Torick," Elmorhirian added.

"Yes, but that usually ends in swift and painful retaliation, so it is only occasionally," Elandir said.

Everyone laughed, particularly at the humorous glint in Torick's eyes.

"I'd be glad of your help," Aedan told them.

"All right then, how about we tour the city this morning and then go to the training field after lunch?" Elandir suggested.

With nods of agreement, their plans were settled and the meal continued leisurely.

"Just pick out whichever ones you feel comfortable with." Elandir gestured to a long weapon cabinet filled with various shaped and sized wooden swords.

Everyone walked up to the cabinet and chose practice weapons that were similar in size and weight to their own, and followed Elandir out of the Elven barracks to the training field. Quite a few other Elves practiced there, but they had one end to themselves. Almost everyone was present though Elnauhir had business to see to, and Makilien's mother and Lorelyn, who were becoming good friends, chose to remain at the house with Leiya. Vonawyn too was absent, but said she'd join them later.

They split up into pairs—Halandor and Makilien's father, Torick and Derrin, Makilien and Sirion, and Aedan and Elmorhirian. Loron and Gilhir were present, but they mostly just observed as did Elandir who also threw in tips and pointers once in a while.

The practice was beneficial to everyone, and they worked hard at it for quite some time. After well over an hour, Makilien and Sirion paused for a break, and Makilien looked over the others. Most of the men had removed their shirts in the heat of the afternoon sun, and she could see red welts and bruises starting to show on various people, mostly the inexperienced. Aedan seemed to have the majority of injuries. His knuckles on his right hand were cracked and bleeding, and bruises were forming on his left shoulder and lower around his ribs while Elmorhirian was unscathed. She felt sympathy for Aedan, but none of the injuries slowed him down, and he seemed to be learning much more than she'd been able to teach him. Under the circumstances, she thought he was doing well considering he was sparring with an Elf.

While Makilien and Sirion watched, Elandir interjected his opinions, though he seemed to be far more interested in pointing out his brother's flaws than offering Aedan any constructive criticism. Clearly, Elmorhirian was getting annoyed, and Makilien and Sirion exchanged glances just before the younger Elf decided he'd had enough.

Calling the match to a halt, Elmorhirian spun around to face his older brother. "I'm getting tired if this, Elandir. Just because I don't do something your way, doesn't make it wrong."

Elandir crossed his arms lazily, looking rather amused at riling his brother. "Well, I do have ten years more experience than you do."

Elmorhirian snorted indignantly. "After how long we've both lived, I don't think your age superiority gives you any advantage over me."

"It gives me more maturity."

"Ha! Sure. Why don't you pick up that sword of yours and prove it."

Elandir raised his eyebrows. "You're sure you want to do it this way?"

"Oh, yes." Elmorhirian already had his sparring sword raised threateningly and a mock smile on his lips.

Elandir just shrugged and reached down for the practice sword at his feet. Everyone else stepped back in anticipation of the brutal battle to follow. For a moment, the two brothers just stood staring at each other, Elmorhirian glaring while Elandir grinned at him. Finally, Elandir said, "Your move, younger brother."

That was all Elmorhirian needed to hear. He attacked Elandir with a speed and agility only an Elf could possess. Elandir easily dodged or blocked the attacks with the same speed and agility. A couple minutes into the fight, Elandir started throwing taunts in between attacks, which infuriated

Elmorhirian all the more, but caused everyone else to laugh. Suddenly, one of Elmorhirian's attacks hit Elandir squarely in the shoulder with an audible smack. He took a quick step back, groaning and rubbing his shoulder.

"Okay, now I know you're serious," he muttered, no longer sounding amused.

After that, the fight went all out. Each gave and received nasty blows causing everyone to cringe between laughter, but neither one of them seemed to notice the pain, yet. All they really managed was to entertain their audience. The fight eventually ended when both of them grabbed the other's wrist. They pushed against each other, but neither of them moved. Breathing hard and pouring sweat, Elandir finally said, "Shall we just call it a draw?"

Elmorhirian said nothing, but realizing he couldn't actually beat his brother, he nodded and they stepped back. That's when the pain set in, and there were groans as they rubbed the bruised areas all over their upper bodies.

"How did you two get into it this time?"

Everyone turned at the sound of Vonawyn's voice. She stood a couple feet behind the group with a pail in one hand and a wooden sword stuck into her belt. Makilien noticed she was not dressed in one of her regular Elven gowns, but in a light, blue cotton shirt with the sleeves rolled up, a pair of dark gray pants, and a lighter gray overdress with a split skirt.

Still sounding indignant, Elmorhirian answered, "Elandir got it into his head to try to convince everyone I'm not a good swordsman."

Vonawyn smirked. "And you tried to teach him a lesson, but it didn't turn out quite like you wanted?"

"No," Elmorhirian muttered. "We're too evenly matched."

Elandir grinned at his scowling brother. "Come on, Elmorhirian, it was a joke," he said persuasively.

Elmorhirian glared hard at him, but then sighed. Elandir smiled. "Does that mean you forgive me?"

His brother contemplated it for a moment, and then gave a reluctant smile. "Of course."

"Good," Elandir replied. He rubbed his shoulder again. "Next time, can we settle things a more peaceful way?"

Now it was Elmorhirian's turn to laugh. "We'll see."

With everything settled between the two of them, they all turned their attention back to Vonawyn who held up the bucket she carried. "I thought you could use some water. It's warm out here."

With a round of thanks, everyone gathered for their turn to drink. Checking them for injuries, Vonawyn said, "None of you look too worse for wear, besides my brothers." Looking at Aedan, she asked, "Who were you sparring with?"

Aedan inclined his head toward her brother. "Elmorhirian."

Vonawyn just nodded quietly, not surprised.

Once everyone's thirst was satisfied, she set the bucket on a nearby bench and pulled out her practice sword. "Am I too late to join in on the fun?"

Elmorhirian laughed. "You haven't practiced in ages."

"Precisely why I'm here," Vonawyn replied dryly. She gave him a certain look that only the children of Elnauhir could give. "I bet I could beat you."

Elmorhirian laughed dismissively. "I highly doubt that."

Vonawyn raised her eyebrows. "Is that so?"

"Yes," Elmorhirian answered, his voice mocking. "That's so."

"Are you prepared to back up that statement?"

Here Elmorhirian paused, realizing he was digging himself into a hole, so Vonawyn goaded him further, "Or are you too scared?"

Elmorhirian narrowed his eyes. "No." He picked up his practice sword again, and faced his sister.

Elandir shook his head. "You just never learn do you? Always letting your mouth get you into trouble."

Elmorhirian shot him a dirty look. "Look who's talking."

"Well?" Vonawyn pressed when he didn't move.

"You challenged me, so you attack," Elmorhirian told her.

"Very well," Vonawyn said, giving a small, almost bored sigh.

But her attack was lightning fast, allowing him barely enough time to raise his sword to block. Everyone watched with great interest, especially Aedan. He was awed by her fluid motion and skill. She was every bit as good as Elmorhirian, perhaps even better. Vonawyn was smaller than her brother, but quicker, which gave her a good advantage. Both blocked each other's attacks successfully, but Elmorhirian had to work much harder.

In a sudden movement, Vonawyn sidestepped to dodge an attack and, at the same time, swung her sword out toward Elmorhirian. The blow landed hard to his right side where one of Elandir's attacks had previously connected. He yelped and grabbed at the throbbing injury. Before anything else could be done, Vonawyn moved behind him and knocked his legs out from under him causing him to land hard on his back. She then pressed the tip of her sword down against his chest, pinning him to the ground.

For a brief moment, only silence surrounded them, but it was followed by low laughter and a couple of snickers, particularly from Elandir and Torick who both applauded Vonawyn's victory.

"Very well done," Torick complimented.

Elmorhirian glared at him and then up at his grinning sister feeling quite humiliated.

"That wasn't fair, Vonawyn. You of all people ought to be able to see how painful my side is," he whined.

"Isn't it a good thing to know your enemy's weakness?" Vonawyn questioned. "And think of it as just retribution."

"For what?" Elmorhirian demanded.

Vonawyn shrugged, tipping her head a little. "You seemed to be needlessly rough on Aedan."

Elmorhirian scoffed. "What?" He threw his hands out in a gesture of disbelief.

But Vonawyn ignored him and gave Aedan a quick smile. Makilien, quite amused by the whole thing, looked over at Aedan and was surprised to find him blushing. She didn't believe she had ever seen him blush before. She looked to Vonawyn who helped her brother off the ground, and then back to Aedan. This time he was staring down at the ground, but his face was still a shade of red.

With echoes of "goodnight" behind him, Aedan left the sitting room and walked through the dim halls of the house. His shoulder ached and his knuckles stung under the thin layer of bandages, but he felt great. He didn't think he'd ever been so content in his life. He loved every moment he had spent here so far. The city was breathtaking and the company . . . well, depending on who it was, they had a way of taking his breath too.

Aedan wondered about Vonawyn as he made his way to his room. Did she feel any of the attraction he experienced around her? He had no idea. *It's way too soon*, he ended up telling himself. He may have found himself taken with her, but she surely didn't feel anything after only one day. And who knew what adversities the future would bring between now and the end of the coming battle, whatever the outcome may be. It hardly seemed a good time to blossom a relationship. Still, he didn't completely banish all hope as he came to his bedroom door.

He turned the knob quietly. Derrin had gone to bed some time ago, and he didn't want to disturb him. However, when he stepped into the room, Aedan found several of the candles lit. Derrin sat in a chair against the wall, his sword in one hand and a cleaning rag in the other. He glanced momentarily at Aedan, only to continue polishing the hilt of the sword.

Aedan closed the door behind himself. "I thought you went to bed."

"I didn't feel like sleeping."

Walking over to his bed, Aedan unclasped his jerkin. "You should have stayed with us. Elandir and Elmorhirian told some great stories."

"I didn't feel like it," Derrin muttered.

Aedan turned back to him and crossed his arms. "What's up, Derrin? You've been moping around ever since we left Andin. How can you not feel content here?"

Derrin barely acknowledged him with a glance. "I'm not sure I like it here."

"Why?"

"I don't know if I like the Elves. They are different. Very different."

Aedan's mouth hung open for a moment. Where had that come from? Then he had a thought. "Does this prejudice have anything to do with Sirion being Half-Elf?"

The muscles in Derrin's jaw tightened, and his fingers squeezed hard around the hilt of his sword, but he did not speak.

"Listen, Derrin," Aedan said firmly, "whether Makilien and Sirion have feelings that go beyond friendship or not, you have to let this go. I understand how you feel, but—"

Derrin rose abruptly. "You have no idea what I feel."

That may have been true two days ago, but not since Aedan had met Vonawyn. He didn't have feelings quite as deep as Derrin had for Makilien, yet, but he could imagine.

"I think I have a pretty good idea."

Derrin just scoffed and shook his head.

"Derrin, Makilien has a right to choose someone else if she wishes," Aedan tried to reason with him.

"Why can't she give me a chance?" Derrin questioned. "A chance to show her I can be every bit of whatever she sees in Sirion." He shoved his sword hard into the scabbard. "All my life I've been looked at as a failure. I've always been a disappointment to my parents. They constantly tell me how perfect my sisters are and how worthless I am just because I don't want to work in the store or be like my father. If Makilien would just give me the chance, I could prove I'm not the failure everyone thinks I am."

Aedan's brows lowered. "You're trying to marry Makilien just to prove a point to your parents?"

"No," Derrin replied. "I love Makilien. I have for years, and that is why I want to marry her, but having a family and building a life on my own, for myself, will show my parents I'm not as worthless as they think."

Aedan sighed heavily. He felt sorry for him. He'd always known Derrin didn't get along well with his business-obsessed parents and two older sisters, but he'd never realized the true extant of misery it caused him.

Aedan shook his head sympathetically. "I never knew all that. I don't believe your parents truly think you are worthless, and I'm sorry they caused you to feel they did. You are not worthless or a failure, and you don't need Makilien to prove that."

Derrin's eyes narrowed defensively, but Aedan continued, "There are other girls, Derrin."

"I want Makilien," he said with stubborn defiance.

Aedan looked hard at him. "But she doesn't want you. If you truly love her, you should let her make her own choice."

Derrin's anger bubbled just below the surface. "I'm going to bed," he muttered.

And that ended the conversation. Aedan stood where he was for a moment with an uncomfortable feeling. The situation was bound to come to a head sooner or later, and he had a strong suspicion it would be ugly.

With a desperate and exasperated prayer, he finally turned to get ready for bed.

:Chapter Ten:

Conflict

Walking down the hall, Sirion rolled up the sleeves of the fresh shirt he'd put on. He had just come from the training field where they'd spent most of the morning sparring. Now lunch would soon be served to the hungry group.

On his way to the dining room, he came around a corner and found Derrin standing against the wall just down from him. He eyed the young man. For days Sirion had sensed the growing hostility between them. Not sure of Derrin's intentions, he moved past, but Derrin stopped him.

"I've got something to say to you."

Sirion slowly turned back, noting how Derrin's blue eyes were narrowed and dark with anger. He raised an eyebrow. "Yes?"

Pushing away from the wall, Derrin jerked his head toward the door at the end of the hall. "Outside."

He stalked off out to the garden. Wondering if the young man had any intention to discuss this civilly, Sirion followed just behind.

They stepped out into the damp, muggy air outside. The day was overcast, and thin bits of fog threaded through the trees. A few yards from the house, they stopped, standing squared off with each other. Folding his arms, Sirion waited, watching Derrin's every move. The way the young man's fists balled told Sirion to be ready to duck at any time.

"You don't have any right to Makilien," Derrin spat, and that started it.

Sirion scoffed. "And you do?"

"I've known her all her life. We grew up together. You've been with her for what? A few weeks total?" Derrin questioned. "I know her far better than you do."

Sirion's brows lowered deeply. "Makilien and I are close. If that bothers you, deal with it. This has nothing to do with how long we've known her, and the length of time doesn't give either of us any kind of rights. The only right that matters in this is Makilien's right to choose whoever she wishes to have any interest in or *not*."

"She'd give me a chance if it weren't for you," Derrin was certain.

"From what I understand, she already chose not to before she ever met me so I don't see how I am ruining your chances."

"Keep away from her and I'll get my chance. I'll show her I'm every bit the man you are and more." Derrin took a step closer as his ire rose until they stood a mere foot apart. If Derrin chose to try to hit him, Sirion wasn't sure what was going to keep him from hitting Derrin right back, if only to knock some sense into him. He was getting altogether tired of Derrin's attitude and unreasonable behavior.

"Why are you so friendly with Makilien anyway? You're a Half-Elf," Derrin spat contemptuously. "Nothing like her. You don't understand the kind of life she lived . . . that we lived. We lived simple lives before all this. Nothing like you, growing up in some Elf palace where you had everything handed to you."

Sirion let his arms fall to his sides and balled his own fists. If he hadn't cared that it would be wrong, he would have sent Derrin to the ground in one swift move. He was sorely tempted to do so, but kept himself in check. His voice dropped to a low, aggravated tone.

"You don't know anything about my life, what I've been through, and the people I've lost."

"But I still know I have more in common with Makilien than you ever will," Derrin insisted, his voice sounding not so much angry, but desperate.

"Which means nothing," Sirion said through gritted teeth. "The choice is still Makilien's."

The declaration and the truth of it once again inflamed Derrin's anger. Sirion knew this time Derrin was going to take a swing at him. Derrin's arm rose a fraction, and Sirion prepared to dodge the blow, but they were both cut short by a throat clearing. Their heads turned toward the house where Vonawyn stood in the doorway. She looked between the two of them, frowning. Finally, she informed them, "Lunch is ready."

Sirion and Derrin glared at each other again, neither moving. At last, Sirion started for the house, but paused and looked Derrin in the eyes.

"No one will *ever* force Makilien into a relationship," he declared. "Whatever you choose to think about us, you will let her make her decisions, and you will accept them. Understand this, I will not stand by and watch if I see her bothered in any way. I will do everything I can to avoid a fight, but if that's what you force this to come to, you better be certain it's what you really want."

Having said his piece, Sirion continued on to the house. At the door, he glanced over his shoulder. Derrin still stood in the garden, his head bent and shoulders drooping. Unexpectedly, Sirion felt his heart moved to pity. He could hardly blame Derrin for trying so hard to win Makilien when he clearly loved her, though he couldn't condone his obsessive unreasonableness. Still, his anger with the young man was much lessened.

Inside, Sirion found Vonawyn giving him a questioning and rather concerned expression.

"Is something wrong?" she asked.

Sirion glanced over his shoulder again. Derrin was finally coming. He shook his head. "There was just a situation that I hope has been settled."

Makilien knew something was up the moment Vonawyn returned to the room with Sirion and Derrin, and it only became more apparent as the meal progressed. For the entire time, Derrin just glowered at his plate, not really in an angry sort of way, but more like he was deeply depressed. Sirion too was quiet and preoccupied, even when Elmorhirian tried to include him in a conversation.

Wanting very much to know what had happened between the two, Makilien pulled Vonawyn aside as soon as lunch was over.

"Do you know why Sirion and Derrin are upset?"

"I found them out in the garden," Vonawyn answered, glancing at them. "I didn't hear anything they said, but I know they were arguing. I walked out just as it looked like Derrin was going to hit Sirion."

Makilien sighed heavily and rubbed her forehead in frustration, feeling a major headache growing.

"What's going on?" Vonawyn wanted to know.

"Derrin is jealous of Sirion because of how close we are, and Derrin has been hinting at marriage for a long time now so obviously he loves me," Makilien explained. "It has been causing all kinds of conflict ever since we left Andin. I've tried to tell him I am not interested in his affection, but he keeps persisting." She shook her head. "I have to make it clear he has to stop. It's just not easy because I know I'm going to have to be pretty harsh to make him understand, and I hate to do that to him."

Vonawyn put her hand sympathetically on Makilien's shoulder. "I will start praying about it right away. I know it will be difficult, but I'm sure it will be for the best."

Makilien nodded in agreement. "It will have to wait until later though. Leiya really wants me to take her for a walk, and I promised I would."

Vonawyn smiled at the mention of the little girl. "You better hurry then. It feels like it could start raining soon."

Leaving the dining room, Makilien found Leiya just down the hall laughing with Elandir and Elmorhirian. The two Elf brothers loved to entertain Leiya. They'd told Makilien her little sister reminded them a lot of Vonawyn when she was little and how they'd played with her. It made Makilien smile to think about.

"Are you ready to go for a walk, Leiya?" Makilien asked as she came up to them.

Leiya nodded eagerly. "I'm ready."

"Aw, you're leaving us?" Elmorhirian pouted.

Leiya giggled. "Just for a little while."

"Well, we won't have any fun until you come back, so don't be gone too long."

"We won't," Leiya promised.

Makilien took Leiya's hand and said, "Let's go to our room to get our cloaks just in case it starts raining while we're out."

They walked upstairs to their bedroom and took their cloaks from the closet. After putting them on, Makilien retrieved her sword from where she'd left it leaning against the nightstand and attached it to her belt. After being stabbed by Gornath in Eldor, she never liked to wander around anywhere without a weapon.

Makilien smiled while Leiya cheerfully chattered on about anything and everything that pertained to Elimar as the two of them walked down one of the city's soft paths. She enjoyed every moment spent with her friends, but Makilien was also glad for a time alone with Leiya. She found herself reminiscing over past events—all the nights she'd taken Leiya to hear Mornash's stories and the nights she'd whispered her own. And now they were here, in one of the very places Makilien had told her about.

They walked past the stable, and then the barracks and training field. There, they came to one of the more elevated foothills within Elimar. They followed the path up, which wound its way around the perimeter of the city. Though not sunny, it was a lovely day for a walk. The quiet, still air and the fog hanging in the trees gave the forest a mysterious, dreamy atmosphere that Makilien and Leiya both enjoyed.

Not quite an hour after they'd left the house, they came to the eastern-most edge of Elimar, a little south of the ford, where the ground rose up a couple feet above the river. Makilien imagined the drop would be much farther had the river been its usual low depth, but it was still swollen and flowing swiftly and turbulently through this section. She cautioned Leiya not to get too close so they stood beside a towering hemlock tree, much too wide for them both to fit their arms around. It had begun to mist, but the thick boughs of the tree kept them dry while they stood and talked.

Aedan's stomach ached. He had never laughed so hard at anything as he did Elandir and Elmorhirian. Gathered on one of the covered terraces with a bunch of the guys, the Elf brothers were giving an account of one of their numerous hunting misadventures. Aedan thoroughly enjoyed it; however his attention shifted when he caught sight of Derrin leave the house and head in the direction Makilien and Leiya had gone. After the tension he'd sensed during lunch, apprehension grew inside him. Yet, he didn't know if he should follow or not. Maybe, if they could have a serious conversation, Makilien would finally get him to understand there would never be anything between them. But what if he refused to accept that?

Torn with indecision, Aedan glanced back at those around him and noticed Sirion too had seen Derrin go. They looked at each other, and Sirion seemed to be just as uncertain. Should they let things play out and hopefully be put to an end by Makilien, or would it be folly not to intervene considering Derrin's unreasonable behavior of late?

"I want to learn how to ride a horse," Leiya announced. "All by myself. Do you think I can do it?"

Makilien smiled. "I'm sure you can. We'll just have to find you a small horse or pony."

"Will you teach me?" Leiya asked.

"I don't think I'd be very good at it," Makilien told her. "Vonawyn would be much better. She taught me."

"Can we ask her when we go back?"

"Sure, but you might have to wait to start learning until we know how much longer we'll be here."

"I can wait," Leiya said patiently, and Makilien smiled.

A moment later, they both looked up when they heard someone coming. Makilien's shoulders sagged when she saw it was Derrin. In a way she'd been avoiding the situation by taking Leiya for a walk though she had promised too anyway, but it looked like the situation had come to her. Drawing in a breath and squaring her shoulders, she looked down at her sister.

"Leiya, why don't you explore a little bit by yourself for a few minutes. You can pick a bouquet of flowers to bring back to Mother."

Leiya nodded. "Okay."

"But stay within sight and don't go near the river," Makilien warned. "We'll be heading back soon before the rain gets any heavier."

Happily, Leiya skipped off to a patch of wildflowers a few yards away. At the same moment, Derrin reached Makilien. *Please, Elohim, help me,* Makilien prayed in earnest. For a second they stood and looked at each other. Derrin stared down at Makilien, his gaze intense, but hopeful and even pleading.

"Makilien, I really need to talk to you."

"Derrin," Makilien tried to keep the conversation from going further, but he stopped her.

"Please," he said. "*Please* just let me say what I want to say."

Makilien shifted. Finally, she nodded. "Speak."

"Makilien, I don't think you understand how much I love you. All these years I haven't simply admired you. I *love* you. There isn't anyone else like you. You are beautiful and intelligent and braver than anyone else I know. You make me feel like I can be all I ever wanted to be, and I just don't know what I'll do without you. I've tried so hard to show you I can be the kind of man you want and can make you happy. Please, Makilien, give me a chance . . . I need you."

Derrin's voice was hoarse with emotion, and tears glinted in his midnight blue eyes. No one had ever poured their heart out so desperately and so pleadingly to Makilien before. It made it difficult to say what she knew she must.

"Derrin, I'm sorry," Makilien murmured, more quietly than she intended, however her certainty increased as she continued, "but you are just not the man for me."

Derrin's expression fell painfully. He looked like he had lost everything that meant anything in his life, and Makilien was sure he felt like he had. Just one pained word followed her declaration.

"Why?"

"I've told you," Makilien tried to say as gently as possible. "We are just not alike."

"But we've known each other for so long," Derrin insisted. "What makes us less alike than you and Sirion? He's so different from us. Everyone here is."

"Derrin." Makilien sighed. "What's between you and me has nothing to do with me and Sirion. And what you don't seem to see is that I am different too," she stressed. "I am no longer the girl you fell in love with. I am more like my friends here. We have the same beliefs, the same goals, and the same things we're fighting for. Please understand that. I don't want to hurt you, I truly don't, but I cannot . . . *will not* have this continue. It *must* end now. Neither of us wants the tension and discomfort this is creating."

Makilien watched him, praying for understanding. The young man looked utterly broken and dejected. Despite the times of irritation and discomfort he'd caused her, Makilien's compassion made her feel sad for him. In a way, she knew exactly how he must feel. Empty, lost, and without purpose. She'd felt that way before leaving Reylaun and realizing the truth that was in Elohim. He was the only One who could provide what Derrin truly needed. Makilien could not do that for him.

She opened her mouth to explain this, but a stifled scream cut her off. Her eyes flew past Derrin and her heart lodged itself in her throat. Like an image from a nightmare, a black-clothed man clutched her precious sister in his grasp.

"Leiya!" she gasped.

Before another second could be wasted, Makilien yanked out her sword.

"You let her go," she demanded.

But the man sneered viciously, and the brush surrounding them cracked as more men burst into the clearing along the river. Makilien had no choice but to face the nearest one as he drew his sword and came for her. However, she did not wait for him to make the first move. She charged at him, taking a desperate swing at his midsection, but her attack was batted off to the side, and she was forced backward toward the rushing river. Makilien attempted another attack, but was foiled again, and she found herself having to move fast in order to defend herself from her foe's counterattack.

Leiya's stifled attempts to cry for help spurred her on as her thundering heart pumped adrenaline through her veins. She glanced toward the man holding her sister. Slowly, he made his way toward the thicker part of the forest. Distracted by the sight and feeling of intense panic at the thought of him getting away, Makilien didn't realize a third man had made his way around behind her. It was too late by the time she sensed his presence. Yet, before he could take a swing at her, there was a solid thump, and he groaned as he fell to his knees, grabbing the back of his neck. Makilien sidestepped away from him, keeping her first opponent at bay with the tip of her sword.

Glancing at the fallen man, she saw Derrin standing behind him with a hefty tree branch. She looked up into his face, feeling a bit stunned. Even after rejecting him, he'd still come to her rescue.

Then she caught sight of the downed man reaching for his sword at his knees.

"Look out!" she warned.

But it was too late. The man whipped his sword around as he stood, and Derrin could not back away in time. The blade cut into his flesh high on his left side. He doubled over, clutching at the wound that dripped blood down the front of his shirt. Before Makilien could stop it, the man shoved Derrin toward the riverbank where he slipped over the edge.

"No!" Makilien shouted, her blood running cold, but she found some small relief when Derrin managed to reach out and catch a root sticking out of the bank. However, being wounded, he could not hold on for long.

Makilien acted in an instant. Swinging widely, she discouraged her original foe from advancing and was able to catch the other man in the back with the tip of her sword. He roared in pain and stumbled a couple of feet before falling to the ground, writhing.

"Help!" Makilien screamed.

Her answer came a moment later when the man holding Leiya gave a cry of pain. Makilien looked over her shoulder. Her sister fell from the man's arms as he clutched at a dagger in his shoulder. Sirion and Aedan burst into the clearing, and Makilien almost melted with relief. Hurrying to Leiya, Sirion scooped her safely into his arms.

In the same moment, Makilien's foe redoubled his attack, and she had to refocus her attention. She did, however, find a moment to glance at Aedan who was coming to her aid and said, "Derrin is in the river!"

Aedan dashed to the riverbank where Derrin only just hung on. Getting down as far as he could, Aedan grabbed the other man's wrist. Despite the intense pain it caused, Derrin reached up to take hold of Aedan's arm with his other hand. Pulling with all his might, Aedan slowly dragged Derrin up the bank.

Suddenly, all the air was forced from Aedan's lungs as something hard—someone's booted foot—drove into his ribs. He didn't have any way of regaining his balance as he tumbled down the bank.

Everything took place so quickly Makilien didn't even realize anything had happened until she heard a splash. She looked to her left. The man she had wounded stood at the river's edge. Aedan and Derrin were nowhere to be seen. A horrible numbing sensation gripped Makilien at the realization that her best friend and Derrin had been swept away. The shock was so great she momentarily forgot her opponent, but fortunately Sirion reached him just before he could do his intended harm. As the man fell, the wounded man at the river ran off into the trees.

Snapping out of her daze, Makilien scrambled to the river-bank and scanned the turbulent water in desperation. But there was nothing. No sign of Aedan or Derrin. She turned and stared at Sirion, eyes filling with tears.

:Chapter Eleven:

The River

Makilien's mind whirled. What would happen to Aedan and Derrin? Could they survive the swollen river, or would they both be drowned? The fear of losing Aedan stabbed deep into her heart, and she barely kept herself from bursting into tears.

Before she or Sirion could take action, half of Elimar seemed to arrive in the clearing—all of their friends and several Elven soldiers. Everyone had weapons drawn, prepared for a fight, but when they saw only Makilien, Sirion, and Leiya, they stopped.

"What happened?" Elandir asked.

Makilien realized everyone looked to her. Trying to calm herself, she recounted the attack. She ended with a tear running down her cheek. Though she wiped it away, more followed.

Elmorhirian hurried to the river to look, but even his keen sight wasn't able to find any sign of the two young men.

"Do you think they could be alive?" Makilien asked, fighting back tears.

Elandir hesitated. "Can they swim?"

"I . . . I don't know," Makilien stammered. "We were never really able to learn in Reylaun."

Elandir's grim expression did not give her hope.

"We have to find them," she said.

"We will," Elandir assured her. Finally, he turned his attention to the two men lying on the ground. "Are they both dead?"

Sirion shook his head and motioned to the man who'd tried to abduct Leiya. "He's only unconscious."

"Where is the third man?"

"He ran off," Sirion answered.

Turning to the soldiers, Elandir instructed, "Two of you take the unconscious man back to the city for questioning, and the rest of you go after the one who escaped."

As the Elves moved to obey, Makilien walked to Sirion, her eyes on Leiya. Her younger sister looked remarkably calm compared to the panic gnawing inside Makilien.

"Are you all right?" she asked.

"I'm all right," Leiya answered with a quick nod.

Sirion placed her into her sister's arms, and Makilien held her tight, tears rolling down her cheeks at the thought of almost losing her too.

"Are *you* all right?" Leiya asked quietly.

Makilien nodded, but could not speak.

"We must get our horses and start searching along the river," Torick said.

Just before the entire group exited the clearing, Makilien left Leiya for a moment and walked back to the river where Aedan's sword lay. As she brushed the dirt from the blade and hilt, she prayed desperately he and Derrin were still alive and would be found.

Back in the city, Lord Elnauhir and the rest of the household met them outside, anxious to know what all the commotion was about.

"What has happened?" the Elf lord asked.

Elandir explained the attack to his father. Everyone looked shaken, especially Makilien's parents. Hanna took Leiya in her arms, holding her close, and Makilien noted the fear in her eyes.

"Were they Zirtan's men?" Elnauhir asked after his son's explanation.

"I'm guessing so, but we don't know for sure," Elandir answered. "We've brought the unconscious man back for questioning. He's being taken to the barracks."

"Good."

Makilien stepped in then with one thing on her mind. "We have to find Aedan and Derrin. If they survived the river, there could be more men out there who could capture them."

Elandir nodded. "We'll get our horses and leave immediately."

Makilien turned with her friends for the stable, but stopped when she heard her mother.

"Makilien, wait."

She turned back to her parents.

"Those men were after you and Leiya," Hanna said. "Won't it be dangerous for you to leave here if there are more men out there seeking your life?"

"Yes, but I have to find Aedan and Derrin."

She caught the pleading look in both her parents' eyes. They wanted her to stay here where she'd be safe. She was torn. Everything inside her wanted to go with her friends, but she also did not want to cause her parents the worry. She heaved a sigh.

Then Sirion quietly said to her, "We will do everything we can to find them."

125

Makilien nodded. She knew this and that it wouldn't make it any more likely they'd find Aedan and Derrin if she were there.

"All right, I'll stay," she murmured, though she could already feel how difficult it would be to sit and wait for them to return.

Aedan plunged beneath the raging water yet again. It roared in his ears and blinded him, making him completely disoriented. Water trickled in through his nose and down his airway, suffocating him. He kicked hard to bring himself back to the surface where he coughed out water and gasped at the precious air.

Doing the best he knew how to stay above the water, he searched the boiling rapids. Finally, he caught sight of Derrin only a few feet away as he popped up above the current. It gave him some small measure of relief that he was alive, but the way things looked, neither of them would be for much longer. He couldn't imagine Derrin, being wounded, could have the strength to keep struggling when his own was nearly spent.

It felt like he'd been battling the water for hours. He had been submerged more times than he could remember and battered against rocks, logs, and whatever other debris was carried along by the angry current. At first each bump had throbbed with pain, but the cold water numbed his body.

But Aedan wasn't prepared to give up just yet. He hadn't come this far just to drown. These rapids had to end. There had to be some place shallow up ahead where they could escape the river. *Elohim,* his heart cried, *save us!*

Just when he felt he had nothing left, the river widened and the current wasn't quite as strong. He tried to stand in the waist deep water, but his legs were swept out from under him on his first attempt. Trying again, he found his footing and was able to remain upright. After a quick search of the area, he spotted Derrin to his right, clinging to a dead tree overhanging the river. With painstaking movements, Aedan worked his way toward him, over the slick riverbed rocks as the water rushed against his body. He could hear the roar of rapids just ahead. If he was swept away this time, it would be over.

At last, he reached the dead tree and grasped one of the smooth, outstretched limbs, working his way to Derrin. The young man was pale and barely conscious. Aedan took him by the arm, and helped him stand.

"We have to make it up the bank."

It would not be easy since the bank was a rock ledge jutting up above the water. Using the tree to climb on, they pulled themselves out of the river. Derrin only made it halfway before Aedan had to drag him, no easy task with the smooth rock surface wet from the mist. After an intense struggle, both collapsed on the bank, gasping for breath.

"Thank You," Aedan breathed skyward.

Derrin moaned in pain, and Aedan remembered his injury. He forced himself to sit up, though his limbs were like lead, and crawled to Derrin's side.

"Let me see," Aedan said, pushing dripping strands of hair away from his face.

Carefully, he lifted Derrin's shirt enough to see the wound. He grimaced. A deep laceration about twice the length of his palm slashed across Derrin's ribs, beginning about midway down his side and angling up toward his chest. Though it did not appear to have broken any ribs or cut into his lung, blood still flowed from the wound.

Aedan cast a desperate glance at their surroundings. Everything was soaking wet. What could he do to help Derrin and stop the bleeding? Finally, he shrugged off his jerkin and pulled out his dagger, which he used to cut a strip of cloth from the bottom edge of his shirt.

"I need you to sit up," he said.

Derrin just gave an exhausted shake of his head. Determined to do something, Aedan moved around behind him and slowly helped him up. Derrin groaned in agony, but made it into a sitting position. Keeping him propped up as best he could, Aedan tied the strip of cloth tightly around Derrin's chest. He then put his jerkin on him.

"I don't know how well that will stop the bleeding, but it's the best I can do."

By now, Aedan had begun shivering so badly his teeth chattered. Though the air was warm, the cold river had chilled them both through.

"We have to get back to Elimar."

But again, Derrin shook his head. "I can't make it. Who knows how far the river carried us."

"We are going to make it," Aedan insisted.

"What's the point?" Derrin asked. "I have nothing. Makilien has rejected me, I have no purpose, and I don't belong anywhere. Just go. Leave me here."

Aedan set his jaw and pushed himself to his feet. "There's a lot more to life than Makilien," he said, "and I'm going to show you that."

With steely determination, he reached down under Derrin's arms and lifted him to his feet. He then put Derrin's right arm around his shoulders to give him support.

"You can either find it in yourself to fight to go on or I can drag you all the way, but whatever it is, we're making it back to Elimar."

Derrin exhaled loudly, and they began walking. It was slow going. Neither of them had the energy to go another few yards let alone the miles separating them from safety. But Aedan would not give up. They'd survived the river—a miraculous feat—now all they had to do was reach the city. It gave him hope to think their friends must be out looking for them. They would never assume them dead. On horseback, it probably would not take long to find them. A couple of hours, maybe.

With this hope spurring them on, they stumbled along the river, keeping well clear of the edge.

In silence, Makilien sat at the window that gave her the best view of the direction her friends had gone. They'd left well over an hour ago, and each minute that passed further twisted the anxious knot in her stomach. Everything was quiet, and Makilien thought she was alone until she detected the slight swish of a dress. She looked up. Vonawyn stood near her, eyes full of sympathy. The Elf touched Makilien's shoulder.

"Are you all right?"

Makilien sighed. "I'm trying not to worry, but it's so hard to keep myself from thinking about the terrible things that could have happened to them." Her voice cracked and she went on, "I couldn't bear to lose Aedan. He's all I've ever had for a brother."

"I understand," Vonawyn told her. "It is never easy when those we love are in peril." She looked off out the window.

"You are always so strong during adversity," Makilien said. "How do you do it?"

"It may seem like it, but truly, it's never any easier for me than for you. I think the only difference between us is I've been alive much longer and have had more times to deal with it."

Makilien nodded and looked back out the window. "I just wish I could be out there. Waiting without any word is so difficult."

"I know."

Makilien sighed again. "I think the next while is going to be very difficult. My parents are so worried about me. They are always going to want me to remain where it is safe, but I don't think that will always be possible."

"They love you and can't bear the thought of losing you," Vonawyn said.

"Yes, even more than some parents, I think." Makilien looked at her hands folded in her lap and then up at her friend. "They've had to endure a lot of sadness. Leiya and I are not the only children they've had. There were a few others between the two of us, but they all died either before or just after birth."

"How awful," Vonawyn murmured.

"It was. When I was really young, I couldn't figure out why Mother was sad all the time. Then, when I was old enough to understand, I shared the sadness. I desperately wanted a brother or sister. I think that's why Aedan and I became so close. Finally, Leiya was born when I was eleven and she lived. Ever since then, Mother and Father have done everything they could to protect us. I was too selfish at the time and thought they were only being unreasonable, but that is why they were so upset when I was so outspoken in Reylaun. They didn't want me to get into trouble."

A long moment of contemplative silence fell between them, but a little smile came to Vonawyn's face. "The other babies your mother had, they are not gone and no longer in existence. Elohim makes special provision for those too young to know the truth. You will get to meet your lost siblings someday."

"I guess I've never thought about that before." Makilien's face also broke into a smile at the thought. "I should tell my parents that. Maybe it will give them some comfort and make them want to accept the truth."

Vonawyn nodded. "Maybe it will."

A moment later, someone entered the house. Makilien rose and both of them went to see who it was. When they reached the foyer, they found Lord Elnauhir speaking to his wife. He'd been gone ever since the others left, questioning the prisoner.

"Have you learned anything?" Makilien asked.

"He will not say much," Elnauhir answered, "but we do know he and the others are in league with Zirtan and were here specifically to capture you and your family. Somehow, they received word you had escaped Reylaun."

Makilien's shoulders sagged. "So nowhere is safe for us except right here within the city."

Elnauhir's expression was grim. "It would seem not. I've doubled the guard around the city to ensure no one can get in."

Aedan shook his head to get his hair out of his eyes, but the wet strands clung to his face. He had hoped since they were out of the river, he and Derrin would be able to dry off, but a steady rain had begun some time ago. He could hardly imagine being much more miserable than they were right now. They were utterly exhausted, and Derrin was getting heavier by the minute.

In a grove of hemlocks along the river, Aedan's foot caught on a root, and they both went down. Derrin groaned, gritting his teeth.

"Sorry," Aedan apologized, helping him sit up.

"This is hopeless," Derrin gasped. "You'd be better off going on without me."

"No," Aedan said stubbornly. He had considered finding shelter for Derrin and then going to find help, but he wondered if there could be more men prowling around in the woods. He couldn't let Derrin face an enemy alone. "We'll rest here for a few minutes and then go on. At least we have some shelter from the rain."

Neither one spoke for a couple of minutes, breathing hard. Aedan wasn't cold anymore, and now that the numbness of it had faded, he ached all over.

"You told me you were going to show me there was more to life than Makilien," Derrin said suddenly. "How do you plan to do that?"

"Depends on if you're willing to consider it or not," Aedan replied.

Derrin laughed dryly.

"You said your life had no purpose."

"It doesn't."

"I felt that way at one time and so did Makilien. I'm sure you remember those days. Then we learned the truth and it gave us purpose."

Derrin shook his head. "You may have found a purpose when you heard about this fight against Zirtan, but that means nothing to me."

"It's not just what's outside of Reylaun and this struggle we're in, Derrin. The truth I'm talking about is in Elohim. Serving Him and living my life for Him is my purpose."

Again, Derrin shook his head, but Aedan insisted, "I think you need to at least consider the things Makilien and I have told you."

"What good will it do me?"

Aedan sighed in exasperation and opened his mouth to explain further, but stopped, staring into the forest.

"What?" Derrin asked.

"I thought I heard something."

"Do you think it's someone looking for us?"

"I don't know. Just keep quiet a minute."

Listening carefully, Aedan could detect nothing at first, but then a twig snapped. A cold sensation prickled along the back of his neck.

"I don't think it's our friends," he murmured.

A moment later, a voice sounded behind them. "What do we have here?"

Aedan spun around and found a man standing a few feet away. He was clothed in black, just as the others had been. Slowly, the man drew his sword, and Aedan gripped the handle of his dagger, a sinking feeling in his stomach.

"What do you want with us?" he demanded.

The man just smirked cruelly at him. "I suggest you drop that dagger of yours."

Aedan pulled it from its sheath, but did not drop it. His heart pounded against his ribs.

The man's gaze hardened. "If you don't drop it, we'll just kill you both."

At his words, several more men came out of the forest, surrounding them. Grimacing, Aedan knew he had no choice. His dagger slipped from his fingers.

:Chapter Twelve:

Enemy Encampment

errin stumbled again. Aedan tried to look back, but the man, who had a firm grip on his arm, shoved him on. He didn't know how long they'd been traveling, only that it was a wonder Derrin was still conscious and enduring the grueling trek. They traveled steadily uphill, stumbling over jagged rocks, and skirting their way around narrow ledges. They'd reached the foothills of the mountains, which loomed up tall before them. Aedan had imagined his first sighting of mountains to be a thrilling experience, but he had no such feelings. All that gripped him now was sheer exhaustion and the beginnings of despair.

Finally, the ground leveled out to reveal a gaping hole cut into the mountainside—the entrance to a large cave. Firelight glowed inside and two men stood on either side of the entrance. A group of five men marched out. The man leading was average sized with black hair, a thin face, and a deep, jagged scar that ran from the bridge of his nose down his right cheek.

"What is this?" he asked the head of the group who had captured Aedan and Derrin.

"We found these two wandering around in the woods. They seemed to be following the river north." The man gestured to Derrin. "That one's wounded."

The man from the cave peered with narrowed eyes, first at Aedan and then at Derrin. "Where do they come from and where were they headed?"

"They won't say."

"Did they have any supplies or weapons?"

"Only this." The man who'd captured them handed the scar-faced man Aedan's dagger, though he hardly glanced at it.

Motioning to those around him, the man from the cave ordered, "Take 'em inside."

Aedan didn't have the energy to put up any kind of fight when he was transferred into the hands of these new men and led to the cave. Inside, he and Derrin were shoved toward a crackling fire where they both fell to their knees.

"I'll go inform the captain," the scar-faced leader told the men. "Watch them."

He walked away, disappearing deeper into the cave, and for a moment, nothing else mattered to Aedan but this chance to finally rest. He glanced at Derrin beside him. The young man appeared to be in so much pain Aedan wondered if he noticed anything that was happening. He turned his face back to the fire, taking in the warmth of the flames.

A few minutes later, the man with the scar returned in the company of another handful of men. He strode forward and glared down at Aedan and Derrin from across the fire. He held up Aedan's dagger. "Which one of you does this belong to?"

Aedan looked at his dagger and then at the man's face, but did not speak. However, when the man glanced at someone behind them, he knew things would likely become unpleasant if he did not talk, potentially causing Derrin more pain.

"It's mine."

The man's cold eyes settled on him. "Where did you get it?"

Aedan found it strange to be questioned about the dagger, but again he answered though he'd rather have kept the information to himself. "It was my father's." He tried to detect a reaction from the man that might give him a hint of why he was being questioned, but saw none.

"What is your name?"

The logs in the fire cracked and popped during the long pause.

"Aedan."

Still no reaction from the man.

When no further questions immediately followed, Aedan took it as his chance to speak. "My friend is badly injured and needs medical care."

He began to stand, disliking to be looked down on, but one of the men behind him kicked him hard in the back of the knee. It buckled and he collapsed again. Biting down hard, he stifled a groan.

After drawing in a deep breath, he looked up at the man again, desperate. "Please, he needs help."

The man glanced over his shoulder before ordering the men behind Aedan and Derrin, "Bring them with me."

They dragged the two of them to their feet and pushed them after the leader. Deep inside the cave, they came to a narrow opening, which led into a small alcove. Here they released their prisoners.

"Guard the entrance," the leader directed one of the men, but neither Aedan nor Derrin noticed. Both dropped to the hard, rock floor at the center of the space. Derrin lay on his back, holding his left side tightly as he dragged in ragged breaths. Aedan looked at him in sympathy, but had no way of helping him.

Resting his arms on his knees, Aedan put his head in his hands. *Where are You, Elohim?* he asked in despair. It was as if he and Derrin were completely hidden from Elohim's view, but even as he thought this, he regretted his lack of faith.

Praying for strength and guidance, he sat quietly until he heard someone coming. He looked up as two men strode in, both with an armful of wood and a well burning torch. Without saying a word, the men built a fire and left a small pile of wood off to the side before leaving again. Their actions surprised Aedan, but it didn't seem to come out of any real desire to help, for no one appeared with medical supplies for Derrin.

Carefully, Aedan helped Derrin closer to the fire where he would be warmer. He took a look at Derrin's wound. To his surprise and relief, it didn't seem to be bleeding anymore.

After that, he too lay down next to the fire. He'd been pushed beyond what he'd thought himself capable of, and now, finally, gave in to the exhaustion of his body.

Makilien's heart nearly stopped at the sound of horses outside. She glanced at each member of her family. They shared her expression. An expression of uncertainty and dread mixed with hope. She stood first, and her family followed her out of their room. Her heart beat hard on the way to the foyer. Supper had already been eaten and darkness had just fallen on the city, yet her friends were only just returning.

Along the way, Makilien prayed Aedan and Derrin had been found and were safe, but she also prayed for strength if they were not. The thought of seeing her best friend draped lifelessly over one of her friends' horses sucked the breath out of her lungs.

They reached the foyer the same time as Vonawyn and her parents and hurried to the door. Elnauhir opened it, and they stepped out onto the lantern-lit front step. Looking down into the dark, rainy gloom, Makilien made out the silhouettes of the group and their horses, but not well enough to gain any answers. She waited, holding her breath and praying hard. Finally, her friends trudged up to the house, Halandor leading the way. She searched his face hopefully, but when their eyes met, she knew he did not have good news.

"Did you find them?" she asked, afraid of the answer.

Halandor shook his head. "No."

Makilien's heart sank, and she struggled to fight against the tears welling in her eyes. Was her best friend gone from her life?

A deep feeling of guilt stung her. In some way, she felt responsible for what had happened. If she could have put a stop to the situation between her and Derrin sooner, he never would have been out talking to her when they'd been attacked. Then he wouldn't have ended up in the river and neither would Aedan. In fact, Derrin probably would never have left Reylaun if not for her, and they all may have been safe right now.

"Are you all right?" Sirion asked, his eyes catching the way her face fell.

"I'll be better once Aedan and Derrin are found," Makilien murmured.

Inside, they gathered in the foyer, those of the search party dripping rainwater onto the floor.

"Could you find any sign of them?" Elnauhir asked.

"No," Elandir answered regretfully. "We searched at least twelve miles downriver. It's possible the rain washed away any sign of them, but if they made it out of the river within our search area, surely we would have come across them."

"Do you think they are dead?" Makilien asked, her voice breaking.

"We can't know," Elandir told her. "At least not until we search the other side of the river. We will do that first thing tomorrow."

With no other information to share, Elandir questioned his father about the man they'd brought in earlier. When the search group was taken to the dining room to be fed, Makilien joined them until her family left for their rooms. She wasn't sure she could sleep, but she followed them, having something important to speak with them about.

When they reached the bedrooms, she said, "I want to go with my friends tomorrow to search for Aedan and Derrin."

"Makilien, those men who attacked wanted to kill you," Hanna stressed. "Who knows how many more may be waiting out there wanting to do the same thing. It's just not safe."

"But that is not going to change," Makilien replied. "I am always going to be in danger, unless we defeat Zirtan and all his men, but I can't just hide here for the rest of my life because of it. Please understand, nothing is going to happen to me unless Elohim wills it and if that is so, then staying here is not going to prevent it anyway. You know all the things I've gone through in the past and how many times I've been near death. Elohim protected me every time, and I trust Him to do so in the future."

Makilien watched her mother's expression, tense with worry. She still did not want Makilien to go, but then Néthyn spoke.

"All right. Go with your friends," he told his daughter. Hanna looked at him questioningly, and he said, "She's right. She cannot stay here forever."

A deep feeling of love and respect rose up in Makilien for her father. She had not expected him to agree with her in this.

"Thank you," she murmured. To her mother she said, "Remember, I am not defenseless, and having my friends with me, we can withstand an attack."

Makilien stared up at the silky canopy over the bed, lit dimly by the moon, which had begun peeking through the clouds. All was silent except for the crickets outside and Leiya's gentle breathing. The little girl was sound asleep as were their parents, but sleep was far from Makilien. In fact, she had not yet even changed into her nightclothes.

In the silent darkness, her mind was overrun. She tried to talk herself into believing she was not responsible for what happened, but the guilt would not leave her. She could hardly bear the thought of losing Aedan, and just as painful was to know Derrin did not believe the truth and what would happen if he died. If only she'd done more to explain it to him. If only.

Makilien exhaled loudly, bombarded by if onlys.

Finally, she sat up and swung her legs over the side of the bed. Leaning forward, she put her head in her hands. *I don't know what to do, Elohim. I know I shouldn't dwell on this and should just trust You, but I feel like I'm at fault for what has happened.*

Knowing that to lie there awake would not do her any good, she slipped out of bed and let herself out of the room. Maybe she'd go to the sitting room and find a book to read to keep her mind from going over everything again and again.

Everyone in the house seemed to be asleep, but when Makilien neared the sitting room, she saw the glow of candle-light. Low voices whispered from the room. At the doorway, she found Elnauhir and Halandor in quiet conversation near the fireplace where a small fire warded off the damp night chill. From what little she had heard, she knew they discussed the men who had attacked.

As quiet as she was, both Elnauhir and Halandor heard her enter and looked to the doorway.

"I'm sorry if I'm interrupting," Makilien apologized.

"No, not at all," Elnauhir assured her. "Is there anything you need?"

Makilien shook her head. "I'm just having a hard time getting to sleep. I thought maybe if I did something to occupy my time it might help."

"Well, feel free to remain here as long as you wish," Elnauhir invited. He turned back to Halandor. "We can discuss this more tomorrow."

Halandor nodded, and Elnauhir turned to leave. Smiling kindly at Makilien, he said, "I will see you in the morning."

"Good night, my lord," she replied.

As the Elf left the room, Makilien faced Halandor who remained standing at the fireplace. Quietly, she joined him.

"What is on your mind?" Halandor asked.

She let out a deep breath, weighed down by her conflicted thoughts. "I feel like it's my fault what happened to Aedan and Derrin, and not knowing if they are alive or dead makes it worse. Just before we were attacked, Derrin poured his heart out to me. I told him things wouldn't work between us and that this whole thing had to end. Even after that he still came to my aid when one of the men tried to attack me from behind. That is how he was wounded and knocked into the river."

She shook her head. "I just feel that if I had tried harder to make him understand long ago, he would not have been there today, and he and Aedan wouldn't be lost right now. It's all my fault we were attacked in the first place. The enemy is after me."

A tear rolled down her cheek. She swiped it away, but more filled her eyes.

"Makilien," Halandor said gently, "none of what has happened is your fault. You may feel like it could have been avoided had you done things differently, but remember, Elohim is in control. I know you are upset about what has happened to Aedan and Derrin, and we all hope and pray they are alive and that we'll find them, but think of what would have happened if they had not been there when you were attacked. You might have been killed or you and Leiya could be in the hands of the enemy.

"And you can't blame yourself for the attack. Zirtan hates us all. Torick and I have helped foil many of his plans. He wants us dead just as much as he does you. He's only targeting you right now because you give many people hope, and hope is something we desperately need to go up against him. That should not make you feel responsible for anything that has or may happen. Everything has its purpose, Makilien. Even that which we don't understand."

Makilien gave a small nod. She knew all this, but to have Halandor tell her cemented it in her mind.

"Thank you, Halandor. Even after everything I've seen and know to be true, I still find myself falling into times of uncertainty and fear."

"We all do," Halandor comforted her.

:Chapter Thirteen:

Branded

T he sun peeked just above the trees as Makilien stood in Antiro's stall and lifted the saddle onto his back. She was glad of the sun. It would make searching easier.

"Are you ready to go find Aedan and Derrin?" Makilien asked her horse as she tightened the cinch.

Antiro bobbed his head up and down.

"Me too."

Makilien glanced up as Vonawyn walk past, dressed in a similar fashion to the day they'd sparred, this time carrying a real sword and a saddle. She entered the stall of a white mare across from Makilien.

"Are you coming with us?" Makilien asked.

"Yes," Vonawyn answered. "It will be more protection for you and, since we know Derrin is injured and Aedan could be too, I can help when we find them."

One corner of Makilien's mouth lifted in a small smile at Vonawyn's optimism.

With a groan, Aedan pushed himself up. His limbs were stiff, and he ached all over. Blinking groggily, he scanned the small alcove of the cave. The torch flickered from its holder at the entrance illuminating a guard still standing there. It didn't appear any of the guards who may have come and gone had thought to put wood on the fire. The ashes were almost as cold as Aedan.

When his eyes landed on Derrin, Aedan watched him closely and was relieved to see him breathing. He seemed to be resting well so Aedan was quiet as he knelt where the fire had been and put a couple pieces of the remaining wood in a pile. He looked at the guard who watched him out of the corner of his eye.

"I need this fire started," Aedan said, expecting the man would light it with the torch, but the guard didn't move. Finally, Aedan lost patience and stood boldly, walking toward the entrance. The guard backed up a step and put his hand around the hilt of his sword, pulling it out an inch. But Aedan stopped at the torch and took it from the holder. The guard peered at him with narrowed eyes as he used the torch to light a new fire.

Once the flames had caught the wood, Aedan returned the torch and sat near the fire to warm himself. He took a deep breath, but winced at the deep ache in his ribs on his right side. Pulling up his shirt, he found a dark bruise almost as wide as his hand and suspected one or more ribs might be cracked.

Resting his arms on his knees, he stared at the flames. He wondered if he'd slept through to morning or if it was sometime in the middle of the night. Within the cave, he had no way to tell.

Sometime later, Derrin stirred. When he came fully awake, he tried to sit up, but fell back, gritting his teeth. Aedan moved to help him. Once Derrin was upright, Aedan asked, "How do you feel?"

"Terrible," Derrin mumbled. He grimaced, arm wrapped around his side. "Do you know how long we've been here?"

Aedan shook his head. "No. I think we were both asleep for a while. The fire was dead when I woke."

A long lapse of silence settled between them as both considered their situation. Finally, Derrin glanced at the guard. "What do you think they're going to do to us?"

Aedan too looked at the man. Several suspicions came to mind, none of which he wanted to voice out loud. "I don't know," he murmured.

Silence prevailed again, and Aedan spent the next few minutes in prayer. All was quiet until footsteps approached outside the alcove. The echoes grew louder until the scar-faced man appeared. He walked up to their guard, and the two spoke quietly. The exchange was brief and, after a quick glance at the captives, the man walked away again.

Aedan and Derrin exchanged glances, not sure what to make of the visit, and all went on as if nothing had happened. However, a few minutes later, the man returned. This time he walked into the alcove and stopped, peering coldly down at the captives. He dropped a small sack and a waterskin at Aedan's feet and walked away without a word.

When he was gone, Aedan picked up the sack. Inside he found four hard biscuits. Compared to what he'd been eating in Elimar, the biscuits were a meager offering, but just the sight of them made his empty stomach growl fiercely. He pulled out two of the biscuits and handed them to Derrin. The young man immediately took a bite, but Aedan paused for a moment to say a silent thanks to Elohim. Any food, no matter how meager, would surely give him strength to endure whatever lay ahead.

Finally, he ate his first biscuit. It was dry and bland, but filling. By the time he'd eaten both, his stomach was satisfied. They shared the water, which wasn't much, but enough to relieve their parched throats.

A short time after they finished, the other man returned yet again. Looking specifically at Aedan this time, he ordered, "You, come with me."

Aedan did not move for a moment, not knowing what it might mean to follow the man, but finally he stood. Maybe by going he could find some way for he and Derrin to escape, or at least convince someone to give Derrin the aid he needed.

An ominous feeling of dread pressed down on Aedan as he followed the man through a series of winding tunnels. When one opened up into another alcove, a little bigger than where he and Derrin had been kept, they stopped. The area was set up like a meeting room with a couple tables and chairs sitting around. Though the surroundings were dim, lit only by one lantern, Aedan could see the tables had maps and parchments scattered across them.

But what captured his greatest attention was the man standing at the table with the lantern. With the man's back turned, Aedan could not see his face, but he was about the same height and build as Aedan. When the scar-faced man addressed him, it partially answered the question of the other man's identity.

"I will take my leave, Captain."

The captain said nothing, and the other man left, leaving Aedan to stand alone. Still, the captain did not speak, engrossed by whatever was on the table before him. Aedan took this time to study the area for an escape. Running wasn't an option. The other man would likely be waiting for him at the end of the tunnel and, even if he wasn't, there were bound to be many more men throughout the cave. He looked for any weapons that might have been carelessly left unguarded, but found none.

At last, the captain spoke, his voice low and deep, stirring something buried within Aedan's memory. His brows lowered. He was sure he'd heard the voice somewhere before, and it put him on edge. Who was this man?

"Your name is Aedan?"

Cautiously, he answered, "Yes."

"And you are from Reylaun."

Aedan's eyes narrowed. "How do you know that?"

A long pause followed, and his heart beat hard for each second that passed in anticipation of the answer.

"I could tell you a lot about where you come from . . . son." Slowly, the man turned, and Aedan felt like he'd taken a punch to the gut. All logic told him his father was dead, yet here stood a man who could not be anyone but his father, Jaeson.

Aedan took a step back, shaking his head. "My father is dead. Killed in a hunting accident."

Jaeson peered at him for a long moment. "It was a story, Aedan, made up for your sake and your mother's."

Aedan's mind whirled. "A story?" He couldn't imagine what would make his father purposely lead his family to believe he had been killed and leave them to deal with the pain of it. "For what reason?"

"I had things I needed to do," his father answered with a calmness Aedan could not understand. "It was better for everyone to believe I was dead."

Bitterness bubbled up inside Aedan. "What could be so important that you would abandon your expectant wife and five-year-old son?"

His father looked him in the eyes. "My loyalties demanded my full attention."

"What loyalties?"

"My loyalties to Lord Zirtan."

Aedan stood frozen. Icy cold coursed through his veins. He couldn't decide which was harder to reconcile with—the fact his father was on the side of evil, the side that wanted him and all his friends dead or enslaved, or the knowledge that he was the son of one of their enemies.

"But . . . Zirtan is evil," he stammered, completely at a loss.

His father's eyes darkened. "Lord Zirtan is not evil. You've been misled."

"No," Aedan insisted firmly. "I haven't. I know the truth. Zirtan wants nothing but death and destruction for those who are opposed to him. People I call my friends."

"Those people are bringing this upon themselves. If they'd only give him their loyalty—"

"To serve Zirtan would be to go against Elohim."

Aedan's father shook his head. "You don't understand—"

"You're right," Aedan cut in again. "I don't understand. I don't understand how you can believe Zirtan is not evil. How could somehow who isn't evil hunt down and kill mercilessly, not just men, but women and children? How could he employ the service of creatures like goblins and Shaikes? How could he cause such pain and destruction? How could he condone a father and husband abandoning his family?"

Tension hung thick in the air for several heart-pounding seconds.

"I planned to return as soon as Zirtan's plans were accomplished. I'm doing this for you in part. For you and the other child your mother had. Once Zirtan has power I will be granted land to rule over. I planned then to come for you and your mother and your brother or sister. You would live as a prince, and someday it would all be passed down to you." In his father's eyes lit a spark of hope and excitement. "And now that you are here, you can help to accomplish that."

Aedan set his jaw. "I want nothing to do with it."

The light in Jaeson's eyes vanished. First he was surprised by his son's refusal, but then his eyes narrowed. "You are my son. You should have some loyalty for your father. I want you at my side."

Holding his gaze without waver, Aedan declared, "My loyalty is first and foremost to Elohim, true Lord and Creator of Dolennar, and I will die before I do anything to aid Zirtan *or* his men."

Again, the darkness returned to his father's eyes. "You're making a rash decision. You will see it whether you come to that conclusion on your own or have to be persuaded. I will give you a chance to think it over."

"You would torture your own son?"

A moment of silence fell before Jaeson answered coldly, "I will do what I must to show you that your place is with me."

Heaving a sigh, Aedan dropped to the cave floor near Derrin, finally ready to give up pacing after what seemed to him to be hours, though he still felt restless and unnerved. His conversation with his father played over and over in his mind, and all kinds of emotions raged inside his heart. He still couldn't understand his father's actions and was angered over the path he had chosen. He was deeply troubled, not only by his father's threat to take further action in an attempt to convince him to join his side, but over the fact he was his son. What would his friends think when they discovered he was the son of one of Zirtan's captains? Nothing, he was sure, but still it ate at him.

Aedan glanced at Derrin. His eyes were closed. Aedan wondered if he was asleep, but then Derrin spoke. "What answer will you give your father when he asks if you've changed your mind?"

"That I haven't."

"And face torture?"

"If I must," Aedan said. "I've faced the consequences of defying Zirtan before."

"Seems to me you could be facing worse than a beating in Reylaun," Derrin remarked.

Aedan frowned. "What's your point?"

"Is it worth it?"

"Yes," Aedan answered without question.

Derrin just shook his head. "It's your life you're gambling with."

Aedan gave him a sidelong glance, but made no reply. Derrin's questions and remarks only fueled the uncertainty gnawing at him, and he wanted none of it.

Time passed, though they had no indicator of it within the stale, dim cave. With it, Aedan's apprehension heightened. He found himself wondering, what if he wasn't as strong as he thought he was? What if his father did find a way to break him? He shook his head, to dispel such thoughts. He could never turn on his friends, could he? Stuck here within the enemy's midst and the situation with his father seemed to make him unsure of anything.

Several hours after Aedan had first been taken to his father, the scar-faced man, whom Aedan had learned was called Rothor, came for him again.

"Your father wants to see you."

Aedan rose to his feet. This was what he had been anticipating, dreading. With all the uncertainties warring in his mind, he feared the outcome of this meeting, but as he followed Rothor, he called out to Elohim. He prayed that no matter what happened, no matter what his father did to him, he would have the strength and courage to withstand, to not be broken.

As he did this, a sense of calm seeped into his heart, and instead of doubt and uncertainty, more pleasant thoughts filled his mind. Thoughts of things Makilien had shared with him, particularly about Meniah. He recalled the things Meniah had said to Makilien. Though he had never met him, Aedan could almost hear Meniah's voice, comforting, encouraging. *You're not alone*, and Aedan knew that was true.

This time, Rothor did not lead Aedan to the alcove where he had met his father, but to the large area at the cave's entrance. Outside, the afternoon sun shone brightly, and Aedan had to squint at the sudden light. A handful of men milled about, but Aedan's eyes locked on his father. The man stood near the entrance, his arms folded across his chest, and Aedan was able to see him better now in the sunlight. His dark hair was the same as Aedan's, falling just past a firm jaw, his eyes an intense dark green. It troubled him to know he looked so much like his father.

In another moment, Aedan stood before him. They eyed each other.

"I don't suppose you've had adequate time to reconsider your position," Jaeson said.

"No," Aedan replied, his jaw set stubbornly.

"Eventually, you will," his father said with complete confidence.

Aedan chose not to waste breath responding. His father was just as convinced of him giving in as he was of resisting. Challenging him wouldn't get Aedan anywhere.

After another brief stare down, Aedan's father motioned past him. Two men took hold of Aedan's arms. At first he tried to pull away from them, but even if he succeeded, where would he go? He couldn't take on everyone.

Following Jaeson, they shoved Aedan toward one side of the cave and forced him to kneel beside some sort of contraption with two metal bands attached to a board. They pulled up his sleeve on his right arm and locked his wrist in one of the bands while the other locked near his elbow leaving his forearm exposed.

Finally, Aedan looked to his father who stood a few feet away, poking the end of a long rod into a smoldering fire. He could only shake his head, hardly able to believe his own father would truly go through with his threats.

His heart hammered inside his chest, and though he dreaded what was to come, he spoke boldly. "Whatever you do to me, I will *never* change my mind."

His father merely glanced at him. "This is where you belong. You are my son. My own flesh and blood. You cannot escape that."

"Maybe," Aedan replied, "but our hearts are entirely different."

Ignoring this, Jaeson told him, "You are one of us now, and every man in Lord Zirtan's service is marked to show their loyalty. We are all proud of that mark and you will learn to be too."

He lifted the rod out of the fire. Aedan's eyes locked on the red hot brand at the end. Panic kicked inside of him at the idea of being scarred for life by a mark identifying him with the enemy. He made a desperate move to pull away, but one of the men twisted his left arm up around his back, shooting pain through his shoulder, and weakening his attempt to escape.

Drawing in ragged breaths, Aedan's mouth went dry as his father approached with the branding iron. When Jaeson stood over him, Aedan closed his eyes, praying urgently to Elohim to help him bear the pain and to live with the shame of the enemy's brand.

The glowing, hot metal seared into his flesh. He clenched his teeth and tried to endure the scorching pain in silence, but a cry escaped him. When Aedan's father finally pulled the brand away, an angry red burn remained. Before Aedan could see it clearly, his father picked up a small bucket and poured a dark liquid over the wound. It was black like ink, but thicker, and oozed along Aedan's arm, covering the burn. Though it was cool to his skin, it did not soothe the pain. Instead, it stung as if he were being burned again. He bit down hard and groaned.

After a long moment of agony, Aedan's father picked up another bucket, this one with water, and poured it over Aedan's arm, washing away the ink. Aedan was repulsed by what appeared. The ink had stained his wounded flesh leaving an ugly, black snake design, beginning at his wrist and winding its way up half his forearm. A mark he would have to live with for the rest of his life, however long it may be.

He hung his head, burdened by the weight of these thoughts.

The men released him, and he pulled his arm free, holding it close to his body as pain still pulsed through his nerves. He pushed to his feet, breathing heavily.

"Rothor will take you back to your friend," Jaeson said. "I hope you will come to the right decision so I will not be forced to take the next step."

Aedan looked at his father, his eyes and face as cold and hard as stone. "Don't count on it."

Chapter Fourteen

Troubled

Aedan was miserable. Whatever had been put on his arm to dye the brand had an ill effect on his body. It had come on slowly, but now, a couple of hours later, he was weak and chilled even as sweat collected on his forehead and trickled down his neck. He stayed near the fire, but it did little good.

He stared into the flames, eyes dull and unfocused, lost inside his ranging thoughts. But a weak groan from Derrin snapped him back to reality. Derrin was weakening. It had been quite some time since he'd said anything.

Forcing himself up, Aedan walked around the fire and knelt at Derrin's side. The young man's face was disturbingly pale and also beaded with sweat. Aedan touched his forehead, finding his skin hot. Derrin peered at him through half-closed eyes.

"You have a fever," Aedan murmured.

"From the look of it, so do you," Derrin observed dryly.

"It's whatever that ink was they put on my arm," Aedan said and focused on unclasping Derrin's jerkin so he could see his wound. When he'd untied the makeshift bandage and pushed aside Derrin's shirt, Aedan's stomach knotted. The wound was inflamed, dark red, almost purple in color, and clearly infected.

He swallowed hard, pulling Derrin's shirt back down without speaking.

"That bad?"

Aedan met Derrin's eyes for a moment and then pushed determinedly to his feet. He walked toward their guard who shot him a warning look, but he would not back down. As Aedan drew closer, the guard yanked out his sword.

"You stay right there," he commanded.

But Aedan kept coming. He only stopped when the point of the man's sword pressed against his chest.

"My friend needs help now or he's going to die."

The guard narrowed his eyes. "Get back in there."

"Not until you get him help."

Aedan felt more pressure on the sword.

"Move or I'll kill you," the guard warned.

"I don't think that would put you in a very good position with my father," Aedan retorted.

The guard glared at him, but Aedan could sense his indecision.

At that moment, Rothor appeared. "What is going on here?"

Both Aedan and the guard looked at him.

"I need help for my friend, and I will not rest until I have it," Aedan declared.

Rothor gave Derrin an irritated glance and turned, disappearing again. Aedan took a step back waiting to see if the other man would bring help. After a minute or two, footsteps returned. Jaeson appeared with Rothor and four other men. They halted at the entrance into the alcove, and Jaeson eyed his son.

"He needs help," Aedan said, gesturing to Derrin, his voice low.

Jaeson glanced at the wounded man, but his eyes refocused on his son. "Since he is such a concern and distraction to you from considering my offer, I will rid you of him. He's no use to us anyway."

Aedan's stomach flip-flopped. Backing toward Derrin, he shook his head. "No, I will not let you kill him."

But Jaeson merely motioned to his men. "Take him."

The men came forward.

"No," Aedan protested.

As soon as one of the men was close enough, he made a fist and swung. It connected with the man's jaw, but Aedan's body was too weak to deliver enough power to do any real damage. He momentarily dazed the man, but a second grabbed Aedan's other arm. Before he could pull free, two men held him in an iron grip. He struggled with all his might but could not escape them.

The other men bent down and grabbed Derrin. He put up a weak, but futile struggle. They yanked him to his feet. He moaned, stumbling as they dragged him away.

"Don't do this!" Aedan pleaded with his father.

He struggled harder, and nearly pulled free of one man, but the other rammed his fist up below Aedan's ribs. He doubled over gasping, almost going to his knees. Before he could recover, something crashed into the back of his skull, and he crumpled to the ground.

Aedan groaned, his head throbbing. He opened his eyes a slit, but saw only a blur. Slowly, he pushed himself up with shaking arms, blinking several times to bring his rock surroundings into focus. Then it hit him, like a cruel slap in the face. Derrin was gone. Dead. He closed his eyes and held his head in his hands. His father had murdered Derrin.

Emotion boiled up inside Aedan. He squeezed his hands into fists.

"I hate him," Aedan whispered to himself. "I hate my own father." He shook his head. *Elohim, help me.*

Between fever and overwhelming emotions, his heart beat hard, pumping blood hotly through his veins. Hard eyes settled on the guard left behind to watch him. In that moment, Aedan made a decision. Whether made foolishly in the midst of his emotions or not, he didn't care. Right now, he was going to escape or die trying. He would not sit around waiting to be tortured or meet Derrin's fate.

His gaze went to the smoldering fire and the small pile of wood beside it. He rose and walked over to it, kneeling as he pretended to tend the fire. The guard glanced over his shoulder. As soon as he looked away again, Aedan took a large chunk of wood in his hand and rose to his feet. He eyed the guard. *I don't know if what I'm about to do is foolish of me or not, Elohim, but my life is entirely in Your hands.*

He approached the guard quietly, but his movements were swift. Just as the guard moved to turn, Aedan slammed the chunk of wood down between his shoulders. The man barely made a sound as he collapsed and lay still. Aedan immediately reached down for his sword.

Once he was sure the man wouldn't rise any time soon, Aedan spun around and jogged down the dim tunnel. His heart pounded in his ears. He spotted the end of the tunnel ahead and the glow of sunlight. Voices drifted toward him. He slowed.

Inching along in silence, he peeked out of the tunnel. Counting only three men at the far side of the cave, he breathed in deep relief. If he was fast, he could make it past them to the entrance. Breathing another deep breath and a prayer, he squeezed the hilt of the sword and dashed out of the tunnel. Two heartbeats later, one of the men shouted. Out of the corner of his eye, he saw them jump up and race after him. But he reached the entrance first, bursting into the afternoon sunshine. He stumbled as it blinded him for a moment, but he did not slow. His feet pounded down the stone ledge leading away from the cave. The jarring movements made his joints ache, but adrenaline pushed him despite his body's protest.

Reaching the bottom of the ledge, Aedan glanced over his shoulder. The men were several yards behind, but showed no sign of giving up their pursuit. His eyes shot forward again, mind scrambling. Which way had they come? He'd been so exhausted he hadn't paid much attention to the unfamiliar country. His instincts told him the river was almost straight ahead. However, in a spilt-second decision, he veered a little to the left to head north.

The forest was thin at the base of the mountain foothills, but just ahead, the trees grew thick. With a burst of speed, he crashed into the undergrowth, branches clawing and slapping at his body. At the stinging impact of one across his chin, he put his arm up to shield his face.

Footing was more treacherous here, full of deadfall and hidden hollows in the ground. He tripped and stumbled but forced himself to keep up the pace. Brush cracked behind him, but he did not look back this time. Soon his lungs burned, especially his right side where his bruised ribs throbbed. How long could he keep up this pace? *As long as it takes*, he told himself. He would run until he was safe or he collapsed.

Speeding through the forest, his foot snagged on a stump. He fell heavily to his knees, groaning as one was bruised against a jagged stone. But he jumped up immediately and kept on. His heart raced, blood pounding in his ears. He risked a glance over his shoulder, but his vision began to blur and darken. He could barely breathe.

I'm not going to—

The thought was never completed. He broke through the brush and nearly collided with the broad chest of a horse. The animal snorted, tossing its head in the air as it pranced backward. Aedan looked up. Relief rushed through his spent muscles.

"Aedan!" Makilien cried.

Gasping, he sank to his knees. "I'm . . . being . . . pursued," he managed through gulps of air.

Elandir, whose horse was now calm, put an arrow to his bowstring. Elmorhirian did the same, and they moved around Aedan to watch the forest where he had appeared. Makilien and Vonawyn were the first to jump down and rush to Aedan's side.

"Are you all right?" Makilien asked. "Are you hurt?"

"No," Aedan answered, shaking his head.

Makilien looked to the forest, searching. Finally, her eyes fell back to Aedan. "Derrin is not with you?"

Aedan met her searching gaze and hung his head. He took a couple deep breaths before managing to speak. "They killed him."

Coldness crept along Makilien's skin, and her heart thudded. She swallowed hard.

Aedan shook his head. "I tried to stop them."

Makilien put her hand on his shoulder to comfort him, fighting her own flood of emotions. Vonawyn glanced at her.

"He has a fever." Of Aedan, she asked, "Are you sure you're not injured?"

"My ribs hurt, but it's not that." He grimaced, hesitating. A thousand different thoughts and fears assaulted him. *What are they going to think?* He shook his head again, forcing the questions away. Slowly, he pulled up his sleeve revealing his dark, scarred and swollen flesh.

Makilien sucked in her breath, and Aedan could feel the others' reactions.

"They did that do you?" Torick asked.

Aedan ground his teeth together. "My father did."

Shock flashed in Makilien's eyes. "Your father?"

"He's alive," Aedan said. "And he's one of them. He serves Zirtan. He wanted me to join him."

As this sank in, Vonawyn looked closely at Aedan's arm.

"Gorrac," she said. "It's mildly poisonous and is causing the fever. But don't worry, it will leave your body in a few days. When we get back to Elimar, I can give you something to help."

She and Makilien helped him up. To Elandir and Elmorhirian, Halandor asked, "Do you see or hear anyone?"

"No," Elandir answered. "Either they spotted us or he lost them." Turning his eyes to Aedan, he asked, "Where were they holding you prisoner?"

"Up in a cave. A couple miles southeast, I think."

"I know that cave," Elmorhirian said. "We've been there before."

"How many men are there?" Elandir wanted to know.

Aedan shook his head. "I'm not sure. At least a dozen."

"Let's get back home," Elandir said. "We'll gather together a group of soldiers and come back."

Back in Elimar, Vonawyn and her mother tended to Aedan. Aside from severely bruised ribs, a nasty bump on the head, and his burn, he had no more physical injuries. However, everyone sensed the toll the ordeal had taken on him mentally. After recounting the entire story, he would say no more about it, but his eyes were troubled.

Following a good meal, Aedan went straight to his room to rest. He slept on and off for a couple of hours, but unsettling dreams and the constant hot and cold of his fever did not afford him a restful sleep. Finally, he sighed and got up again. Wandering the halls, he came to the garden terrace and walked out, sitting on the railing. The sun's warmth and the tranquil setting soothed him more than any rest had so far.

Looking down, he pulled up his sleeve, his forehead creasing as his brows lowered in disgust. He pushed his sleeve back into place, turning his eyes to the garden.

"Do you want to be alone?"

Aedan's head swung around to the opposite end of the terrace where Vonawyn stood. She was so silent, he wondered if she'd been there all along or had just arrived.

"No, please join me . . . if you'd like."

She crossed the terrace to the rail where she looked at him, her warm brown eyes more soothing to him than any of the surroundings.

"The shock of all this must be difficult," she said in understanding.

Aedan gave a little shrug, but then nodded. "It's just overwhelming to see someone you've believed dead for years, and to see what my father is . . ." He shook his head, his teeth clenching. "He abandoned us to serve Zirtan."

"How old were you when he left?"

"Only five."

"Do you remember much about him then?"

"Bits and pieces. More emotions than memories. I craved his attention, but he never seemed to have much interest in me. I still remember him and my mother arguing all the time. Always when he was preparing to leave. After we received the news of his death, Mother never spoke of him. She seemed more angry than sad."

He paused before shaking his head again, staring out at the garden, but not really seeing it. "I'm almost sure now she knew he just left us and wasn't really killed."

"It's difficult for a child to grow up amidst such turmoil," Vonawyn said, her voice soft with sympathy.

"And just as difficult for a Mother to raise a child alone, especially with another born only weeks later." Aedan sighed heavily. "I was forced to grow up fast. Even at such a young age I felt I had to take care of Mother and Rommia. And after all that, I now come face to face with my father, and all he wants is to force me to join him."

Rubbing his arm, his eyes settled back on Vonawyn. There had been so much building inside him that he hadn't wanted to talk about, but somehow it all came out so easily with her. And now, he realized, it had helped.

"I don't know what may come of it, but I believe you were meant to meet your father," Vonawyn said. "It doesn't seem to me to be only coincidence."

Aedan sat silent for a moment, considering that. Vonawyn gave him a warming smile.

"While you were resting, I made this for you." She came closer and gave him a soft fabric vambrace. The outside was heavy, dark green linen while the inside was lined with a softer material. "It will hide the brand."

She took it back from him and pushed up his sleeve, lacing the vambrace in place. Aedan lifted his arm to look at it. It did perfectly cover the brand. He stared at Vonawyn, awed by her kindness and desire to help.

"Thank you," he murmured.

Vonawyn gave him a smile that made her eyes sparkle. "You're welcome."

:Chapter Fifteen:

Capital City

Tears glittered in Makilien's eyes. The new memorial stone sat at her feet with a cold finality to it. In deep sorrow, she lamented how quickly things could change from good to bad. They'd held a funeral service for Derrin that morning, placing the memorial stone with his name on it inside of Elimar's cemetery, a peaceful area surrounded by white birch trees. Makilien had wanted to say something—something in honor of his memory—but she hadn't known what.

Now, standing alone at the site, she whispered, "I'm sorry you had to deal with such disappointment. I will always be grateful for the way you saved my life."

Two tears slid down her cheeks. She struggled against the temptation to blame herself for Derrin's death. It was hard not to feel some responsibility.

She looked down to the object in her hands, a bundle of small flowers. Each flower had five teardrop-shaped, blue petals that were glassy smooth and almost appeared wet. Mourner's Tears she'd been told they were called. Many of the graves around her were decorated with them. Bending down, she placed the little bouquet on Derrin's memorial stone.

In silence, she contemplated the events leading up to this moment. A short time later, she sensed, more than heard, someone approach her from behind. She looked over her shoulder and met Sirion's compassionate gaze. He walked up beside her and stared down at the memorial stone before looking back to her. Taking in the sight of her downcast face, he asked, "Will you be all right?"

Makilien nodded slowly. "It's just hard. The battle hasn't even been fought yet and already we've lost someone. What burdens me the most is the knowledge that Derrin probably never believed the truth. I wish I could have done more to help him understand."

Sirion sighed. He had his own regrets concerning Derrin. He wished he'd had time to repair their strained relationship. But he knew neither he nor Makilien should dwell on their regrets.

"I'm sure you did everything you could," Sirion said. "If he refused to believe anything you told him, that was his choice, and not a failing on your part."

"I know. I just feel very sad." Though she'd never been close to Derrin, she had known him since they were children, and her heart mourned the loss of his life.

Sirion's hand came comfortingly to her shoulder, and they stood for another few moments. Finally, Makilien turned, and they walked through the city.

Upon entering Lord Elnauhir's house, they found most of the men inside the large study near the sitting room. Telcar, the general of Lord Elnauhir's armies, was present. He and a group of Elves had been out searching for Zirtan's men and had apparently returned while Makilien was gone.

Some glanced at Makilien and Sirion as they entered, but remained quiet while the dignified, black-haired Elf spoke.

"We swept a large area to the south, and it is as Elandir and Elmorhirian expected. They left the cave before we could reach them yesterday and fled north. We found several trails leading away. We don't know if they have kept on going or are still somewhere close by. They could have given up and returned to Zirtan, or they could still be around just waiting for Makilien and her family to venture outside of the city."

Lord Elnauhir rubbed his chin pondering this. Speaking his thoughts aloud, he said, "They are safe within the city?"

"Yes, my lord," Telcar assured him. "No one could get in undetected, and if the enemy wished to attack, they would need a large force to do so, one we would be aware of before any attack came."

Elnauhir turned his thoughtful eyes to Makilien. "Still, considering the circumstances, I think it might be wise for you and your family to travel on to Minarald. The journey would be risky, but I believe Lord Darand's palace would be the safest place for you now."

Makilien agreed. "I believe so too."

"We'll make sure to have a group large enough to discourage any attackers along the way," Halandor said.

"I can go with you," Elandir offered.

"Me too," Elmorhirian chimed in.

Looking to their father, Elandir asked, "May we go?"

"We shall all go," Elnauhir told them. "I wish to speak to Lord Darand face to face." He turned to Telcar. "I will leave you in charge of the city and will send word as soon as you must lead our soldiers to Minarald."

"Yes, my lord," Telcar replied.

"How soon will we leave?" Makilien asked.

"In the morning," Elnauhir answered, "before Zirtan's men make any more attempts on your life if that is indeed their plan."

In a flurry of activity and travel, three days rushed past and brought the large group from Elimar to gaze upon the magnificent granite walls of Eldor's capital city. The group, fifteen people in all, slowed their steady traveling pace a few hundred yards from Minarald's open iron gates. Makilien tilted her head back to look up at the walls, her mind reliving her time spent in the city and the night of battle. She found no sign of the struggle. The walls and the gate had been repaired, and she even noticed recent additions. Tall, wooden trebuchets stood at regular intervals along the top of the wall, at least twenty in number.

"I see more has been done to fortify the wall," she commented.

"Yes," Halandor replied. "The men of Beldon have built the trebuchets. They are masters at constructing siege weaponry. Scaffolds have also been built along the inside of the wall to give us more space to fight. We hope this time we may last longer on the wall before having to face Zirtan on an open battlefield."

Once through the grand archway of the gate, the horses' hooves clopped on the hard, stone pavement as they made their way toward the heart of the city. The streets were busy as the city's inhabitants hurried to do their final errands for the day. At first, no one seemed to notice their group, but then a murmuring grew and people stopped to look at them. Makilien couldn't understand why until she heard her name rising above the commotion. A child pointed and exclaimed, "Look, it's Makilien!"

The excited chatter increased, soon alerting everyone ahead of them. Makilien glanced at the people, flashing them a smile, feeling shy amidst such an uproar. She rode tucked in between Halandor and Sirion, but couldn't find any way to hide herself behind either of them.

The excitement followed them all the way to the royal stable where they left their horses with the stablemen and continued on foot toward the palace. At last, the commotion died away.

"I can't believe so many actually remember me," Makilien said. "I'm sure I hardly seemed of any importance."

"People love heroes," Torick replied. "Especially those who come along during their lifetime."

"I hope all the excitement goes away."

Torick responded dryly, "Don't worry, people can also be fickle and forget things very easily."

In a moment, they came to the wall surrounding the palace. Passing through the gate, they entered the courtyard and paused for a moment while Makilien's family and Aedan gazed at the palace rising high above them in magnificent splendor. The granite walls and each of the three rows of tall windows reflected the golden glow of the late afternoon sun. From one wide middle balcony hung an enormous, royal blue banner with Eldor's symbol of a kingly lion embroidered in shimmering silver thread. The sight filled Makilien with awe all over again.

In silent admiration, the group moved on, passing the pond and fountain sparkling in the courtyard's center before coming to the wide length of steps leading up to the entrance of the palace. Two guards stood in front of the double, carved oak doors. They each bowed respectfully to Lord Elnauhir and pushed the doors open before them.

Inside, they walked down a large hall with a towering arched ceiling, and that brought them to the open door of the throne room. The light, amplified by reflective granite walls, made the room bright, and the tapestries and banners added splashes of rich color. Not much furniture graced the room, but the most prominent piece was the mahogany throne centered at the far end, raised up on its marble platform.

But the appearance of the room captured Makilien's attention only for a moment. Around one table at the far end, five men rose and faced them, joyful smiles warming their faces. Lord Darand headed the group, followed by Darian, Nirgon, Lord Glorlad, and Lord Andron. The lords and the general met them at the center of the room. After greeting Elnauhir, Darand turned glad eyes to Makilien.

A wide smile broke across his face as he said, "Makilien, how thankful I was to receive word that you were safe and now to see it with my own eyes. I cannot tell you what joy it gives me to have you here once again."

"And I can't fully express my joy at being here, my lord." She gave the kind king a hug. "I have dreamed of returning for a long time."

"Thank Elohim for bringing it to pass," Darand replied.

Makilien nodded, wholly in agreement and turned to motion her family forward. "My lord, this is my father, Néthyn, my mother, Hanna, my sister, Leiya, and my friend, Aedan."

She smiled as the king went to each one in turn, greeting them warmly before encompassing all to say, "Welcome to Minarald. I hope you will enjoy your time here for however long peace may be granted to us."

"Thank you, my lord," Néthyn spoke for the family, and Aedan too said his thanks.

By this time, Makilien turned to the rest of the group, embracing Darian and Nirgon and exchanging friendly greetings with Glorlad and Andron.

Once the commotion of their arrival had settled, Lord Darand questioned Lord Elnauhir. "What brings you to Minarald so soon, my lord?"

"I felt it would be best to be here to discuss the recent findings of our spies and any more information we may receive," Elnauhir replied. "And I personally wanted to be sure Makilien and her family reached here safely. The enemy had a camp nearby Elimar we were unaware of. They must have been watching the city because a few days ago they attacked Makilien at the river and tried to abduct her and her sister."

"A bold move," Darand said in surprise.

"Yes, and we were concerned there may be another attempt," Elnauhir went on. "I believed here would be the safest place for them at this time."

Darand nodded and turned once more to Makilien and her family.

"I assure you that you are safe here. After what happened with Gornath on your last visit, Makilien, I have the palace closely guarded by my most trusted soldiers. I can't guarantee complete safety outside the palace grounds, but with an escort, I believe you can safely travel the city."

"I'm not sure we will stray far from the palace anyway," Makilien replied. "It seems my presence has caused quite a stir among the people."

"Yes, I'm sure they were quite excited and will be eager to catch a glimpse of you, but they will not cause you any harm. Actually, I believe they make it yet safer for you here. We cannot know for sure if there are enemy spies in the city, but the people will not stand by and watch if something were to happen to you."

Makilien felt a certain amount of peace knowing the people would stand up to defend her.

:Chapter Sixteen:

Griffons and Dragons

D azzling shafts of early morning sun poured through the twelve arched windows high on the wall and filled the gallery with light. Aedan was fascinated by the room's contents. Life-size statues of men and some women stood in two perfectly straight lines along each side of the room. The white marble figures were sculpted to the most precise detail. Most were the likeness of great soldiers, equipped with battle gear and well-armed, though some of the statues were of more scholarly men. They stood proud, yet each man or woman had their head bowed.

He moved slowly from statue to statue, reading the names and inscriptions on the pedestals. They spoke of the deeds done by each man for which they were honored. He found the statues on the right hand side to be of Eldor's kings, while those on the left were of the country's heroes. Between each statue on the wall hung either a painting or tapestry depicting some important moment in the country's history. Depictions of battles, celebrations, coronations, and even of some more sobering occasions.

They filled Aedan with a sense of determination. Though he had not been born in Eldor, he felt a great love for it and a deep desire to defend it. To follow in the footsteps of these honored men.

When he had reached the end of the room, he stopped. Here, below a tall, decorative arch, were seven statues—four men and three women. He read the name on the pedestal of the man in the middle, *Baltar*, and realized these were the seven people who had founded Eldor. Above each of the statues, following the shape of the arch, seven stars were carved into the wall, and in the middle was the carving of the crowned lion, Eldor's proud symbol. Aedan stood silent and admired the kingly depiction.

A short time later, footsteps echoed behind him. He turned as Prince Darian came to his side.

"It's quite a room, isn't it?" the prince said.

"I've never seen anything like it."

"When I was a child, I used to come here and imagine my statue among the kings." The prince chuckled at his childish actions and shook his head. "Then, when I was a bit older and had less prideful daydreams, I'd come to inspire myself to be more like the men here. I still do once in a while."

"They certainly do inspire," Aedan agreed.

"Each person played a very important role in our history." Darian paused, remembering many of the stories he'd learned during his history studies and then went on, "But they knew their accomplishments were only made possible by Elohim. That is why their heads are bowed. Their victories and their strengths were not of their own power that they should be exalted."

Aedan gazed again at the statues. He found it all incredible —the history, the strength, and the faith.

"I wish I had been born here," he said.

"You're welcome to call Eldor home," Darian told him.

Aedan smiled. He would do that.

"Are you hungry?" the prince asked after a moment. "Breakfast will soon be served."

Aedan nodded and the two of them turned to leave. On the way out, Darian said, "If you like the Kings Gallery, I'm sure you'd enjoy the armory. I can show it to you after breakfast. Do you have any combat training?"

"I can use a bow, and Makilien taught me the sword, but I need more practice and experience."

"In that case, perhaps we can go to the barracks later as well and spar for a while."

Aedan touched his side. His ribs were still a little sore, but not enough to hinder him. "I would like that."

"Excellent," Darian said with a grin.

When they entered the dining room, nearly everyone was present and prepared to take their seats for the morning meal.

Upon walking in, Leiya greeted them brightly.

"Good morning, Aedan. Good morning, Prince Darian."

"Good morning, Leiya," the young men replied.

Her wide brown eyes focusing on Aedan, Leiya said, "After breakfast, Makilien is going to take us to the av…" She paused and made a face, trying to remember how to say the word. "…aver…avarary."

With a chuckle, Makilien joined them and supplied the word her sister struggled for. "The aviary."

"Yes, the *aviary*," Leiya repeated, speaking slowly to make sure she pronounced each syllable correctly. "She is going to introduce us to Arphen. None of the dragons are here though," she said with disappointment.

"Lord Darand said one of them should be here any day now to report on any activity along the Claron River," Makilien replied. "So you won't have to wait long to meet one."

Leiya skipped along between Makilien and Aedan, talking excitedly on their way to the aviary. The large structure stood only a few blocks from the palace. When they arrived, they stepped through the tall, wide doorway. Inside the open building, light streamed through the windows, and the cool air smelled of straw. In one of the sunny spots on the floor were three griffons. The magnificent creatures had smooth, dark coats, and their bodies were as lions, but great wings extended from their shoulders. Instead of paws on their front legs, they had sharp curved talons like eagles. Their heads were also eagle-like with curved yellow beaks and watchful brown eyes. The only difference were the feathered, cat-like ears on the sides of their heads.

One of the griffons sat upright, using its beak to preen the feathers of its wings. The other two lay on their sides, enjoying the warmth of the sunlight. It was one of these two griffons who first noticed their arrival and rose to his feet. Makilien recognized him right away to be Arphen.

"Well, well, we have visitors," the creature said in his kind voice. The corners of his beak lifted in a smile as he approached them, followed by the other two griffons.

"Makilien," Arphen said, "How wonderful to see you here. I heard news of your arrival and was very much hoping you would come to visit."

"I am very glad to see you again, Arphen," Makilien replied. "I'm equally glad to be able to introduce my sister Leiya and my friend Aedan."

Arphen bowed his head to them. "It is a great pleasure to meet you both."

"And a pleasure for us as well," Aedan replied. "Especially after all Makilien has told us of you."

With a smile, Arphen shifted his keen gaze to Leiya who stood very close to her sister. Makilien smiled, remembering how intimidated she'd first been by Arphen.

"You, little one, have very pretty eyes," Arphen said.

Leiya giggled, losing a bit of fear. "Thank you."

Arphen's smiled widened, and he turned his eyes to Makilien. "I would like to introduce you each to my companions." He turned to the two griffons behind him. "This is Tôr and Vyl."

Tôr, another male griffon, looked almost the same as Arphen. A person who did not know them would have had difficulty telling them apart. Vyl, however, a female griffon, was a bit smaller than the other two and her coat and wing feathers were darker, almost black in places.

"Tôr, Vyl, I'm very pleased to meet you," Makilien told them.

"We are most pleased and honored to meet you, Makilien," Vyl replied, her voice beautiful and melodic, yet strong.

"And you, Aedan and Leiya," Tôr added, his voice a bit deeper than Arphen's. "It is always a pleasure to meet those from the north who have not fallen for the enemy's lies."

"Coming from the north, it is an incredible pleasure to meet you as well," Aedan said.

"I can't imagine how different things must be in an area where truth is oppressed," Vyl remarked.

"Very different."

"Which makes us all the more thankful you are all here," Arphen said. "And know the truth."

Minarald truly did seem like home to Aedan after his first full day in the city. He felt like he had always belonged here. He thoroughly enjoyed the company of those he had met, particularly the prince and General Nirgon. Much of his time so far had been spent in their presence.

Prince Darian had taken him to the barracks as he'd offered, and after a tour of the amazing armory, they'd sparred together. Now on this second day, Nirgon took time out of his busy schedule to join the two of them and instruct Aedan, who was honored to have the interest of the general.

They trained for the majority of the morning. Aedan's ribs were sore from the activity, but he barely noticed it.

In rapid succession, he moved through a series of precisely-timed movements, working hard on his fluidity and form. He stepped forward with each of the prince's back steps, attacking and then parrying Darian's counterattacks. Metal rang, for they were not using practice swords this time. Finally, they came to the end of their drill and stopped.

"Excellent," Nirgon praised as he drew closer. "Aedan, you have great skill at wielding a large blade. One of the best I've seen in a long time."

"Thank you, General," Aedan replied, a little out of breath. "Your instruction has been very helpful."

"I do not know if you plan to join us when Zirtan's forces arrive, but we could certainly use more warriors like you," Darian said.

Aedan shook his head modestly. "I'm sure there are warriors who are far more skilled than me, but I do intend to fight in the battle."

"Well, I for one will be proud to fight alongside you," Darian told him.

"As will I," Nirgon added.

Aedan smiled. It felt good to have their respect, though he didn't consider himself to be nearly as valuable as most of the others around him. Nirgon said he was skilled, but it didn't change the fact that he was terribly inexperienced compared to these battle-tested warriors. Even Makilien had fought through battle and various other skirmishes. Yet, he knew all too soon his time to prove himself would come.

"I would think it's just about time for lunch," Darian remarked, breaking Aedan from his thoughts. "I don't know about you, but a morning of training always works up my appetite."

Aedan agreed and slid his sword into the scabbard as he and Darian turned to leave the barracks' training field. On the way, they passed many companies of soldiers all training hard. Aedan spotted many young men around his age or even younger and wondered if, like him, they had not yet seen their first real battle.

Quiet and contemplative over these thoughts, Aedan did not immediately notice a new arrival when they entered the palace courtyard, but when he looked up he stopped for a moment, in awe. Standing at the base of the palace steps was the most amazing creature he'd ever seen—a magnificent dragon with brilliant, ruby-red scales glinting like polished armor.

"It's Carmine." Darian grinned at Aedan. "Let us see what news he has brought from their patrol along the river."

Aedan and Darian crossed the courtyard and joined the group of people who had gathered around the dragon.

"...None of Zirtan's men have been spotted yet," Carmine informed Lord Darand. "I flew briefly over his fortress. They are still massing inside, and his furnaces burn day and night to provide the army with weapons and armor."

"Have they constructed any siege weapons?" Darand asked.

"I did see several catapults, my lord. I'm sure they will try to utilize them as they were very effective last time."

Darand nodded, his lips in a grim line.

Carmine waited a moment before he went on, "As I have said, we have not spotted any of Zirtan's men along the river; however, three days ago I saw seven men at the river's edge. When they spotted me, they fled into the forest."

"You do not believe these were men of Zirtan?" Darand questioned.

"No, my lord. They were clothed very differently—in brown and green. They were skilled at disappearing within the trees. I circled the area several times, but could find no other sign of them."

"That is strange," Darand murmured. "I did not think there were any men in Rhûnland besides those of Zirtan."

"Nor did I."

Makilien glanced at the faces of her friends, wondering what this information might mean, if anything at all. When she spotted Aedan, she beckoned him closer and waited for an opportunity to speak.

"Thank you for your report, Carmine," Lord Darand said. "You may go and take your rest."

Carmine bowed his noble head.

"Thank you, my lord."

As the group dispersed, Makilien motioned for Aedan to follow and stepped forward.

"Carmine," she said before he could fly way.

He turned to face her and smiled. "Yes, Makilien?"

"I have not yet introduced you to someone. This is my friend, Aedan."

The dragon turned his keen gaze to Aedan, the irises of his large eyes a deep red. Not the kind of red eyes Aedan would have imagined for some evil creature, but a rich red that gave him a sense of the dragon's wisdom and strength.

"Aedan, how pleased I am to meet you," Carmine said.

"And I you," Aedan replied. "It is a great pleasure for me to finally meet one of your kind."

"I look forward to getting to know you," Carmine told him. "Any friend of Makilien's is a friend of mine. Come to the aviary sometime before I leave and we can speak more."

"I will."

The dragon nodded his head to both Aedan and Makilien, and then extended his great wings. With a hard flap, he lifted into the air and flew off to the aviary. Once his majestic form had disappeared from sight, Makilien smiled at Aedan who breathed, "Incredible."

"Isn't he? I can't wait for you to meet the others. Seeing all three of them together is amazing. Their colors are so beautiful."

The two of them turned to the palace. Inside, they walked into the throne room where the others were in the middle of a discussion concerning the men Carmine had seen. Curious over the mystery of it, Makilien asked, "Has Rhûnland ever been inhabited by people?"

"Yes," Darand answered. "Quite a few generations ago, people from the south settled there, much like our ancestors settled Eldor. Both my grandfather and father reached out to them in friendship, but they rejected forming an alliance. They were not unfriendly, but they wanted to keep to themselves. We kept some contact with them, but twenty or so years ago, all communication ended, and recent scouting of the area has turned up no sign of them. All their cities and settlements are gone. We assumed one of three things. Either they returned to the south, they joined Zirtan, or he wiped them out. That there could still be people living there comes as quite a surprise."

"I know you did not have much contact with them, but what type of people were they? What kind of characteristics?" Makilien asked curiously.

"I only saw them once when I visited with my father, but they were less fair in color than most of us. Darker complexions and all dark haired. A very strong people—tall and lean. I think all they wanted was peace, but it seemed to me they could be very fierce warriors if threatened. As I said, they were not unfriendly. Very hospitable in fact, yet they were distant and perhaps distrustful of us."

Makilien quietly contemplated this as the rest of the group went on, discussing the other news Carmine had delivered.

Though everyone else seemed to have moved on from the subject, the people of Rhûnland stuck in her mind. A curiosity lingered throughout the afternoon and evening that would not let her forget what she'd learned, but why?

:Chapter Seventeen:

A Daring Plan

The hall was dim and silent as Makilien made her way along, mindful of those sleeping just beyond the closed doors. Before reaching the steps, which led downstairs, she turned to her right and approached a large glass door. She pulled it open and stepped out onto a wide balcony. Walking to the railing, she looked out over the quiet city.

Memories flooded her mind. This was the very place where she'd spoken to Meniah the night before he'd sacrificed himself for them and where he'd told her that Elohim had great plans for her. She hadn't truly believed it at the time, but then Elohim had used her to defeat Zendon, and now, perhaps, He had even more for her to do for Eldor.

Makilien stared off toward the east where golden rays of light painted the horizon, slowly spreading across the dawn sky. The early morning silence settled peacefully around her as she closed her eyes and prayed.

Gradually, the sun climbed above the horizon, bathing her in warmth. Birds sang and the city stirred. Makilien drew in a deep breath. She knew what she had to do.

Leaving the balcony, she walked downstairs, determination in her stride. The palace was quiet, yet voices came from the throne room. She stepped inside and found Lord Darand, Halandor, Torick, Loron, Sirion, and Aedan standing in a group. The closest of her friends and just the ones she sought. When she came to them, she said, "I have an idea."

Everyone turned to her, expressions questioning.

"What sort of idea?" Lord Darand asked.

"Yesterday, when Carmine told us about the men he saw in Rhûnland, it just would not leave my mind. I spent much of last night thinking and praying about it, and I just finished praying again now." Makilien paused, thinking it through one last time. "I want to go to Rhûnland. If there are still men there who have not joined Zirtan, and if we could convince them to fight with us, it would certainly put us in a better position than we are in now."

All were silent for a moment, processing her idea. Finally, Lord Darand cautioned, "We do not know for sure the men Carmine saw were those from Rhûnland or that they would not be hostile toward us. They still could be sided with Zirtan, and the country itself is dangerous. It is practically Zirtan's doorstep."

"I have given a lot of thought to the dangers, but I also think there must be a reason I have been unable to put this out of my mind. And I actually have more to my plans."

She walked over to a table where a map lay. Her friends followed.

"I was looking at a map last night and thinking about the dragons who left Eldor. If it is true they fled to the mountains, I'd think the most logical place for them to hide would be here near this forest." Makilien pointed on the map to a small forest deep in the heart of the Irrin Mountains to the east. "If I were to go to Rhûnland to try to find help, why not also search for the missing dragons and try to gain their aid? Indiya, Emaril, and Carmine are a huge asset to us in battle. Think of how even a few more dragons could aid us."

She watched her friends exchange glances with each other and noted the uncertainty in their eyes.

"It is a very daring plan, Makilien," Lord Darand said at length. "With all the dangers, there is a good chance you would not return from a quest like this."

"I know," Makilien replied quietly, "but I really believe this is something Elohim wants me to do, and I must have the courage to do it, despite the danger."

Darand released a long sigh. "You truly do believe it is Elohim's will?"

"I do," Makilien answered. She'd prayed for hours, and even though she had no real assurances, somehow she just knew.

"Then, as much as my heart wishes for you to remain here, I cannot stand in your way," Darand said. "You must do what you believe Elohim wants of you."

Makilien gave him a smile, touched by his concern.

Before she could speak again, Aedan announced, "I will go with you."

Makilien looked from the king as each of her friends gave a nod.

"I do not want to put anyone else in danger," she told them. "I believe I'm supposed to do this, but I could be wrong."

"You are not putting anyone in danger," Torick replied. "We are endangering ourselves, and gladly so if it means doing what we can to protect you and help you succeed."

Though she hated to consider losing any of them in this mission, Makilien had to smile. She was truly amazed by the group of friends she was blessed with and that they were so willing to follow her into an uncertain future.

"When do you wish to leave?" Darand asked.

"As soon as possible," Makilien answered. "Who knows when Zirtan will decide to march, and we need to find help before then."

The king agreed. "I will send for Nirgon and Carmine. Nirgon may have some ideas and advice, and Carmine knows the area around the Claron River better than anyone. He may also have more information concerning the dragons."

"Yes, I do want to hear from him in this matter," Makilien replied.

Several minutes after Darand sent for the general and Carmine, they arrived at the palace. Instead of meeting the dragon in the courtyard as usual, he came inside to the throne room. He looked especially majestic in the royal space.

By this time, Eredan, Prince Darian, and the other lords had also joined them and listened with interest as Makilien explained her plans.

"It will be a dangerous mission," Elnauhir said. "But who are we to question the will of Elohim? It may be the entire outcome of this war will rest on such an act that must be carried out in faith."

"Still, are you sure of this, Makilien?" Lord Darand felt burdened to ask. "You need not be one who goes."

"Yes, I am sure," she answered. "Meniah told me once that Elohim had great plans for me. I did not believe how it could be at the time, and I still don't understand why He chose me, but if He has more planned for me to help Eldor, I won't let fear get in the way of that. And I won't send someone else to do it for me."

"Very well then." Darand turned to Nirgon. "What thoughts do you have?"

"Well, I agree with Lord Elnauhir it will be dangerous, but it could make a huge impact. More men willing to fight with us would certainly strengthen our defenses. And a larger group of dragons would be invaluable."

"Do you believe there could still be a good number of men living in Rhûnland who have not allied themselves with Zirtan?"

"I think it is more possible than we first thought. If they are hiding within the Darrow Forest, then they easily could have gone undetected for all these years."

"What about you, Carmine?" Lord Darand asked. "What have you to say? Do you think Makilien can find the dragons who left?"

"I think the area she plans to search is a good one. I've long thought of searching it myself. I'm sure they have hidden well, so finding them will not be easy, and perhaps impossible, but that is the place to look."

"If she does find them, do you think she could convince them to fight with us?"

Carmine tilted his head. "That is as uncertain as finding them. They left because they lost trust in the Human race. To convince them to fight with us would be no easy task. It's been many years since they left. Those surviving may still harbor mistrust and anger and would have passed those emotions down to their offspring. Everything rests on whether or not this is Elohim's plan and He has been working on their hearts."

"I think it would be a good idea," Nirgon said, "to have someone go to represent each of our countries."

"Yes, that would be wise," Darand agreed. "Halandor and Torick will represent Eldor, Loron can represent the Eldorian Elves, and Sirion will represent Althilion." He looked to Lord Andron. "That means we need someone willing to go to represent Beldon."

Eredan stepped forward. "I will go, if it pleases you, my lord."

Andron looked at him quietly for a moment. He hated the thought of losing his general and closest friend, but he understood the importance of this mission.

"Yes," he replied. "You may go."

Darand nodded in approval of the group and said, "Good. That covers all of our allied countries. And Makilien and Aedan, you two will represent all those oppressed under Zirtan's rule and the reason we must not let him achieve victory."

Makilien and Aedan glanced at each other, feeling the importance of that responsibility.

Then Carmine said, "I too will join you. Should we find the dragons, if there are still those surviving from the original group, they will remember me and may be more willing to aid us."

"Good," Darand said again. "You also know well the lands you will be traveling and will be able to spot any danger from far off."

With their plans established, all the members of the group left the throne room to prepare for their journey. On the way upstairs, Makilien looked at Aedan.

"Thanks for coming with me. I know you are aware of how dangerous this will be."

Aedan gave her a smile that so often cheered her in tough times. "I'm in this with you until the end . . . whatever that end may be."

Makilien returned his smile.

When she reached her bedroom door, she paused to pray silently. She had to give her parents the news of her plans, and knew they would not want her to go once they learned of the great danger it presented. But she needed them to understand why she had to do this. It could be one of the key elements upon which everything rested. *Please help them understand, Elohim. And please turn their hearts toward You so they may have the same assurances and comfort I have.*

She opened her door quietly in case Leiya was still asleep, but found her sister getting dressed.

"Good morning," the little girl said, smiling brightly.

"Good morning, Leiya." She came closer to help her finish dressing and braid her hair.

"What are we going to do today?" Leiya asked.

Makilien said nothing for a moment. "Well, Leiya, I have to leave the city this morning."

Leiya's eyes widened with question. "Where are you going?"

"Some of our friends and I are going to try to find more help for the battle. Remember the other dragons I told you about who left Eldor?"

Leiya nodded.

"We're going to try to find them and find more men," Makilien explained.

"When will you be back?" Leiya asked.

Makilien shook her head. "I'm not sure."

Her sister didn't say anything, her face resigned. It always amazed Makilien how readily Leiya accepted things.

"Are Mother and Father awake?" Makilien asked after a moment.

"I think so. I thought I heard them talking."

Makilien stepped to the door of their parents' bedroom and knocked lightly. When she heard her mother's voice, she opened the door and walked in. Leiya followed. After they shared good mornings, Makilien broke the news to her parents.

"I need to talk to you. I'm going to be leaving here after breakfast."

"To go where?" Hanna asked, her voice already tinged with apprehension.

With some hesitation, Makilien explained the details of her plans and her need to go. At the end, she said, "I can't lie to you. It will be dangerous and . . . there's a chance I won't come back, but this could affect the outcome of the war. I know how much you worry about me and Leiya and how afraid you are to lose us, but I don't know what else I can say to comfort you other than I know Elohim will protect me, and if something does happen, it will be His will.

"I wish more than anything there could be peace and we could just live, but we are at war and there won't be peace unless we are victorious. In order for that to happen, many people are going to lose their lives before the end. If I can make a difference, I have to be willing to make that sacrifice."

Tears welled in her mother's eyes, yet both her parents looked on her with understanding, especially her father.

"Go," he said, his voice low with emotion. "It would be selfish of us to keep you here if you might be able to do something to help all these people. You were used once before to bring victory, who's to say you won't be again."

It surprised Makilien to hear her father speak in such a way. Could he have finally believed the truth? She searched his eyes, but her mother spoke before she could question him.

"When will you go?"

"Right away, as soon as we've had breakfast. Most of my friends and Carmine are going with me."

It comforted her mother to know this.

"I need to pack, and then we can go down to breakfast."

Makilien turned back to her room. Great hope kindled in her heart at what her father had said. If he did not yet believe, she prayed he would soon.

"Ready for our next adventure?" Makilien ran her fingers through Antiro's thick, black mane.

The horse nickered eagerly and pawed the ground.

"It's going to be another dangerous adventure, and I'm not sure what is going to end up happening to us," Makilien told him quietly. "You can stay here."

But she received an indignant snort in reply as Antiro shook his head.

Makilien smiled and murmured, "Brave horse."

He nuzzled her cheek making her smile widen.

She glanced around the palace courtyard. Everyone appeared to be ready to depart. Her parents and Leiya stood waiting at the base of the palace steps. Makilien left Antiro to say her goodbyes. Her mother was on the brink of tears when she reached them. For a moment, they struggled for what to say. It was hard for Makilien to think of dying before seeing them again, but she knew it must be worse for her parents.

"Be careful," Hanna pleaded, a tear sliding down one cheek.

Tears welled up in Makilien's eyes, and she hugged her mother tightly. "I will."

Next she turned to her father. They too hugged, and Néthyn whispered in his daughter's ear, "I'm proud of you, Makilien."

Eyes moist, she smiled at him. "Thank you."

Finally, she knelt by Leiya and gave her little sister a tight hug.

"I love you, Leiya," she said. "You are the best little sister I could ever have."

Leiya's smile beamed. "You're the best big sister ever." She then became more serious. "I will keep praying for you while you're gone. Elohim will protect you."

Makilien smiled at her confidence. "Thank you, Leiya."

She said goodbye to each of them. Her mother shed a few more tears, and Makilien barely held hers in check. Just before she walked away from them, she faced her parents with all seriousness.

"Whatever happens, please, think about everything I've told you about Meniah and Elohim. Please." She pleaded with them through her eyes.

Slowly, her father nodded first and then her mother, and though it was one of the more difficult things she'd ever done, Makilien turned away from them. Before returning to Antiro, she walked over to Vonawyn.

"I need to ask you, if something happens to me, will you please help my family? I don't know how they would be able to bear it, but I know you could help them." Vonawyn was so strong and supportive. Makilien knew she was just the one to console her parents if they had to face tragedy.

"Yes, I will," she promised, "but I pray I will not have to." Reaching out, she hugged Makilien. "You will constantly be in my thoughts and prayers. I will pray for everyone's safety and your success."

"Thank you so much, Vonawyn."

As Makilien turned toward the horses, she saw Sirion speaking with her parents. With a teary smile, her mother gave Sirion a hug, and it brought a warm smile to Makilien's face. When Sirion joined her at the horses, she asked, "What did you say to my parents?"

Sirion glanced at her, giving her a little smile. "I told them not to worry because we were all going to take care of you."

Makilien's own smile grew wider. "Thank you."

Now it was time to go. Everyone mounted up, and Nirgon spoke to the group.

"I will show you to the east gate," he said. "We will try to avoid anyone along the way so that if Zirtan does have spies in the city, perhaps they will not know you have left."

"And I will fly ahead to scout the road," Carmine told them. "I will join you tonight when you set up camp."

He spread his wings and launched into the sky. As he disappeared over the wall, the group moved out, following Nirgon. Makilien glanced once over her shoulder to her family, wondering if she'd see them again and what might befall her and her friends on this journey.

:Chapter Eighteen:

Perilous Journey

Makilien had never traveled to the far east of Eldor, but the scenery changed little and wouldn't for a couple of days, she was told. They had easy traveling throughout the day and put many miles behind them before the sun dipped low. For the night, they found a hill to set up camp. They had not seen Carmine all day, but as they unsaddled their horses, the dragon appeared in the sky and landed near them.

"We should have an uneventful night," he announced. "I thoroughly checked the area and saw nothing of anyone who might wish us harm."

"Good," Torick replied. "If we can make it to Rhûnland undetected, it will be very good."

Once the horses had been cared for, they set up their camp and gathered what wood they could find on the open plain. With a quick burst of flame from Carmine, they had a fire going and heated their supper.

As Makilien ate, she glanced up at Carmine who sat just within the firelight, his scales glowing like rubies. "Carmine, was there a particular dragon who led those who left Eldor?"

"Yes," he answered, with a slow nod of his head. "My brother, Saras."

Makilien raised her eyebrows. This was unexpected news, but it could be a benefit to their mission. "So he could still be leading them now?"

Carmine nodded again.

"Do you think you could convince him to return to Eldor?"

Carmine's eyes narrowed a little as he thought. "I don't know," he admitted. "Saras was very stubborn and thought little of Humans. He could never understand why I chose to stand with them. Perhaps time has changed him, but to a dragon it really hasn't been so long."

The path they traveled along Eldor's southern border was an easy path. Each day dawned with no bad weather to slow their progress. The nights were quiet and uneventful giving Makilien increased optimism they would reach Rhûnland undetected by the enemy.

However, their fifth night on the trail, only two days before they'd reach the river, their hope of secrecy came to an end. Not long after they had eaten supper and were preparing to bed down, disturbed rocks tumbled down in the mountain foothills. They were not large rocks, but still echoed loudly in the quietness of the night.

Everyone stilled and listened. At first, no other noise broke the silence, but then Makilien caught a swishing sound almost too faint for her to perceive before it disappeared.

"Something just flew away," Sirion said.

Makilien looked around at her friends. "What do you think it was?"

"It was too large to be an eagle or an owl," Carmine said, "but too small to possibly be a dragon."

That left only one other possibility.

"A death vulture?" Makilien guessed.

"I believe so," Carmine replied, a grave edge to his voice.

"So Zirtan will now know we're here."

"We will have to be even more cautious from now on," Halandor said, "and be wary of ambush points. I don't know if the vultures will be able to tell Zirtan who is in our group, but we will pray they don't."

Makilien slept restlessly that night, ever wondering if Zirtan would take action to try to stop them or if their relatively small group would be of little concern. She prayed for the latter. After all, Zirtan would not know what they were up to and therefore wouldn't have a great reason to be alarmed. Especially if he did not know she was in this group. How she hoped and prayed the vulture they'd heard would not be able to bring their enemy specific details.

No other sounds disturbed them throughout the night, and morning dawned with nothing amiss. Carmine scouted the area as the group had breakfast and returned with nothing to report. He'd found no sign of the enemy.

They saddled the horses, and after a group prayer, they once again continued on their journey.

The terrain had begun to change now. The rolling green hills of western Eldor gave way to hard, rocky soil where tough grasses grew in thick clumps. Jagged boulders scattered the foothills providing the enemy numerous places to lurk and set up an ambush. Makilien's nerves were on edge and every sense on high alert.

The sun rising before them, climbed slowly upward with each hour. Before they knew it, the warmth shone at their backs on its descent. The quiet day lulled everyone into a false sense of security. Makilien had just begun to hope they would escape any confrontations when a piercing screech echoed in the mountains.

The horses stopped, prancing nervously as their riders looked about. Several large, dark shapes hurtled toward them at blinding speed. One dove straight for Makilien. Razor sharp talons latched onto her shoulders, and with a strong upward tug, she was lifted right off of Antiro's back. Her horse gave a frantic whinny as she fought against the giant vulture's grip. Fortunately, it did not have a secure hold on her, and her struggles proved life-saving. The evil bird's talons dug into her skin, but then ripped through her dress.

Ten feet she fell. Her legs collapsed on impact, and her right side slammed into a large rock when she hit the ground. Gasping for the air that had been forced from her lungs, Makilien scrambled to her feet. Ducking low, she rushed back toward the horses. Crouched near Antiro, the vultures would have a hard time reaching her.

Carmine's enraged roar echoed in the distance. Makilien glanced briefly over her shoulder to see him racing from where he'd been scouting ahead. Everyone was on the ground now, ducking and dodging the numerous death vultures' talons. Though Makilien was the only one light enough for them to actually carry away, their sharp talons could do lethal damage.

Some of the horses panicked as her friends tried to keep them from running off. Loron and Sirion attempted to shoot the birds out of the sky, but their aim and speed were reduced by the chaos.

Carmine arrived a moment later. A panicked screech rang out overhead as he grabbed one of the death vultures out of the air. With the dragon now here, Makilien thought the attack would end, but more death vultures flew from the rocks. At least twenty of them all together swarmed the group. A handful would be no match for Carmine, but while five of them kept Makilien and her friends at bay, the majority of the birds attacked the dragon from every direction.

He clawed and bit at them and flamed some, but the evil birds were relentless. They latched onto him, prying at his scales with their talons and beaks, and ripping at the membranes of his wings. He roared fiercely as he fought but could not gain control.

Makilien watched in wide-eyed horror, unable to do anything to help him. She could barely stand to see it. *We have to do something!* But what? She and her friends were struggling to survive against their own set of death vultures.

Just as all hope seemed lost, a great roar blasted through the sounds of struggle and two blurs of blue and green dove toward Carmine. Well aimed streams of fire shot down, and the death vultures shrieked as their black feathers burst into flames. They scattered in all directions, most dropping to the ground in a trail of gray smoke. Those that survived retreated to the mountains and soon disappeared.

Carmine came to a heavy landing, and the two other dragons landed on either side of him—Indiya and Emaril. Makilien and her friends left the horses and hurried to the dragons. Blood oozed and trickled down Carmine's scales from several areas and from the tears in his wings.

"Are you all right?" Indiya asked in her strong voice as she inspected him.

Carmine nodded, breathing heavily in and out. "Yes, I'm all right."

"It looks like your wings could use a few stitches," Loron pointed out.

Carmine flexed his wings and agreed as Loron turned back to the horses to get the medical supplies.

"How did you know we were in trouble?" Carmine asked the other two dragons.

"Indiya heard you," Emaril answered.

"Barely," she added. "I thought maybe it was nothing, but thank Elohim we were close enough and decided to check." The beautiful blue dragon eyed the group, noting Makilien was with them. "What are you all doing way out here?"

While Loron tended Carmine's injuries, they shared their plans with Indiya and Emaril. Both were very interested, particularly in the missing dragons.

"Do you think it's really possible to find them?" Indiya asked.

"If Elohim wills it," Carmine answered. "I know there must be a reason Makilien feels called to do this. Whether or not it means we will find them, I cannot say."

The wide Claron River flowed before them. Pale gray stones littered the shore on each side, and crackled under the horses' hooves as they shifted restlessly. To cross would be to leave Eldor and enter into the country of Rhûnland.

From what Makilien could see, the terrain was much like what they'd traveled the last two days, yet more rough and wild. At first glance it appeared to be a treeless plain scattered with numerous dark rocks, but far off in the distance to the south, the horizon was dark with the trees of a forest. It was there Carmine had spotted the mysterious group of men.

"Are you certain you do not want one of us to go instead?"

Makilien turned to look at the dragons as Indiya questioned Carmine.

The red dragon nodded in answer. "Yes, I am certain. My injuries are only slight, and if we do find the dragons and my brother still leads them, I want to be the one to talk to him. I know both of you desire to join us, but remember, the people of Eldor and our allies all depend on your warnings when Zirtan marches to attack. It is important for you to remain here."

"We understand," Emaril replied.

Makilien remained with the two dragons as her group prepared to ride on. "Thank you for coming to our rescue yesterday. I don't think we would have survived had you not shown up."

Indiya smiled, her head dipping close. "Praise Elohim we did. It has been wonderful to see you again, Makilien."

"I'm glad to have been able to see you too."

With final farewells, Makilien and her friends moved their horses to the river and crossed. In the middle, the river came up to the horse's bellies, but they were able to cross easily. Carmine flew overhead, lower than usual, hoping not to alert anyone to their presence.

The horses stepped lightly across the rocks on the opposite shore, and the group turned south toward the forest ahead. The ground was hard and the grass dry, less rain falling here than in Eldor. Travel was no longer as easy. The horses often stumbled on the numerous rocks, forcing them to travel at a slower pace.

Gradually, the forest drew near through the hours. All were on alert for signs of Human population, but the open country seemed void of life. They stayed along the bank of the river, and, just before sundown, it brought them to the edge of the forest. At the tree line, they stopped. This would be their nighttime campsite.

Makilien gazed up at tall, broadleaf trees. They were different than she was used to. Their foliage was darker than the trees of the other forests she'd visited. The leaves were also quite large, the same size as her hand with her fingers spread apart, and shaped similar to maple leaves. Their dark coloring made the forest even more dim than it would usually be, and it was eerily quiet. Men or creatures certainly would not have to try hard to stay hidden in the shadows.

:Chapter Nineteen:

Caught

A chilly breeze swept across Makilien's neck, making her shiver as she secured her supplies. The newly risen sun lacked warmth, hidden behind a blanket of clouds.

With plenty of daylight ahead, the group rode out as soon as everyone was saddled up. Makilien gazed at the strange forest. The more she looked at it, the more she realized it wasn't exactly eerie, just different from anything she'd seen before. The tall, dark-leafed trees appeared gloomy and menacing at night, but in daylight they were rather beautiful and intriguing. The forest definitely held an air of mystery.

After they had gone a ways, she navigated Antiro up beside Halandor so she could ask, "What kinds of trees are the dark ones?"

"Darrow trees," Halandor answered. "That's where the forest gets its name. They are unique to the country, particularly this area. Eldor used to trade for darrow lumber. It's a very hard, dark wood. I believe there are some pieces of furniture at the palace that are made with darrow wood."

Makilien would have to ask Lord Darand about them when they made it back . . . if they made it back.

Finally, around mid-morning, Carmine landed at the river's edge and joined them.

"This is the place I saw the men," he announced.

Everyone dismounted, and Halandor, Torick, and Loron searched for signs that may still be visible. The rest of the group remained with the horses so they would not trample any clues. After a thorough search of the beach, they moved toward the forest and searched the perimeter. Just before they were about to give up and discuss their next move, Halandor stopped.

"There is a faint trail here."

They gathered around him. Makilien had to look closely, but she did see where the ground was more packed down than in other areas.

"It could just be a deer trail," Halandor went on, "but it appears to be all we are going to find. We could follow it and see if we find any more signs."

The rest of the group agreed, and they mounted up. Halandor took the lead. The trees were too thick for Carmine to be able to track their progress from the air, so he followed on foot.

Inside the forest, the ground was littered with darrow leaves. They were soft and muffled the sound of their travel. The forest canopy was so thick it didn't allow enough sunlight for much else to grow. Thriving unusually close together for their size, the trees stood straight and tall like thousands of dark pillars supporting an immense roof riddled with small holes, which allowed thin shafts of light to penetrate. The air around them was still and had a strong, yet not unpleasant, earthy smell. It was strangely quiet like Althilion, though it did not quite share the other forest's sense of peace.

They moved in a slow, single file line, winding their way to the southeast. The trail remained faint. At times they lost it completely, and Halandor would have to dismount and search the area to find it again, but he always did. They kept alert for other signs along the way, but found nothing. Not even any defined tracks to tell them what type of trail they might be following.

They had an odd sense that time stood still within the forest, but Makilien did notice the shafts of sunlight, which had slanted toward them at the beginning of the day, slowly shifted until they shone straight down. At this time, the group came upon a bit of a clearing and stopped. Not only did the sunlight tell them midday had arrived, but so did their hungry stomachs.

"We'll rest and have lunch here while we decide our next move," Halandor said.

They dismounted and let the horses graze on what little grass they could find among the fallen darrow leaves. After taking some dried meat and fruit from her pack, Makilien looked up. The canopy was still thick, but she could see a bit more of the sky here in the clearing. She was glad. The forest had a strange way of making her feel as though she'd never see the sky or open space again. Everything was so close and closed in.

Staring deep into the shadows of the trees, Halandor asked, "Should we continue to follow the trail or widen our search?"

"We've only gone a few miles," Torick pointed out. "And the fact that we've found no deer tracks or any other animals leads me to have some suspicion it still could be a trail more used by men. It would make sense if the men of Rhûnland are hiding here that they would disguise their trails and would live deeper within the forest than we've traveled."

Halandor agreed with this assessment. Catching brief nods by the others, he said, "Then we'll continue to follow the trail and see where it brings us by nightfall."

Anxious to be on their way, they only took a brief time for their lunch. As Makilien returned uneaten food to her pack, Antiro looked up and stared intently into the forest to his right. Makilien looked from him to the rest of the group. Loron, Sirion, and Carmine too watched the forest suspiciously.

"What is it?" Torick asked, his voice low.

"Something's out there," Loron murmured.

"How far away?" Halandor questioned.

"Not far."

Everyone stood very still and strained to listen. A moment later, the loud crackle of a limb breaking echoed eerily in the trees. Makilien's skin prickled. Her heart pounded as her hand moved toward her sword. The hair on her neck rose, and she sensed a presence behind her. Before she could react, a strong arm wrapped around her, and a razor-sharp blade pressed against her throat. She gasped. Her friends spun around, drawing their swords. But they froze, eyes wide and fearful.

"No one move or she dies."

Icy fear flowed through Makilien's blood. No mistaking that voice. Jorin. Her heart hit hard against her ribs. How had he found her here? She waited breathlessly. Would he just kill her on the spot this time and not risk losing her again?

"Drop your weapons," Jorin ordered, his voice as sharp as his blade.

Makilien's friends looked at each other, hesitating. Without weapons, how could they save her?

"Now!" Jorin snapped.

Makilien winced as the tip of the dagger sliced into her skin, and a thin stream of blood trickled down her neck. Her friends obeyed and dropped their weapons.

"Yours too," Jorin told Makilien.

Carefully, she slid her sword from the scabbard. Her mind raced for a way she might use it to get free, but it was futile. Any attempt would end in instant death. Once the blade was free, she dropped the sword at her feet.

Carmine growled, his red eyes narrowed and flashing.

Jorin glared at Makilien's friends. "Keep your lizard at bay or I'll kill her right now."

Carmine backed off, but his ferocious expression lingered, thin wisps of smoke curling around his nostrils.

A tense moment of silence fell between them. Eyes remained fastened on Makilien and her captor as everyone searched for a way to rescue her. But they were caught in an impossible situation.

"You two," Jorin said suddenly. Makilien could not tell who he referred to, but Sirion and Aedan look at each other. Then Jorin ordered, "Get your horses."

Watching Jorin the entire time, Sirion and Aedan left the group and retrieved Falene and Lokye. Antiro flattened his ears and snorted angrily, pawing the ground. Makilien glanced at him, but Jorin paid him no heed.

In this time, four other men came out of the trees from the direction they'd first detected movement and joined Jorin.

"Well done," he praised them, and Makilien realized they'd been used as a distraction.

To the remaining group, Jorin warned, "Do not follow us. If we even suspect you have, one of them will die."

With that threat, Jorin backed away and pulled Makilien along with him. He ordered the other men to guard Sirion and Aedan.

"What about the others?" one of the men asked. "Aren't we going to kill them?"

Jorin set his dark eyes on the group, and Makilien's heart pounded in fearful anticipation of his reply, praying with all her might that her friends would be spared.

At last, Jorin said, "Lord Zirtan wants them to witness their countries fall. Leave them."

Makilien sighed with relief, but it was overshadowed when she, Sirion, and Aedan were forced deeper into the forest. Jorin kept the lead, holding Makilien in front of him, the dagger still to her neck. She walked with great care, afraid that tripping would cause him to cut her throat.

Dread consumed her as the grim reality of the situation set in. What would happen now? What could her friends do? If they tried to rescue the three of them, one or more of them would die. But death was imminent if Jorin brought them to his intended destination, so what action could be taken? And what of the mission? Had it already failed? If only she would have thought to try to tell her friends to go on without them. Victory over Zirtan was more important than her life, and she knew Sirion and Aedan would feel the same. But it was too late now.

Several minutes later, Makilien spotted a group of horses and one man standing guard. When they reached him, Jorin said, "Get the shackles."

The man dug around in one of the horse's saddlebags and produced three pairs of shackles. He brought them to Jorin.

"Shackle her."

The man clamped the rough shackles around Makilien's wrists. Only then did Jorin finally take the knife from her throat. Makilien let out a quiet sigh just before Jorin shoved her toward one of the horses, a tall black horse about the size of Antiro, but it did not share Antiro's friendly eyes. The horse snorted and stomped impatiently as they approached.

"Mount up," Jorin instructed.

Makilien looked warily at the horse and pulled herself up. As soon as she was seated, Jorin took a length of rope and tied her shackles to the saddle. She glanced to Sirion and Aedan and found they too had been secured to their horses.

Her gaze locked with Sirion's when he looked up. His brown eyes were shadowed with worry. Makilien let her head bow and her eyes close for a silent prayer. *We are powerless, Elohim. We can't save ourselves from this. Help us please. You're the only hope we have.*

In another moment, Jorin mounted behind Makilien. He gave his horse a sharp kick and the animal lunged forward. Makilien gripped the saddle. The other men followed, leading Sirion and Aedan along with them.

The sun was a fiery red-orange ball low on the horizon when at long last the horses all came to a halt. Having been pushed hard all afternoon, the steeds panted heavily, and Makilien pitied the poor animals.

She hung her head and released a heavy sigh. She ached everywhere from the rough ride. Jorin's horse was not nearly as smooth-gaited as Antiro, and Makilien could not reach the saddle's stirrups to help brace herself against all the bumps and jars. She cast her eyes around the area. They'd left the forest a couple of hours ago and once more traveled the rocky plains, but the forest lay just to their right as they traveled east.

"Set up camp here," Jorin barked out orders, making Makilien flinch.

The men jumped down immediately to obey. Jorin too dismounted. He turned to Makilien to untie the shackles from the saddle before he dragged her off the horse with no concern for her comfort. When she reached the ground, her ankle twisted painfully. She bit back a groan, but had to walk with a slight limp when he led her to one lone tree near the edge of camp.

Taking a key from the inside pocket of his long, black leather coat, Jorin unlocked one of Makilien's shackles and ordered her to sit. She sank down at the base of the tree, and he shackled her arms around it. Makilien shifted uncomfortably, her muscles strained to be stretched back around the wide trunk.

Once she was secured, Sirion and Aedan were chained in the same manner and left alone as Jorin and his men focused on their camp and supper.

Makilien sighed. "We've sure fallen into a mess this time." She frowned to herself and turned questioning eyes to Sirion who sat just beside her. "I don't understand. I know why they took me, and I know why they took Aedan, but why you?"

Sirion shook his head. "I don't know. I've been trying to figure it out myself. I've been part of a lot of plans against Zirtan, but I can't think of any specific incident they'd want me for like they do you. I would think Halandor and Torick would be of more interest."

"It doesn't make sense," Makilien murmured.

They fell silent for several moments, wondering. Finally, she asked, "How far are we from Zirtan's fortress?"

"Five, maybe six days," Sirion answered. "Not a lot of time to find a way out of this."

Lowering her voice even more, Makilien asked, "Do you think the others will come after us?"

"I know they will," Sirion replied with certainty. "They'll stay far enough away not to be detected until they can come up with a way to try to save us. They won't just let us go. I wouldn't."

Makilien agreed. The knowledge of that was both comforting and concerning. What would happen if Jorin realized they were behind them? He promised she, Sirion, or Aedan would die, and he meant every word of it. To think of it made Makilien shudder. Would one of them have to die in order for the other two to live?

:Chapter Twenty:

Unpleasant Company

M akilien shivered, chilled to the bone. She stared longingly at the fire where Jorin's men slept, but it was too far away to offer any bit of warmth. She tried to shift her arms and winced. They were sore and tingling. She glanced at Sirion who caught her eye, but they said nothing. Finally, Makilien's eyes turned to the eastern sky, which had begun to glow with a golden light to signal the beginning of a new day of uncertainties.

With a wave of defeat trying to overcome her heart, Makilien closed her eyes and prayed, *This is so hopeless, Elohim. I don't know what is going to happen to us. If it is Your will, please rescue us from this . . . all of us. If not, give us strength to face our enemies and not falter under fear and intimidation.*

In a short time, Jorin's men rose and put together a quick breakfast. Makilien tried not to think about the gnawing ache in her stomach as she watched them. She had no hope of getting nourishment; however, just before they were about to leave, Jorin and two of his men walked over to the tree. In his hand, he held a bowl. One of the men unchained them, and Jorin extended the bowl to Makilien.

"Eat quickly. We leave as soon as the horses are saddled." His voice was hard and told them he was not acting out of charity, but only so they would not faint from hunger before they reached their destination.

Makilien took the bowl. In it was a thick mixture of dried meat and beans, barely enough for one person, let alone three. She looked uncertainly at Sirion and Aedan.

"You two eat it," Sirion said.

Makilien shook her head. "No, we all need food."

"It's all right," he insisted. "I'm Half-Elf. I can go longer without it."

Makilien still didn't feel it was right, but to discuss it further meant wasting the little time they had to eat. With reluctance, she turned to Aedan. Jorin hadn't provided utensils so they had to use their hands. Fortunately it was not very messy, but the humiliation of it stabbed at them.

While eating, Makilien glanced at the two men who still stood by. Both had their hands on their swords and no doubt had orders from Jorin to kill them immediately should they do anything to try to escape.

Wincing, Makilien tried to move her shackles up away from her wrists, but they were too tight to go far. After two days of rough treatment, the metal edges had dug into her skin, rubbing it raw, until finally she had open sores that oozed with blood. She looked at Sirion and then Aedan, her eyes settling on their stained shackles.

One of the two men who stood guard over them shifted. Makilien glanced up at him from where she sat in a close circle with her friends in the dry grass while the rest of Jorin's company ate a brief lunch. It was the only respite they would get from riding until later that evening.

She sighed, and her eyes met Sirion's for a moment. They'd been forbidden to speak to each other, even at night, though Jorin couldn't prevent them from secretly whispering. Escape was always on their minds, and had been mentioned cautiously, but right now any possibility of that seemed far out of reach.

As Jorin and his men finished their meal with no sign of offering any nourishment to the prisoners, Makilien noticed Sirion look to the east, listening intently. Then a look of apprehension came to his eyes, and he mouthed the words, "Someone's coming."

Makilien's heart pounded. Could it be the rest of their group? And, if it was, what would happen? Could they be rescued without someone dying?

Not knowing what else to do, they sat silent, but kept a close watch on the men. Soon, Makilien caught the sound of hoof beats coming hard and fast. Jorin and his men noticed it a moment later.

"Horses!"

At this word, Jorin yanked out his sword and strode toward the captives. Makilien swallowed hard as she glanced at his menacing blade and then up into his dark eyes. Glaring down at them, he said, "If it is your friends, you will die."

He stood over them, ready and willing to strike, and they waited, all looking to the east as the sound of horses grew louder. Makilien breathed in, praying desperately this would not be the end for one or all of them.

After several tense seconds, a dozen horses appeared over the rise a couple hundred yards away. Huge horses bearing fearsome riders. It took only a moment for Makilien to realize the riders were Shaikes.

The horses thundered toward them. They were tall and muscular, all black with long manes and feathered fetlocks. Makilien noticed right away how similar they looked to Antiro and for a moment wondered if this was where he'd come from. Maybe her beloved horse had been bred by Zirtan to carry the massive Shaikes.

The Shaikes were not what anyone had expected, and in an odd way, it relieved Makilien. Since the Shaikes were in service to Zirtan, it gave Jorin no reason to kill her or her friends. She let out a breath as thirteen Shaike riders yanked their steeds to a halt at the edge of camp. Jorin slid his sword into its scabbard. For a moment, the only sound was the heavy panting of the sweat covered horses. Then the Shaike at the head of the group, a fierce looking brute with three strips of black hair left to grow on his otherwise shaved head, growled deeply, "Jorin."

"Gorgon, what are you doing here?" Jorin asked, voice taut.

"We came to give you assistance."

Though Makilien could not see his face, Jorin visibly tensed.

"I am quite capable of handling this without assistance."

The Shaike shifted in his saddle, one of his thick eyebrows rising. "Seein' as how you made such a mess of things last time, I'm not quite sure I believe that."

"I have the three of them right here." Jorin swept his hand back to motion to his captives. "They are quite secure and will not escape."

Gorgon peered at them, his fierce yellow eyes narrowing as a wicked grin stretched across his face. He slid down from his horse, landing heavily before striding toward them. Coming to a halt next to Jorin, he peered down at the prisoners. Makilien and her friends looked up at him, feeling especially small and powerless under the piercing gaze of this giant of a beast who stood even taller than Jorin.

With his evil, fanged grin leering at them, the Shaike suddenly reached down. His huge hand clamped around Makilien's neck, jerking her to her feet and pulling her close. She grimaced as his foul breath hit her face and tried to step away, but he would not let go.

"So this is the famous Makilien."

A low, evil chuckle rumbled from his chest. His grip around her throat tightened. Makilien choked as her airway was cut off. She reached up and pulled at his thick fingers to loosen his hold, but they would not budge. In fact, her struggles only made him squeeze tighter. Black spots danced in her vision as her throat was slowly crushed.

As she slipped toward unconsciousness, Sirion jumped up and rammed his shoulder into the Shaike's chest. The beast barely moved, but in the surprise of the action, he released Makilien. She stumbled back and dropped to her knees, gasping and coughing as air rushed into her depleted lungs.

Gorgon latched onto Sirion and threw him to the ground. Makilien's heart squeezed when Sirion gasped in pain after the cruel Shaike kicked him in the stomach. Aedan jumped up now, also ramming the Shaike to stop him from kicking Sirion again. With an enraged roar, Gorgon pulled out his giant long sword.

"No!" Makilien cried weakly.

But her cry was overwhelmed by Jorin.

"Stop!" He pushed his way in between the captives and Gorgon. "I would prefer to take them in alive."

The Shaike glared at Jorin, and then down at Makilien and her friends, his eyes flickering dangerously. Finally, he shoved his sword back into its scabbard with a low growl.

Makilien crawled over to Sirion as he pushed himself to his knees. He breathed hard and winced.

"Are you all right?" Makilien whispered, tears stinging her eyes. "None of your ribs are broken are they?" She could only imagine how forceful the kick from a Shaike would be.

Sirion shook his head, erasing the pain from his face. "No, I'm fine." Concern switched to her now. "Are you?"

"Yes," Makilien murmured.

Suddenly overcome by what had just taken place, two tears dripped from her eyes. She brushed them from her face before any of their captors could see and blinked back the rest. Sirion touched her hand for a moment, and she gave him a weak smile, but was reassured by the strength in his eyes.

"We must get moving," Jorin announced. Speaking to Gorgon, he went on, "Their friends might be following us. I don't want to give them time to catch up."

Gorgon turned to the other twelve Shaikes who had remained on their horses.

"Razhak!" he bellowed.

One of the Shaikes kicked his horse forward.

"Take the others and backtrack along Jorin's trail to see if anyone is following," Gorgon instructed. "If you find anyone, kill them."

Razhak nodded and kicked his horse again, sending it into a gallop. In a cloud of dust, the other Shaikes followed him.

Night fell as Jorin's company set up camp. Chained to the nearest tree, Makilien and her friends watched and listened to their conversation and the raucous laughter from Gorgon. All seemed particularly pleased as their prisoners sat helplessly.

When they'd been forgotten by the boisterous group, Sirion spoke in a whisper, his eyes still focused on the men. "Tomorrow, you two are going to escape."

Makilien and Aedan turned their heads to look at him.

"What?" Makilien asked, not understanding.

"Tomorrow, I will distract the guards. It should give you just enough time to get to Falene and Lokye. Take them and ride away as fast as you can."

"What about you?"

Sirion did not speak.

Horrified by the import of his silence, Makilien shook her head. "Sirion, no. I will not leave you here. Jorin will kill you the moment he sees we are running."

"We could be less than two days from Zirtan's fortress," Sirion spoke in a grave tone. "If we don't do something, we will *all* die."

"There must be another way," Makilien said desperately.

"There isn't."

The cold reality of that statement hit her hard. Before she could protest further, Aedan said, "I'll do it. Sirion, you take Makilien and go."

"No. I won't leave either of you," she insisted.

But Sirion spoke firmly, putting a decided end to the debate. "I will do it, and when I do, you both must go. It will be tomorrow, during lunch, when only two guards are watching us."

Makilien swallowed, heart breaking. Tears ran down her face. Sirion was right, they had no other way of escape, but how could she just ride off and leave him to his death? Yet, if she did not succeed when he acted, then his sacrifice would be in vain. She had no choice.

Sniffling at her tears, Makilien felt Sirion shift to take her hand in his and squeeze it. She looked at him, her lip trembling as she tried to stop crying before Jorin and his men noticed. She longed to try to talk Sirion out of his plan, but the determination in his eyes told her she would not be successful.

Oh, Elohim, please provide another way, she begged, but she had an awful feeling this sacrifice was necessary.

:Chapter Twenty-one:

Dark Arrows

T he cold, dark hours of the night offered Makilien no moment of rest, no peace. How could she sleep knowing in a few hours she would lose one of her closest friends? She prayed continually for Elohim's intervention, and also for strength to act should things play out as they were.

As the sun sparkled above the horizon, the men packed up camp, and Jorin offered the prisoners their meager breakfast. But even on the verge of starving, Makilien's unsettled stomach nearly rebelled at the food.

A somber gloom shadowed the captives as they began their day's travel. Dread weighed heavy in Makilien's heart. She wanted more than anything to find an escape for all three of them, but her attempts failed. After three days of little food and sleep, she was mentally drained. She found no hope of being able to formulate some miraculous escape plan.

In a blur of discomfort, exhaustion, and sadness, the morning hours passed by. The sun inevitably climbed higher, and, before long, midday was upon them. Makilien's stomach tied in a dreadful knot when Jorin jerked his horse to a stop. The men dismounted and put the prisoners in a group, as usual, and Jorin chose two men to guard them.

Drawing in a shaky breath, Makilien watched Sirion look at Jorin and the men preparing lunch and then at their guards, waiting for the right moment. Her heart wept inside her at what she had to do. She tried to be resolved, but felt far from it. For a moment, her eyes locked with Sirion's, begging him not to go through with this, but he cared more about giving her and Aedan a chance than saving his own life.

Jorin and his men were soon busy with their meal and the guards' attention shifted more to the surroundings than their quiet, pitiful prisoners. Makilien tried to slow her heart pounding hard against her ribs, knowing Sirion would soon make his move. She worked hard to focus and be alert, not wanting to mess things up.

Then the moment came. Makilien's stomach did a flip-flop as Sirion began to rise. Her mind screamed no, but she kept her mouth clamped shut. However, Sirion paused, listening. He looked to the west and sat again before any of the men noticed. Makilien and Aedan peered at him questioningly.

"Horses," he whispered.

A new feeling of dread settled over them, wondering if it was the Shaikes Gorgon had sent after their friends and what news they might bring.

"How many?" Makilien asked.

Sirion listened a moment before answering. "Two."

"No talking!" one of the guard's snapped.

They glanced up at him and said nothing more as the sound of hoof beats reached Makilien's hearing. Jorin and his men heard it too. Pulling out their swords, they surrounded Makilien, Sirion, and Aedan. But soon, only two Shaikes rode into camp. Their horses were near to exhaustion, and one Shaike had drying blood oozing down his arm.

Gorgon strode up to them. "Did you find them? Are they dead?"

Makilien held her breath, awaiting the answer.

"We found them," the uninjured Shaike affirmed. "They attacked us by surprise. We couldn't overtake them. We were the only two who survived."

Gorgon's voice lowered menacingly. "Did you kill *any* of them?"

The two Shaikes exchanged glances before the uninjured one answered reluctantly, "No."

Makilien let out a gasping breath. *Thank You, Elohim!*

But Gorgon was anything but pleased. He growled fiercely.

"Fools!" Reaching up, he grabbed the Shaike's armor and jerked him from his horse, throwing him to the ground. "How do you know they aren't tracking you! You probably led them straight to us!"

In rage, Gorgon yanked out his sword and placed the tip at the other Shaike's neck. "You are going to get on your horse and ride back the way you came. When you find them again, you are going to kill as many of them as you can, and you will not come riding back here. If you do, I will kill you myself!"

To punctuate his words, he slashed his sword across the Shaike's exposed shoulder. The creature's dark red blood trickled from the wound.

"Now get up and get riding!"

The Shaike jumped up and mounted his horse. Without another word, the two Shaikes spun their mounts around and rode off to certain death.

Once the sound of hooves had died away, one of Jorin's men spoke.

"They can't be far behind us."

Another of the men chimed in, "I knew we shoulda killed 'em."

Slow and deliberate, Jorin turned. His eyes settled on the prisoners, narrowing. An icy chill raced up Makilien's spine, and she swallowed.

"I told them there would be consequences if they followed," Jorin uttered darkly.

"What are you gonna do?" one of the men asked, more than a hint of eagerness in his voice.

"We'll kill one of them and leave their body here to show the others I am serious, and that they had better not continue following."

Makilien's eyes went to Sirion and Aedan, her heart reacting in a hard, stumbling series of beats.

"Which one?" Gorgon asked, baring his teeth in a wicked grin.

Jorin's eyes swept over each of them.

Finally, he said without pity, "The Half-Elf."

Makilien's chest squeezed tight and tears flowed into her eyes. It was only a matter of time before they were all killed, she knew this, but she wasn't ready to see one of her friends die. She never would be.

Gorgon strode toward them, and an agonized plea burst from Makilien. "Please, Jorin, please, don't do this!"

But it was regarded with nothing more than contempt.

Gorgon reached down and grabbed a handful of Sirion's hair, dragging him to his feet. Makilien and Aedan jumped up in a desperate desire to intervene, but Jorin's men grabbed them and held them back. Gorgon yanked Sirion away from his friends and held him in an iron grip, facing Jorin. Utterly helpless, the prisoners watched Jorin reach to his belt and withdraw a long, curved dagger.

"No, Jorin, please!" Makilien cried, her voice trembling.

Ignoring her cry, Jorin approached Sirion who breathed heavily, but said not a word. Makilien shook her head, intense panic and desperation pumping adrenaline through her veins. She pulled hard against her captors. This time, her left arm slipped out of one man's grip. With a sharp yank, she pulled her other arm free. Before either of the men could restrain her, she rushed forward and took a stand between Jorin and Sirion.

"Makilien, no!" Sirion implored, but Makilien kept her gaze focused on Jorin. His eyes darkened with anger and hatred for her.

"You don't know how foolish you are," he spat, his voice taut with rage.

"If I am foolish for trying to protect someone very dear to me, then so be it."

"Move," Jorin ordered in a tone that told her if she refused, he would be hard pressed not to unleash his full fury on her.

Drawing in a deep breath, Makilien prepared herself for whatever action he might take. Sirion begged her to move away, but she just could not do it. In a quiet yet confident voice, she declared, "No."

Jorin's eyes widened at the fact she would dare to defy him. Makilien sensed it coming and braced herself as he raised his hand and backhanded her with all the anger-fueled strength he possessed. She collapsed at his feet, dazed with the pain that exploded in her head. Her senses numbed as she slipped toward the beckoning darkness of unconsciousness. But Sirion's face flashed in her mind, and she forced herself to focus. Gritting her teeth, she struggled to push herself to her hands and knees. At the coppery taste in her mouth, she spit blood and a stream of it trickled down from her lip.

Groaning, she swayed and stumbled as she rose to her feet, and though she stood unsteadily, blinking to stay focused, she faced Jorin, unafraid. She would rather die here trying to defend Sirion than just let him be killed only so she'd live long enough to face Zirtan.

But as much as Jorin desired to strike her down where she stood, he wanted more to bring her to his master alive. To see her suffer at his hands. Fighting the consuming heat of his rage, Jorin grabbed her by the arm and dragged her stumbling back to his men.

"Keep hold of her!"

The men nodded timidly and held Makilien tight as Jorin turned back to finish with Sirion. Crushed by the weight of helplessness now that she'd tried everything possible, a sob broke from Makilien and tears ran freely down her cheeks.

"No," she cried as Jorin approached Sirion. Her shoulders shook as she wept bitterly. "Elohim, please stop this!"

Void of all compassion, Jorin came to stand in front of Sirion. He glared at the young man who held his iron gaze with more confidence and acceptance than most men who had fallen at Jorin's hand. Somewhere deep inside, Jorin had a begrudging admiration for that, but he hastily destroyed that emotion and the weakness it could cause. Heedless of the mournful tears and cries behind him, Jorin raised his dagger.

Sobbing, Makilien squeezed her eyes shut, hardly able to endure the agony. It was as if she'd been stabbed herself to hear the horrible, gut-wrenching sound of flesh being penetrated. Sheer horror gripped her heart, and her legs went weak. A cry of pain pierced the air. But Makilien realized in an instant it had not come from Sirion. Her eyes opened, blinking rapidly at the tears blurring her vision.

Eyes wide, she watched Jorin drop to his knees. Embedded deep in the back of his left shoulder was a dark-shafted arrow. All stood frozen for a moment before Makilien took it as her chance to act. She yanked against her captors, but the action snapped them out of their daze, and they held fast. However, a dark streak shot from the forest trees a few yards away and hit one of the men squarely in the chest. He fell with a gasp at Makilien's side. The other man released her, scrambling away in fear.

As soon as she was free, Makilien reached down and pulled the dead man's sword from its scabbard. Straightening, her eyes flew around the area. Jorin's men were in a frenzied panic. Aedan too had managed to get free and find a sword. Makilien's gaze then searched for Sirion. She found him just in time to see Gorgon throw him to the ground and pin him with his foot. The cruel beast drew his sword and raised it above his head. He swung downward, but the blade did not reach its victim. Instead, it crashed into Makilien's sword.

Before Gorgon could react, Makilien swung wide, her sword slicing into the Shaike's middle. Blood spilled from the wound, and Gorgon roared in pain, but even this was not enough to stop the creature. He raised his sword again to cleave her in half. However, there came the sound of multiple solid thuds, and Gorgon roared again. His sword fell from his hands, and he toppled over with three arrows in his back.

Sirion jumped up, and Aedan joined them. Breathing hard, the three friends looked around and realized they were the only ones left standing. An eerie silence settled as they peered at the forest. Exchanging uncertain glances, they waited to see if the attackers would show themselves.

Brush rustled in the trees. A moment later, a large group of men burst from the forest. Moving swiftly, they surrounded Makilien, Sirion, and Aedan. They were fierce looking, clothed in dark green linen and brown leather. All stood tall like Jorin, and had dark olive skin and raven black hair. With dark brown eyes and stern expressions, they peered at the three captives. Makilien glanced over her shoulder, heart sinking. A Shaike stood with the men.

After a tense moment, one of the men strode forward, carrying an impressive long sword. His long black hair was tied back away from his strong, proud face. Scrutinizing their quarry, the man spoke. His words were of the Western language, but they were spoken with a rich accent, though his tone was sharp. "Drop your swords."

Makilien and Aedan glanced at each other, but with their hesitance came the subtle but distinct wooden creak of the other men drawing their longbows back a little farther. Makilien dropped the sword at her feet, as did Aedan. As soon as they were unarmed, a couple of the men rushed in to take hold of them, dragging them away from each other none too gently. Makilien struggled at first, but realized this was pointless. Her attention returned to the leader of the group as he gave orders to his men in a language she could not understand.

A couple of the men hurried off to where the horses had wandered, while the rest searched the bodies of Jorin's men. Makilien watched them closely, searching for any small sign that these men might turn out to be their saviors and not simply a new group of captors. Clearly, they weren't in direct service to Zirtan, but the presence of the Shaike caused concern.

A pained moan came from nearby. Makilien's eyes snapped to the source. One of the men had rolled Jorin over. She had believed Jorin to be dead, but now found he was only unconscious. The man standing over him spoke to their leader who looked at Jorin in disgust and gave his man a brief answer. With his leader's approval, the man pulled out his sword and raised it above Jorin.

"Stop!" The exclamation burst from Makilien before she realized she had spoken.

All eyes turned to her. For the life of her, she could not figure out what prompted her to intervene, to want mercy for the evil man, but something inside her just could not stand by and watch Jorin killed in cold blood, even after the cruelty he'd displayed.

At a loss, she stammered, "He—he's unconscious and unarmed."

The leader, eyes narrowed, peered at her shrewdly before finally giving another order. The man scowled down at Jorin, but re-sheathed his sword.

By now, the other men had returned with the horses and all weapons and supplies had been gathered. The leader spoke to them, and they all hurried toward the trees, bringing Makilien and her friends with them. Makilien looked to Sirion and Aedan as they entered the forest. What would become of them now?

:Chapter Twenty-two:

Gébrale

It felt as though they had been traveling for hours, but it was difficult to say for sure in the dark, closed-in forest. Not only had Makilien lost sense of time, but also direction as they wound their way through the darrow trees. It seemed they made many twists and turns along the way, never traveling in a straight line for long. She couldn't decide if the men did it to disorient them, or if it only felt this way.

One thing she could say for them was that they were not cruel like their previous captors. They took care to make sure their prisoners received enough water during the trek, and though they traveled quickly, it was not a grueling pace. And, at one point, they had even provided Makilien with a wet cloth for her bleeding lip. However, they did not say anything, leastwise not anything Makilien, Sirion, or Aedan could understand.

At last, their journey came to an end when the forest cleared a little. It was not completely open, but the trees were more widely spaced, and nestled between the thick, dark trunks stood sturdy cottages. Makilien found about a dozen of them within her sight, but there appeared to be many more deeper within the forest. The cottages were dark grayish in color, constructed of darrow wood, and thatched with grass from the plains.

She did not see anyone until they had gone beyond the first cottages. Then they passed people on the cleared paths winding their way through the forest village. Men, women, and children, all bearing an attractive olive complexion and black hair, stopped to stare at them as they passed by. Though their gaze was not cruel, Makilien did sense an aloofness and uncertainty regarding their presence. The people likely had not had any outsiders in their village for many years and she, Sirion, and Aedan certainly appeared very different within their midst.

Makilien took in everything with curiosity. In a way, the simple life these people lived was reminiscent of life in Reylaun. Besides the cottages, she noticed a blacksmith shed, a carpentry shop, and more than one stable. She quickly came to realize horses were an important commodity to this community. She saw many of them—tall, powerful animals—well-suited to the people to which they belonged.

Well within the village, they came at last to a stop. Before them stood a small building, which appeared to Makilien to be much like the corn cribs in Reylaun. Whether or not that was its intended purpose, it looked like it would now be used to secure her and her friends. The leader of the group swung the door open and motioned them inside. Quietly, Makilien, Sirion, and Aedan obeyed, and the door slammed shut behind them.

Standing in the middle of the space, dim light filtering through the slats of the walls, they looked at each other. They were filthy, battered, and exhausted, but alive. And they were sure now they had found the men they had been seeking, even if it had not come about in the way they'd planned.

"Are you all right?" Sirion asked Makilien, breaking the silence, his eyes settling on the bruising to her face and her cut and swollen lip.

She nodded slowly. She had a nasty headache, and the side of her face and her lip still stung, but she'd endured worse. Worn out, she sank to the ground and leaned back against the wall. Sirion and Aedan did the same.

"I wonder how long they'll keep us here before we get a chance to talk to them," Aedan said.

"I don't know," Makilien murmured. She glanced over her shoulder to look through the slats but did not see anyone. "I could be wrong, but they don't seem to intend us harm. They have to know we are not sided with Zirtan, and apparently, neither are they."

"What do you think about the Shaike?" Aedan asked.

"He is the one thing that doesn't make sense," Makilien said. "I don't know what it means for us, but I do know Elohim must have some plan for bringing us here like this."

Her companions agreed. In the silence that fell between them, they each considered what had transpired only a short time ago. A flood of emotion and deep thankfulness welled up inside of Makilien.

"Thank Elohim they arrived when they did," she said, her voice trembling a little. She turned her eyes to Sirion. "When I heard Jorin get shot, I . . . I thought for sure he had stabbed you. I could hardly bear the pain of it."

Sirion gave her a reassuring smile and let out a deep breath, still feeling the relief of that moment. In all the things he'd been through, he didn't think he'd ever been so certain he was going to die.

"Praise Elohim," he said quietly.

Makilien nodded. "Praise Elohim."

For an hour they sat, mainly in restful silence, thankful that, though still prisoners, their peril was not as certain. As the light around them grew dimmer with the late hour of the day, footsteps approached. When the door swung open, they looked up to see the man who had been in command. The three of them rose as he stepped inside. Eyeing them, he said, "Let me see your chains."

Makilien, who stood closest, raised her arms. The man stepped closer, and she realized in his hand he held a key. Using it, he unlocked the shackles from her wrists before moving on to Sirion and Aedan. After tossing the shackles away, the man faced them again.

"My name is Gébrale. I am the captain and leader of these people. Who are you and where do you come from?"

His gaze landed first on Makilien, and she could see a hard glint of distrust in his dark eyes.

"My name is Makilien. I come from Reylaun, a small village in Aldûlir."

Gébrale's eyes narrowed keenly as he studied her for a moment. Then his gaze shifted to Sirion and Aedan who each gave their names. Still looking at them with suspicion, Gébrale motioned outside.

"Come with me."

They stepped from the building. A couple of men waited outside and followed as an escort as Gébrale led them through the village. The sunlight was dim now, but torches and lanterns had been lit around each of the cottages, giving the village a warm orange glow.

Not far from where they had been kept, they came to a cottage, distinct from the others in that it was larger, and stepped inside. Only a couple candles flickered so it was dim, yet warm and comfortable. Leaving the entry, they came to a large room for sitting or meeting. Inside this room stood a woman. She was young, just a few years older than Makilien, her almost waist-length black hair framing a lovely face.

Turning to them, Gébrale said, "This is my sister, Demera. She will tend to your injuries."

Though her brown eyes were curious and questioning, Demera smiled kindly at them. "Come," she invited in a soft, accented voice, motioning to a couple of chairs. "Sit."

Makilien, Sirion, and Aedan did as she bid and took seats.

With a basin and cloth in hand, the woman came to Makilien first. Pulling up a stool, she sat and cleaned the blood from Makilien's face. Her touch was light and gentle.

"What is your name?" she asked.

When Makilien answered, Demera cast a brief glance at her brother. In this moment, Makilien realized news of her actions had traveled even to this remote village.

After tending Makilien's face and cleaning and bandaging her wrists, Demera moved on to Sirion and finally Aedan. It felt good to receive care after suffering the opposite for days.

Almost immediately after Demera finished, Gébrale's men returned accompanying three women, each carrying a tray. They set the trays on a low table, and Makilien and her friends beheld platters of venison, vegetables, cheese, and fresh bread. Their mouths watered, reminding them of how hungry they were.

"Please, eat," Demera invited generously.

They did so gratefully, and little was said during this time. Gébrale and Demera remained with them, and Gébrale watched them closely. His scrutiny may have been discomforting had they not been so preoccupied with the delicious food.

At last, Makilien's stomach filled contentedly. Though still wearied by the ordeal, her mind was now free to focus again on the mission that had brought them to Rhûnland, and the providence of Elohim to have brought them to this very village.

Noting when she had finished, Gébrale spoke. "You told me your name is Makilien."

She nodded to affirm it.

"We've heard that name spoken among Zirtan's men. It is an intensely hated name to them." He paused a moment, peering at her. "It is said the young woman bearing it killed Zirtan's general, Zendon, during their attack on Minarald last summer. Is this true?"

"Yes, it is true," Makilien acknowledged.

"You are the Makilien they speak of," he stated more than asked.

She gave a nod. "I am."

Gébrale looked rather pleased with his assessment, but his voice held a distinct tone of curiosity. "And how did you accomplish so great a feat?"

"I didn't. Elohim did. I was merely His tool to defeat Zendon and bring victory. Had it not been His will, I never would have even survived to see the battle."

Now Gébrale sat silent for a long moment in contemplation. Finally, he asked, "So this is the reason you were being held prisoner?"

"Yes. Three days ago we were ambushed and taken captive. The man you were going to have killed, this was his second attempt to bring me to Zirtan. His name is Jorin . . . Zendon's brother."

Gébrale's dark eyes widened. "Zendon's brother? And you stepped in to save him?"

"I don't believe it would be Elohim's will to just stand by and let a man be killed mercilessly, even if he is on the side of the enemy," Makilien spoke with confidence.

Silence again followed, and she decided it was a good time to ask, "Captain, do you and your people have any sympathies for Zirtan and his men?"

"No," he answered firmly. "Our sympathies are for ourselves."

"Have you had trouble with Zirtan?"

Gébrale's expression hardened and anger ignited in his eyes. "He has driven us from our lands, and forced us to hide within the forest where his men cannot find us. He's destroyed our settlements, robbed us of our possessions, killed our people, and enslaved many of us." He ended with a weary sigh.

"And you can do nothing because there are not enough of you to stop him."

Gébrale gave a slow nod.

Makilien took a deep breath. It was the perfect opportunity to make her proposition, the very reason she and the others had left Eldor, but suddenly, she was nervous. She licked her lips, saying a quick, silent prayer.

"I know all you want is to live in peace and keep to yourselves," she said carefully, "but sometimes you have to fight for that, and if you're not strong enough on your own, you ally

241

yourself with those who want the same as you. Captain, before we were captured, our group had come to Rhûnland in search of your people."

Suspicion jumped into Gébrale's eyes, but Makilien entreated, "I understand your people have never wanted to enter into an alliance with Eldor or any of the countries to the west, but I believe Elohim called me here to ask you to join us in our fight against Zirtan. The battle is near, and Zirtan's force far outnumbers our own, but the outcome is in the hands of Elohim, and you may be one of the pivotal pieces He uses to bring victory, as I was."

Gébrale peered at her, his look cold and uninterested. "My people verge on extinction. I have a force of less than two-thousand men-at-arms. I can find no wisdom in sending them to face a force the size of Zirtan's."

"But if we are victorious, you will gain your lands back and will be able to live in peace as you desire," Makilien tried to encourage him.

"When most, if not all, of my men are slain, what use will it be? You may be confident in your belief in Elohim and victory, but I am not," he declared.

Makilien's heart sank as she struggled to know what more she should say to change his mind. Finally, she decided to let it go for now. Gébrale did not seem to be in the mood to discuss or consider her proposition any further.

Reinforcing this, the captain rose abruptly. Demera rose with him and asked a question in their language. Gébrale's reply was short and did not seem to please her as they began to argue. She put her hands on her hips and spoke firmly. Gébrale looked hard at her, but finally gave in and turned his still intense eyes to Makilien and the others.

"Come," he snapped.

Makilien, Sirion, and Aedan followed in silence and were escorted outside once again. Night had fully fallen, cloaking the village in a thick, yet quietly peaceful darkness.

Just when Makilien wondered where they would be taken, they came to a large building. Walking inside, Gébrale's men lit several torches revealing the interior as an open meeting hall. Gébrale gave the men a series of orders. Two left and two others went to light a fire in the open fire pit at the center of the hall. When the other men had returned, they carried with them three straw pallets and blankets.

"You will sleep here tonight," Gébrale said, his voice clipped and preoccupied. But then he turned, leveling them with a cold gaze. "The door will be guarded throughout the night. Do not try to escape."

"We won't, Captain," Makilien assured him.

With that, Gébrale and his men strode out, pulling the doors shut behind them. Silence settled in the hall. Exhausted, Makilien turned to one of the pallets near the fire and sank down. Sirion and Aedan joined her.

Staring at the dancing flames, Makilien asked wearily, "Do you think he will consider anything I said?"

"I don't know," Sirion murmured. "He is hard to read. They all are."

Makilien sighed, plagued with a wave of uncertainty, and turned regretfully to her friend. "I don't know if I did very well trying to convince him. You should have been the one to speak to him. You have much more experience and greater standing than I do."

Sirion shook his head and encouraged, "You are the one who felt called to come here. We came to protect and support you. You did well. It's in Elohim's hands to work on their hearts as to whether or not they will join us."

:Chapter Twenty-three:

An Unlikely Ally

Makilien watched Sirion poke at the dying red embers of the fire. Her eyes switched briefly to a bright patch of sunlight on the floor shining from one of the hall windows, but it would soon disappear as the morning sun climbed higher. She breathed out a sigh. She always hated waiting, especially in dealing with something like this. But hating it didn't make the wait any shorter. It took another hour yet before the door of the hall opened. She, Sirion, and Aedan rose as Gébrale and four of his men entered.

"Come," he ordered without any further words.

The three of them followed.

Outside was cool, but refreshing as golden shafts of sunlight shone through the thin blanket of mist gathered in the forest canopy. Through the village they walked, passing many villagers already in the midst of their daily activities. As the night before, they once again came to the large house where they'd eaten supper. Inside the entry, they met Demera, and Gébrale turned to face them.

"Before your breakfast, we will give you a chance to clean up and provide you with fresh clothing," he announced, his tone not softening. To Makilien, he said, "You will go with my sister."

Makilien glanced at Sirion and Aedan, but was not afraid. With a nod, she followed Demera through the large house. Down a long hall, Demera opened a door, and they stepped into a spacious bedroom.

"There is a wash basin and clothing there." Demera gestured to a tall screened panel standing in one corner.

Gladly, Makilien stepped behind the screen to wash up as Demera waited at the foot of a large darrow wood bed. She then changed into the new clothes. They were similar to those Demera wore—a pair of brown suede pants, a forest green shirt, and a chestnut brown, knee-length leather jerkin. The ends of the jerkin tapered to a point in the middle, and beautiful tooling decorated the armholes and neckline.

Stepping out from behind the screen, Makilien found Demera there to offer her a hairbrush. She accepted it with a smile and worked the brush through the snarls and tangles of her hair. As she did so, she glanced at the other woman.

"How long have your people lived here in the forest?" she ventured to ask.

"Twelve years," Demera answered. Her voice carried a wistful tone as she clearly recalled life before they had taken to the forest.

Gently, Makilien asked, "How did it come to this?"

Demera blew out a long sigh. "One by one our cities fell to Zirtan's armies until they marched on Tûrenth, our capital city. My father did all he could to defend our people, but he fell alongside most of our soldiers. We had no choice but to flee or be taken captive."

"Was your father the king?" Makilien asked as the real-ization hit her.

"He was."

"I'm terribly sorry," Makilien said softly. "For all your loss."

Demera only nodded, and Makilien let a moment of silence pass before she spoke again with caution. "We would like to help you get your lands back."

Demera looked steadily at her, but said not a word.

Sirion and Aedan stood at the table where a large wash basin sat. Gébrale and two of his men stood by the door watching them. They said nothing as they cleaned up, focused on their own thoughts and musings. A sudden question from Gébrale several minutes later surprised them.

"Why do you cover your arm?"

They looked to him and realized his question had been directed to Aedan. Aedan glanced at his arm, covered with the vambrace Vonawyn had made, and then his eyes rose to Sirion's. Both remained silent. Gébrale took a step toward them.

"Show me," he instructed.

Aedan hesitated, struggling with uncertainty. How would these men react to discover he bore the mark of Zirtan's men? Would it ruin their chances to gain their trust entirely? Would they believe it had been forced on him?

When he did not obey the command, Gébrale's voice sharpened. "If you will not remove it and show me, I will order my men do it."

Aedan released a sigh, praying to Elohim to help him with his struggle of shame and that this would not turn the men of Rhûnland completely against them. With great reluctance, he unlaced the vambrace and pulled it from his arm revealing the ugly snake brand.

Immediately, Gébrale's eyes darkened and has face grew hard. "Servant of Zirtan!" he hissed.

"No," Aedan insisted. "I am not."

"You bear the mark of the enemy!" Gébrale motioned to his men. "Take him away and lock him up."

"I am not one of Zirtan's men," Aedan tried to make him understand, but even so, Gébrale's men came forward.

Sirion stepped between them. "Stop," he commanded, his voice echoing with the authority of his noble birth.

Gébrale's men paused.

To Gébrale, Sirion said, "Let him at least explain how he got the mark. He speaks the truth. He is not one of Zirtan's men."

Though Gébrale's face did not soften, he turned his eyes back to Aedan expectantly.

Taking this chance, Aedan told the captain of his father, and of his capture and his father's plan to force him to join them.

"I would die before I'd join Zirtan's forces," he concluded with heartfelt conviction.

But Gébrale was not convinced, his eyes icy with distrust. "A convenient story, one I will not so easily accept."

He motioned to the guards again. "Take him."

Sirion again placed himself between them, but Gébrale forcibly pushed him aside, one hand on his sword. "Do not interfere unless you wish to join him."

Sirion clenched his jaw, fighting the urge to argue. It would do no good for anyone to have both himself and Aedan locked away. He caught Aedan's eyes, hoping to convey that he and Makilien would do whatever they must to get him out.

With a look of regret and resignation, Aedan put up no struggle as the men grabbed him by the arms and led him from the room. Gébrale stayed behind and cast his hard eyes once more on Sirion.

"Finish up. Your breakfast is waiting," he said shortly.

Holding the man's gaze for a moment longer, Sirion turned to do so and a tense silence fell on the room. He cleaned up and dressed in the fresh clothing he'd been provided before Gébrale escorted him to the room where they'd had supper. Makilien and Demera waited there. As they walked in, Gébrale said something to Demera, his voice clipped.

Her brows rose in surprise. A short exchange followed. Gébrale spoke with obvious displeasure, but his sister's voice, though questioning, was calm. Finally, Gébrale turned and walked out. Demera hurried after him, saying something more. The doors closed behind them.

Makilien hurried to Sirion's side.

"What happened? Where is Aedan?"

Sirion turned to her, grimacing. "Gébrale insisted on knowing what was beneath his vambrace."

"He saw the brand?"

Sirion nodded. "Yes, and he had his men take Aedan and lock him up somewhere. We tried to explain and convince him that Aedan did not receive it willingly, but Gébrale refused to believe it."

Makilien breathed out a deep sigh. "We will have to try to convince him again once he's had time to consider it."

She turned and sank down on the couch, not even thinking about the breakfast that waited on the table. Sirion sat beside her.

"I wish the others were here," Makilien murmured. "None of this is going well. I still think Halandor would be a much better person to talk to Gébrale. And I'm afraid for them wandering around looking for us so close to Zirtan's fortress. Who knows where they are."

Sirion agreed. "Maybe we can convince Gébrale to let us go out looking for them."

Makilien nodded, but had to admit she did not have much hope. With Aedan now locked up and suspected of serving Zirtan, Gébrale's distrust of them would be at its highest.

Aedan peered out between the slats of the corn crib, watching an occasional villager pass by. Finally, he pushed away from the wall and took the few steps to the other end of the structure. He was restless . . . and starving.

"How am I going to convince them?" he murmured, shaking his head.

He wondered if he would have believed himself if he were in Gébrale's position. Probably not.

Heavy footsteps approached the corn crib. Aedan looked to his left. Through the slats, he saw a towering figure—the Shaike. His curiosity heightened. He hadn't seen the creature since their trek the day before. It baffled him. If Gébrale wouldn't even believe he'd been forced to receive Zirtan's mark, how in Dolennar was a Shaike allowed to live within their midst?

The Shaike stopped at the wall of the corn crib, and Aedan looked up into his piercing yellow eyes as the creature peered in. His expression seemed to be set in a permanent scowl.

"I brought you breakfast," the Shaike said suddenly, his voice low and edged with a growl.

A plate slipped through the slats. Aedan took it, finding a hearty meal.

"And water."

A waterskin came through next.

"Thanks," Aedan replied glancing from the food back to what he could see of the Shaike's face.

He set the waterskin on the ground beside him and picked up the fork lying on the edge of the plate. Silently offering a quick prayer of thanks, he took a bite, savoring the rich food. Chewing, he watched the Shaike out of the corner of his eye. The creature stood, arms crossed, and had not moved. What more could he want?

Taking notice of Aedan's frequent glances, the Shaike said, "My name is Tanzim."

Aedan swallowed and stared at him. Was that friendliness in his tone? From what he knew of Shaikes, they were all cruel beasts, but there was something very different about this Shaike.

"I'm Aedan."

The Shaike grunted. "Pleased to meet you."

Aedan's brows rose. A friendly and polite Shaike?

"You don't serve Zirtan, do you?" That much was obvious, but Aedan wasn't sure what else to say.

Tanzim shook his head fervently. "No."

"I've never heard of a Shaike who does not serve Zirtan."

Tanzim shrugged his massive shoulders. "Not many leave his service."

"Why did you leave?" Aedan asked, becoming ever more interested in this giant being who contradicted everything he knew of the race.

Tanzim was silent for a moment and rubbed his arm where he too had a snake tattoo, among others. "I got tired of the killing . . . so I escaped."

"How did you come to be here?" Aedan settled back against the wall to eat, anxious to hear the Shaike's story.

"It ain't hard for one of us to get out of the fortress. Hiding's the hard part. After I escaped, I figured the forest would be the safest place. Gébrale's men found me a few days later and held me prisoner until they trusted me."

"How long did that take?"

"Months."

Aedan released another sigh. That didn't bode well for him.

But Tanzim said, "Don't worry. It won't take so long for you. You're not a Shaike."

"With this mark, I might as well be."

Still, the Shaike insisted, "I don't think Elohim will keep you here so long."

Aedan nearly choked on his food. "You believe in Elohim?"

Tanzim gave a firm nod. "I do," he said with as much conviction as Aedan had heard from anyone.

Aedan realized he shouldn't be surprised, but it was an amazing thing nonetheless. "How did you come to believe in Him?"

"Gébrale's sister. She visited me when I was a prisoner. She taught me all about Him."

"That is incredible," Aedan murmured. "Forgive me, but I never really thought it possible."

The Shaike smiled at him, a rather odd looking expression since his appearance was so fierce, but Aedan smiled easily in return.

"Most people would not believe it."

"Tell me more," Aedan requested. He found he liked the company of this Shaike, and talking to him was certainly preferable to sitting alone wondering if he'd ever earn Gébrale's trust.

Makilien stared out the window though her mind was elsewhere. Behind her, Sirion sat quietly on the couch, also lost in thought, their half-eaten breakfast still sitting on the table before him. They felt forgotten and wondered what Gébrale might do with them considering the mood in which he'd left.

At last, Makilien pulled herself away from the window and once again took a seat beside Sirion. He looked at her, noting the concern in her eyes.

"I'm sure all will turn out," he comforted. "Gébrale is a hard man, but I don't believe he will harm any of us."

She gave him a quick smile. "I'm sure you're right. I just wish Aedan was here. I want to know for sure he is all right. You know how he has been struggling with that mark. This is bound to make it worse."

Before Sirion could reply, heavy footsteps approached and the door swung open. Makilien and Sirion rose as Gébrale strode into the room. His smoldering eyes landed on each of them.

"My scouts have just reported finding a company of four riders and a red dragon three miles from here. Somehow they have managed to track us."

Makilien exchanged a look of relief and excitement with Sirion. Four riders meant no one had been killed by the Shaikes. Turning back to Gébrale, she said, "Captain, those are the others from our company. Our friends."

Though she hoped that would ease his mind, Gébrale's expression remained hard. "They are well armed, and I will not have them coming into our village that way. But neither will I risk sending any of my men to confront them."

It took a moment before realization hit Makilien. If a different alternative could not be found, Gébrale would just have her friends killed to avoid the risk of attack.

"Captain," she said urgently. "Send us out to them. They will disarm. I promise it. None of us want trouble."

Gébrale peered closely at her. "I will send one of you." His eyes shifted to Sirion. "You will go. You will have them all disarm completely. Should any of them resist . . . word will be sent immediately back here to kill your friends." He glanced at Makilien as he said this.

Makilien wasn't entirely sure she believed he would really do it. Still, Sirion would make sure that chance was not taken.

"The same goes should the dragon show any aggression," Gébrale went on. "Do you understand?"

Sirion gave a firm nod. "I understand."

"Come with me."

Before leaving, Sirion turned to Makilien. His eyes held confidence, yet concern lingered. "I'll be back shortly with the others. Everything will be fine."

:Chapter Twenty-four:

Reunited

Makilien paced and rubbed her arms against apprehension. It seemed Sirion had been gone a long while, but time ticked by so slowly, she could not be sure.

"Everything will be fine," she repeated his words to comfort herself.

It was the only sound besides her footsteps. The house seemed abandoned. She was aware there must be guards outside the room, but there had been no sign of their presence. Pausing by the window, she prayed, wishing she could see out the front of the house so she'd know when anyone arrived.

At last, footsteps approached, loud compared to the silence all morning. She turned. The door opened, and Gébrale walked in. At the stern look on his face, Makilien knew a brief moment of fear, but then he said in a softer tone, "Your friends are here."

Makilien couldn't suppress a smile. Her heart beat excitedly as she followed him. Just outside, the whole group waited. Grins sprang to their faces. Makilien passed Gébrale and rushed out to them, coming first to Halandor, giving him a tight hug.

"No one was hurt by the Shaikes, were they?" she asked.

Halandor shook his head. "No. We're all fine."

She glanced over her friends to confirm it.

"How did you escape?"

Makilien's eyes returned to Halandor. "It's quite a story. Certainly the hand of Elohim."

She then went on to greet each of the others, including Antiro who was overjoyed to be reunited with her. After the reunion, the group noticed Gébrale and several of his men waiting nearby. The captain stepped forward, his expression serious and hard to read, as usual.

"My men will see that your horses are looked after. You will all come with me."

Makilien and her friends obeyed, following Gébrale and a few of his men through the village. When they reached the meeting hall, he took them inside. Turning to them, he said, "You shall remain here until I have discussed with my men what is to be done. I warn you, do not try to oppose us or escape. Our village may be small, but our men are mighty." He glanced pointedly at Carmine as he said this. Obviously, the meeting hall would do little to contain him if he wished to escape.

They took the warning in silence. Makilien had hoped by now Gébrale would see they were no threat, but she understood his concern for his people.

Just before he left them, Makilien stepped forward with an earnest request. "Captain, will you please bring Aedan here to join us. I know how hard it must be to trust us, especially someone with Zirtan's mark. But, Captain, I have known Aedan my entire life. He is my best friend, and there is no one I would more readily trust with my life."

Gébrale's eyes rested on her for a moment before scanning the rest. When they returned to Makilien, he said in his usual cool tone, "I shall think about it."

With this, he left them, and the group focused once again on each other.

"Well, I am assuming we have found the men of Rhûn-land," Torick said.

Makilien half smiled. "Yes, and now the hard part—convincing them we're friends and to help us against Zirtan. They have Aedan locked up because Gébrale saw the brand. We haven't seen Aedan since early this morning."

"Have you spoken with them concerning our mission?" Carmine asked.

"Yes, I spoke briefly to Gébrale last night. He refused to consider helping us and clearly still does not trust us. It's as Lord Darand said. It seems they want to keep to themselves and not get involved in our fight.

"I've talked privately to Gébrale's sister, Demera. I think she is much more open to us. I learned from her that Gébrale is actually heir to be king. Their father was king at the time Zirtan attacked them twelve years ago. Gébrale has not taken up the kingship because they don't have a kingdom. But he has a lot resting on him, and I think he is afraid of making a decision that will result in complete destruction for their people. I'm sure that is why he is so reluctant to trust us or consider joining us. I hope, now that you're here, one of you will know better what to say to him than I did."

Halandor nodded. "We'll talk to him, but I don't think the outcome of this is going to rest on us or our words."

They waited some time for Gébrale to return, but they had much to discuss about the last four days. Halandor told of how they'd followed a few miles behind Jorin and his men, praying for the right opportunity to rescue the captives. Then how they'd met with the Shaikes, resulting in a fierce, but brief battle, and finally they'd found where Jorin's men had been killed.

At last, as evening descended, the hall doors opened. Gébrale stepped inside and stopped before the group. He said nothing at first, but motioned someone in. A moment later, Aedan appeared.

Makilien grinned and said his name in delight. She hurried to meet him and gave him a hug.

"Are you all right?" she asked quietly.

"I'm fine," Aedan told her with a smile. "Thanks to you . . . and a new friend."

Makilien's brows rose with curiosity.

"I'll explain later," Aedan said in amusement as Gébrale approached behind him.

Everyone faced the captain. Makilien noticed immediately his expression was less guarded than usual.

"I apologize for the wait," he told them. "I hope you can understand my caution."

All nodded, and Makilien gave him a warm smile, "We understand."

"If you will come with me, supper is being prepared." Gébrale cleared his throat and went on a bit reluctantly. "My sister . . . and I would like you to join us."

Four torches lit the clear spring at the edge of the village as stars twinkled through the holes in the forest canopy. The firelight flickered on the polished silver, horse head pommel of a long sword, very kingly in its construction. Gébrale turned the weapon absently in his hands, staring at the hilt. This sword was the only thing he had of his father's. The only thing that had not been carried off by Zirtan's horde when Tûrenth was raided and the people fled for their lives. He could still remember every detail of that day—the screams and cries, the death, the destruction of their beloved city. He wanted never to see his people have to face that again, but was it foolish to think they would forever be safe here? He wanted to believe so, but the question filled his heart with turmoil.

"What keeps you up this night?"

Gébrale looked up at the soft voice as Demera sat on the bench beside him, her inquisitive eyes studying his face.

With a labored sigh, Gébrale answered, "Many things."

Demera watched him stare at the clear, still water of the spring before she said, "Makilien and her friends?" She'd seen Halandor speaking for a long time with her brother and knew he had much to think on.

At first Gébrale did not respond, but then nodded in affirmation.

"Why will you not help them?"

Gébrale's dark brows drew together as he stared at his sister. "You would help them?"

Demera did not answer, but Gébrale suspected the answer in her heart was yes.

"I'm trying to protect our people," he suddenly felt the need to defend himself and his decisions. "Would you have us all be slaughtered?"

Demera's frown matched her brother's. "I love and care for our people just as much as you. Do not accuse me of being irresponsible and unconcerned with their lives."

Gébrale's expression fell apologetically, and Demera continued in a softer tone, "I want nothing more than for them all to be safe, but I also don't want for us and the generations to follow to hide here in the forest in fear as Zirtan takes over Dolennar."

"So you do believe I should go to war with the Eldorians against a force that vastly outnumbers us to a fate that could be the end of us all?"

"I believe you should consider where we are and what might happen if Zirtan gains control. We may not be safe here for much longer. I want you to consider perhaps Makilien is right and Elohim called her here to seek our help . . . I believe He did."

Gébrale hung his head under the weight of all that rested on him. How could he know what the right decision truly was? "I wish I had your faith . . . the faith of our father."

The frustration Demera had been struggling with for her brother and his stubbornness melted. She laid her hand on Gébrale's arm. "You can. It's always been available to you. You know what I believe, what our father believed. You know the truth . . . all you have to do is choose to believe it too."

Without another word, Demera rose and left him alone. Sighing deeply, Gébrale looked up through the trees to the stars as a war of indecision raged in his heart.

"We should be able to reach the mountains in four days," Halandor said to the group.

Once sure everything was attached to Antiro's saddle, Makilien turned to Carmine. "Do you remember seeing any passable areas that will take us up into the mountains?"

"Not specifically," the dragon answered. "But once we are closer, I will look for a path for you."

Makilien's gaze moved over the others who were nearly finished packing their horses with belongings and fresh supplies. She then looked to Gébrale's house. No one had seen him at all this morning, not even during breakfast with Demera. The night before, he had given them permission to leave since their time was short, but still refused to fight alongside them. Great disappointment stung Makilien's heart at this. She'd felt so sure she'd been called here, but she tried to trust that good would still come of it.

When everyone was ready to leave, she said, "I will go find Demera and tell her we are going."

Just as she moved toward the house, they spotted Demera and Tanzim coming, along with Gébrale. In his hand, Gébrale held the reins of a magnificent gray horse. Upon reaching them, he looked over the group, his eyes stopping on Makilien.

"Are you all prepared to leave?"

"Yes, we were just about to go."

Gébrale paused for a long moment before he spoke again. "I was up most of the night thinking . . . praying. I realize now that refusing to stand against Zirtan with those who would be our friends would likely lead to us having to stand against him alone in the future. Had we accepted Eldor's friendship and alliance earlier, it may have been that our country would not have fallen into ruin. I do not wish to repeat that mistake. I and my soldiers would be honored to fight alongside Eldor and her allies." To Makilien, he said, "After many years of pride and stubbornness, I finally believe as you do. And I also believe you were called here to us."

Tears pooled in Makilien eyes at this wonderful turn of events, and she exchanged smiles with her friends.

"Captain, I cannot tell you how happy and how grateful we are," she replied. "Or how grateful everyone will be in Minarald when they receive the news."

"As I have said, we are not a large force, and I do not know how much more strength we can add to your army, but I hope our presence will make a difference."

"I'm sure it will, Captain."

Gébrale gave her a kind smile that twinkled in his eyes. When his gaze moved past her, his brows lowered a little.

"What are you grinning at?"

Makilien glanced over to see the goofy grin on Tanzim's face.

"I knew you'd come around one day," the Shaike answered.

Gébrale laughed dryly and shook his head. "I hope I am not forever remembered as the man who took longer to believe the truth than a Shaike."

Tanzim chuckled deep in his throat, and the others joined in out of the pure joy of the moment.

Once they'd had a good laugh, Gébrale became serious once more. "I know you are anxious to be on your way so I ask, with your permission, that I may join you. Since you seek the dragons, I may be able to offer you aid. I believe I may know where they live."

This captured everyone's attention. Gébrale continued, "I know of a path up into the mountains. It will not be an easy trek, but it is passable as far as I know. Farther to the west in the heart of the mountains is one mountain that towers high above all others in the area. For decades my people have told stories of that mountain and of dragons who inhabit it. I can't say for sure if that is where they reside, but there must be some truth behind the stories."

"We'd be glad to have you join us if you are not needed here," Halandor told him.

"I've already discussed this with Demera and my men. She will oversee the preparation of our soldiers and lead them to Eldor along with help from Moréas, my right hand man. And Tanzim has already assured me that he will not let any harm befall her." He smiled. "My sister is as strong and capable a leader as I am, if not more so."

Demera shrugged modestly, and her brother turned to say goodbye. Farewells were spoken by the remainder of the group. At last, everyone mounted up, and with their new ally, they began the journey back west, to the mountains and their next uncertain task—to find the dragons.

:Chapter Twenty-five:

Eborin

From the edge of a sheer drop-off, Makilien and her friends stared into the valley below. A vast pine forest lay nestled between the mountains. Makilien glanced over her shoulder, down along the winding path that had led them up to this precipice. It had been a long, tiring journey up through the mountains. One they'd begun over two days ago.

When Makilien's eyes swung back around, they settled on a glimmering white mountain peak, towering high above the others, exactly as Gébrale had described it. It would take a good two days or more of travel through the forest to reach it. She looked to Carmine standing at the cliff edge.

"Do you think the dragons could live on that mountain?"

"We will not know for sure until we reach there, but I believe it's the best guess we can make," Carmine answered. "Its height gives an advantage for spotting enemies that would appeal to a dragon. And there must be a reason for the stories."

Makilien looked at the others, and they nodded in agreement, though she noticed Gébrale shake his head.

"All the time I was growing up, children were warned never to come to this mountain," he said. "Now I march straight toward it."

"Are you sure you want to go any farther now that you've brought us here?" Makilien asked, hating the idea of possibly leading him to his death. "Things may not go well after this."

Gébrale gave her a smile. "Of course. This is important. An army of dragons would be an incredible asset in battle."

Makilien smiled in return and turned back to Carmine. "Does there seem to be a way down?"

"Yes, but it will not be easy. You will not be able to ride."

Everyone dismounted. Leading the horses on foot, the group began their descent with extreme caution along a narrow, winding ledge. Most places it was barely wide enough for the horses and many times they'd send rocks and dirt crashing down the mountain face. All were tense and silent as they guided their mounts, some of which were more frightened and skittish than others. Silent prayers were said throughout the journey.

Finally, after the strenuous couple hour trek, they reached the valley floor with no major incident. Directly before them now lay the forest they had seen from above. At ground level, it was much different. The dark pines towering above them were the largest Makilien had ever seen. Even Carmine who landed beside them looked small next to the trees.

"I will join you on foot from here," he said. "I'm sure whatever happens, if there are dragons near, they will be aware of our presence before we are aware of theirs."

Makilien gave a quick nod. They had discussed sending Carmine on ahead to search, but he was unwilling to leave the group of riders alone. Now Makilien was glad he stayed with them.

They let the horses rest for a short time before mounting again and riding into the forest. The giant boughs of the pines blocked out much sunlight, and the uneven ground was thick with tall ferns and spongy, dark green moss. Vegetation rustled in the cool breeze, but there was no sign of life. The wild, mysterious atmosphere of the forest put everyone on edge. Even Gébrale who was used to thick woods peered around with apprehension.

It was difficult to tell how far they traveled, but mid-afternoon was well upon them when suddenly Carmine ordered, "Stop!"

Everyone halted immediately.

"What is it?" Torick asked, his voice low and edged with concern.

"I smell smoke . . . from dragon fire."

Halandor peered into the trees. "Are you sure?"

Before Carmine could answer, a thunderous roar shattered the stillness of the forest. The horses whinnied in fear, and icy tingles raced up Makilien's spine. All eyes rose toward the treetops. In a blur, a large, dark shape rocketed across the sky. Another deafening roar echoed, and the sound of beating wings surrounded them.

A great burst of scorching flames exploded in front of the group. Makilien threw her arm up to shield her face from the heat. The horses shrieked and snorted in panic. As the area before them burned, streaks of color raced through the trees, and streams of fire appeared on all sides.

Makilien and her friends squeezed in close to each other to keep away from the flames. All had a hand on their weapons, but only sheer willpower kept them from drawing. Appearing harmless may be their only chance of survival. *Please Elohim,* Makilien cried out. *Protect us. Keep these dragons from killing us.*

With a crackling ring of fire burning around them, blocking any possible route of escape, a deep, menacing voice growled down from above.

"If any one of you draws a weapon, you will all die."

Everyone slowly moved their hands away from their swords and looked up. Now, perched in the thick branches right above them, were four dragons, ready to pour down a cascade of fire should any of them make a wrong move. Makilien gazed up, wide-eyed, both frightened and in awe.

Each dragon was different in color. One, a female, was a beautiful white with hints of other colors when her scales caught the light, like an opal. Of the other three males, one was golden brown like polished bronze, another a dark red-orange, and the last was a forest green, darker than Emaril. All glared down at them with their brightly colored eyes, and each time they exhaled, the air around their nostrils shimmered with heat.

In silence, they waited. Then, out of the corner of her eye, Makilien caught movement, and something landed on the forest floor. Everyone turned to look as a fifth dragon stepped heedlessly through the ring of flames and scorched earth. No one dared to move. With cold blue eyes, the dragon glared down upon the riders. The smoke and flames rising behind him outlined his muscular form and glinted on his coal black scales making him the most fearsome and intimidating creature Makilien had ever encountered. Goose bumps rose up on her arms, and she had to swallow down a lump in her throat.

"For what business do you dare enter here?" the dragon growled in the same deep voice they'd heard before. "Do you wish to bring trophies back to your homeland?"

Makilien took a deep breath to keep her voice from trembling as she spoke. "No. We do not come to bring you harm. We are here in peace. We only come seeking aid."

The dragon snorted, sending two streams of curling smoke from his nostrils. "We do not aid Humans."

"Would you allow us to explain our situation?" Makilien asked pleadingly.

The dragon narrowed his glinting eyes. "Who are you?"

"Makilien."

The dragon showed no reaction and looked now to Carmine, examining him as the red dragon spoke.

"I am Carmine, brother of Saras who led the dragons to these mountains. Does he still lead you?"

This time, the dragon did react, though Makilien barely caught it. He seemed surprised and his voice softened just a little. "Saras is dead," he informed them. "Killed by those foul death vultures."

Carmine's head lowered in sadness, and sympathy rose up in Makilien.

"I'm sorry, Carmine," she murmured.

He gave her a slow nod, before focusing once more on the other dragon. "When did it happen?"

"Some years ago," the black dragon answered. Then, in an instant, his voice was like steel again and his eyes flashed back to Makilien. "You should not have come here. These are our mountains. We want nothing to do with the Human race. Those who dare to search for us do not leave alive." He blew more smoke to punctuate this declaration.

Stepping forward, Carmine stood face to face with him. The two were almost the same size, yet Carmine was a bit larger, a testament to his age. Both were a fearsome sight as they sized each other up.

"You would just murder the Humans?" Carmine asked, his voice as hard and menacing as the other dragon's.

"They murdered us," the black dragon tried to justify his statement.

Carmine growled in displeasure. "You cannot judge the entire Human race by the actions of a few. Those here would not murder a dragon."

"I have no proof of that," the black dragon responded, his voice too coming out in a growl.

Carmine rose up a little taller. "If you want to kill the Humans, you'll have to go through me first."

With a deep, arrogant laugh, the black dragon retorted, "Do you forget? I have four other dragons on my side."

"And I have the Creator on mine," Carmine countered.

The black dragon's arrogance seemed to evaporate as he could not find an appropriate comeback to this. In the following moment of silence, Carmine studied the younger dragon closely through his narrowed red eyes. Something about the black dragon sparked his memory.

"I know you," he said, voice lowering.

For the first time, the black dragon backed down a little. Taking a step back, he shook his head and insisted, "You are mistaken."

"Who are your parents?" Carmine wanted to know.

The black dragon turned a little, almost if he were trying to hide his face from Carmine, and refused to answer.

Carmine continued to study him until his eyes opened wider in recognition. "Wait . . . Eborin. You are Eborin, my brother's son."

The black dragon's neck and wings drooped a fraction before he drew himself up again to his full, menacing height and faced Carmine fully once more.

"Yes, I am Eborin . . . Uncle." Though family, his voice was ice cold.

"Eborin, surely you know you can trust me and that these Humans are my friends and will not harm you or the dragons with you."

"I do not trust you at all," Eborin declared. "You chose the Humans over your own kind. You are with them now."

Carmine's eyes narrowed again and his voice rose. "We dragons were created to aid the Human and Elven races. Most forgot that charge, but I have not. And neither did those who remained with me. We remembered our purpose. Clearly, you and the others did not."

"We will give no service to those who would murder us in cold blood just to sell us off piece by piece," Eborin spat, glaring at Makilien and the others in the group.

"As I said, those people are but a few compared to those who would gratefully welcome your assistance," Carmine tried to tell him. "Times have changed in your absence. The people of Eldor and her allies no longer fear dragons, and those who would murder us are no friends of the people. Killing dragons is considered murder within Eldor's borders."

"The damage to our race has already been done. Humans are not worthy of our assistance."

Makilien cut in before Carmine could reply to him and entreated, "Please, will you at least consider what we've come to ask of you?"

Eborin turned his chilling gaze toward her. "And just what have you come to ask of us?"

She hurried to speak while she had the chance. "As you may know, Zirtan will soon march on Minarald to try to destroy Eldor and all our allies. We came to beg you for aid. We are outnumbered and lack the strength he is bringing against us. We do not even ask for a lasting friendship with you. Only that you fight alongside us in this battle. After that, you may return here, and no one will bother you.

"Zirtan is trying to gain control of all Dolennar. Those who do not want to be oppressed by his rule must join together to stop him. Even here may not be safe for you if he succeeds in his domination. It is the kind of men he has on his side who are the ones who want to kill you."

Eborin sneered. "You ask us to risk our lives to fight with you?"

Makilien nodded. "Yes."

It was then Gébrale joined her. "I am Gébrale, son of Alec, the last king of Rhûnland. Our people are much like you. I felt the same about going to war alongside Eldor. I did not want to risk the lives of my people, but I can see now if Zirtan conquers those who oppose him, none of us will be safe. Once he gains full control, one way or another it will affect us all. I understand that now and have sent my army to Eldor to fight with them."

Eborin scoffed. "You are a fool." He glared again at Makilien. "Did your king send you here?"

Makilien shook her head and spoke with quiet confidence. "No, Elohim sent me."

Eborin said nothing for a moment, but then stated cruelly, "Well, it looks as if He has sent you to your death."

The dragon turned before Makilien could reply. To Carmine, he said, "You and the Elf I will show mercy. You two may go, but the Humans stay until I have decided what is to be done with them."

Carmine snorted angrily, glaring at his nephew. "We will stay and share in whatever fate you determine for them."

"Very well," Eborin retorted, "if you choose to be fools." He looked to Makilien and her friends. "Disarm and throw your weapons away."

They did as he commanded. They had no choice.

Eborin gazed up into the trees where the four others still perched. "Wythel, stay here with the others and watch them. Should any of them attempt to escape or regain their weapons, kill them all."

The white female dragon nodded. "We will."

"Malachi, you come with me," Eborin ordered.

With those words, Eborin launched himself up into the sky and the dark green dragon followed. In a moment, both were gone from sight.

:Chapter Twenty-six:

Dragon's Den

Makilien held her head in her hands as she sat and prayed. Little talk was exchanged between the group since the dragons could hear every word. Makilien was at a loss. She hadn't known what to expect when they reached this point, but it was not as she had hoped. Maybe she'd been naïve, but she truly had not expected the dragons to be so hostile toward them. She'd been prepared for their refusal to help fight, but she had never imagined the dragons would actually kill them.

Worried she'd led all her friends to their deaths, Makilien continued to pray earnestly for deliverance. She tried to comfort herself with the confidence she had that they were supposed to be here after what had taken place with Gébrale and his people. It had appeared as if they were going to fail there too, but Elohim had come through as always. Surely He would do the same here. Yet, if the dragons did kill them, at least they had accomplished something, and Eldor would have the aid of Rhûnland.

Close to an hour later, they heard the flap of wings and looked up. In a moment, Malachi, the green dragon, landed before them. Carmine approached him. He had known this dragon well before they all left.

"Malachi," he said, his voice cautious, yet friendly.

"Carmine," the other dragon responded with comfortable familiarity.

"It is good to see you," Carmine told him.

"And you as well," Malachi replied, but his deep voice halted uncertainly.

"What is it?"

Malachi hesitated. "Eborin wants me to bring Makilien to him."

Everyone's eyes swung to Makilien and then back to the green dragon.

"Will he kill her?" Carmine asked.

"I don't know," Malachi admitted. "He said he wants to speak with her. I don't know what he plans after that."

"Well, she's not going anywhere," Torick declared, and continued, despite warning growls from the dragons above, "If he wants to speak to her, he can come and speak to all of us."

Knowing full well if she refused to go and Eborin was forced to return he would no doubt kill them all, Makilien quickly stepped in.

"No, Torick," she said and faced Malachi. "I'll go with you."

"Makilien, there's a good chance that dragon will kill you if you go," Torick replied, concern heavy in his voice.

"And if we make him angry by refusing to cooperate and he comes back here, he'll probably kill us all. Either way, we are powerless. At least this way I can try to talk to him and convince him to release or help us." Makilien's eyes came to focus on Halandor who was clearly conflicted. "It's the only choice we have."

With reluctance, he nodded though it pained him deeply. With his agreement, the others seemed to see too that they could do nothing and had to let things play out as they were.

"We must go then," Malachi said.

Makilien glanced at all her friends, wishing she could hug each of them, but there was no time. Her eyes caught Sirion's for a moment as she turned. She saw the fear in his eyes and sensed his struggle to keep from taking some sort of action.

"Pray," was all Makilien could say, and she walked over to Malachi.

The dragon looked at her and then at her friends. "I am sorry. It is not my desire to do this."

He then took her by the arms and extended his wings. In a moment, they sailed into the sky, Makilien dangling beneath him. The breath was sucked from Makilien's lungs as they rapidly ascended. She looked down at her friends, but in a second they shrank from sight, and all she could see were the treetops.

Malachi climbed steadily until the forest looked small beneath them, and Makilien could see miles and miles of mountain peaks. They flew westward, straight toward the towering mountain they had spotted earlier. At this altitude, the air was cold and numbed Makilien's face and arms. It was certainly not like the exhilarating flight she'd taken with Indiya. Dangling from the claws of a strange dragon who could suddenly release her if he wished and the thought of what could be coming made her stomach twist and churn.

After a few minutes, the tall mountain loomed just before them, and Makilien spotted a large rock ledge jutting out from the mountain. Malachi angled downward and, flapping hard, set her gently on the ledge, coming to land behind her. Straight ahead yawned the black opening of a cave.

Makilien rubbed the goose bumps on her arms as her whole body trembled. It was very cold up here—with snow still among the rocks—and her summer dress did little to offer warmth, but it wasn't only the chill affecting her. Fear worked hard to wrap its way around her heart.

"Eborin is waiting in the cave," Malachi told her.

Makilien looked over her shoulder into the dragon's pale green eyes, and he gave her a remorseful look. She turned back to the cave and swallowed. She forced herself to take a step, but then stopped. Sinking down to one knee, she closed her eyes.

"Elohim," she murmured. "I know You are in control of whatever is about to happen. My life is always in Your hands. Not this dragon's, not Zirtan's, not anyone's, only Yours. If I die now, I know it will bring me to You and Your Kingdom. But if there is a way of escape, if there is more I can do, please show me. And whatever happens, give me courage to outweigh my fear and give me the right words to speak."

She stayed kneeling, calling to mind the memory of her time with Meniah when he'd appeared to her as she so often did in times of struggle. *You will never be alone. Take courage in that always,* he had said.

"I will," she murmured.

Opening her eyes, she rose. After taking a deep breath, Makilien strode toward the cave. At the entrance, she slowed a little to make her way more cautiously in the darkness that crept around her, each step diminishing more and more of the outside light. Finally, she rounded a corner and the light faded entirely. She paused for a moment, slowly breathing in and out, before shuffling along the hard floor, her hand feeling the way along the rock wall to her right. The air was not stale, but the darkness felt thick and suffocating, and chilled her whole body.

Her heart rate increased as did her trembling as she wondered how much farther she would have to go before something happened. Would she end up running right into Eborin? She couldn't see her own hand in the darkness, let alone a black dragon. Or would he suddenly flame her or snap her up in his jaws? Worst was the knowledge that he could see just as well in the dark as he could in the light while she was completely blind. *You will never be alone,* she repeated over and over to herself.

The cave seemed to go on forever. Makilien had begun to wonder if Eborin would just let her wander around for hours while he watched in cruel amusement when she spotted a small light spot to her left. Focusing on it, she realized two spots hung in the darkness. She had no time to figure out they were moving closer before she saw clearly they were the eerie glow of blue dragon eyes. Eborin's warm breath drifted across her cheek.

Makilien froze and tried with all her might to slow her heart, which beat so hard she thought it might fail her.

"Did your friends try to resist Malachi bringing you here?" Eborin's voice resonated in the vast enclosed space.

Makilien swallowed and had to lick her dry lips before answering. "They wanted to, but I agreed to come."

"Did you?" Eborin droned. "Why?"

"I knew we would all be killed if we resisted. At least right now they are all alive." Though still terrified, she found her confidence building as she spoke.

The clear, pale light of Eborin's eyes moved closer as his face came within inches of hers. "You would sacrifice yourself to let your friends live?"

"Yes," Makilien answered softly.

"Why?" the dragon questioned again.

"Because I love them. They would do the same for me. And someone I loved once sacrificed himself for me and others. I want to be like him."

Eborin backed away, saying nothing for a few moments. Finally, when he spoke again, his voice was low and even colder.

"You are the same Makilien they say killed Zendon."

She nodded. "Yes."

His eyes moved as he paced in front of her, his sharp claws clicking against the rock. As Makilien watched him, the image of a cat toying with a mouse just before it killed sprang to mind. This was exactly how she felt. She was the mouse and Eborin was the cat. She swallowed again.

"You were a fool to come here looking for us," Eborin growled.

"I don't feel like a fool for doing what I believe Elohim wanted of me," Makilien replied.

A blinding flash of light and flames leapt toward her. She threw her arms up to shield herself as she fell back against the wall. The scorching heat stung her skin, but it was not enough to cause any real injury. Once the heat died away, she lowered her arms. Breathing heavily, she stood up straight, facing Eborin. Though all she could see were his glowing eyes, she faced him with determination.

Both stood where they were for a moment. Then Eborin came close again, and she could almost feel the rumble of his voice.

"Do you know how much pain I could cause you?"

"Yes."

The dragon's hot breath swept by her face again. "Most grown men would be cowering before me now, yet here you stand face to face with me. Are you not afraid?"

"I am very afraid," Makilien told him, her voice trembling a little with honesty.

"You do not seem to be."

"That is because my courage is not my own. It comes from Elohim. He is my hope, my strength, and my courage. He is right here with me now and wherever I go. If it is not His will I die here, He will be my protection."

She watched Eborin's eyes narrow, but then they backed away as it seemed the dragon sat down. A long exhalation of air blew from his nostrils and then silence as he stared at her, unblinking.

"You are a strange Human," he said finally. His voice had lost its hard edge, taking on a more curious tone. "Many speak like you, yet falter when tested."

"Maybe that's true," Makilien replied cautiously, "but maybe you've grown to think worse of Humans than is always necessary. Most of the people I know and have met truly are kind, generous, gracious, and noble. But I do know too of the cruelty of others. There are both sides. That is why we will soon find ourselves in a battle where many if not all of the people I love may die."

"Hmm," Eborin rumbled thoughtfully.

Makilien held her breath, wondering, waiting.

"Come," the dragon instructed suddenly. "It is too cold for you here."

Makilien had forgotten all about the cold during their discussion, but now she was frozen.

"This way." The glow of Eborin's eyes moved off in the direction Makilien had first come.

She followed the barely visible light and the sound of his claws on the rock. He moved slowly, allowing her to keep up. She didn't know quite what to make of his sudden concern, but she was thankful. Finally, they came around the corner where light flooded in. Makilien squinted as she stepped outside, but her eyes adjusted quickly.

"We will return her to her friends," Eborin told Malachi.

The corners of the green dragon's mouth turned up just a little, and he approached Makilien.

"This time, please, ride on my back. It will be more comfortable for you," he said as he crouched before her.

A smile came to Makilien's face, and she crawled up, holding one of the dark spines on his neck. In a moment, they were in the air, following behind Eborin. For this flight, Makilien's heart was much lighter, and she thanked Elohim to still be alive.

In only a short time they arrived again near the eastern edge of the forest where thin trails of smoke rose above the treetops from the smoldering vegetation. Dropping down through the trees, the two dragons landed near Makilien's friends. All eyes turned, and Makilien could see their joy and relief when they spotted her. She slid off of Malachi and walked to her friends, but Eborin cut off any chance to speak.

To Makilien and her friends, he said, "You will remain here until we return." Then, looking up to the dragons in the trees, he ordered, "All of you, come with me."

The dragons looked at each other, and all five of them flew away, leaving only Makilien and her friends. As soon as the dragons were out of sight, everyone surrounded her.

"Are you all right?" Halandor asked. "You're shaking."

Makilien gave a quick nod, releasing a nervous laugh. "I'm really cold and was really scared, but I'm all right."

Sirion grabbed a blanket from one of the horses and put it around her shoulders. She smiled in thanks, and Torick asked, "What happened?"

"I'm not really sure," she admitted. "I think Eborin was testing me. He tried purposely to scare me while we were speaking, but he never tried to kill me. I don't know what will happen now, but his attitude seemed to have changed."

Not knowing how long the dragons might be gone, the group set up camp and made a small fire for Makilien to warm herself. From there she gave the details of her brief encounter with Eborin. The change in the dragon gave them all hope, and no longer did they fear they would be killed.

The bright orange and pink of sunset painted the sky when the group rose at the approach of wings. Eborin and Malachi appeared above the trees as they descended and came to land at the edge of camp. The black dragon stepped forward and focused on Makilien.

"Somehow, you have convinced me there may be some good in the Human race," he said, sounding rather perturbed about this. He was quick to add, "I still have no love for Humans, nor do I have any desire to help in your war. However, after speaking with many of the dragons here, I was surprised to learn most of them do wish to help you. So, despite how I feel, we will give you aid."

Makilien could not stop the flow of tears that filled her eyes and coursed their way down her cheeks. "Thank you so much."

For the briefest moment, an emotional expression lit Eborin's eyes that suggested he wasn't as cynical toward Humans as he let on, but he hid it quickly. "I am only doing the will of the other dragons."

"Still, thank you."

"How many of the dragons will join us?" Carmine asked.

"Forty-seven of the oldest and most experienced," Eborin answered. "The young ones will remain here, out of danger."

Eyes widened and looks of amazement and excitement were exchanged. Forty-seven more dragons on their side would give them a huge advantage against Zirtan's troops. Makilien could hardly imagine so many dragons all together, fighting in battle.

"You may remain here and leave whenever you wish," Eborin told the group.

"We will leave in the morning," Halandor replied. "We must return to Eldor before Zirtan arrives there."

Eborin nodded. "Then we will leave you for the night."

As quickly as the two dragons had appeared, they left again.

:Chapter Twenty-seven:

Return

"Once we reach the Claron River, perhaps Indiya or Emaril can escort you the remainder of the way while I fly on ahead to bring the news of our success to Lord Darand."

Makilien nodded in response to Carmine. "Yes, I'm sure they all wonder what has happened to us by now. My family is probably sick with worry after all this time."

She turned back to finish saddling Antiro.

Just as the group had finished packing up their camp, Eborin and Malachi came down through the trees. Everyone stopped to face the dragons.

"Last night I sent scouts to check on the activity in Zirtan's fortress," Eborin announced. He paused. "They have just returned with the news that Zirtan's force is massing to leave."

"Are they sure of this?" Carmine asked.

"Yes," Eborin answered gravely. "The army may already have left by now."

Makilien traded glances with her friends, fear squeezing her stomach.

"Do you think we can reach the river before they do?" she asked.

Halandor shook his head. "I don't know. We all know how quickly Zirtan's army can move . . . especially if he is leading them."

"What are we going to do?"

No one had an answer to this as silence hung over them. To be trapped here in the mountains while Zirtan's force marched on Minarald was a terrible possibility.

Eborin stared intently at them, debating. Finally, against his better judgment, he said, "There is another way to Minarald."

All eyes turned to him hopefully.

"There is a hidden passage through the mountains," he went on. "Only we dragons know of it. It will take you almost directly to the city within four days."

"Where is it?" Makilien asked eagerly.

Eborin stepped closer and looked down on them, his eyes narrowed. "First, you must swear *never* to share its location with anyone. You are to be the only ones to know it exists. Don't even tell anyone how you reached the city. Do you understand?"

Under his intense stare, they nodded solemnly.

"We won't tell anyone," Makilien promised. "Our only concern is reaching Minarald in time."

Eborin continued to stare, questioning his decision to do this. At last, he sighed. "Very well, Malachi will lead you to the passage. The rest of us will come in a few days."

"Thank you, Eborin," Makilien spoke with all the sincerity in her heart.

The dragon gave the slightest nod of his head.

"Be sure to come before Zirtan reaches the city," Carmine told him. "There is still dragon armor in the armories. There should be enough for all."

Eborin did not reply. Instead he told them, "You should go . . . before I change my mind."

Though Makilien believed he was more sympathetic than he let on, everyone turned to mount their horses. With Malachi leading the way, they turned to the northwest and rode away from camp.

For most of the morning they traveled through the forest, which gradually rose until the trees thinned out and they were once again at the foot of the mountains. Expertly, Malachi led them along steep cliffs, around deep gullies, massive, jagged boulders, and other impassable terrain they never could have navigated on their own.

A few hours after leaving the forest, they came around a sharp bend and found, nestled between two mountain peaks, a passage just wide enough for two horses to pass side by side. Here they stopped.

"This is it," Malachi said. "The way is clear and easy from here."

"Thank you," Makilien told him with a grateful smile. "I can't tell you how thankful we are to have a way to reach Minarald in time."

"I am glad I could show it to you," Malachi replied. "I will return now to our mountain, but I will see you in a few days."

They said goodbye to him, and he flew off. After allowing the horses to rest for a while, the group mounted up again and rode two at a time into the passage.

"We should be getting close by now," Torick remarked, eyeing the steep rock walls rising around them.

After four days in the mountains, everyone shared the same restlessness, anxious for a glimpse of the open plains of Eldor. Around every bend, they hoped to find the way out of the maze like passage they were following.

Makilien hoped they had not gone wrong somewhere along the way. She didn't believe so, but it was a concern. Carmine could have told them how much farther they had yet to go, but they had all urged him to go on ahead to Minarald on their second day so he could warn Lord Darand of Zirtan's approach.

Just as these thoughts of the dragon entered Makilien's mind, a shadow passed over the group. Everyone looked up and smiled as Carmine descended and landed before them.

"Is everyone faring well?" he asked. "Has the way been difficult?"

Halandor shook his head. "No, but I think we are all wondering how much farther we have to go. Everything is starting to look the same."

Carmine smiled. "Only another two miles and you will be out of the mountains. Then its three miles to Minarald."

The group breathed a collective sigh of relief.

"I came to see that you were well, but also to tell you Zirtan's force crossed the Claron River two days ago," Carmine went on. "They should reach the city within three days."

"How are preparations coming?" Halandor asked.

"Very well," Carmine answered, with a satisfied nod. "The outer city is nearly evacuated, though there are still families coming from the villages."

"Has my sister arrived?" Gébrale wanted to know.

The dragon nodded. "Yes, she and the army arrived three days ago. Rest assured, Lord Darand has made your sister quite comfortable at the palace."

Gébrale's smile showed how glad he was to hear this.

"And my family knows we're safe?" Makilien asked.

With his own smile, Carmine said, "I told them myself. I don't think I have to tell you how relieved they were."

Excitement bubbled inside Makilien at the thought of seeing them.

With this news, they rode on. This time Carmine remained with them, flying just overhead as they traveled the remaining two miles of the mountain passage. At last, coming up over one final ridge, the rolling green Eldorian plains appeared and gave everyone increased energy and enthusiasm. Now out of the mountains, they urged the horses on at a greater speed.

In a short time, they spotted Minarald in the distance, a most welcome sight for all. When they arrived and rode through the gate, things were far different than normal since the evacuation had already taken place. They saw only soldiers, and the streets were unnaturally quiet for daytime. It caused a solemn silence to fall over the group as they rode on to the stable.

Turning to Gébrale who took in the sight of the city with some wonder, Halandor said, "It's a shame you can't see it when it is thriving with life."

Gébrale gave a short nod, but said, "I pray there will still be the opportunity."

Word of their arrival had reached the palace ahead of them, and just as they entered the courtyard after tending to the horses, the doors opened and a large group spilled out to meet them. Joy jumped in Makilien's heart, and she ran forward to be surrounded by her family. She hugged each of them tightly, savoring the moment.

"Oh, Makilien!" her mother cried, cupping Makilien's face in her hands as she looked at her daughter through teary eyes. "We are so glad you're safe! We were so worried. It's been so long."

"I know, it has. I missed all of you so much."

"You truly are all right, aren't you?" She frowned at the bruises still visible on her daughter's face.

"Yes," Makilien assured her. "So much happened, and we have much to tell you about, but Elohim protected us all."

"We look forward to hearing of it," Néthyn said, his hand on her shoulder.

Makilien wasn't sure they'd be so eager if they knew of all the danger the group had faced, but she just smiled.

"I would have cried," Leiya stated with all seriousness.

Makilien grinned at her. "I think I was too scared to cry," she replied as the two of them spoke of her encounter with Eborin as they prepared for bed.

"Did he really breathe fire at you?" Leiya asked, her eyes round and bright with imagined fear.

"Yes, though thankfully he didn't want to kill me or I would have been roasted on the spot," Makilien told her dramatically.

"I wish I could see a dragon breathe fire."

"I'm sure you will sometime. Maybe Carmine, or Indiya and Emaril can show you."

Leiya nodded and then said excitedly, "I met Indiya and Emaril."

"Did you?"

"Yes. Three days ago they came here to talk to Lord Darand. Indiya's really beautiful, isn't she?"

"She sure is."

"I love her blue scales. Blue is my favorite." Leiya paused as Makilien helped her slip into her nightgown. "When will the other dragons get here?"

"I'm not sure," Makilien answered. "They said they would be here in a few days so any time, I guess."

Leiya crawled into bed. "I'm excited to see them, but I'm a little scared to see Eborin," she admitted.

Makilien chuckled and sat beside her. "He can be pretty scary, but don't worry. He may not really like us, but he won't hurt us. I'm very thankful to have him on our side for the battle."

"Do you think we'll be able to win now?" Leiya asked, looking up at her sister with hopeful eyes.

Makilien released a small sigh. "I can't say for sure. We have a lot more help now than we did before, but ultimately, it is all in Elohim's hands. He will control the outcome."

"I can't wait until it's all over."

Makilien nodded, hoping, praying she and all her loved ones would still be here when it was. So easily she could lose everyone she was close to. *Help me not think of that,* she prayed in her heart.

In the moment of quietness, there came a knock at the door separating their room from their parents'.

"Come in," Makilien called.

The door opened, and Hanna and Néthyn stepped into the room. With warm smiles for their two daughters, they walked to the bed.

"Are you two ready for sleep?" Hanna asked.

They both nodded. Sleeping in a real bed snuggled next to her sister sounded wonderful to Makilien.

Leiya crawled to the edge of the bed and gave both their parents a hug and kiss goodnight. When it was Makilien's turn, she hugged her mother for a long moment, and Hanna said, "I'm so happy I have you both here and safe for now."

Makilien smiled. "I love you."

"I love you, too," Hanna replied, touching her cheek.

Makilien turned then to her father. Before she had a chance to say goodnight, he asked her, "Are you too tired to talk?"

Makilien shook her head. Néthyn said a final goodnight to Leiya, and as Hanna tucked her under the covers, Makilien followed her father out to the balcony. Outside it was clear and cool, and a beautiful starry night. For a moment, she looked east to the moonlit plains, thinking of the army that would soon destroy the peacefulness. But she put that out of her mind and turned to her father, curious to know what he wanted to say.

"I've been looking forward to telling you this ever since you arrived," he began. He paused, smiling contently as he gave her the news. "I finally believe the truth you tried to share for so long."

Makilien's breath caught, and tears welled up in her eyes. She had to blink quickly to keep them from falling.

"Really?" she murmured, her voice wavering with emotion.

His smile growing, her father nodded.

Makilien put her arms around him. "I am so happy!"

As they parted again, she asked, "What made you change your mind?"

"General Nirgon," Néthyn answered. "We talked a lot while you were away. He helped me see what I did not before."

Makilien smiled widely, her eyes moist and sparkling, and her heart full of gratitude. For a moment she could not speak, but then she asked, "What about Mother?"

"I think she is more open, but she's not ready yet."

Nodding, Makilien prayed in her heart that her mother would soon see the truth.

"When were you able to talk to General Nirgon?"

"He has been training me ever since you and the others left," Néthyn explained. "Prince Darian knew my desire to continue training, and when he asked the general to find someone able to do that, he offered to see to it personally."

This news came as a surprise to Makilien, but she was very thankful Nirgon had taken time to train her father despite how busy he must be. She couldn't think of anyone more qualified to teach him all he needed to know to defend himself and his loved ones.

"We trained hard," Néthyn went on. "Before we began, I asked him to prepare me for battle."

Makilien's brows lowered. This was the first she'd heard of her father joining them when Zirtan arrived.

"You are going to fight with us?"

"Yes," her father answered with all seriousness.

Makilien exhaled slowly. The thought of losing her father in battle put a tight knot in her stomach. She wanted to know her family was safe, all of them, but how could she ever ask her father not to fight?

"I need to do this, Makilien," Néthyn said, sensing her uncertainty. "I have never fought for anything in my life . . . not even my family." He had to pause as his voice choked up and tears filled his eyes. "I should have fought for you, Makilien, in Reylaun. I did nothing as you suffered. I am so sorry."

Seeing her father's regret and emotion, Makilien could no longer hold back tears. They streamed down her cheeks as she shook her head. "No, don't be sorry. I did what I had to do. I was willing to accept the consequences. There was nothing you could have done to stop that."

"I could have stood up for you and tried to defend you . . . even if it meant facing the same consequences with you."

"But Mother and Leiya needed you. It would have been awful for them to have us both enduring punishment. We both did what we needed to do." Makilien drew in a trembling breath. "You and Mother have always done the best for me and Leiya and did everything you could to take care of us and keep us safe, even when I didn't see it. I love you so much."

With those emotional words, they hugged tightly.

"I love you, Makilien. I am so proud of who you've become and the things you've done."

Makilien rested her head against her father's shoulder as she stood in his strong arms. A few more tears leaked out as she prayed desperately that Elohim would bring victory in the coming battle and peace for her family.

:Chapter Twenty-eight:

Disaster

An eerie calm rested over the city. As good as it would have felt to sleep in and get the extra rest, anxious anticipation had Makilien up well before her sister or her parents. Downstairs in the throne room, she stood with her friends as they discussed battle strategy with Lord Darand and General Nirgon.

"How long do you think we can last on the wall?" Makilien questioned when she had an opportunity.

"With more room to fight and the added dragons, I don't see why we could not hold out for at least a few days," Nirgon answered. "It all rests on our ability to keep from being overrun and protecting the gate. If it is breached, we'll have no choice but to leave the wall."

"Do you think they will breach the gate?"

"Unfortunately, I think it is inevitable. They will get through one way or another, but our goal will be to try to even our forces before we have to meet Zirtan on the battlefield."

"Do we know yet how large a force Zirtan really has?" Makilien asked.

"No," Nirgon answered, "but Carmine, Indiya, and Emaril are out scouting now, and one of them will bring back more details on the army."

"What else needs to be done before Zirtan arrives?" Darand asked.

"The walls need to be stocked with extra arrows. Our archers will be our main defense if we are to last. Supplies also need to be moved to the buildings closest to the wall. If we last as long as we hope, the men will need nourishment, providing we are given any respite. We should also have extra weapons nearby. I'll see that those preparations are begun right after breakfast."

Gathering a bundle of arrows in her arms from one of the carts, Makilien climbed the steps to the top of the wall. Large barrels and crates were set along the length of the parapet every few feet. She walked to the nearest one that was not yet full and placed the bundle of arrows inside it. Straightening, she put her hands on her hips and looked about her, getting familiar with the new additions and where everything was. She'd been entirely naïve to the process of battle last time, but now she wanted to be as knowledgeable as possible.

Exhaling slowly, Makilien turned back to the stairs.

"What is that?" a nearby soldier asked.

She glanced over her shoulder. A group of soldiers murmured to each other and pointed to the east. Instantly, dread gripped her stomach wondering if somehow Zirtan had arrived already. She too looked to the east. In the distance, she saw nothing on the ground, but small dark specks dotted the sky.

She peered closely, trying to distinguish what they could be, but it was impossible to tell.

"Maybe it's the dragons," one of the soldiers suggested.

Makilien searched down the wall, and when she spotted Sirion, she ran to him.

"Sirion, what is that in the sky to the east?"

He looked up from his work and followed her line of sight, focusing on the dark objects.

"Are they the dragons?"

Sirion squinted. It took a moment before the objects were close enough for him to identify. When he had, his eyes widened, and Makilien caught the flash of fear in them.

"They're death vultures!

The word spread rapidly through the soldiers.

"Everyone, get your bows!" one of the captains commanded.

Makilien and Sirion looked at each other. Neither had their bows with them, but one of the weapon carts held many. They ran to the stairs and down to the cart, each grabbing a bow. On the way back to the top, Sirion suddenly turned and stopped Makilien.

"Be careful," he said, his voice low with concern. "Remember they can pick you up."

Makilien gave him a quick nod.

When they reached the top of the wall again, the vultures were close enough for Makilien and the rest of the soldiers to recognize. Everyone stood, bows ready, wondering what the evil birds had in mind. A chill raced across Makilien's skin. Hundreds of death vultures filled the horizon.

Less than a mile from the city, the vultures swooped down to the ground before flying up again to great heights. The soldiers frowned, not understanding what the birds were doing. But then, everyone came to the same realization that in the vultures' talons, they each carried great mountain stones.

Sirion grimaced. "They are going to drop them on the city."

Makilien's heart beat hard, knowing the terrible damage that would cause. "What do we do?"

Sirion looked at her, his expression grave as he shook his head. "I don't know."

And Makilien knew with stomach-turning dread that without Carmine, Indiya, and Emaril there to fend off the attack, they could do nothing. They still had the griffons, but they were no match for hundreds of death vultures, and at the height the birds flew, only the few Elves present had any hope of hitting them with their arrows.

Hearts pounding, everyone watched in riveted horror, looking high up into the sky as the birds reached the city. At first, nothing seemed to happen, but then, all at once, stones dropped, raining down as deadly projectiles. Makilien's heart beat hard three times, and then the stones reached them. Deafening crashes erupted everywhere. Rocks tumbled through the streets and smashed into buildings and the wall. A violent shudder ran through the stones beneath Makilien's feet.

Panicked shouting joined the crashes. Arrows streaked into the air. Makilien grabbed an arrow and drew back the bowstring as far as she was able. She took aim at one of the approaching vultures. Just as she released the arrow, a rock smashed into the wall only a few feet away, making her stumble. Before she could regain her balance, another hit, closer this time, and showered her with debris. In the midst of the chaos,

Sirion grabbed her by the arm and moved her toward the stairs.

"Get off the wall, now!"

Makilien scrambled to the stairs, taking them as fast as she could, heart drumming in her ears. Halfway down, a rock ripped into the wall directly above her. Pieces of stone sprayed into the air. Makilien screamed and ducked, but a fragment smashed into the side of her head. She fell forward. The only thought in her dazed mind was not to fall from the edge of the stairs as she tumbled down leaving bruises all over her body.

At last, she stopped. Her vision was blurred and her hearing echoed, but her instinct to survive made her push to her feet. However, a searing pain shot through her right knee and she stumbled. *I must get away from here!* her mind screamed. She tried to look around, but something leaked into her eye. She wiped her face, her hand coming away smeared with red.

In the confusion, she heard the echo of her name. She tried to move again, but strong arms lifted her up. Blinking, her eyes focused on Sirion's face. As he carried her away from the wall, Makilien's senses finally returned to normal.

When they came to the arched doorway of a nearby building, they took shelter beneath it. Clinging to Sirion, Makilien could only watch and listen as stones rained down all over the city. The horrific crashes exploded around them mingled with shouts, screams, the desperate screeches of griffons, and the crumbling of the city's structures. Tears stung Makilien's eyes in both anger and fear. Who and what would be left once the vultures finished?

Trapped right at the center of the nightmarish scene, it seemed to go on forever, but a ray of hope came in a resounding roar that echoed across the city. Makilien and Sirion looked up to see streaks of fire shoot across the sky, engulfing several death vultures. The birds shrieked as dragons of all colors flew overhead. The showering of rocks ended as charred vultures fell to the ground.

Cautiously, Sirion carried Makilien out of their shelter. By now, the death vultures retreated eastward with at least twenty dragons in pursuit. Breathing heavily, Makilien's eyes focused on the wall and she nearly burst into tears at the destruction. Significant damage had been done, particularly near the gate and to many of the trebuchets. But the most horrible were the many soldiers lying dead and wounded.

For a long moment, Makilien and Sirion could only stare in shock. They snapped out of it when they noticed someone approaching them. A great wave of relief overcame Makilien when she realized it was Halandor, and he was uninjured. His expression reflected deep concern to see Makilien as blood ran down the side of her face.

"Are you all right?" he asked breathlessly.

"I think so," she answered. Her head and leg hurt, but she didn't think anything was seriously wrong. She prayed she had no broken bones in her leg. She seemed to be able to move it all right, but her knee throbbed with sharp pain and blood soaked through the edges of a rip in her pants.

"Who else was here at the wall?" Sirion asked.

"Aedan, Loron, Torick, and Eredan I know for sure," Halandor answered.

"Have you seen them?"

Halandor shook his head. "Take Makilien back to the palace, and see if everyone is all right there. I will look for the others."

Sirion nodded and turned for the palace. Along the way, they passed destruction unlike anything they'd witnessed before. The city, normally so proud and beautiful, was scarred, the streets littered with debris and shrouded in dust. Makilien put her hand to her mouth and coughed as they passed through the swirling particles. Things were strangely quiet now. Growing fear for her family and friends closed around Makilien's throat, her heart thudding against her ribs. She glanced up at Sirion. His face was set, strong and determined as always, but he too wondered what losses they might face as a result of this attack.

At last, they reached the palace courtyard, and Makilien released a sigh. Only a small portion of the third floor showed any damage. They stepped inside to chaos. Guards and servants rushed around them. Sirion ignored them, taking Makilien directly to the throne room. When they entered, joy filled Makilien's heart to find her mother and sister. Lord Darand and Darian were present as well with the other lords and Vonawyn.

"Makilien!" Hanna rushed to her daughter, gasping at the sight of so much blood. "Are you all right?"

"I think I'll be fine," Makilien answered, but her mind was on something else. "Where's Father?"

Hanna, face already white with fear, shook her head. "I don't know. We think he was helping the general."

Makilien swallowed hard, but did her best not to show her worry, knowing it would only add to her mother's concern.

Vonawyn joined them, her eyes quick to assess Makilien's injuries, and instructed Sirion take her to the healing quarters. Hanna and Leiya followed. Sirion set Makilien carefully down on one of the beds, and Vonawyn examined her wounds.

"Will I be able to walk?" Makilien asked after a moment, watching her steadily.

"You have a nasty gash across your knee, but nothing seems to be broken. It will be painful when you put your weight on it. You'll have to see once I finish cleaning and bandaging it," Vonawyn answered.

Makilien blew out a sigh. The last thing she wanted was to be stuck here when so many needed help. "I need to find my father," she said.

"Don't worry. Just rest here," Sirion told her. "I will go out and find him."

Makilien's gaze lifted to him. The calm determination in his brown eyes gave her comfort and assurance.

"Thank you."

With a nod, he left the healing quarters.

While Vonawyn tended the injuries, Makilien relayed what had happened at the wall. As soon as Vonawyn had finished, she helped Makilien stand. Carefully, she put weight on her leg. Hot pain stabbed through her knee.

"How does it feel?" Vonawyn asked.

Makilien bit her lip in frustration. "It hurts," she finally admitted.

"Just wait here for a moment," Vonawyn told her and disappeared into another room. When she returned, she carried a crutch. "You should try to keep your weight off it . . . at least whenever you can. This will help."

Makilien took the crutch. "Thanks, Vonawyn."

Back in the throne room, soldiers came and went, giving Darand grim reports of the devastation. The king took it all with quiet acceptance, but his eyes betrayed the deep regret in his heart and the uncertainty over what this surprise attack would mean for their defenses.

A short time later, one of the entrance guards brought word to him. "My lord, there are several dragons in the courtyard. They seek audience with you."

Most everyone followed the king from the palace. Outside they beheld a stunning sight. Dragons filled the courtyard, and a few even perched on the surrounding wall. Though Makilien did not take time to count them, she knew they must be all of the dragon warriors Eborin had promised. Such a large number and colorful array of the creatures awed those gathered. There were dragons in all colors and shades —greens, blues, aqua, gold, red, lavender, and violet.

At the base of the palace steps stood Eborin, tall and majestic, his black scales gleaming in the sunlight. A stern look hardened his face, but Makilien knew they need not fear him. Wythel and Malachi stood at his side. Lord Darand descended the stairs, eyes falling from one dragon to another until he stood before their leaders.

"Lord of Eldor," the black dragon addressed the king. He dipped his head in a gesture of respect Makilien would not have expected from him. "I am Eborin," he went on, "leader of the dragons of the Irrin Mountains."

"I am most honored to meet you, Great Dragon," Darand replied, his voice a bit breathless. "I hope in some way I will be able to express the gratitude I have for the aid you have granted us. In the battle to come and for the rescue you provided today. Our city would have been utterly destroyed had the death vultures been allowed to continue their attack."

"It is regrettable we could not have been here sooner . . . to prevent the attack." Eborin's uncharacteristic sympathy put a small smile on Makilien's face. He glanced at her then, eyeing her bandages and still bloodied clothing before going on, "I hope you have not suffered too great a loss."

"I am still waiting for word on how many lives were lost," Darand replied. "Any number is severe to us, but we are thankful to have been spared much greater devastation."

He glanced over the assembly of dragons again. "Now that you are here, you are welcome to our aviary. I am sure you will all be comfortable there."

"Those who wish to stay there may, but I will stay in the mountains until the time for battle has come," Eborin told him. There was a decided edge to his voice, yet it was not unkind.

Before they could continue, shadows passed over those gathered, and Carmine, Indiya, and Emaril came to land in the courtyard, their expressions taut with distress.

"What happened?" Carmine asked, his voice rumbling with both anger and sorrow over the damage they'd seen from the air.

At first he cast a suspicious eye on Eborin, but Lord Darand was quick to explain. "Death vultures. They dropped stones on the city. Thankfully, Eborin and the others drove them away before they could finish the destruction."

Indiya peered at the king, her eyes troubled. "How many were lost in the attack?"

Darand shook his head, spreading his hands helplessly. "I don't know yet. I am waiting to find out." Now that Carmine, Indiya, and Emaril had returned, they could answer another question the king had been waiting on. "What information do you have on Zirtan's army? Were you able to tell how many he has in his force?"

All three dragons looked at each other, reluctant to speak. Carmine glanced around the courtyard, before focusing again on Darand.

"It is as we feared, a force much larger than we faced before," Carmine reported. "About twice the size at least . . . one-hundred twenty to one-hundred forty thousand."

A dreadful silence followed his words. Men and dragons looked at each other as this news settled into their minds.

Finally, Darand spoke, his expression projecting strength, but standing near him, Makilien noticed the uncertainty tingeing his voice. "And how far away are they?"

"They should arrive here no later than evening on the day after tomorrow."

"I will give the information to Nirgon as soon as he gets here," the king said with a nod, and added more quietly, "which I pray he does."

After these words, Darand requested, "Will you, Indiya, and Emaril show the dragons who wish to remain in the city to the aviary and see that all they need is provided for them?"

Carmine nodded. "Yes, my lord."

Nearly every dragon in the courtyard followed him. Only Eborin and Wythel did not. They flew instead in the direction of the mountains.

Slowly, everyone turned back to the palace. As they ascended the stairs, Makilien stepped away from her mother and sister for a moment and came to Darand's side.

"My lord," she said, her voice lowered, "How many do we have in our army?"

Lord Darand looked at her. The hesitancy in his eyes said he wanted to keep the truth from her, but he knew he could not. "With Gébrale's men, we had just over forty-two thousand . . . after the attack today, I'm not sure."

Fear and dread descended like a heavy, smothering blanket upon Makilien. Zirtan possessed a force of almost one-hundred thousand more warriors than they did. If they had barely achieved victory against seventy-thousand, how could they survive double that?

:Chapter Twenty-nine:

Before the Storm

Struggle waged a battle in Makilien's heart. A struggle against the fear of the coming enemy, the worry for her father and friends who had not yet shown up at the palace, and her frustration with the injuries preventing her from going out to search for them. She tried hard to keep the struggle hidden for her mother and sister's sake. If she allowed her true emotions to show, it would tell how dire the situation truly was, and she wanted to spare them, at least for the moment.

At last, Makilien looked up to see Sirion enter the throne room, her father and Aedan with him.

"Oh, thank You, Elohim," she breathed.

Rising from her seat at one of the tables, Makilien used her crutch to limp over and meet them.

"Father!" She hugged him for a long moment. "Are you all right?" she asked. His clothing was layered with dust, but she could see no injuries.

"Yes, I'm fine," he assured her.

Hanna and Leiya joined them. Makilien's mother had tears in her eyes as she embraced her husband.

Now Makilien turned to Aedan. Other than a few scratches on his face, he too appeared uninjured. After confirming this, she asked, "Have you seen any of the others?"

Aedan nodded. "Torick, Loron, Eredan, and Tanzim are all fine."

"What about General Nirgon?" Makilien asked, knowing that losing their general would be a devastating blow, one they might not recover from.

"He too is fine," Sirion told her. "He was with your father when I found him."

Makilien exhaled, words of thanks already whispering from her heart.

"He went to assess the damage at the wall," Sirion went on. "He will be here shortly."

"Lord Darand will be glad to hear from him," Makilien said.

Sirion glanced at the king, and said, "I am going back out to see what I can do to help."

Both he and Aedan turned to leave, but Makilien held Sirion back for a moment.

"Thank you," she expressed with deep gratitude, "for finding my father for me and bringing him here."

A smile touched Sirion's face. "You're welcome."

All were anxiously awaiting news when Nirgon entered the palace. With him came Arphen. Makilien gasped when she saw the griffon. Large patches of his dark fur were stained with blood from numerous wounds. Almost as disturbing was

310

the grim look on the general's face. Makilien's stomach knotted as they all gathered round one of the tables.

"What can you tell us, Nirgon?" Lord Darand asked, a slight tremor in his voice. "Do you know how many have been slain?"

The general gave a heavy sigh. "From what I've seen and heard, I know the death toll is at least four hundred. About fifty were civilians . . . the rest were soldiers."

Burdened by the weight of this, Lord Darand hung his head and leaned against the table. The real battle had not yet even begun and already they were three-hundred fifty soldiers less.

"There is also much loss amongst the griffons," Arphen reported with great regret. "Eighteen are dead and another fifteen are severely injured."

"And what of the damage?" the king went on after allowing a moment for the information to sink in.

"Though there are areas of damage throughout the city, the main targets were the barracks and the wall," Nirgon told him. "Half the barracks is destroyed. That is where we lost the greatest number of soldiers. The wall too sustained heavy damage, particularly at the gate. It has been significantly weakened."

The knot in Makilien's stomach pulled tighter. All through the room she could sense the despair at the general's words. To lose so many men and their greatest defense, it seemed all had turned against them even after the allies they had gained.

"Can any repairs be made in the time we have?" Darand wanted to know.

"We will do what we can, but it will be minimal."

Lord Darand straightened. His voice rising with a determined confidence, he said, "I want to speak to all lords and captains. I want to hear all thoughts and opinions on how we can counter what's been done."

Within a half hour, all lords, generals, and high ranking captains from each of the four countries gathered in the throne room, including Arphen, Tôr, Carmine, and Malachi who had joined them in Eborin's place. Makilien's mother and Leiya had left the room, but Makilien and her father remained. The room buzzed with talk of the attack, but when Lord Darand held up his hand, everyone fell silent.

"We have suffered a devastating blow with the attack today. As many of you know, the death toll is at least four-hundred and may be rising as we speak. The barracks is badly damaged, as is the wall. The wall was our greatest defense, but now we cannot be sure how long it will last. We must discuss how best we can now defend it to hold out as long as possible."

"The gate is the weakest point," Nirgon informed them. "It is there we must focus our defense. We will place most of the archers above the gate to prevent it from being overrun." He looked to Carmine and Malachi. "That too will be the focus of the dragons."

Carmine nodded. "Catapults and trolls would cause the most damage. We will target them specifically."

"How long do you believe we can hold out with the damage that has been sustained?" Lord Darand asked Nirgon.

The general gave this a long moment of thought. "A day . . . two days . . . not much more than that if Zirtan focuses on these weaknesses. No matter how well we prepare and make our plans, the sheer size of his army will overrun us, and unfortunately, after this attack, it will happen sooner than we all hoped."

With desperation growing inside her, Makilien asked, "Is there anything we have, anything else we can do, to give us an advantage against such a force?"

Nirgon looked at her and shook his head. "I think we've done all we can."

Silence settled around the table for a sobering moment. Then, breaking that silence, Lord Elnauhir spoke.

"We are not strong enough to defeat Zirtan's army." The words hung darkly in the room. "We all know this," the Elf lord continued, forcing all to come to terms with the cold reality of their circumstances. "The only hope we have of victory is in Elohim and His intervention. Still, we must do what we can to defend ourselves. Last time, Elohim gave us victory through Makilien and her defeat of Zendon. We witnessed how our enemies faltered without leadership. That may again be our hope for victory."

"You mean we must try to defeat Zirtan himself?" Nirgon asked.

"Only Elohim can truly defeat him," Elnauhir answered. "None of us can. However, we know sometime in the last few hundred years, Zirtan took on a physical, Human-like body in order to set in motion his conquest. We cannot kill *him*, but we may be able to kill his physical form. If he is not physically there to command his army, it may send them into a panic."

"I agree," Nirgon said after thinking it over for a moment. "To see Zirtan defeated could be a killing blow to the confidence of his men. Fear is one of Zirtan's greatest weapons, but perhaps it could be ours as well."

"I cannot say for sure whether such a thing is possible or what kind of dark power Zirtan may possess. Anyone who challenges him is quite likely to die in the attempt, but in the end, the risk could be worth everything."

Elnauhir looked into the eyes of each and every one of them, and they nodded in agreement. Each one knew right there if they came upon Zirtan during the battle, they would do whatever they could to try to defeat him . . . no matter the cost.

Makilien exhaled and rolled onto her back. Her stomach twisted and squeezed. She stared toward the door out to the balcony. Though the light was dim, dawn had broken. Knowing that to continue trying to sleep would be pointless, she sat up and slipped quietly out of bed. The day had come. Zirtan's force would arrive in a matter of hours.

Careful to stay quiet, Makilien walked out to the balcony, noting the dull ache in her knee, and stood at the railing. Her gaze swept across the city. It lay silent in the early morning, but at the wall was much activity. Anything that could be done to strengthen and secure the gate had become the number one priority. Thousands of men worked together, putting up braces, piling up stones, and repairing scaffolds and trebuchets. They had so little time, they worked in teams all through the night. How Makilien prayed the work was not done in vain.

"Makilien."

The small voice snapped Makilien out of her thoughts and prayers, and she looked over her shoulder. Leiya stood in the doorway.

"I'm sorry, Leiya, did I wake you?"

The little girl shook her head. "I couldn't sleep."

She walked out and came to stand beside her sister. Resting her arms and her chin on the railing, she sighed and stared east.

"Looks like a storm is coming," she said.

Makilien too looked east. The sky above them stretched out in a deep blue, but black clouds rimmed the horizon. Occasionally, the far off clouds illuminated with eerie, yellow flashes.

"It seems like the weather is always affected by the approach of evil," Makilien murmured, remembering the foul weather and fearful storm that had erupted the day Meniah was killed and the battle had begun.

"When will Zirtan get here?" Leiya asked, her quiet voice edged with fear.

Makilien paused, trying to hold back fear of her own. "This afternoon," she answered finally. "He will be here by this afternoon."

Voice now trembling, Leiya admitted, "I'm scared."

Looking down at her precious little sister, Makilien put her arm around Leiya's shoulders and held her close. *So am I.*

"They are less than two leagues away. The first of them should reach here within two hours."

The throne room fell silent following Carmine's words. All looked to the king. His expression hardening, Lord Darand nodded.

"It is time for our final preparations," he said, his voice steady and even. "Nirgon, see that the men are ready and begin moving everyone into position. Zirtan is not likely to attack before nightfall, but we must be prepared."

The general gave a quick nod and turned to leave. The other lords gave similar orders to their generals.

Turning back to Carmine, Darand went on, "Bring the dragons to the barracks armory to be armored, and have word sent to Eborin."

"Yes, my lord," the dragon replied.

Rapidly, the room thinned out as everyone who had a job to do left the palace. Once again, Darand's eyes moved along those who remained—Makilien and her friends, and the lords.

In a quieter voice than before, the king said, "The time has come for battle. Let us all prepare as best we can. I will meet all of you back here when you are finished. We will go to the wall together."

Everyone gave a silent nod and turned to leave the throne room.

Walking the dim halls to the palace armory, Makilien looked up at her father, trying to hide the uncertainty in her voice.

"Halandor will help make sure you have everything you need," she said, not sure where she would be preparing.

Néthyn said nothing but put his arm around her shoulders. Makilien gave him a small smile.

At the entrance of the armory, Vonawyn beckoned for her to follow. She led the way to a door just down the hall, and they entered a large, open room. First Makilien saw her mother and Leiya there, waiting to help her prepare. Then she noticed not only Demera, but a large group of Elf woman, at least fifty of them. Many were young like Vonawyn. What surprised her was that all were in the process of suiting up for battle. She looked at Vonawyn, brows raised in question.

"We cannot take the places of all those who were slain in the death vultures' attack," Vonawyn said, "but we are capable of replacing some."

Noticing her use of *we*, Makilien asked, "You are going to fight?"

Vonawyn nodded, a look of steely determination in her features. "We have all been trained well. What good is it if we don't use it to help defend our families, friends, and homes when it is needed most?"

Makilien gave her a grim smile. "It will be an honor to fight alongside you."

Vonawyn smiled in return. "And you, Lady Makilien, Swordmaiden of Eldor."

With a fresh wave of determination, Makilien turned to where her mother and sister waited and began to change. She put on a royal blue dress and the Elven chain-mail Vonawyn had given her. Over the top, she buttoned a black suede jerkin and black skirt nearly identical to those of her ceremony clothes. Next came the vambraces for her arms and the greaves for her legs. She braided her hair securely and equipped her weapons. This time she added a small fighting axe to the collection. Finally, she faced her mother.

Tears collected in Hanna's eyes and caused Makilien's to sting.

"I'm so afraid for you, Makilien," Hanna murmured, "but I'm so proud of you. Proud of who and what you are. I never could have imagined it."

Makilien reached out to hug her, wishing never to leave her mother's soft embrace. "Neither could I."

By now, Vonawyn and the others finished. Makilien turned to them and focused on her friend. Vonawyn was armored in thin, but strong plate-mail that shone with a tint of dusty blue. The well-fitting breastplate and leaf-shaped pauldrons were emblazoned with swirling vine-like designs and dotted with stars. Armed with a bow, sword, and two long knives, the Elf maiden looked to be a truly formidable opponent indeed.

"Are you ready?" Vonawyn asked.

Makilien's pulse spiked at that question. Could one ever truly be ready? But she answered, "Yes."

Sirion adjusted the straps of his leather pauldrons and flexed his arms to make sure he was not restricted in any way. After checking that all his weapons were secure, he knew he was as prepared as he was ever going to be. Exhaling slowly, his eyes scanned the large hall of the armory, full of every weapon and piece of armor anyone might desire, all crafted by the city's most skilled artisans.

At one armor-laden table stood Lord Darand and Prince Darian. With aid from two assistants, they donned polished silver plate-mail depicting the crowned lion of Eldor. Across the table were Lord Elnauhir and his sons. For a moment, Sirion allowed himself to wonder what it would be like to be like them—to have his father here at his side. The deep sorrow of years past stung acutely, but before he could dwell on it, his uncle approached—his father since the age of seven.

"Sirion," the wise Elf lord said with all the love of a father in his eyes.

"Uncle," Sirion replied.

For a moment there was silence as he watched his uncle search for the right words. It seemed at the time it mattered most, it was most difficult. Things that weren't said now, may never have a chance to be said again.

Finally, Glorlad spoke, "I wanted to tell you what a blessing it has been to watch you grow and to have raised you. Your parents . . . your father, would have been so proud of the man you have become. You are the most unselfish person I know, just like your father was."

Emotion pressed down on Sirion's chest causing a lump to rise in his throat. He cleared it once before speaking. "Thank you, Uncle. It was your teaching and guidance that made me who I am. Thank you for raising me as a son."

"And a son you will always be to me, Sirion."

He pulled Sirion into an embrace, something that did not occur often, but Sirion welcomed it.

When they parted, Glorlad clapped Sirion on the shoulder and turned as they both took in the sight of their comrades. This time, Sirion's eyes landed on Aedan. He too was without a father or even someone like a father. Knowing well from the feelings he'd just experienced how painful that was, Sirion left his uncle for a moment and walked over to him to offer whatever encouragement and support he could. The other young man was almost finished, armored in dark-ringed chain-mail and just tightening the last buckle of a pair of thick leather vambraces.

"Ready?" Sirion asked him.

Aedan gave a strong nod. "Yes."

Sirion admired his calm confidence. It was a rare thing, especially in those facing their first battle. He too admired Aedan's desire to fight for people and countries he had no ties to, only friendship—friendship that had been developed over so short a time.

"We're fortunate to have men like you with us," Sirion said.

Aedan looked at him, gratitude lighting his eyes. "Thanks. I'm just glad I can be here to help. I want peace for everyone. I've known so little of it myself."

Sirion gave a slow nod and extended his hand, clasping it around Aedan's forearm. Aedan did the same. Today they were brothers in arms, and they drew strength from each other.

:Chapter Thirty:

To War

A sobering atmosphere of uncertainty and suppressed fear shadowed the group as everyone and their loved ones re-gathered in the throne room. Makilien stood with her mother and sister, and her father joined them as soon as he and the men had entered. A bit of a smile lifted Makilien's lips as she admired her father. His choice of armor consisted of a long-sleeved, knee-length chain-mail hauberk and steel plated leather greaves. Makilien's heart swelled with pride to see the warrior he had become. But it failed to ease any of the difficulty of the next few minutes. Minutes that may be the last her family would spend together.

The tears in Hanna's eyes nearly reached overflowing as she looked between her husband and daughter. "I wish there was a way to keep you both here with me, but I know you must do what you have to do." Her voice trembled, and she had to pause before going on, "And I know all I can do is pray." She focused her eyes on Makilien. "I believe it now, everything you tried to tell us. If it were not true, what hope would I have of both of you returning to me?"

Finally, the tears fell, and she choked back a sob. Néthyn immediately took his wife in his arms. Makilien's eyes filled, and her throat constricted. She swallowed hard to try to ease the tightness.

For a long moment, her parents held each other, and they kissed tenderly.

"I love you," Néthyn murmured.

Hanna touched his cheek. "I love you."

When they parted, Hanna opened her arms to her daughter with a weak smile. Taking a shaky breath, Makilien stepped into her mother's embrace.

"My baby," Hanna whispered in her ear. "I love you so much."

"I love you too."

Makilien did not want to let go and held tightly for several moments in which her heart ached. When she did let go, she saw the deep fear and sorrow in her mother's eyes and the fresh tears running down her face. Makilien longed for a way to give her comfort, but she knew the greatest source of comfort was Elohim.

Finally, she forced herself to turn away else she too would have succumbed to tears. She now faced her father who held Leiya in his arms. The little girl wrapped her arms tight around his neck and laid her head on his shoulder, her cheeks wet with unrelenting tears.

"Please come back," she pleaded with a sob.

"Oh, Leiya." Néthyn's voice was soft, but he could not assure her.

"I love you, Papa," Leiya cried.

"I love you too, sweetheart."

When he set her down, Néthyn wiped the tears from his young daughter's face. Looking into her wide eyes, he said, "Remember everything Makilien has told you about Elohim.

He will always be with you and your mother, and with me and Makilien."

"I—I will, Papa," Leiya promised, choking a little.

As he rose, he kissed her on the top of the head. Makilien then knelt before her sister. She determinedly willed herself not to cry, to be strong, to have hope that this would not be the last time her family would be together.

Leiya's lip trembled, and neither of them seemed able to speak so Makilien drew her sister into a hug. Closing her eyes against tears, Makilien felt the shuddering of Leiya's quiet sobs. She bit her lip and then whispered, "I love you, Leiya."

"I love . . . you too," Leiya barely managed. She clung to Makilien. "I don't want you to go."

"I know," Makilien replied, voice breaking.

Not knowing how much longer she could hold back her sorrow, Makilien parted from her sister and rose. Glancing around the throne room, her eyes fell on her friends and those they had said their goodbyes to. *How do things come to this?* she asked herself. Families and friends torn viciously apart by war.

To the dismay of their families, it came time to leave. With longing looks at those they loved, the warriors turned and solemnly followed Lord Darand. At the door of the throne room, Makilien cast one last, desperate look over her shoulder at her mother and sister. Tears glistened on their faces as they stood together, Leiya leaning against their mother, clutching her skirt for comfort. A numbing chill encased Makilien. What if the two of them were left all alone in this world that was still so new to them?

When they were out of sight, the intense buildup of emotion overwhelmed Makilien. She could hardly breathe against the tightening of her chest and throat. She tried to swallow, but the inside of her mouth had dried up. Just before they reached the front doors, she fell behind the others, desperately fighting to hold back the suffocating flood of sorrow and fear rising within her. When her father noticed, he turned to her.

"Makilien, are you all right?"

"Yes," she gasped. "Go on. I'll catch up."

Néthyn looked at her anxiously. "Are you sure?"

Makilien gave a quick nod, knowing her voice would give away the terrible state she was in. Her father hesitated, troubled over how pale she was.

Gathering her strength, Makilien insisted, "I just need a minute."

She attempted a smile, but knew it fell painfully short.

With great reluctance, her father turned and followed the others.

Once they had left the palace, Makilien bent over, bracing her hands against her knees. She tried to breathe deeply and fight the sorrow, but the hopeless expressions on her mother and Leiya's faces, the thought of losing everyone she loved, it all crashed in on her at once. She squeezed her eyes shut, shaking her head in a desperate act of resistance. But a choked sob broke free and two tears leaked from her eyes. After this, she knew she'd lost the battle. She sank to her knees and buried her face in her hands. Tears of agony ran through her fingers.

"Elohim!" she cried out. "Please! Please bring us all back together again. Please save all of those I love from death."

Deep inside, her heart continued to cry these words.

"Without You we are without hope. Please give us victory."

Struggling for strength and courage, feeling they had deserted her, she felt a hand clasp around her shoulder. Through tears she looked up and focused on Sirion. His eyes were pained with heartache for the sorrow she suffered. Gently, he helped her to her feet and gathered her into his arms. Makilien rested her head against his chest and continued to cry, letting it all drain out in her tears as she drew comfort from being near him.

"I don't want to lose anyone," she said weakly. "I'm terrified of it."

Sirion rested his cheek against her head and spoke what he knew to be true. "Elohim has the outcome already set. Whatever happens in the next hours, the next days, nothing will be out of His control. If we find we must deal with loss, it will be intensely painful, but He will help us bear it."

As two more hot tears rolled down her face, Makilien squeezed her eyes shut and nodded. Sirion was right. He spoke with experience of the pain of loss. Finally, she reached up and wiped away tears as Sirion let her go.

"Thank you," she said, looking gratefully up into his eyes. "I get overwhelmed sometimes and need someone to help me see things clearly again."

Sirion smiled, the height of kindness and caring, and it immediately calmed Makilien inside.

"All right," she said, feeling strength and resolve returning to her heart. "I'm ready now."

She stared up at him, holding his steady brown eyes. They just stood, not speaking, not moving. Something in Sirion's gaze made Makilien wait. She held her breath. *Say it*, she found herself hoping. But, as the silence lengthened, she reluctantly tore her eyes away. They couldn't stand there forever. She turned to catch up with the others.

"Makilien, wait."

She turned back, her heart beating a little harder.

This time, Sirion was ready to speak. "I need to say something to you before we leave. I'm not sure how you will feel about this, but I know if I don't say it now, I may not get another chance." Caught between the uncertainty of battle and what he might have done given more time and better circumstances, he exhaled heavily, eyes searching hers. "I love you, Makilien."

Though she had just gained control of her emotions, Makilien cried out softly, but the smile that broke across her face told Sirion everything he needed to know.

"In all we've been through together," he said, "especially in the last few weeks, I have greatly admired who you have become since we first met. Your devotion to Elohim and your willingness and bravery to follow His will no matter the consequences. Your friendship means everything to me. But the other day when the vultures attacked, when I saw you fall and wondered if you could be dead or badly hurt, I was terrified, and I knew then without a doubt that I love you."

"I love you too," she said, eyes shining through her tears. From the beginning there had been something special in their friendship, and in her heart, she'd known for a while it was even more.

No matter what happened beyond this point, the knowledge that she loved him brought a calm and a joy to his heart. He pulled her back into his arms and just held her tight, for now, for this little bit of time.

"This is why I am so afraid I might lose you," Makilien said, voice breaking.

Sirion did not reply, but she knew he felt the same. As they parted, he kissed her on the forehead and smiled saying, "At least, whatever happens, there is nothing left unsaid between us."

Makilien nodded, eyes fixed on the face she had so dearly come to love, even more so than she'd realized. She'd always held such great admiration for him—for his selfless kindness and faith. And, for just a moment, she reflected on how wonderfully blessed she was to have found herself occupying this special place in his heart.

The smile still lingering, Sirion held his hand out to her. She took it and squeezed it tightly. Together they walked out of the palace.

Outside in the courtyard, two servants waited with Antiro and Falene. The others were gone. As they descended the steps, Makilien looked up at the sky. The storm clouds she'd seen with Leiya that morning were overhead now, dark and menacing. A chill, damp breeze blew her skirt against her legs. Rain would surely fall soon.

Their two loyal steeds stood proud and regal looking, armored in polished plate-mail. Antiro bobbed his head as Makilien approached. Smiling, she rubbed him under the chin.

"Ready to face our foes in battles once again?"

Arching his neck, Antiro pawed at the ground.

"Always my brave horse," Makilien murmured.

She and Sirion mounted and rode out. Passing through the courtyard gate and the inner city, all was deathly quiet in anticipation even though this part of the city was filled to capacity. Doors and shutters were closed tight as if somehow it would keep out the evil approaching from the east. *If only it could*, Makilien lamented.

When they reached the inner city gate, she shook her head.

"What is it?" Sirion asked, his voice mingling with the echoing clops of the horses' hooves on the stone.

Makilien looked at him. "I was just thinking how quickly things can come to change. A little over a year ago I was just a captive farm girl longing for answers to the questions burning in my heart. Now, for the second time, I am in a battle that will affect everything we know. It's hard to believe." She let out a small, mirthless laugh.

"The ways of Elohim are often mysterious."

A smile came to Makilien's face. This was why she loved Sirion—always faithful, always encouraging in the midst of trial. "They are indeed."

In a short time, the two of them arrived at the wall finding it an altogether different scene than the quiet inner city. The wall and the wide area below teemed with activity. Thousands of soldiers moved about, tending to final preparations, and getting into position. After leaving Antiro and Falene in the area prepared for the horses, Makilien and Sirion moved through the crowd finally coming to Lord Darand, the other lords, and their friends near the gate. Everyone had their attention directed farther down the wall.

Turning that way, Makilien saw Indiya and Emaril speaking. Carmine stood nearby, but only listened. While Indiya appeared calm, Emaril seemed more agitated, his wings rising and falling with his voice.

"What is going on over there?" she asked.

"We're not sure," Halandor answered. "They have been speaking for a while."

Silently, they watched again. If Loron or the other Elves had been able to make out words, they didn't say. A few moments later, Indiya lowered her head and gave a little nod. Emaril appeared relieved. Everyone's attention then shifted to Carmine who turned to join the group at the gate.

"Is there a problem?" Lord Darand asked.

Carmine looked over his shoulder at the other two dragons and then back to the king.

"Indiya has just shared with us that she is with child."

Eyebrows rose and looks were exchanged at the surprise of such news.

Carmine went on, "There was some debate between her and Emaril as to whether or not she should still join us."

"Will she?" the king wondered.

Carmine glanced back once more and shook his head. "She was quite determined, but Emaril has talked her out of it."

By this time, Indiya and Emaril had come to join them as well.

"I hear congratulations are in order," Darand said to the pair.

Indiya smiled widely, her sapphire eyes sparkling.

"How long have you known?" Darand asked.

"Not long," Indiya told them. "A few days."

"And you are going to sit this battle out?"

Indiya glanced at Emaril whose expression was adamant. She then nodded. "As much as I want to help here, I know it would be unwise to risk my life at this time. I will remain at the palace. That way, should anything happen, I can still offer some protection to the people there."

"I must say I am glad to hear it," the king said. "We do not want to lose you or the baby." He looked at Emaril. With one more word of congratulations, he said, "Once you are finished here, you and Carmine may take your positions on the wall, but take your time."

The dragons nodded. As they said their farewells to Indiya, Makilien turned to her friends. "That was unexpected."

"Yes," Vonawyn agreed. "And if not for this wretched war, it would be quite a time to celebrate." She faced Makilien and Aedan who stood near. "Dragons only give birth once every fifty years or so, if at all. That is why they are so rare and the loss of one's life is such a tragedy."

Makilien glanced at Indiya. "I hope this goes well so we can celebrate."

"So do I."

At that moment, a shadow passed overhead, and Eborin and the other dragons of the Irrin Mountains landed behind the wall wherever they found room. All wore gleaming armor provided for them at the barracks armory. They were a magnificently fierce sight. Eborin came forward, bowing his head to Lord Darand.

"Where would you like us? We are at your command," he humbled himself to their authority, the authority of men.

"Zirtan may now know we have more dragons thanks to the death vultures, but he does not know how many. I say we keep it that way," Nirgon said. "For now, stay behind the wall. When the onslaught becomes more than we can manage, I will call you out. It will give us some element of surprise."

"As you wish, General," Eborin replied, and he turned to join the others and relay the orders to those who had not heard.

Nirgon watched him a moment before turning to Lord Darand and the others. "Our force has all gathered. Everyone is here. Warriors from almost every corner and race of our known world."

All eyes took in the sight of each other. Their diverse group represented all the peoples who had gathered here against a common enemy. It gave Makilien goose bumps to think of the true magnitude of it. But even with all the many who had come, the overwhelming circumstances remained on everyone's mind. A force still marched on them, only a few miles away, a force that had the size and strength to crush them all.

:Chapter Thirty-one:

Enemy Lies

"**Z**irtan's force is coming!"

The dreaded call echoed down the length of the wall. Makilien's heart thudded. She strained her eyes to see the horizon, but a steady rain now fell, limiting visibility. The patter of raindrops was the only sound as everyone seemed to hold their breath in wait. No one moved.

And then, a couple of minutes after the call had gone out, she spotted something—something darker than the gray gloom on the horizon—and slowly rising above the pelting of the rain was an eerie rumble. Murmurs ran through the soldiers.

Makilien stood, transfixed, as the dark smudge in the east grew into a solid black line, stretching across the horizon. She swallowed hard. A chill crawled along her skin underneath her rain-soaked clothing, and she shivered.

The army moved swiftly for one so large. It was not long before Makilien could distinguish the ranks within the mass of soldiers. Just as in their previous meeting, the army appeared to bypass the city and gathered directly to the north about a mile off. Now the entire eastern horizon and most of the north was filled with the black army of Zirtan.

Makilien looked back at her father who stood just behind her. His face was like steel, but his eyes betrayed the fear inside. The same fear that clawed inside Makilien too. They'd heard for weeks of Zirtan's force, but to see it made the nightmare real.

For many minutes, all watched the streams of enemies mass to the north. It seemed to Makilien to last much longer than last time, proof of Zirtan's increased numbers. As the march continued, she realized Nirgon had joined them. He watched the amassing army for a moment and glanced at the storm clouds blanketing the sky.

"With this weather, darkness will fall earlier than usual," he said.

They nodded in silent agreement. Battle would soon be upon them.

It took another hour for Zirtan to fully gather his force. By this time, much of the light had dwindled. The rain had died to a light mist, but the clouds remained dark and foreboding. Makilien heard the powerful flap of wings and looked to see Carmine leave the wall. For a few minutes he was gone. When he did return, he gave his report to Nirgon and the other commanders. Makilien was just close enough to hear what he said.

"They are forming ranks. It does not appear they will wait long to attack, if they wait at all. There were no siege towers, but there are many catapults and trolls. I also spotted several ballistae. I can only assume they are for us dragons. Zirtan must have learned from last time that we can be very damaging to his men and machines."

Nirgon, his mouth set in a grim line, gave him a nod.

"Thank you, Carmine. Make sure the rest of the dragons are aware of this danger."

"Lord Darand!" an Elf called out. "Three riders approach the city!"

All eyes went north. Though, for most, they were hard to distinguish at first, they spotted the riders. Swiftly their black steeds carried them across the distance to the city. Commotion trickled along the wall, and Lord Darand, Nirgon, and the lords descended one of the stairs. A command to open the gate echoed from below. Anxious to see what would take place, Makilien and her friends moved down the wall until they stood over the gate with Elimar's Elven archers. Below them, Lord Darand and the others rode out, coming to a halt several yards away to await the enemy.

A hundred yards from the lords, the dark riders reined their mounts and approached with slow, ominous steps. Makilien's eyes locked on the rider in the middle, a man unlike any she had ever before seen. He was clothed entirely in black and wore no armor, but a heavy cape swept back over his shoulders. His appearance was youthful, yet gaunt. He had a thin face with a prominent jaw line and cheekbones. His skin was pale and his eyes like coal. Straight black hair framed his face and lay across his shoulders.

A numbing chill raced through Makilien's veins, wrapping icy hands around her heart. All at once she knew with dreadful certainty this was Zirtan—the very embodiment of evil.

Just before he and the other riders halted before the lords, Zirtan glanced up at the wall. The breath was sucked from Makilien's lungs, for it appeared as if he looked directly at her. His gaze burned with malice and seemed to rip away every bit of courage she possessed. Fear gripped her greater than any she'd experienced before, and she began to tremble, feeling utterly exposed and defenseless. She shrank back from the parapet, more like a terrified child than a warrior.

Then a hand came strong and protectively to her back, and she jumped a little. She tore her eyes away from Zirtan, and they met Sirion's. In them, she found love and strength and was reminded not only of those she had around her, but of Elohim. He was always at her side, everlasting, the provider of all hope and protection. His was the ultimate power, far greater than any the enemy could ever display. Makilien breathed deep, and her courage flowed back. Now, she looked upon the enemy again.

Her focus landed on the other two riders. The one on Zirtan's left looked like a typical enemy soldier. He bore the large red banner of Zirtan depicting a black serpent and a jagged sword.

The third rider, on Zirtan's right, however, was much more significant. His head was covered with a dark helmet, the lower part of his face hidden by a cloth. Long, dark brown hair fell in front of his chest. He wore a black cape lined with crimson, and his armor glinted black like Eborin's scales. The armor was the most notable aspect of his appearance. It was constructed elegantly, mirroring that of the Elves, yet wherever there was a corner, it was spiked viciously. *The Dark Elf!* His dark eyes scanned the wall, particularly above the gate where most of the Elves stood. Makilien could feel animosity build among her Elven friends and their army.

The Dark Elf's eyes then dropped as his master began to speak and all attention turned in an instant.

"Lords," the word came forth low and saturated with mockery as Zirtan addressed the group.

"Zirtan," Lord Darand replied through clenched teeth.

"Your defense, though noble, is foolish," Zirtan went on, his voice like satin and dripping with pride. "You see my army and you know the size of your own. You cannot win. Victory is impossible. All lives will be lost, unless . . ."

He paused, letting the dire reality grip them all before making his offer. "Unless you surrender. Surrender to me, and all lives will be spared. You have nothing to fear," he cooed, taking on the tone of a loving father. "I ask only for your co-operation. Violence need not be necessary. Do you not wish to return to your homes . . . to your loved ones? Why cause them to suffer needlessly by your deaths? Only allow me to enter peacefully and you may all go to your homes and families. Is that not what you desire?"

Dead silence. Even the rain had ceased for the moment. Makilien's gaze shifted nervously. Had anyone around her been affected by the deceitful allure of Zirtan's words? Even she'd had desire tugging at her mind, willing her to surrender, telling her that's all she had to do to avoid this struggle. She swallowed hard, remembering the last time someone had tried to sway her with tempting words.

"No." Darand's voice defiantly shattered the dangerous silence. "Your lies will not sway these people, Deceiver. We will not hand over our lives and the lives of our loved ones to evil. We will die before we allow you to set foot beyond our gate."

There seemed to be a collective exhale of breath.

Zirtan's face contorted in a terrible rage. "Fools! Then die you shall. And you," he spat at Darand, "I shall see to personally."

He peered up at the soldiers on the wall, his voice rising to a level that reached the ears of every person gathered. "You will all die here by the hand of my force, and any who remain alive within the city after the battle is finished will become my slaves and endure pain and torture beyond what you could imagine. By the declaration of your king, hope for you has been thrown away."

With these chilling words, all talk ended. Zirtan jerked his horse around, and he and his men galloped off, leaving Eldor's army with mounting fear lurking in everyone's heart.

Slowly, the lords turned and rode back through the gate. Makilien caught a glimpse of Lord Darand's face, set determinedly, but pale. Murmurs raced along the wall. Casting her eyes about, Makilien found looks of hopelessness and uncertainty on many faces, questioning their stand.

As the gate groaned closed and the braces were replaced, Makilien stood with shaken confidence and fear that only by the words of the enemy, their army would crumble. All hope seemed to be fading fast when Nirgon appeared. Boldly, he stepped up onto the parapet and looked down upon the army. All eyes rose to him.

"Soldiers!" he cried out, his voice strong amidst the uncertainty. "Stand fast! Do not be shaken by the lies of the enemy! Do not give in to fear, for that is his greatest weapon. I see out there a devastating force, same as you. An army driven by hate and cruelty more than three times the size of our own. An army capable of leveling every stone within this city. But do you know what I see here? An army brought together by friendship and loyalty, fighting for freedom and what is right and true. And soldiers, we have the advantage! They may have the numbers, but we have a power on our side greater than anything that could be brought against us. We have Elohim! And through Him we have strength, courage, and hope to defeat any evil. So do not look out there and be frightened, but look to Him and be strengthened!"

Fists and weapons were thrust into the air as a deafening cheer broke through the army. Warm tears rolled down Makilien's cheeks as she joined in. Hope had been restored to the heart of their army.

Nirgon held up a hand, and everyone fell silent again.

"In the next hours and days, your fortitude, your strength, your courage will be tested like never before, so do not let yourselves look away from the One who is our strength. Cling to Him in your hearts. Now, let us fight! Let us fight for victory!"

Another cheer, even louder than before, rose up, echoing across the full length of the wall. Nirgon stepped down from the parapet, and everyone moved to their positions with renewed vigor.

Makilien and her friends returned to their spots to the right of the gate, those who had skill with a bow moving to the front. Makilien, Sirion, and Loron stood there, as well as Vonawyn, Elandir, and Elmorhirian who chose to fight alongside their friends.

In silence, they watched Zirtan's army prepare to march on the city. No one said anything until Aedan, who stood just behind Vonawyn, said her name. She turned, looking up at him curiously.

"Yes?"

Aedan glanced at those around them, but he knew as well as anyone the uncertainty of lasting the night. In light of this, it didn't matter that he had an audience when he spoke. Time was far too short to wait.

"When this is over . . . if we both survive . . . I would really like to get to know you better. If you would like to, maybe we could spend some time together."

He swallowed in uncertainty, but Vonawyn smiled sweetly. "I'd like that," she told him.

A relieved and happy smile came to Aedan's face.

"Aw!" Elandir and Elmorhirian echoed.

Vonawyn's cheeks grew a little rosy. "Oh, shush you two."

"No, seriously," Elmorhirian replied and Elandir finished, "We most heartily approve."

Smiles passed around. Makilien felt Sirion take her hand, and they shared their own smile, not realizing this gesture did not go unnoticed. A good number of their friends immediately prayed Elohim would spare both of the young couples the heartache of losing each other.

The joy of the moment was brief. A low murmuring rose and the words, "Here they come," reached their ears. Looking out, Makilien could see the steady forward march of Zirtan's army. It was slow, calculated, and confident, different from the undisciplined race toward the city last time. This time, the army was commanded by its master. He would drive them toward total destruction of the opposing force. There would be no mercy and, above all, no retreat. He would drive them on to the death of the very last warrior if he had to.

The rolling rumble they had heard before increased in intensity as the distance between them was eaten up beneath the feet of the soldiers. Makilien squeezed the grip of her bow. The black mass of soldiers stretched out far beyond what she could see.

Taking her eyes away from the enemy, she looked over their own army. Small though they were, determination flashed in the eyes of the soldiers. They stood erect in neat ranks lining the wall. All had their weapons ready. Some manned the surviving trebuchets. Carmine and Emaril flanked the Elven archers at the gate, and the griffons were at their positions on the rooftops. Only about half as many were present as would have been before the vulture attack, but they were ready. And though she could not see them, Makilien knew more soldiers and dragons waited below to join the fight. A small army, yet mighty when faced with the enemy's destruction.

Only another couple hundred yards. Makilien could soon make out the snarling faces of goblins and Shaikes and hear their shrieks and growls.

"Archers, make ready!" the command came from Nirgon.

Makilien pulled an arrow from her quiver and fit it to her bowstring. Glancing to her left, she caught Sirion's eye, and they shared looks of grim determination.

Another several yards the enemy advanced.

"Prepare to fire!"

Makilien raised her bow and drew the string back to her cheek. She picked out an enemy form and focused on it. She made herself take a long, deep breath, but couldn't slow the rapid pounding of her heart. Peering down her arrow, she knew as soon as the command for the volley was given, the slaughter of both sides would begin.

:Chapter Thirty-two:

Onslaught

"**F**ire!"

At the command, Makilien let her bowstring slip from her fingers. Thousands of dark streaks shot through the air, and, with audible impacts, pierced their targets. The air filled with ear-piercing shrieks as the first line of goblins, save a few, fell. But it did nothing to slow the advance of those behind.

As Makilien reached for another arrow, ranks of enemy archers surged forward. She had only time to fire once before she had to duck below the parapet. An answering hail of arrows flew toward the wall. Though everyone tried to shield themselves, many arrows found targets. Soldiers screamed and fell.

Before the enemy had time to fire again, Carmine flew from the wall followed by Emaril. The red dragon climbed high and dove almost straight down toward the archers. Skimming right over the top of them, he coated the creatures in liquid fire and flames. Many of the archers collapsed in smoldering heaps.

Emaril dove behind him, taking out another couple ranks before he was through. This gave Eldor's soldiers time to redouble their attack. One arrow after another, Makilien fired into the fray until her quiver was nearly empty, but the enemy continued to rush forward. As her final arrows were spent, goblins and Shaikes reached the base of the wall.

Anticipating their next move, Makilien pulled her fighting axe from its holster. Just as anticipated, dark, pronged hooks were slung up by the Shaikes. They flew over the parapet and clattered loudly on the stone as the ropes were yanked taut. Raising her axe to sever the nearest one, Makilien stopped short, discovering something that affected their whole strategy. Zirtan had learned from last time. Instead of rope attached directly to the hook, several feet of chain stretched between them making it impossible to cut.

No!

In a moment, Makilien's father, Halandor, and Sirion were at her side.

"Try to pry it away from the wall and over the parapet," Halandor instructed, his voice urgent over the clamor below.

The four of them grabbed the prongs of the hook and pulled with all their strength. At first, it barely moved. The rope tugged as goblins climbed, and they knew they did not have much time. *Come on!* Makilien shouted to herself, gritting her teeth.

Straining every muscle, the foursome felt the hook slide a couple of inches. Finally, it began to move steadily, and just before the goblins reached the top, the hook slid over the edge of the parapet. Frenzied shrieks sounded followed by several solid thumps.

All along the wall, soldiers struggled to move the hooks. Some were successful while others were not. At first, the soldiers were ready for the goblins, and the first several dozen up the ropes were struck down, but a few goblins managed to sneak through and made way for others.

Grabbing arrows from the nearest barrel, Makilien fired down upon the mass of creatures waiting to scale the wall. They were so numerous it seemed to do little good, but she kept on. The ringing clash of swords echoed near her, and she looked to her right, finding a swarm of goblins had broken through a line of soldiers and were making their way along the wall toward her.

Carmine growled, circling just above the gate. The goblins were relentless—thousands of them swarming like an army of angry ants. More and more they slipped past the soldiers. *They are going to be overrun.* Carmine grimaced. It appeared too much like last time. *Especially if the Shaikes have a chance to join the fight.* The goblins were only the first wave to occupy the soldiers while allowing more deadly enemies to scale the wall.

Knowing his fire had not completely rebuilt, but feeling he had to take action, Carmine turned and dove. Gliding just along the base of the wall, a cascade of flames rose in his throat and poured out of his open jaws. The scores of goblins waiting to climb the ropes retreated in a panic, but most could not get away in time. Many tried to slash at the dragon, but he was just above their reach. The fire seared right through their armor and flesh, dropping them instantly.

Arrows bounced off Carmine's armor, and one pierced his left wing, but he did not stop his attack. When finally his fire had died, he flapped his wings hard to ascend. As he rose, he spotted the chain of one of the grappling hooks just above him. Racing past it, he grabbed it in his claws.

The weight of almost a dozen goblins jerked his limbs, but flapping harder, he carried the hook and rope up into the air and away from the wall. A couple of the goblins let go, but the rest clung to the rope for their lives.

Higher and higher Carmine climbed until, without warning, he folded his wings and began to free fall. A moment later, he extended them again. Air caught the membranes and he slowed immediately. At the almost instant stop, the goblins lost their grips and fell squealing into the roiling mass of their comrades.

Still carrying the grappling hook, Carmine flew over the wall and dropped it in an empty spot on the other side. He then turned and flew over to Emaril who circled nearby.

"When you can, target the goblins at the base of the wall and then get rid of the grappling hooks," he instructed. "Take them behind the wall so they cannot be used again."

The other dragon nodded and swooped downward. On the opposite side of the gate Carmine had covered, he flew along the base and flamed the goblins. Carmine also flew back down to the wall. This time, he grabbed two grappling hooks at once. The weight was almost too much for him to carry, but he managed to bring them up to a lethal height. After detaching the goblins, he once again discarded the hooks behind the wall.

As he circled around for more, he noticed quite a bit of commotion farther out in the enemy's ranks. Flying higher to stay out of range of arrows, he surveyed the area. When he had his answer, he flew back and called to Emaril, "They're bringing up the ballistae! Beware!"

Makilien squeezed the hilt of her sword and watched the group of goblins move through the soldiers. The evil little creatures weaseled their way along, sneaking past distracted warriors, slashing and backstabbing any in their path. She cast a quick glance over her shoulder to be sure none were coming from the other way.

Finally, one of the goblins turned up just in front of her. She was ready. The last thing the creature saw was the blur of her blade. As it collapsed, two more goblins jumped out behind it. Aware of the danger, they snarled and pointed their blades at Makilien. Glaring at them, she raised her sword high and brought it down. It clashed loudly with the first goblin's sword. The second goblin hopped to Makilien's right, hoping to catch her unaware from the side, but she spun and blocked its attack.

The first goblin tried to make a move, but swinging her sword widely, Makilien forced the creature back. With an idea formulating, she pretended to put all her focus on the other goblin and grasped her fighting axe with her left hand. Seeing her attention was averted, the first goblin lunged forward to drive his sword through her middle. At the last second, Makilien side stepped and the creature's momentum took it right past her. She yanked out her fighting axe and swung backwards. The blade embedded itself deep in the goblin's back. With a deafening squeal, it fell flat on its face, and before the other goblin realized what had taken place, it found itself impaled by Makilien's sword. Giving her a final defiant snarl, it too fell.

Makilien scanned the area for more, but any nearby had been dealt with. Wiping her blade on her skirt, she returned it to its scabbard, reached down to retrieve her axe, and took out her bow once more. She hurried to her original position where immense relief swept through her to find all her friends unharmed. Standing between Sirion and Vonawyn, she joined them in firing down upon the goblins. Hordes of bodies already littered the base of the wall. She could hardly imagine what it would be like when it was over.

"Look out! Archers!" Sirion warned.

He dragged her down with him as everyone ducked. The arrows ricocheted on the parapet. Again, screams penetrated the air.

Crouched beside him, Makilien looked at Sirion. "How are we doing?"

He gave a little shrug. "Better than last time . . . but I'm afraid of what will happen once full darkness sets in."

It gave Makilien some small hope to know they were keeping things under control, but Sirion was right. They had the advantage while daylight remained, but once night fell, the advantage would go to their enemies. With a glance at the dim sky, she knew their advantage would fade fast.

For the next half hour, the archers and soldiers were able to keep the goblins at bay. Since the creatures could not gain ground, no Shaikes climbed the ropes. Carmine and Emaril were instrumental in keeping the numbers down as they carried away many of the grappling hooks.

Just as darkness fell, a roar echoed overhead. Makilien looked up right as a large projectile streaked past Carmine, very nearly taking out his right wing. She gasped, but the dragon was unharmed. *Thank you, Elohim!* Her eyes swung out past the parapet, and, in the gloom, made out the shapes of several ballistae. Built like giant crossbows, they fired large, spear-like arrows. She prayed none would hit their targets.

Now that darkness had engulfed them completely, torches were lit, but it did little to offer the soldiers light. Makilien wished the moon would break through the clouds, but she had little hope of that, for it had begun to rain again.

In this cold, wet darkness, she came to the realization that no more goblins climbed the ropes. As soon as the remaining creatures on the wall were killed, fighting ceased. She strained to see what Zirtan's army was up to, but even with the scattered torches, she could not make out much through the darkness and rain.

"What is happening?" she asked as she and her friends gathered once more.

After a moment of silence, Torick spoke, his voice grim. "They are regrouping."

"The first attack may have been only to test our strength," Halandor said.

Makilien slowly drew in a breath, shivering.

Before anything more could be said between them, a sound caught their attention. It was only a slight clamor among the enemy at first, but it rapidly intensified, engulfing the whole army. Enemy warriors beat upon their armor, the Shaikes roared savagely, and the goblins broke into a wild shrieking. The sound was chilling and roared in their ears, rising in a terrifying echo into the night.

Makilien swallowed hard. Had she not her faith to sustain her courage, she would have cowered in fear.

:Chapter Thirty-three:
Dark Hours

In a screaming, tangled horde, the goblins rushed the wall again. New grappling hooks were hurled over the parapet by the Shaikes coming behind, much more numerous than before. Just as the soldiers rushed to get rid of as many as they could, hundreds of goblin archers fired at the wall. A thick hail of arrows hurtled toward the soldiers. This time they were offered no respite between volleys until Carmine and Emaril attacked. But that gave Eldor's army only a brief couple of minutes before they were fired upon again.

Heart pounding, Makilien ducked and dodged, several arrows slicing the air barely inches from her body. But the arrows were not her only concern. Three grappling hooks had landed nearby that she and her friends had been unable to move. Just as she was expecting, goblins popped up over the wall in seconds. They were so quick and agile most made it successfully over before anyone could knock them off the parapet.

Makilien loosed her sword. She had a feeling she would no longer find the opportunity to use her bow. Only a few feet away, a group of goblins poured onto the wall. Gripping her sword tightly, she swung hard. With gasping shrieks, three goblins crumpled at her feet. Two more clutched at their wounds. Infuriated, they lunged recklessly. Makilien kicked one away and stabbed through the chest armor of the other.

Without a moment to breathe, a fresh goblin assailed her. She blocked its strike, but the creature was too quick for her to counterattack. Four attacks in a row she had to block. Finally, on the fifth, the goblin swung wide for her stomach. She jumped back, but was ready for her attack. As the goblin completed its failed swing, she slashed down across its exposed shoulder. It stumbled, and she drove her sword into its side.

Makilien gasped for breath, but did not let her guard down. Her eyes darted from one struggle to another. Everywhere battle raged, and massive hordes of goblins swarmed the ranks. But the soldiers fought hard, determined not to let the enemy breach their defense.

Still, the goblins had accomplished their goal. Makilien groaned to see a Shaike lug itself over the parapet before her. Straightening, it looked around, and its glinting eyes locked on her. With a guttural growl, it lumbered toward her and raised its massive sword. Makilien raised hers to block, already grimacing.

The Shaike's blade came down with such powerful force that when it met Makilien's, her hands stung so badly she wanted to let go, but she held tight though her sword was driven toward the ground. Again, the Shaike raised its blade. She retreated a step while her mind scrambled for a way to defeat the monster. Her hands numbed on the second strike, and she struggled to keep her sword. Her heart raced, and she realized she might not survive another blow.

As the Shaike's arms rose for a third attack, a dagger suddenly plunged into the creature's body just above its breastplate near the neck. The beast howled, and Makilien rushed forward. As the Shaike reached for the dagger, she stabbed her sword through the gap between its armor at its side. With that, the Shaike collapsed in a heap.

Standing on the other side of the body was Sirion.

"Thanks," Makilien gasped.

He nodded and reached down for his dagger.

"Stay with me, if you can," Sirion told her over the ruckus of the battle.

Makilien nodded, remembering how well they had fought together last time. "I will."

Watching each other's backs, they took down any foe that came their way. Between the two of them, they were easily able to take on the Shaikes who managed to reach the top, a great relief to Makilien. It too enabled them to go to the aid of multiple soldiers who would have been overwhelmed.

A resounding crash of metal exploded, and a vibration trembled through the stones under Makilien's feet. She and Sirion glanced at each other, and Sirion rushed to the parapet to look over. When he turned back to her, he said, "Trolls, at the gate."

"Already?"

"Zirtan is going for a quick victory."

A knot of fear twisted Makilien's stomach, but overwhelming determination forced it down. Determination to show Zirtan victory wasn't achieved only by power and brute force.

Another crash rang out. The dark shape of one of the dragons dove downward. Fire jetted from his mouth, illuminating the gate. Makilien came to the parapet and saw six trolls carrying a long battering ram. Carmine had been the one to attack, and Emaril quickly joined him.

As two cascades of fire rained down, the trolls bellowed their pain and anger. They would not last long; however, numerous trolls stood nearby to replace the fallen.

Abruptly, Emaril's fire stopped and he roared. Makilien gasped, afraid he'd been hit with an arrow from a ballista, but then she saw something else. Black as the night sky, death vultures attacked from above. They latched onto Emaril and he lost altitude, falling dangerously close to the enemy horde. Carmine was forced to stop his attack on the trolls in order to go to his aid. He had just enough fire left to scorch the birds clinging to the other dragon. The two of them rose to a safer height, but more death vultures attacked them. With the dragons' fire spent, it turned into a bloody struggle of teeth and talons.

And that was all the longer Makilien and Sirion could watch. A new wave of goblins and Shaikes reached the top of the wall, and they were assailed by numerous opponents. The battle intensified, and Makilien could sense desperation growing. Zirtan's force was gaining the advantage.

On the wall, swords clashed as men cried out, hewn down by their shrieking, snarling enemies. Above it rose the frantic screeches of death vultures mixed with the pained roars of the dragons and griffons. Makilien caught sight of something fall from the sky, but could not tell if it was friend or foe. Metal clashed again at the gate.

Just when it seemed they would not be able to hold off much longer, Nirgon's voice echoed over the struggle. A moment passed and dark forms flew into the sky from behind the wall. Before the enemy could see it coming, the entire area lit up almost as if it were daylight. Like a fiery curtain, molten liquid and flames poured down on the enemy ranks from the mouths of more than forty dragons.

The firelight shimmered on their armor and lit up their scales, filling the night sky overhead with a dazzling, but deadly rainbow of color. Shrieks and roars of panic rose from the enemy force as they scrambled to get away from the approaching dragons, but they had nowhere to run. Even the goblins and Shaikes on the wall were distracted by the carnage being poured out on their army, and many of them fell to Eldor's warriors.

Makilien could not help but smile grimly, knowing neither Zirtan nor his army could have expected this. She could only imagine what the sight was like from across the battlefield where Zirtan likely gave his commands—the sky filled with more dragons than anyone had laid eyes on in decades.

But any hope of victory was still far off. Yet, this gave a much needed boost to the army's moral, and with a defiant cheer, they fought fiercely with renewed strength and confidence.

Witnessing the devastating attack the dragons had unleashed on their enemy caused fresh adrenaline to surge through Aedan's veins. With the death vultures screeching fearfully overhead, now overwhelmed by the number of dragons, Aedan slashed his broadsword through a group of goblins. In a moment, they all fell, headless. Wielding the large blade had become as natural as breathing. Always in his heart he'd been a warrior and felt that fighting for the lives of the people he cared about was something he'd been born to do.

A Shaike appeared in his path. This beast was the third he'd come upon, and he'd learned attacking first gave him an advantage. Before the Shaike could make a move, Aedan charged forward. The Shaike reacted just fast enough to block his sword, but Aedan did not relent. He attacked again and again, throwing the Shaike off balance. It stumbled back a step, and that became its undoing as it unwittingly lowered its sword. In that moment, Aedan lunged, throwing all his weight behind his blade. It cut through the Shaike's leather armor, and the beast fell backwards.

As it hit the wall at his feet, Aedan looked ahead to see what else may be behind it. A few yards down from him, he caught the glint of silver plate-mail and realized it was Darian. Caught unaware, a Shaike came up behind the prince and slammed him down to the stone. Aedan's heart stumbled as the Shaike raised its sword to deliver a killing blow.

He sprinted forward. A goblin stepped in his path, but with one deft swing, it fell to the side. Everything seemed to slow as the Shaike's blade fell. With a shout, Aedan drove his sword into the Shaike's back. The Shaike gave a choked howl, and Aedan pulled his sword free, letting the creature fall.

His eyes went immediately to the prince. Darian sat up, shaking his head to clear his senses. Aedan extended his hand. Looking gratefully up at him, Darian took it, and Aedan pulled him to his feet.

"Thank you," the prince said. "I didn't see that one coming."

Makilien's muscles burned from prolonged exertion. Her legs, forearms, shoulders, and back were on fire, but her determination ran strong. She could not tell how much time had passed—thick darkness still lay upon them—but she knew they had lasted far longer on the wall than last time.

"Right!" Sirion shouted in warning.

Makilien spun to her right and threw up her sword. That very instant, a Shaike's blade crashed into it. The force drove her into Sirion's back, but she stopped the blow that could have easily beheaded them both. This was all the time Sirion needed to drop the goblin before him. He spun around Makilien and attacked the Shaike before the beast could swing again. Makilien joined in, attacking from the left.

The creature's body had not even fully fallen before a great explosion rocked the wall. The stone beneath Makilien seemed to fall away, and she fell forward. Her knees and palms hit hard, and she winced at the stinging pain. Sirion grabbed her and pulled her close to shield her as stones rained down around them. Makilien covered her head and listened to the debris settle.

Finally, Makilien and Sirion looked up, a bit dazed. Sirion stood first and helped Makilien to her feet. They both turned their gaze down the wall. Not three feet away, a crater had been carved into the top section, ten feet wide and five feet deep. *Catapults*, Makilien thought, heart sinking. Nothing else could cause such damage.

A burst of light came from the battlefield as one of the dragons attacked the catapult responsible. Almost immediately, there came a pained roar and the fire died. In the light of the flames licking the catapult's frame, the dragon fell into the roiling mass of enemy soldiers. Her throat constricted, tears springing to her eyes. Could it be Carmine or Emaril? She shook her head. She couldn't think of it. She just couldn't.

Makilien forced her mind back to the fight. She realized she'd dropped her sword when she'd fallen and looked around for it. Sirion spotted it first and handed it to her.

"Thanks," Makilien said, but her voice shook a little, still shaken by the catapult attack and fallen dragon.

As she and Sirion moved away from the crater to where the battle was still being fought in earnest, she saw two more fire streams appear at the catapult and prayed no more dragons would be killed. She prayed too that none of her friends or her father had been killed in the destruction caused by the catapult.

:Chapter Thirty-four:

Siege

The pale, colorless light of dawn had never been so welcome. To be able to see their enemies more clearly gave the soldiers confidence to push on. Behind gray clouds, the sun climbed and the light grew. With it, the enemies upon the wall seemed to fall more rapidly, and the stream of goblins and Shaikes climbing the ropes slowed.

At last, an hour after dawn, the bombardment stopped entirely, and Zirtan's force pulled back, just out of bow range. The remaining creatures on the wall fought furiously, left by their comrades to face their doom, but they were overwhelmed. With that, fighting came to an unexpected but welcome cease.

Drawing in ragged breaths, Makilien wiped her sword, slid it into its scabbard, and let her weary arms fall to her sides. Her eyes cast out over the battlefield. Innumerable bodies littered the base of the wall, and gray smoke curled into the sky from smoldering mounds and charred war machines. Past the ruin, Zirtan's army stretched out as far as she could see. She did not know how they could lose so many, yet never appear to decrease in number. Still, she felt a grim satisfaction and relief that Eldor had held the wall, even against the overwhelming force. They had lasted the night, something Zirtan, in his arrogance, surely had not expected of them.

Then Makilien's gaze turned to their own forces. Dead and wounded soldiers, their bodies broken, lay strewn across the wall, the pale granite stained crimson. In three places, the parapet had been shattered by catapult attacks, but the wall and the gate stood strong as did the remaining force. Resolve still flickered behind the expressions of weariness.

Makilien turned when she sensed someone behind her. She looked up into Sirion's face, breathing out a sigh. Both shared the same appearance, tired-eyed, their faces and armor spattered with dark blood. They just stood for a moment, overwhelmed by the exhaustion of more than twelve hours of continuous battle, but thankful to be standing here now.

Sirion's eyes looked past her for a moment. "Let's find the others."

Makilien nodded, her mind immediately turning to her father and the rest.

As the adrenaline that had sustained her wore off, pain spread through every part of her body, especially her knee. She took a couple steps, but all her strength melted away, and she stumbled. Sirion caught her by the arm. She tried to walk again, but could not manage without a severe limp. She looked down and realized her pant leg from the knee down was stained with blood.

Hand still holding her up, Sirion asked, "Are you injured?"

Makilien shook her head. "My wound from the death vultures' attack . . . all the activity must have reopened it."

"We should try to find Vonawyn and have her look at it," Sirion said. "Here, I'll carry you."

Carefully, he lifted her up into his arms.

Zirtan's flashing eyes glared upon the walls of the city—still erect, still strong—and the number of soldiers still defending it. He squeezed the reins in his hand, his leather gauntlet stretching tight across his fist. Those nearby stood with bated breath, not daring to move for fear the fiery hatred in their commander's gaze might be unleashed upon them in some brutal explosion of fury.

At last, Zirtan slid off his horse and threw its reins at one of his men. He stormed toward a group of his captains who cowered at his approach. Looming over them, he demanded in an icy voice, "What is this? Why are those walls still standing? Why am I still standing here when I should be on the throne at the palace?"

All eyes turned to the highest ranking captain in the group, as more than one man took a discreet step back. The captain glanced at each of them, cursing their cowardice and disloyalty. With a hint of a scowl crossing his face, he drew himself up and turned to face Zirtan with more than a little fire in his belly. But that fire was doused the moment he locked eyes with his commander, seeming to wither under the chilling gaze. He swallowed hard, trying to speak with some authority, but his voice came out weak and halting.

"Th-they are stronger than we anticipated and . . . better prepared."

Zirtan bent closer to the captain, his face inches away, and it seemed to the man as if he grew a bit larger. "Look around you. I have a force unlike any they have ever seen. They are but a handful in comparison. They should have been crushed *by now!*"

"M-my lord," the captain stammered. "If you'd like, we can attack again immediately."

Zirtan's eyes narrowed to dark slits, and he said nothing for a long, torturous moment. Finally, he growled, "No. Let them consider the horrors another night will bring." He turned to go, yet spun to face the captains once more, encompassing all this time. "But as soon as darkness has fallen, I expect you to get me into that city, do you understand?"

His gaze pierced each of them, and they knew if they did not fulfill this command, their lives would be forfeit. They nodded, pale faces grim.

Turning more slowly this time, Zirtan's eyes settled again upon the walls of Minarald. "Tonight, I want all focus to be on the gate. Aim all available catapults there. Break it down. And the dragons—shoot down as many of them as you can. Make the lizards regret they ever threw their lot in with Eldor."

"Makilien!"

The relief brought by the sound of Halandor's voice soothed every ache and pain. She looked up to see him, her father, Torick, and Elmorhirian. None appeared to be injured, for which she thanked Elohim.

Néthyn reached his daughter first. "Are you all right?"

"Yes, it's just the wound from the other day," Makilien assured him.

"Elmorhirian, have you seen Vonawyn?" Sirion asked.

The Elf nodded. "I just saw her with Elandir and Loron. I'll get her."

"I'll take Makilien down to the medical supply house."
Elmorhirian nodded again and hurried off.

"What about Aedan?" Makilien asked her remaining friends. "Has anyone seen him?"

They shook their heads, but Torick said, "I'll find him."

"Thank you, Torick."

Néthyn following, Sirion carried Makilien down from the wall. Along the way, Makilien's eyes searched the faces of soldiers for those she recognized. Near the gate she spotted Nirgon and Elnauhir, and Carmine and Emaril were among some of the dragons from the mountains.

When they reached the building that had been designated as the gathering point for the wounded, a great number of injured soldiers had already gathered. Those not wounded worked to do all they could for them. Makilien grimaced and looked down at her knees to block out the sight of so many terrible wounds.

Gently, Sirion set her down by the building so she could rest against it, and he and Néthyn knelt beside her. With a heavy sigh, Makilien leaned her head back. "Do you think Zirtan will wait until nightfall to attack again?"

Sirion nodded. "He knows we can't fight as well in the dark. He might as well wait for the advantage."

"But we did well, didn't we?"

"We did." Sirion flashed an encouraging grin. "Better than I feared we would. I didn't know if we could hold on throughout the night. We couldn't have without the dragons."

Makilien agreed. The dragons had saved them from early defeat.

In another few moments, Vonawyn came, working her way through the soldiers. Following behind was Aedan. A weary, but glad smile stretched across Makilien's face. Vonawyn knelt beside her, and Aedan stood to the side with Sirion and Néthyn.

"Is it your knee?" Vonawyn asked.

"Yes."

"Let's have a look at it."

Vonawyn helped Makilien pull off her boot and carefully roll up her pant leg. The bandage around her knee was almost completely soaked with blood. Vonawyn unwound the bandage, exposing the wound.

"How does it look?" Makilien asked, leaning forward.

"The edges are inflamed. I don't think it's infected, but it is still bleeding." Vonawyn laid the bandage back over the gash. "I think it would be best to stitch it."

While she dug through the supply pack she had brought with her, Makilien shifted her leg and winced. Being exposed to the air made her gash sting. Wetting a cloth with a water flask, Vonawyn cleaned the wound. Then she picked up a small glass vial. She looked apologetically at Makilien.

"This will be painful, but it will cleanse the wound. I want to make sure it doesn't get infected once I sew it up."

Makilien breathed in and braced herself. "Do whatever you have to."

Vonawyn tipped the vial and a clear liquid trickled onto Makilien's knee. In an instant, it felt as if a hot poker had been touched to the wound. She sucked in her breath and gritted her teeth.

After a minute or two, the pain subsided to a throbbing ache. By this time, Vonawyn had threaded a thin needle.

"I'm afraid this isn't going to feel very good either," she warned.

Makilien bunched a handful of her dress skirt in her fist as Vonawyn began to stitch up the gash. Biting down, Makilien swallowed hard as her friend worked. Nothing was said until Vonawyn had finished. Speaking tentatively, the Elf maiden said, "With a lot of exertion, the stitches could rip. I can wrap your knee tightly to help prevent that, but it will limit your mobility and could hinder you in battle." She paused. "You could . . . go back to the palace."

Makilien shook her head. "Call me stubborn, but no, I can't leave now."

"Are you sure? You won't be in the best condition to fight."

"I'm sure. Many won't be in good condition by the end of this, but none of us must give up. Just wrap it tight. I'll manage."

"All right."

Vonawyn went back to work. Once the bandages were in place, Sirion and Néthyn helped Makilien up.

"Try to stay off it as much as you can," Vonawyn said. "We should have thought to bring your crutch."

"I can help her get around," Sirion offered.

"Good." Vonawyn packed up the medical supplies. "Now, I'm going to see to the other wounded. More and more are being brought here."

"Is there anything I can do to help?" Aedan asked.

"Yes, come with me," Vonawyn answered, and the two of them walked away.

Peering through half-closed eyes, Makilien shifted against the wall, trying to find a more comfortable position on the hard ground near the backside of one of the stairs. She tried to rest as much as she could, even sleep. But it was always fitful, and she'd only doze off for short periods of time. Inside, she was apprehensive of being wakened to a call to arms. Her friends had come and gone during the day, taking rest for short times before offering to help somewhere.

Right now, Sirion and Elmorhirian lay off to her left, their slow, even breathing telling Makilien they were both in a deep sleep despite how much commotion droned on around them. She stared down at Sirion's restful face. She had grown up believing she would never love anyone. But now she did, more deeply than she could put into words. She ached for this to all be over so she could discover what more was in store for the two of them.

With a sigh, she glanced toward the gate. More braces were being added. A small smile came to her face when she spotted Tanzim. She didn't think she'd seen him stop working all day, and his strength was greatly appreciated. He could easily do the work of three men. And no one showed the slightest misgiving about working side by side with one of the very creatures they'd been fighting so fiercely only hours ago.

In times like this, she thought, it didn't matter what you looked like, where you were from, or what your station was. Everyone had the same goal and worked equally hard for it. She saw this in the way all the lords pitched in to help with even their lowest ranked soldiers.

Makilien's eyes lifted to the sky. The day had dragged out slowly, but the long shadows and dimming light signaled dusk was finally descending. When she looked down again, her gaze landed on Halandor. Sirion and Elmorhirian both woke at his approach.

"General Nirgon is soon going to begin getting everyone into position," he announced. "He is meeting with the lords and captains now to discuss the strategy for tonight."

Sirion rose with Elmorhirian and helped Makilien up. They followed Halandor to the large group assembling nearby, anxious to hear the discussion. As they joined their friends, they were just in time to hear Gébrale speak.

"Why not place my men above the gate? Darrow wood bows and spears are the strongest here. We may not be able to kill the trolls, but we can certainly dissuade them from attacking the gate. That would allow the dragons to focus on the wall and the siege weapons."

Nirgon nodded. "Yes, and be far safer for them. Flying stationary above the gate created an easy target for the ballistae. Tonight then, your men will have the charge of protecting the gate."

"And protect it we shall," Gébrale promised.

With the last few adjustments to their strategy, the leaders dispersed to give orders. In moments, soldiers filed up the wall stairs for another night of battle. With help from Sirion, Makilien made her way up, and they all went to their positions. She glanced down the wall both ways. It looked almost the same as the night before, but tonight she could tell they were spread out a bit thinner.

Her attention was drawn from the soldiers when Nirgon came as he had the evening before and stood upon the parapet. Tonight, he looked more grim, a cut along his chin and blood spattering his armor, but a fire burned in his eyes.

"Soldiers, I stand here with great pride in all of you. Last night, you fought with all courage. Once again, Zirtan's force will come upon us, bent on destroying everything we hold dear. But we've proved we can stand against him. The night will be long, one of the longest you've ever faced, but don't give up. Continue to look to Elohim and fight hard. We can weaken Zirtan's force if we hold our ground. Stand fast and stand together!"

A loud cheer rose across the wall as the general stepped down. Determination beat in the hearts of all as they stared defiantly at their enemy.

The echoing cheer drifted across the battlefield.

"Fools!" Zirtan spat. "Filled with a false hope of victory. I will show them."

His eyes landed on the rider to his right.

Feeling the intensity of his gaze, the Dark Elf looked to his master. Even he could not control the involuntary shiver that crawled across his skin under the scrutiny of those breath-snatching eyes. He hadn't the faintest doubt as to the evilness of the figure beside him, nor to how low he'd sunk to be serving such evil.

"It's time to put an end to this. Ride forward and make sure the captains do their jobs. I want the city taken. If they cannot fulfill my commands, bring them to me."

Slow and deliberate, the Dark Elf nodded and pressed his spurred heels into the sides of his steed. Zirtan watched him ride away, satisfied he had at least one person with enough guts and will to do his duty. Then, grinning savagely to himself, he said, "Tonight, the city will be mine."

:Chapter Thirty-five:

The Battle Rages

Zirtan's force crashed against the wall like a tidal wave. Despite numerous volleys of arrows, they could not slow the surge. Grappling hooks were hurled over the parapet, and the goblin's raced up the ropes as fast as their long, agile limbs could carry them.

Makilien emptied her quiver into the enemy mass, but did not refill it. Goblins drew near, and she pulled out her sword. The creatures fought through the soldiers ferociously. Many men went down, overwhelmed. From both ways they came, but Makilien knew Sirion had her back and she had his.

Hooting and snarling, the goblins charged forward, flailing their weapons. The first ones to come within Makilien's reach did not realize their peril until it was too late. Two dropped dead while a third fell mortally wounded. But for the three that had fallen, five more took their place.

With narrowed eyes, they jeered, brandishing their blades. Makilien glared back and reached for her fighting axe. She had little experience fighting with two weapons, but now she had to learn fast. She needed this advantage since her knee kept her from moving and turning as quickly as she needed to defend herself.

Three of the goblins jumped in to attack at once. Makilien swung both weapons. Her sword crashed against two of the goblin's blades. She missed with her axe, but it kept the third goblin from coming too close. The creatures attacked again. She blocked with her weapons, and while she held one goblin's sword up with her axe, she delivered a hard kick to its stomach.

As it tumbled backwards, she turned to the other two and swung her axe. The sharp blade connected with one goblin's ribs, and it fell to the side. Twisting her sword around, she slashed across the other goblin's chest. It too fell, and Makilien turned just in time to block an attack from the goblin she'd kicked. She surprised it with a sudden counter attack using her axe and drove her sword through its mid-section.

The moment it fell, three more goblins leaped over the fallen bodies. Makilien had to take a step back to avoid them as they pressed in fearlessly.

With two goblin-laden ropes in his claws, Carmine soared upwards. Stars were just appearing in the sky above, and the moon climbed above the horizon. *At least our army will have some light to see by,* he thought, if it was not blotted out by smoke.

After ridding the rope of the clinging goblins, Carmine flew the ropes over the wall and dropped them. He then met up with Malachi.

"Goblins are filling the wall," the green dragon reported. "The Shaikes will soon follow."

Carmine looked down at the soldiers, fighting with everything they had. And sneaking between the ranks were nearly as many goblins. He growled.

"Zirtan wants his victory, and he wants it now." His gaze fell back to Malachi. "Come. We must slow the goblins. You take the right side of the gate, and I'll take the left."

Malachi nodded and they both dove downwards to the base of the wall, unleashing a flood of fire. And slow the goblins it did, but only for a short time. Though a charred heap now lay along the wall, several bodies deep, it did not deter the goblins who came behind.

Carmine growled again. What they were doing was not enough. They had to do something more. He dove down to grab another two grappling hooks. Wishing he could carry more, an idea sprang to mind. On his descent, he reached out and slashed his sharp claws across a rope. It was not severed, but several strands snapped and it would only be a matter of time before it broke completely, especially if the Shaikes began to climb.

Banking upwards, Carmine grabbed two of the grappling hooks. As he flew higher, he called to some of the nearby dragons, "Try to slash the ropes on the way down!"

The dragons nodded and followed his example.

"Carmine!"

He dropped the grappling hooks behind the wall and curved around to meet Emaril.

"What is it?"

"They are bringing the catapults."

Carmine looked out over the enemy army, keen eyes picking out the siege weapons, numerous in number, and slowly rolling forward. On either side of each catapult were ballistae.

"They are going to do whatever they can to stop us from destroying them," he said. "Warn the others."

Emaril nodded and flew to the nearest group of dragons. Carmine, however, dove lower, just above the wall.

"The catapults are coming!" he warned the soldiers. At each trebuchet he stopped, telling the men there to aim for the catapults and ballistae once they were within range.

The blow came out of nowhere. Makilien turned to finish off a goblin and, in the next moment, she hit ground. Hot pain pulsed across the back of her head. She groaned. Everything was hazy. She shook her head and rolled to her side. Looking up, she spotted in the darkness the towering silhouette of a Shaike. Its sword glinted with moonlight as it raised it above its head. But Makilien realized the attack was not meant for her. Panic cleared her senses in an instant.

"Sirion! Behind you!"

He spun around as the Shaike brought its blade down. Makilien gasped as Sirion jumped back, and the attack only missed him by inches. But, in his haste, he stumbled and fell against the parapet leaving him vulnerable to the Shaike's next attack.

Makilien frantically searched for her sword and scooped it up. Scrambling to her knees, she slashed the blade across the back of the Shaike's legs as it was about to finish Sirion off. The beast howled as its knees buckled. Sirion regained his balance and delivered a heavy-handed blow to the Shaike's neck.

After it had fallen, Sirion came to Makilien and helped her to her feet.

"Are you all right?"

Makilien winced, her head still throbbing. "I think so."

She touched the back of her head. When she pulled it away, fresh blood mingled with that which already covered her hands. She glanced up at Sirion, catching the worry in his eyes, but both knew nothing could be done. They had no choice but to turn back to the fight. Now that the goblins had cleared the way, Shaikes would soon show up all over the wall. It seemed they came faster this night, and soon the fight escalated.

Back in their spots, Makilien watched a grappling hook a couple of yards away where she suspected the Shaike had come from. Sure enough, another Shaike appeared. This one Makilien did not give the chance to attack. Pulling out her axe, she dashed over to the grappling hook. With a quick strike, the creature lost its hold and fell into the swarming mass below.

Makilien risked a glance over the parapet. Only a couple feet down, two goblins raced up the rope. Not feeling confident she could stop both of them from reaching the top, she backed away and waited.

Aedan knew the Shaike was coming behind him. He could hear its heavy footsteps. But he didn't dare take his eyes away from the one that loomed before him, demanding all his attention and skill. His heart hammered. He had to do something. He would be dead in moments if he did not.

Barely dodging an attack, Aedan drove his sword down hard. The Shaike blocked it, seeming unfazed; however, it gave

Aedan a second to glance over his shoulder. The Shaike behind him raised its blade. He waited for two heartbeats and suddenly dropped down.

The Shaike's blade descended, but instead of felling Aedan, it slashed deep into the other Shaike's chest. The beast roared and collapsed. Before the remaining Shaike could figure out what had happened, Aedan jumped up and drove his sword into the creature's ribs.

He exhaled loudly in relief as the Shaike toppled over. He then spun around to find his next opponent, but was knocked off his feet as a massive chunk of stone crashed into the wall just yards away. The catapult attacks had begun.

Scrambling up, he stared at the large crater that had been left and thought of how many soldiers had been lost at once. They'd never even seen their doom coming.

He turned to scan the sea of chaos taking place in the opposite direction. Almost immediately, his eyes caught on long dark hair and femininely-shaped Elven armor. *Vonawyn!* He knew without a doubt it was her. His heart lodged in his throat. A Shaike had her by the neck, and though one of her long knives was embedded in its chest, the beast didn't seem affected.

Aedan bolted forward, little concerned with anything but reaching Vonawyn before it was too late. Fear knotted his stomach knowing the beast could crush the Elf's throat and break her neck with ease. His eyes locked on her weakening struggle, Aedan shoved past both friend and enemy to reach her side.

The Shaike began to raise its sword to finish her off, but Aedan reached it first. With all his strength, he swung his broadsword down. The Shaike gave a deafening roar as its severed arm dropped at its feet, fist still clenched around the hilt of its sword. Vonawyn fell from its grasp, gasping.

Heart racing at how close Vonawyn had come to being killed, Aedan unleashed a devastating attack to finish off the Shaike, but he was blind to what was behind him. He heard Vonawyn's choked cry, "Aedan!"

He spun around as the glint of metal hurtled toward him. Instinctively, he put his arm up to shield his head. Devastating force crashed down on his arm. The blade slipped down past his chain-mail finding flesh just above the vambrace. With a cry, he fell to his knees. The Shaike loomed over him, its sword already raised again for a killing blow. In that moment came a roar, and the point of a sword punched out through the attacking Shaike's chest. The creature froze and then fell off to the side. Standing behind him was another towering figure, and Aedan looked up into Tanzim's fierce expression.

"Thanks," he gasped, though pain stole his voice.

Vonawyn was there in an instant and dropped down next to him. Eyes wide, she said his name in fear. He clutched his bleeding arm to his stomach, afraid of what damage had been done. The pain was so intense, he could not tell. Finally, he moved it away from his body. He had to know. Moving it slowly at first, he came the relieving discovery that the bone had not been broken.

"I'm all right," he assured Vonawyn. "Are you hurt?"

"No."

Aedan pushed to his feet, helping Vonawyn up with him. He bent to pick up his sword, and Vonawyn retrieved her other knife. Sharing grim looks, Aedan, Vonawyn, and Tanzim turned their attention to the battle just as a second catapult attack rocked the wall. Immediately following was yet another.

This time the metallic clang told Aedan it had impacted the gate. If it continued, he wondered how many hits it would take before the gate was breached.

Makilien felt the vibration of the catapult attack even from where she stood. While she was distracted, two long-fingered hands latched onto her right arm. She looked down, right into the hideous face of a goblin. It snarled, mouth open to reveal its long, pointed teeth. It tried to bite her hand, but Makilien moved too quickly.

"Oh, no, you don't," she muttered as she twisted her arm away from its mouth and shoved the creature. She swung her sword at its back as it stumbled away, but only the very tip met flesh.

The goblin squealed in pain, but then turned in a rage and dove for Makilien's legs. She jumped away, yet the goblin still caught one of her ankles. She fell hard to her hands and knees, her sword falling beside her. Not realizing how close she had come to the edge of the wall, one of her arms slipped over and her chest hit the stones, taking her breath away. Looking down, there was nothing but dark cobblestone littered with bodies sixty feet below.

Panic jolted through her, and she scrambled backward. But a forceful shove to her shoulders pushed her another dangerous few inches over the edge. She screamed at the terror of feeling she might topple over. A satisfied hiss came from the goblin. Bracing herself any way she could from going over, Makilien rolled to try to get away. But the goblin was on top of her again, and this time its hands went around her throat. She struggled to pry them off, but the goblin held tight. Inch by inch, it worked her farther over the edge.

Bringing her knee up into the creature's stomach, Makilien felt its grip loosen. She grabbed one of its wrists and pulled its hand away from her throat, but the other stayed. The goblin squeezed, hoping to weaken her with lack of air and push her over the edge to her death.

Makilien fought desperately to break free of its hold, but despite being smaller, the goblin was shockingly strong, and its long arms kept its vulnerable head out of reach of any attack. Spots danced in Makilien's vision. *Elohim, help!* Her hold on the goblin's wrist weakened and then failed. The goblin's vicious, grinning face turned into a hazy form.

Makilien's limbs numbed, but someone grabbed her free hand. She heard the thump of something being struck, and instantly her airway opened up. Gasping for air, she felt herself being pulled away from the edge and into someone's arms. As she coughed and dragged in deep breaths, she watched the goblin claw madly at the edge of the wall, but there was nothing for it to grasp and it disappeared. Its panicked shrieks pierced the darkness and ended abruptly.

Shaking and still gasping, Makilien looked up at Sirion. She didn't say anything, but the relief in her eyes was enough.

In the brief time the two had been distracted, goblins and Shaikes crowded in around them, and they found little room to defend. With the edge of the wall behind them, they stood shoulder to shoulder, mindful not to get pressed back too far. The fight was fierce, but finally they regained ground.

Out of the darkness, a resounding crash came again. Another attack on the gate. A minute later, two more followed. Makilien grimaced. Zirtan was not relying only on trolls to break through this time. Their plans had been thwarted yet again. Dragon fire lit up the sky here and there, but most lasted only briefly. A roar of pain echoed just before another projectile hit the gate.

"The catapults are too heavily armed," Sirion said gravely, during a lull. "They are surrounded by ballistae and archers. The dragons can barely get close enough to do any damage without sacrificing themselves."

Makilien swallowed hard. If the dragons could not stop the catapults, it was only a matter of time before the gate was broken and hordes of enemy soldiers would pour into the city.

The night drew on without respite, punctuated every so often by catapult fire, either at the gate or elsewhere. Soldiers, weary from two nights of battle, found their defense weakening. The enemy seemed to outnumber them on the wall. Makilien believed this would be it, their last stand for freedom, but then dawn broke across the sky. As the light grew, the fighting slowed once more. The sun rose, and the enemies ceased climbing the ropes. At last, everything became quiet.

For a long moment, it seemed everyone just stood where they were. Makilien had never been so dead-tired in all her life. She almost couldn't stand as she cast her eyes listlessly over the carnage. So many lives had been slain.

Then, slowly, soldiers moved toward the stairs. Gathering her energy, she re-sheathed her sword. Sirion came to stand next to her. She looked at him, thankful he had survived the night, and managed a weak smile. Sirion smiled in return and put his arm around her shoulders. Helping her support her injured knee, the two of them made their way to the stairs.

:Chapter Thirty-six:

Care for the Wounded

"You should have someone look at your head," Sirion said as he helped Makilien sit at the base of the wall.

She touched the back of her head. Her hair was matted and sticky with blood.

"I'll see if I can find Vonawyn," Sirion told her.

Makilien nodded and leaned against the wall. It hurt her head, but she was too exhausted to care. For the next several minutes, she sat drifting in and out of sleep. Finally, when she opened her eyes again, she blinked, bringing Sirion into focus. Beside him walked Vonawyn and Aedan. She breathed out a sigh, but when she saw the blood glistening down Aedan's arm, she rose.

"Are you all right?" she asked.

"Yes, don't worry," Aedan assured her. "I wasn't paying enough attention, and a Shaike came up behind me. Thankfully it was my arm and not my head. What about you?"

"A Shaike hit me in the back of the head. Thankfully with his hand and not his sword."

Tired, little smiles grew between the two of them.

"Let's see about getting those injuries tended to," Vonawyn said, and led the way to the medical house.

Aedan insisted Makilien go first so Vonawyn got down and carefully inspected Makilien's wound.

"You have a long cut along the back of your head. It bled a lot, but is not deep and is not still bleeding," she said. "I'll clean it and it should be fine."

Once the cut had been tended, Vonawyn went on to change the bandages around Makilien's knee. As her friend worked, Makilien asked, "Did anyone see my father or anyone else since the fighting stopped?"

Her three companions shook their heads.

"I've only seen my brothers," Vonawyn told her.

And that was all anyone knew. Makilien sighed, worry settling in.

Finished with Makilien, Vonawyn moved on to Aedan. Sirion helped him remove his chain-mail, and Vonawyn rolled up his bloodstained sleeve. Everyone grimaced at the large open wound just above Aedan's elbow.

"It's quite deep," Vonawyn said. "It looks like it may go all the way to the bone. I'll have to clean and stitch it."

Makilien waited until Vonawyn had finished and Aedan had slipped back into his chain-mail to get up.

"I need to find my father."

Sirion and Aedan volunteered to go with her.

"My skills are needed here," Vonawyn told them. "But come tell me when you've found everyone."

Makilien gave her a nod, and she, Sirion, and Aedan worked their way through the injured soldiers to the wall, checking along the way for their friends among the wounded.

Earnestly, they searched the faces of the crowd for anyone familiar, soon spotting Lord Darand and Darian with Nirgon. Carmine and Emaril stood alongside Eborin at the gate while the other dragons were scattered throughout the area. Makilien was glad to see only a few dragons appeared to be missing. As they continued on, they met up with Lord Glorlad, and then Lord Elnauhir and his sons. Halandor and Loron joined them with Torick and Gilhir following shortly.

"Has anyone seen my father?" Makilien asked, her voice edged with panic. It was odd not to find him with her friends.

"No, I haven't," Halandor answered regretfully, and the others shook their heads.

Makilien's stomach twisted in a tight knot. She took a deep breath, trying to remain calm, but fear gnawed at her.

"I'll help you find him," Halandor was quick to offer.

He joined Makilien and the others in the search. They worked their way from one end of the crowd to the other, but still found nothing. Dread clutched Makilien's heart. *He has to be all right*, she told herself. *Oh, Elohim, please let us find him all right.*

Halandor gave Makilien's shoulder a gentle, reassuring squeeze. "We could have missed him," he said, keeping his voice light and hopeful. "We'll go through again."

Once more they moved through the soldiers, calling Néthyn's name and asking anyone they could if they'd seen him. Makilien prayed they'd just missed him. But no one could say they had come across him, and Néthyn did not appear amidst the faces. When they reached the other side of the gate near one of the stairs, they stopped.

Here, Torick joined them and asked, "Nothing yet?"

Halandor shook his head.

Makilien's chest tightened with tears waiting to be spilled. Something had happened. In her heart she knew it, but she tried to cling to hope. She looked desperately into the faces of her friends, voice breaking as she asked, "Now what?"

"We'll keep looking," Halandor assured her, but he was more solemn now. "We need to check the wounded at the medical house and check the men still on the wall."

Makilien knew this included the dead.

"I can check the medical house," Torick offered.

"I'll go with you," Aedan said, knowing two people could search faster.

Halandor nodded, and the two of them walked off. That left Makilien, Halandor, and Sirion to search the wall. Makilien struggled to prepare herself for what they might find as they climbed the stairs. Her stomach churned, clenching and turning. She wanted to sink to her knees and cry, to have someone tell her it would be all right, but she had to search. She had to find him.

They fanned out across the wall. Uninjured soldiers worked quickly to carry their wounded comrades down to the medical house, but they were not even close to aiding everyone yet. Hundreds of bodies littered the wall. Some of the soldiers moaned and cried out in pain.

Carefully, Makilien stepped around each body, grimacing and giving sympathetic looks to those who were conscious. All she could do was tell them help was coming as she continued searching for the familiar face of her father. She had to blink rapidly at times to keep her eyes from blurring with tears. She felt she might be sick as the roiling of her stomach increased with the smell of blood.

"Father, where are you?" she murmured to herself.

Unpleasant thoughts raced through Makilien's despairing mind. What if he had been shot? Or slain by a Shaike? Maybe he'd even been killed in one of the catapult attacks. She knew how easy it could be to fall over the edge. It could have happened to him too. The terrible thoughts of death clamored to overwhelm her, but she shook her head and drew in a deep breath to rid her mind of such images.

She paused to blink away the tears that had collected and looked around. One of the craters left by the night's catapult attacks was a few yards ahead. Jagged rocks lay scattered around it. Among the rocks, bodies lay, covered in dust and debris. None of them moved.

Makilien's eyes swept over them, but caught on one. The dark brown jerkin and chain-mail did not belong to any of the Elves or the soldiers of Eldor, Beldon, or Rhûnland. Makilien's heart first missed a beat and then pounded against her ribs. She took a step forward, hesitantly, scared to move at first, terrified of what she would find. But just that step closer and she knew.

"Father!"

She scrambled to his side, dropping to her knees. She brushed the rocks off his back, and, using all her strength, rolled him over. Makilien gasped and fear knifed through her. Blood stained the front of her father's jerkin from high on the left side, and a crimson pool of it had collected on the stones where he'd lain. Blood too stained one side of his pale face.

"Father!" A sob broke from Makilien's chest and she cried, "Please, Elohim, don't let him be dead!"

She could not tell if he was breathing.

Sirion and Halandor knelt next to Makilien, and Sirion put his fingers to Néthyn's neck. Makilien's frantic eyes locked on his face. Her heart pounded in her ears as she held her breath, waiting. *Please!* she pled over and over.

Finally, Sirion looked up. "He's alive."

Makilien let out her breath, faint with relief.

"But his pulse is weak," Sirion continued. "It looks like he's lost a lot of blood. We need to get him to Vonawyn."

Moving quickly, Halandor slipped his arms under Néthyn's shoulders and Sirion took his legs. Carefully, they lifted him up and hurried toward the stairs. Makilien led the way, frequently looking over her shoulder and praying her father would survive.

When they neared the medical house, Makilien spotted Vonawyn and called her friend's name. When the Elf saw Halandor and Sirion carrying Néthyn, she rushed to meet them. She took in the sight of his wounds and instructed, "Bring him over here."

She led them through the gathering wounded and stopped where she had room enough to work. Halandor and Sirion gently lowered Néthyn to the ground.

"We need to get his chain-mail and shirt off so I can see the wound," Vonawyn told them, her voice calm yet tinged with the concern she didn't allow to show.

With everyone helping, they removed Néthyn's jerkin and armor and slowly pulled his shirt off, exposing his injury. Beginning at his collarbone, a jagged wound ran down to the middle of his chest.

"A Shaike must have done this," Vonawyn murmured, more to herself than anyone. She lightly ran her fingers along his ribs. "No bones are broken from what I can tell. There is bruising."

Fresh blood oozed from the wound. Vonawyn handed Makilien her father's shirt. "Press this to the wound to stop the bleeding while I gather supplies. I'll be right back."

Makilien did as instructed and used both hands to press the shirt to the wound. Her eyes settled on her father's face. The blood from some unseen wound contrasted starkly with his ashen skin. She longed for him to open his eyes. She knew he was alive, she could feel the rise and fall of his chest under her hands, but he looked dead.

Tears welled in her eyes, and her throat closed. She blinked. Two tears spilled down her cheeks, leaving glistening tracks through the grime. Makilien sniffed and wiped her face with the back of her hand. Sirion rested his hand on her back, and Halandor said, "I'm sure he will be all right, Makilien. He's strong, and Vonawyn will take care of him."

She nodded and sniffed again. "I just hate to see him like this." She paused, fighting a flood of tears. "He could have died so easily."

"But he's still here," Halandor told her gently.

Makilien nodded again and worked to gain control over her emotions.

In a few minutes, Vonawyn returned. Aedan and Torick followed after her, their faces expressing their concern. Makilien moved to give Vonawyn room to work and knelt so she could rest her father's head in her lap.

Vonawyn first took time to look at his head wound.

"There's a gash along his temple, but it's not serious." She then refocused on the wound to his chest. From her supplies, she withdrew a cloth and waterskin. After wetting the cloth, she cleaned away the blood around the wound. Finally, she picked up a full vial of antiseptic. She glanced at the men. "I will need you to hold him. It's likely the pain will wake him."

Halandor and Sirion held him down so he would not move and further injure himself. Vonawyn removed the cap from the vial and began to pour. At first, Néthyn did not respond, which concerned Makilien, but then he stirred as the cleansing liquid seeped deep into his wound. He groaned and tried to get up, but Halandor and Sirion stopped him. His eyes blinked open several times, but were not yet seeing clearly.

"It's all right, Father. It's all right," Makilien murmured. "We're just helping you. The pain will lessen."

Her father groaned again, grimacing. It hurt Makilien to see him in pain. Finally, his eyes blinked open again and focused on her face.

"Makilien," he said hoarsely.

Through tears, she smiled. "Yes, I'm here."

Vonawyn handed Makilien the waterskin. "Give him some water."

She let a little water trickle into her father's mouth. His eyes had closed, but he looked relieved to have a drink. When they opened again, he asked, "What happened?"

"It looks like you were injured by a Shaike and then probably knocked unconscious by debris from a catapult attack," Makilien answered.

Cringing, he nodded. "Yes, I remember now."

By this time Vonawyn had threaded a needle and was about to begin stitching the wound. Makilien hoped it would not cause her father too much more pain.

"Did the gate hold?" Néthyn questioned.

"Yes," Makilien answered. "Zirtan's army has again withdrawn for the day."

Her father slowly exhaled.

Vonawyn looked at Makilien, ready to begin stitching.

"Father, Vonawyn is going to stitch your wound, all right?"

Néthyn gave another weak nod.

Vonawyn was a swift worker, for which Makilien was glad. Her father grimaced, but it did not take long to finish. Vonawyn wiped away the fresh blood and focused on Néthyn's face.

"I am going to have you taken to the palace. It would be far too dangerous for you to try to fight again in your condition."

Néthyn sighed, but was too weak to protest the decision.

"We'll get a stretcher," Torick said.

When he and Aedan returned, they lifted Néthyn onto the stretcher and Halandor and Sirion prepared to carry it.

"I'm going with," Makilien said. "It will be difficult for my mother and Leiya to see him injured."

"When you get there," Vonawyn replied, "have my mother finish cleaning away the blood and clean the wound to his head."

Makilien nodded, expression turning serious. Her voice dropped low. "He will be all right, won't he?"

Vonawyn gave her a reassuring smile. "Yes. His chainmail took the brunt of the attack. It saved his life."

Makilien blew out a sigh. "Thank you for taking care of him, Vonawyn."

The Elf smiled and touched her arm before turning to put a clean cloth over Néthyn's wound to protect it on the way.

Halandor and Sirion lifted the stretcher and started for the palace. Makilien walked alongside her father, keeping a close watch on him and hoping he would still be conscious when they arrived, for her mother's sake. She could not help but be glad to know her father would be safe at the palace, though he would not wish to leave the battle.

When they arrived, they took Makilien's father in through the throne room. The commotion of their arrival soon brought many of the servants as well as Lorelyn, Makilien's mother, and Leiya.

"Néthyn!"

Makilien went quickly to her mother to ease her distress. "He's all right, Mother. He's injured, but he'll be all right."

Hanna hurried to her husband's side and took his hand. Néthyn smiled weakly up at her. Leiya rushed to stand next to her mother. Makilien hated for her to see their father still bloodied, but she did not stop her.

"Papa," Leiya said in a wavering voice.

Néthyn released Hanna's hand for a moment and touched Leiya's face. "I'm all right."

In the intense emotion of the moment, Makilien struggled not to succumb again to tears. Drawing a deep breath, she turned to Lorelyn. "Vonawyn told me to ask you if you would finish cleaning and treating my father's wounds."

Lorelyn nodded. "Of course. Bring him to the healing quarters."

Halandor and Sirion turned. Hanna and Leiya stayed right at Néthyn's side. Along the way, Lorelyn looked at Makilien with a hopeful smile.

"Vonawyn, she's all right?"

"Yes, she is fine," Makilien assured her, scolding herself for not even thinking to tell the poor Elf woman sooner how her family had faired the last two nights of battle. "Lord Elnauhir and your sons are as well. I saw each of them before I came here."

Relief relaxed Lorelyn's pensive expression, and she asked after the others.

In the healing quarters, Makilien took Leiya aside while Lorelyn and Hanna tended Néthyn. She thought it best not to let her little sister see their father's grievous wound. Leiya seemed quite content with this time with Makilien and immediately asked about the battle. Makilien told her what she could, but spared any of the gruesome details.

"Mama let me watch a little from our balcony," Leiya told her, the little girl's eyes wide and expressive. "It looked scary."

"It is scary."

"There are so many bad guys."

Makilien nodded silently, for a moment carried away by the scenes of battle so fresh in her mind.

"Sometimes, when I wake up at night, Mama is still out watching." Once again, Leiya captured her attention. Her little sister's expression drooped. "I think she cries when she watches."

Makilien looked over her shoulder at their mother, her heart hurting with compassion and concern. Her mother did look very weary.

"I hear her praying too," Leiya went on as she perked up a little. She quickly added, "And I pray."

Makilien smiled at her. "That's very good, Leiya."

When Hanna and Lorelyn had finished with Néthyn, he was brought upstairs and made comfortable in bed. Now that he had been seen to, Halandor and Sirion prepared to return to the wall. Before they left, Halandor came to the bedside. His voice lowered as he spoke to Néthyn.

"If Zirtan breaks through our defenses and his army reaches the second gate, take your family, Lorelyn, and anyone else here and get out of the city. There are gates to the west. You will have to go through the outer edge, but I don't think you will be noticed. Flee to Elimar. You will only have a couple of days before Zirtan spreads his army out across the country to make sure he has complete control. From Elimar, you can figure out where to go so you will not be enslaved or directly under his rule. Even if you have to return to Reylaun."

Slowly, Néthyn nodded. The gravity of Halandor's instructions settled heavily in the room. A shiver of dread raced through Makilien's body. An escape plan for her family, though greatly appreciated, made defeat seem too certain.

Both Halandor and Sirion turned to leave then. At the door, Sirion paused. He glanced back at Makilien and motioned to her. She went to him, meeting his eyes.

"Makilien, if it is what you want, stay here with your family," he told her, his tone serious, almost pleading. "You do not need to come back to the wall."

Makilien opened her mouth to speak, but no words came. She wanted to stay. She really did.

Sirion touched her arm and gave it a squeeze. For a long moment, they just stood there, realizing if she stayed, this could very well be the last time they were together. Finally, he turned and walked down the hall to where Halandor waited. Eyes glued to them, tears rose up inside Makilien. Desperation willed her to call Sirion back. She wanted him to stay with her. To be safely away from another night of battle. But she bit her tongue as indecision and struggle warred within her heart. Should she stay here with her family or follow him where they would likely both lose their lives?

As the two men disappeared from sight, Makilien breathed a deep sigh and returned to her father's bedside, still undecided. On the edge of the mattress, Makilien sat with Leiya while their mother sat on the other side. It made her heart glad to see that her father could rest comfortably. She was so proud of him. He'd fought and survived two nights of fierce battle. She was also relieved he'd be here with her mother and Leiya whatever happened.

No one said much. It was enough just to be together for this time. But Makilien was preoccupied. Over and over she changed her mind, causing terrible turmoil inside. *I don't know what to do, Elohim,* she prayed in desperation. *What choice is the right one for me to make? Should I stay with my family or go back?*

She had no immediate answer, but as she sorted through all her jumbled thoughts and emotions, things slowly became clearer as definite thoughts formed, giving her peace when she finally made her decision.

An hour passed by. Makilien cherished every moment of it. How dearly she loved her family. She gazed at her mother. Though the woman's husband lay injured, she looked happy— happy to have him and her children with her.

It hurt Makilien to take that away again, but she said in a quiet, yet confident tone, "I think it's time I return to the wall."

They all looked at her.

"You're not staying?" Her mother's eyes were painfully pleading.

Makilien's resolve wavered a little, but she had made up her mind. "I am a fighter. I always have been. Even years ago back in Reylaun." She said this with a cross between a laugh and a sob. Pausing a moment to control the emotions trying to rise up and overwhelm her, she went on, "I want so desperately to stay with you, but . . . I just can't walk away from this now. I have to see it through."

Though it pained every thread of her being, Hanna nodded. This acceptance from her mother was itself nearly enough to destroy Makilien's hold on her emotions. She moved around the bed and wrapped her arms around the older woman.

"I know I must let you go and trust Elohim to bring you back to me," Hanna said with as much strength as she could manage.

Makilien held her for a long moment, tears gathering against her closed eyelids. "I love you, Mother."

Hanna rubbed her back and squeezed her tight before finally letting go. Makilien then went to her father. He took her hand in his. "I'm so proud of the way you fight for what is right and what you love."

Makilien smiled even through teary eyes. However, a grim expression replaced it. She leaned closer to him and lowered her voice hoping maybe her mother may not hear, at least not enough to understand the implication of her words.

"I saw the gate before we came here. I don't think it's going to hold. Be ready to get Mother and Leiya away from here."

Makilien watched two tears slide down her father's cheeks and could not stop her own. He squeezed her hand, knowing she did not expect to see them again.

"I love you, my brave daughter."

"I love you too."

Makilien kissed his cheek and straightened, wiping her tears and hoping her mother did not suspect what her father knew.

She walked around the bed again to hug Leiya.

"Take good care of Father now, all right?"

Leiya nodded, making a strong effort not to cry. "All right."

Makilien walked to the door, but paused to look back at them.

"I love you all so much."

She then walked out into the hall and closed the door, heart heavy.

:Chapter Thirty-seven:

The Element
of Surprise

Tears trailed down Makilien's face as she made her way through the deserted heart of the city. She wiped her cheeks, but the tears still flowed. She couldn't stop them nor did she really want to.

When she reached the wall, the full horror of war, which she'd briefly escaped, assailed her. Grim-faced soldiers moved about, many battered and bloody, and all battle weary. The cries of the wounded echoed from the medical house. Glancing that way, it seemed there were more soldiers than could be cared for. A breeze sent smoke over the wall carrying with it the smell of not only charred wood, but bodies as well, and the scent of blood.

Makilien immediately felt sick and her head throbbed. Trying to block it out, she slowly worked her way through the crowd, searching. It was with great relief her eyes fell on Sirion standing with Halandor and Torick. She hurried to join them. They were at first surprised to see her, but taking in the sight of her ashen face, they were more concerned.

"Are you all right?" Halandor asked.

397

Makilien took a deep breath, trying to calm her body. "It all just hit me as I came back, the horror of all this." She paused, shaking her head. "I think I'll be all right in a few minutes."

But she didn't feel like she would be all right. A cold sweat made her both chilled and too warm. Her head buzzed as her stomach twisted. She took another deep breath attempting to settle it, but, finally, it was too much. She went down on one knee and emptied what little was in her stomach. It made her feel a little better, but all her energy was gone. After a moment, Sirion held out his hand and helped her up. Her friends each bore understanding expressions.

"You should rest," Halandor said with a hand on her shoulder.

"And drink some water," Torick added. "You may not be able to keep it down right away, but you are dehydrated."

He handed her a waterskin. She took a couple sips, and, though it didn't settle well at first, it stayed down. She knew her body craved it.

"You should eat when you can too," Halandor told her.

They led her down the wall to a less busy and crowded area and told her to sit down.

"Try to get some sleep," Halandor said.

Makilien hesitated and bit her lip.

"What is it?" he asked gently, seeing the uncertainty in her eyes.

With a sigh, Makilien hung her head. "After two nights of battle, I'm afraid if I try to sleep, that is all I will see."

"Would it help knowing I'll stay right here, and if not me, someone else?" Sirion asked.

Makilien looked into his kind face and then at Halandor and Torick. Finally, she nodded. It would not take away the images, but at least she'd have someone to comfort her if she could not sleep.

Before she lay down, Sirion pulled off his jerkin. He turned it inside out, folded it into bundle, and set it down for her to use as a pillow. She smiled at him.

"Thank you."

Though only cold stone lay beneath her when she lay down, her whole body thanked her for the rest. She closed her eyes. Her memories from the battle did indeed flood in, but she forced her mind on other things. She thought of Meniah and prayed for rest. She needed it for the coming night.

Black figures loomed up in a dark haze, and the roar of battle surrounded Makilien. She tried to raise her sword, but the weight of it was more than she could manage. Desperately, she tried again. Fear gripped her as enemies drew in . . .

Makilien sat upright with a gasp. Her heart hammered against her chest, and her eyes darted around. Though she sat in shadow, the area was bright with sunlight. Slowly, she exhaled, thankful to have awakened from the dreams that seemed to haunt every moment of sleep.

"Are you all right?"

She looked over her shoulder. Halandor sat against the wall near her. His eyes showed the signs of weariness, and Makilien hoped she had not just wakened him.

"I'm fine," she murmured. "Just dreams."

She wiped the back of her hand against her damp forehead. In adjusting her chain-mail, she found her clothing was also damp with sweat and clung to her body. Trying to ignore the unpleasantness of it, she sat back against the wall. Her stomach gave a sudden growl of fierce hunger.

"Sirion and Torick went to get some food," Halandor told her.

Though hungry, Makilien didn't feel she had much of an appetite. She would eat, however, just for the nourishment.

Watching the soldiers pass nearby, she sighed deeply. "The gate won't hold another night, will it?"

She turned her eyes and met Halandor's gaze. In his expression was bleak acceptance of the truth.

"No," he answered, "it won't."

A moment of silence stretched out between them, both considering exactly what that meant. Finally, Makilien spoke, though her voice wavered more than she wanted. "What are we going to do?"

"I spoke earlier with General Nirgon," Halandor said with enough strength in his tone to encourage her. "He was going to speak with the lords about riding out to meet Zirtan instead of waiting for the gate to fall."

Makilien consider this action. One way or another, they would face Zirtan on the battlefield tonight. Why not do it on their terms?

"How long did I sleep?" she asked, wondering how much time they had left.

"A few hours," Halandor answered. "It's a little after five o'clock now."

In a moment, Sirion and Torick returned with enough food for everyone. They divided it up between them and before eating, Halandor offered a prayer of thanks that they could take this advantage of rest and nourishment even with their enemies so near.

While they ate, they talked of the last two nights of battle, sharing their experiences. Aedan and Vonawyn joined them shortly after they began. It was apparently at Aedan's insistence that Vonawyn leave the medical house where she'd worked all day. Makilien was glad she did so, for the heavy weariness clearly showed in her friend's face.

They had nearly finished their meal when Loron also joined the group.

"It has been decided," he said. "We will ride out to meet Zirtan."

No one spoke, but Halandor gave a nod.

"General Nirgon believes it might be a good idea to ride out soon and take Zirtan by surprise," Loron went on. "It would at least give us a brief advantage. His men won't be prepared and we'll have a couple of hours of daylight left."

Everyone agreed with this logic and Loron added, "The general is with the lords now on the wall making the final decision."

Anxious to know what decision would be made, everyone rose and climbed one of the stairs to the top of the wall. Near the gate, all the lords stood in a group. Along with them, Eborin and Carmine stood over the men. It seemed a decision had already been reached. As they approached, Nirgon nodded to the lords. "I will inform the captains."

The group dispersed. When Nirgon turned and saw Makilien and the others, he stopped to speak with them.

"We are going to ride out to meet Zirtan and catch him by surprise. We will ride within the hour."

"We will be ready," Halandor replied.

Nirgon nodded, and before he moved away, he focused on Makilien. "How is your father? I heard he was injured."

"He will be all right," Makilien answered. "He is at the palace with my mother and sister."

"Good. It does me good to know he will recover," Nirgon said.

"Thank you for your concern, General."

Nirgon smiled and moved on to prepare their army for their last bold move against Zirtan.

As her friends spoke to the lords who lingered behind, Makilien stepped to the parapet to stare out over the immense ocean of enemies that would await them as soon as the gate opened. She could hardly believe it still appeared as though they had not lost many men. With a look over her shoulder, Makilien compared their army. The number of wounded who lay at the medical house seemed to match those who were still standing. Only half of their force remained.

She looked out over the wall once again, and the sheer size of the brutal enemy force was all too apparent. They outnumbered Eldor's shrinking army by at least five to one. Makilien knew with dreadful certainty in that moment that, unless a miracle took place, they stood no chance of victory. They hadn't the strength or numbers to take on such a force.

She breathed deeply and gazed up into the sky. *Will you save us this time, Elohim?* She truly did not know. Perhaps defeat was part of His overall plan for the future. Slowly, her mindset changed from optimism to grim acceptance of their fate. A miracle may come, but her hope was dim. Standing there, she told her Lord, *I am ready to die if it will further Your plans and Your glory.* Peace came with this declaration, yet sadness settled in her heart, for not only might she die, but all her friends as well.

In the midst of these thoughts, she sensed their presence as they surrounded her at the parapet. She turned to face them. Halandor, Loron, Torick, Sirion, Gilhir, Aedan, Vonawyn and her brothers were all there. They seemed to know the realization she'd come to and had the same acceptance in their eyes.

For a long moment, only silence hung between them, but then Torick spoke, quite softly at first as his eyes shifted between each person. "I don't do well with speeches or flowery words . . ." he paused, clearing his throat, "but I would like each of you to know what an honor it is for me to have fought beside you . . . to have served our Lord and our countries with you, and to have shared your friendship over all my long years. If this is where we find our paths end, I am greatly encouraged that it will only be the beginning of a life we will share together forever."

Tears welled up in Makilien's eyes. Rarely did Torick share the things in his heart with such deep emotion.

Halandor rested his hand on Torick's shoulder. "And I as well, my friend." He looked around to encompass everyone. "I've known no greater friends, nor warriors of such courage."

Finally, tears flowed from Makilien's eyes. Though goodbye was not spoken, these words of farewell cut deep into her heart. She spoke next, though it was with difficulty. Her voice trembled as she tried to form words out of the emotions in her heart.

"All of you remember what I was when I first met you. I can hardly believe where I am now, and each of you has made an impact in my life. You've helped me become who I am. Thank you."

More words were spoken, everyone taking a moment to say the things they wanted their friends to know. Makilien's tears fell freely, as did Vonawyn's. Makilien believed it was the first time she had ever witnessed the Elf cry. Even the eyes of the men held tears.

By now, most everyone had left the wall and gathered at the gate. Makilien and her friends moved to do the same. Once the entire army was mounted and present, Nirgon called for everyone's attention. Atop a tall, white stallion, his gaze swept over the army.

"Soldiers." His voice rang out across the courtyard, and all eyes focused on their general. "When this gate opens, we will need to move quickly for our attack to be effective and catch Zirtan off guard. Once out of the gate, all riders of Eldor, ride with me. Captain Gébrale and Lord Andron will take the riders of Rhûnland and Beldon to the right flank, and the Elves will follow Lord Elnauhir and Lord Glorlad to the left. The dragons will precede us from the air and take out the first lines of Zirtan's army."

The general paused for only a moment. "Before we ride out, I want to take this moment to go to Elohim. In Him is our only hope for victory."

Nirgon bowed his head, and all throughout the army, men did the same. Makilien closed her eyes and made her own plea in her heart as the general began, "Elohim, we come to You facing our greatest enemy and a force far beyond our strength to face. We have no hope, but in You. I pray, by Your hand, we might achieve victory if that is Your will for us. Give us protection, strength, and courage in these next hours and guide each of us through the decisions and actions we must take."

Though Nirgon's voice was strong, it quieted at the end, and Makilien barely heard him say amen. As she opened her eyes and looked around, she saw how exhaustion and the uncertainty of what was to come had taken a toll on everyone.

Her gaze turned back to Nirgon who faced the army again and said, "Zirtan may very well overcome us today . . . but let us show him those who are bound together in the truth of Elohim will not back down and will not give in to fear. We will stand firm in Elohim who is our fortress and our strength, and we will not be shaken. If the outcome today is to be for Zirtan, we will not grant him an easy victory. We will fight this battle with courage until the very last breath!"

His words lit a fire of grim determination in each one of them, and a loud cheer rose up, reverberating against the city walls and surrounding the entire army. Anticipation pounding in their hearts, Makilien and Sirion looked at each other. Sirion reached out and took Makilien's hand. Squeezing it gently, he brought it to his lips for a moment before reluctantly letting go.

Zirtan stalked across the field, scowling and cursing the people within the city.

"After two nights of vicious battle, how can they still cheer?" he raged. "They have nothing to hope for!"

Once night fell, their doom would come. There would be no more waiting. His men would fight until victory was achieved. Until every last man behind that wall lay dead.

"My lord!"

Zirtan's head jerked up at the sound of his captain's cry. The man pointed frantically toward the city. Zirtan's eyes went to the wall and widened in surprise. The city gate was opening. At first, gleeful triumph filled him. Eldor's pathetic army finally realized its doom and was surrendering. But then, he saw something he did not expect. The city's mounted army poured from the gate and with great speed, moved into formation to attack. He could not believe it. It could not be possible. Their small army was really coming to attack his massive force?

Once every rider had left the gate, the army charged across the plain, and up over Minarald's walls came the army of dragons. Spreading out in a long line across the sky, they flew just ahead of the advancing riders.

"This can't be," Zirtan muttered under his breath.

But the words of his captain confirmed it. "My lord, they are going to attack!"

Anger rose up in Zirtan so violently a couple of his men took a step back at the fury in their leader's expression. In a venomous voice, he commanded, "Then get ready to meet them!"

:Chapter Thirty-eight:

Bitter Rivals

A wide cascade of fire poured out upon the enemy, hiding them momentarily behind a shimmering curtain of flames and smoke. The riders slowed to let the fire consume their enemies and die away, but it was only a moment or two before the distance between the two armies closed. Makilien squeezed Antiro's reins tight as the painful thudding of her heart pounded against her ribs. The sound of it in her ears was drowned out by the thundering of hooves. The terrain and the seconds passed in a blur.

And all at once, a terrifying crash erupted as the armies met. Horses shrieked as they collapsed, impaled on enemy blades. Men screamed, but the riders still standing pushed on, pummeling their enemies, gaining as much ground as they could until their momentum faded. The charge ceased and vicious battle ensued. At first, Eldor's soldiers had the upper hand—the surprise attack worked and many enemy soldiers fell before them—but soon, Zirtan's men recovered and pressed in savagely.

With her sword in her right hand, Makilien pulled out her fighting axe with her left and used both weapons against the enemies closing in on either side of her. Many of her attacks were successful, but defending against so many used every bit of concentration. The pain in her muscles from so many days of battle worked hard to distract her, but she had to force it away.

Eldor's soldiers made a good stand while daylight lasted. They stood firm and their numbers remained strong, infused with confidence and a dim, but desperate hope of survival. But they could not stop dusk from falling, and the threat of coming darkness robbed their advantage. As if signaling the change in momentum, night gathered in around them, smothering the spark of hope.

Makilien barely had an opportunity to take her eyes from the fight, but as the sunlight faded, she took a moment to look around her, wondering if she fought alone or if a friendly face battled nearby. Out of the corner of her eye, she recognized Lord Darand. She focused in his direction and realized something was wrong. His horse stumbled, and, to Makilien's horror, fell, disappearing in the fray.

"Lord Darand!" she screamed, but her voice was lost in the clamor.

Fearing for the king's life, Makilien pushed Antiro through the mass around them and came at last to the spot where the king had fallen. Relief pulsed through her when she arrived and found Darand still alive and fighting for his life on the ground. Makilien jumped off of Antiro to aid him.

Once the immediate danger had been dealt with, Makilien turned to the king.

"My lord, take Antiro!"

Darand shook his head. "No."

But Makilien took his arm and looked him determinedly in the eyes. "Please, my lord."

Darand still hesitated, but any argument now would mean the death of both of them. Finally, he stepped around to Antiro's side and mounted.

"Antiro, keep Lord Darand safe," Makilien instructed.

Her horse gave a reluctant, but obedient nicker, and Makilien was forced to take her eyes from him to focus on the battle. At first, she felt lost in the fight. From the ground, she was much shorter than all her foes, save the goblins, and so many surrounded her. The beginnings of panic clutched her heart, but lifting her sword, she cut into the enemy. Most did not notice her coming, focused on other, more prominent threats. Makilien used this to her advantage. She pushed on, gaining small amounts of ground at a time, grimly satisfied with her success.

Entirely occupied by the two Shaikes in her path, Makilien drew her sword back, preparing for a surprise attack, but before she could swing forward again, a crushing force latched onto her arm and gave a yank. Landing hard on her back, she gasped and found her arm caught in the strong jaws of a mountain wolf. Fortunately, her vambrace kept its teeth from reaching flesh.

Now that she was on the ground, the wolf released her arm and lunged for her head. She threw her sword up just in time. The wolf's teeth clamped down on the blade. Makilien gave her sword a jerk. The wolf yelped as the sharp edge cut its mouth, and it jumped back. Scrambling to get up, Makilien only managed to scoot back a few feet before the wolf came at her again. She kicked it hard in the snout as it came close. The wolf snarled, but it gave her just enough time to get to her feet.

Holding the beast off with the point of her sword, Makilien and the wolf circled their small portion of the battlefield. The wolf growled and snapped, saliva dripping from its jaws. Breathing hard, Makilien glanced over her shoulder, fearing an attack from behind. During this apparent distraction, the wolf leapt. But Makilien jumped to the side just in time and delivered a powerful downward stroke to the wolf's neck. With a short, pained howl, it fell and did not rise.

Makilien spun around to meet any more enemies coming close. As her gaze darted amongst the roiling sea of combatants, she rejoiced at discovering a familiar face.

"Sirion!"

Even over the roar of battle, her voice reached him. He turned, sharing Makilien's relief. They fought through the enemies between them. Sirion too was on foot, and Makilien hoped it was not because poor Falene had been slain.

"Where's Antiro?" Sirion asked when at last they reached each other.

"I gave him to Lord Darand. His horse was killed," Makilien answered. "What about Falene?"

"She was injured," Sirion said. "I had to leave her."

Those were the only words they were able to exchange. Their enemies pressed in, and they turned to fight. Makilien was deeply relieved to have found Sirion. When the end came, she hoped it would come fighting beside him.

Now that darkness had fallen, the raging battle spread out over a massive area before the city. Makilien found it some surprise their army had been able to so steadfastly hold their ground for this long. She anticipated things to change quickly as the night progressed, but for now, it gave her encouragement.

After felling one of Zirtan's men and a goblin that had tried to take her by surprise, Makilien raised her sword to meet another enemy coming from the side. When she faced him fully, she gasped and her sword dropped to her side while she stared wide-eyed. As soon as he had slain his opponent, Sirion spun around. He too just stared at the fierce warrior dressed in the typical black and red garb of Zirtan's men.

"Derrin?" Makilien almost couldn't believe it to be him. The cold, hard cruelty of his expression was not familiar. "We . . . we thought you were dead!"

Derrin's eyes cut right into her. "And were relieved, no doubt."

Makilien's mouth opened in shock and she quickly said, "Derrin, no. We mourned your death." She just stared at him for a moment, trying to let his appearance sink in. "What happened? How are you still alive? What are you doing with Zirtan's men?"

"I *am* one of his men," Derrin declared. "I offered them my loyalty in exchange for my life."

The shock of this hit hard, and Makilien didn't even think before saying, "You don't have to stay with them. You can join our fight now."

Derrin laughed scornfully at this suggestion. "Join a lost cause?" he scoffed. "No, I've found where I belong. I have respect and power. I have everything I want . . . almost."

Apprehension tingled up Makilien's spine at the cruel edge to his voice. This wasn't the same Derrin she'd known all her life in Reylaun. Time with the enemy had given him a dangerous and dark confidence.

"I have an offer for you," he went on, his voice never softening. "Come with me and your life will be spared. You can escape the certain doom of your army if you'll just lay down your weapons and surrender to me."

Makilien almost laughed at the absurdity of such an offer, but her hard tone matched his, leaving no question in her answer. "I certainly will not go anywhere with you, and neither will I abandon my friends in this fight. I will fight to victory or to death, whichever one Elohim has ahead of me."

"Then you leave me no choice, but to persuade you to reconsider." Derrin raised his sword as he took a step forward.

Makilien gripped hers again in both hands bringing it to a defensive position, but Sirion stepped in front of her.

"Come any closer to her and you'll regret it," he said, leveling Derrin with a warning glare.

Derrin just smirked, his blatant arrogance scaring Makilien. She could hardly imagine it, but what if he had the means to back up his confidence?

"Spoken like a man intent on protecting the woman he loves," Derrin replied, his smirk growing into a malicious grin.

"That is exactly my intent," Sirion said, his voice low and determined.

"So you do love her?"

"I do."

Derrin turned icy blue eyes to Makilien. "Just friends, that's what you tried to make me think. You're a liar, and I knew it all along."

"I didn't lie to you," Makilien shot back, angered by the accusation. "The relationship between Sirion and me was never any of your business, so I didn't talk about it. There was never anything between you and me. I've told you that over and over. There never was before I met Sirion, and there never will be now."

"But you should have chosen me!" Derrin's simmering anger finally erupted. "*I* am the one who has always been there. *I* am the one who always yearned for your love."

"If you truly loved me, you'd walk away. Or better yet, leave Zirtan's army and fight with us."

Derrin gave a cold, cruel laugh, though it was edged with barely controlled rage. "As I said, why would I join the losing side? No, I'm quite happy where I am. Zirtan has promised me a place among his closest men. The only thing I don't have yet is you."

"You're mad, Derrin," Makilien said, shaking her head. "You've been obsessed with me for all these years and you've let your obsession drive you to madness."

"You don't understand!"

"How can I? This behavior and the action you have taken is not the Derrin I've always known. You refuse to see I am not the only thing worth living for, and it's driven you to this. If you turn to Elohim, He can give you—"

"Enough!" Derrin spat. "I do not want to hear about Elohim."

Makilien's brows lowered, as did her voice. "Then we are done talking."

Derrin glared back at her. "Very well, if that is what you want. But if I can't have you, then I won't let him have you either."

He pointed his sword at Sirion.

"Derrin, this is crazy!" Makilien cried.

Seeing the unquenchable fury in his eyes, Sirion raised his sword and approached Derrin, but Makilien grabbed him by the arm.

"Sirion, no!"

He turned to her, his expression set, yet calm. "This has to end somewhere, Makilien. If all he'll settle for is a fight then I am more than willing to fight for you."

Makilien looked into his eyes and the certainty and determination there. "But Sirion . . ."

Gently but firmly, he pushed her aside and murmured, "Stay back."

He turned to Derrin who stood waiting, looking only too eager to face his rival.

Cold fear spread through Makilien. Sirion was one of the most skilled warriors she knew. Surely Derrin of all people would be no match for him, but Derrin's fearless manner gave her a horrible feeling that was not so.

Sirion stood and raised his sword, waiting for Derrin to move in attack. And attack he did. He flew at Sirion and unleashed a brutal series of attacks. Sirion barely had time to place his sword in the right spots to block. Fresh and well rested, he would have fared better, but the long days of battle had destroyed his Half-Elven advantage. The force and skill of Derrin's attack took him by surprise. The enemy had taught him well, *very* well.

Derrin remained on the offensive, driving his opponent back. Sirion carefully defended, paying close attention to the other man's style, looking for a weakness. He had to admit, Derrin's attacks were nearly flawless, but they were too rash and fueled by blind rage. Eventually, Sirion found where he left himself open.

Once he had a good understanding of how Derrin fought, Sirion began his counterattack. It rattled Derrin at first, but he recovered in a moment, and any time Sirion took the opportunity to advance, it only fueled Derrin's anger. With every one of Sirion's attacks, Derrin responded in an instant with two more. Back and forth they traded blows, their swords shrieking as they met and parted. Sirion hoped to find Derrin slowing, but the man seemed tireless.

Sweat poured down the sides of Sirion's face and neck. His muscles cramped with fatigue. Then, with a loud clang, their swords locked. Standing chest to chest, they looked each other in the eyes. Hatred spewed from Derrin's, and Sirion just shook his head in pity.

Just as he put his weight behind his blade to force the other man away, Derrin drove his armored elbow into the side of Sirion's head. Sirion stumbled, dazed, and heard Makilien scream. She tried to come to his aid, but Derrin shot her such an icy look, it froze her in place.

Warm blood trickled from the gash running from just below Sirion's eye down past his cheekbone. Derrin had taken first blood and with it he already savored victory. But Sirion's survival instinct kicked in on high. His fatigue momentarily forgotten, he spun around and drove into Derrin with a force he had not anticipated. Derrin now found himself on the defense. Sirion's speed returned to him, and he summoned all of his Elven training.

Just as quickly as Derrin had caught him by surprise, Sirion put a deep gash in the inside of Derrin's right arm. Before he could recover, Sirion slashed across the top of Derrin's knee and drove the pommel of his sword into his shoulder. With a gasp, Derrin fell hard to his back. The point of Sirion's sword was at his throat in an instant. Sirion stared down at him, breathing hard, his face dripping sweat and blood. Derrin glared up at him.

"Go ahead," he goaded. "Kill me."

But Sirion shook his head. "No." He bent down to look Derrin in the eyes. "Remember this. I had you at my mercy, and I let you live hoping one day you will see the truth Makilien tried to share with you. The truth that is in Elohim. I will not send you into eternity knowing you are without it."

He straightened and walked to Makilien. Her face was still pale with the fear of watching him and Derrin duel. He touched her shoulder reassuringly, and the two of them turned. Soon they were once again engaged in battle leaving Derrin to stumble off to nurse his wounded body and pride.

:Chapter Thirty-nine:

The Last Stand

On the ground, Aedan cut through a group of goblins that all fell shrieking. Armor glinted to his right, and he spun to meet his next foe. The moonlight had a distinct way of reflecting on the enemy's dark armor that distinguished them from ally soldiers. The man tried to take his head, but Aedan ducked and caught the man in the chest with his blade.

A short blast of dragon fire nearby lit up the night as the man fell. Aedan surveyed the area and caught sight of a couple fellow soldiers, but everywhere surrounding them were hordes of enemy men. Eldor's army was engulfed in a sea of black.

He threw himself at his next opponent, his sword coming down hard. The man blocked it and counterattacked. He swung low for Aedan's knees and then diagonally, aiming for his chest. Aedan dodged the first attack and blocked the second. He then came at the man with his own series of attacks, but each was unsuccessful as the man was quick and strong. On the last attack, their swords locked for a moment and Aedan looked into the moonlit face of his foe. Familiarity hit him immediately, and recognition was quick to enter the other man's eyes.

"Father," Aedan murmured.

He took a step back, stunned for a moment, but all the cruel deeds his father had done raced into his mind. The mark his father had forced him to bear, the abandonment as a child, and the evilness of his father's heart. Who knew how many countless others he had hurt or killed? Aedan's anger over this ignited within. He raised his sword and attacked his father with the intent to stop him from ever harming anyone again.

Seeing the wrath, his father anticipated a brutal fight. He prepared and blocked each of his son's successive attacks. When Aedan's momentum slowed, his father came at him with the same fierceness he'd just unleashed, but Aedan was not shaken. Though both were almost equal in skill, Aedan sensed his father didn't possess his measure of youthful strength.

The war raging around them faded into the background as their focus settled solely on each other. The fight ranged over a large area of the battlefield. Everyone seemed to move out of their way as the two fierce combatants came near. Aedan's muscles ached at the constant back and forth blows, but he refused to acknowledge the signals of pain they sent to his brain.

When Jaeson's sword suddenly found Aedan's shoulder, the chain-mail saved him from injury, but the reality of it gave him a fresh burst of fury. His emotion driven strength and speed were finally wearing down his father's defense. Jaeson slowed, and his moves lost their forcefulness and precise placement.

Sensing this decline in his father's tactics, Aedan upped his attacks. He hacked at his father's blade, driving him backwards. Jaeson stumbled once, and both he and Aedan knew the fight would soon end. When their swords came together, Jaeson made one last desperate effort. He grabbed one of Aedan's wrists and dropped his sword to grab the other. Aedan yanked against him, but his father held fast, attempting to wrestle him to the ground. Pushing and jerking, Aedan tried to break free of the iron grip.

After a hard-fought struggle, he moved himself into a position to drive his knee up into his father's stomach. Jaeson gasped and released Aedan's wrists as he doubled over. Before he could straighten, Aedan slammed the pommel of his sword down between his father's shoulders. As the man collapsed, Aedan picked up his father's sword and flung it far out of reach. Slowly, Jaeson pushed to his knees and looked up.

"You've become a fierce warrior," he rasped between gulps of air. "Exactly what I would expect from my son."

"Quiet!" Aedan snapped. "I may be your son, but it's not something I'll ever be proud of."

Jaeson swayed with the exhaustion of the fight. "You are the victor. Go ahead and take what you are after."

At this provocation, Aedan raised his sword above his head, poised to strike. He stood, sword suspended in the air, arms shaking and mind flooding with all his father's horrible deeds. Right here he could end them for good. His anger waged a bitter fight and his emotions screamed at him to do it, but he lowered his blade. To kill his father here, like this, would only be revenge. He couldn't go through with that.

Aedan watched a smirk grow on his father's face. Now, instead of the selfish anger that had been driving him, his fury changed to a righteous anger for the atrocities Zirtan and men like his father committed. Taking his father by surprise, he grabbed his jerkin and yanked him close. The smirk left Jaeson's face in an instant as he peered into his son's intense eyes.

419

"Do you even see what is going on here?" Aedan demanded, chest heaving. "Can't you see the lives you are destroying? The pain and the sorrow inflicted on those who are innocent? Look around you!" he shouted, jerking his father and gesturing with his sword to the raging battle being fought around them. "Good men are dying by the thousands! Men who have not gathered for selfish gain or some cruel quest for domination, but men who are here to protect their families—their wives and their children—who sit behind the city walls fearing for the lives of their men, most of whom will never again come home to them.

"Can you not see the evilness of Zirtan? He gives no value to life, but one day he will meet his end and pay for the pain he has caused, and so will those who have followed him," he said with heated emphasis. "Elohim is real, Father, and He is in control. How else do you think Eldor has stood against Zirtan's force for this long? How else could a young woman have defeated Zirtan's general? Zirtan may gain victory tonight, but in the end the victory will be Elohim's. Consider carefully which side you truly want to be on when you stand before Him someday."

Aedan stared hard at his father. He'd spoken with all the conviction in his heart, yet he still found himself surprised when something crept into his father's eyes. Deep in their depths a tiny spark lit as if something dawned there. The hardness of his father's expression had softened.

Aedan's heart beat with desperate hope. Had his words penetrated the cold wall around his father's heart? Did he finally see the evil in Zirtan, the one he had been following for so many years? Everything inside of Aedan begged Elohim for his father's understanding. Holding his breath, he waited for him to speak.

But Jaeson's eyes suddenly darted past Aedan and widened. "Behind you," he warned.

Aedan looked over his shoulder to find the mountainous silhouette of a Shaike. The creature's sword was already hurtling toward his head. With barely any time to act, Aedan threw himself to the ground and the blade sailed right over him. He scrambled up in time to block the next strike and came after the Shaike with his own attack. As he had done before, Aedan was unrelenting, and soon the Shaike dropped before him.

When he was certain it would not rise, he turned quickly to the spot where he'd left his father. Deep disappointment crushed his heart. His father was gone.

Aedan hung his head and groaned. He'd been close, so close, to making an impact on his father. He'd seen it in his expression and in his warning of danger. There had been an opening, a softening of his heart. But now what would happen? Would he ever give it any thought again?

Please, Elohim, give me strength, Makilien's plea whispered desperately from her heart. She was spent, barely able to move to defend against her foes. With each one she wondered if it would be her last. She looked often to Sirion, terrified to see him fall, and her heart aching for him to see her die. But how much time was left before one of the two took place?

A dragon soared overhead, the flap of its wings sending down gusts of air. Fire poured down, and a troll bellowed close by. Makilien glanced up into the starry sky. Malachi hovered, illuminated by his firelight. The troll tried to get away, but its lumbering gate was too slow.

In the light, Makilien was able to see several more trolls nearby, slowly moving through the battle, leaving a wide path of destruction. As soon as the one was dead, Malachi flew to the next. The troll flailed its arms and club, but the dragon was out of reach. Yet, just before his fire consumed it, a loud mechanical noise came from somewhere behind Makilien. A dark streak shot into the sky, and Malachi gave a horrible, pained roar as he was struck. He flapped awkwardly in the air for a moment before plummeting.

"No!" Makilien cried.

The cold, cruel reality of what had just happened gripped her and sucked her breath away. She watched the dragon slam to the ground where he lay still. Hot tears poured down her cheeks.

"Malachi," she wept.

Sirion's arm came tightly around her shoulders, offering comfort, but in the next instant, urgency cut into his voice as he said her name. She looked up to see a troll towering above them with his great club raised over its head. As the club came down, Sirion pushed Makilien forward. She stumbled and fell, rolling to get away from the troll who hammered the club with devastating force into the ground only a couple feet away. Makilien started to rise as the troll raised the club up again, but this time the creature swung the club low in a wide arc. She dropped back down to her stomach to avoid being struck. The massive club flew right over her, taking out all the soldiers near the troll, friend and enemy.

Makilien pushed to her knees and crawled to safety behind the troll, out of danger of its club. She scrambled to her feet, frantic eyes searching.

"Sirion!" she screamed.

But his face did not appear anywhere, nor did he answer her call. She tried again and again, screaming until her voice was hoarse. As soon as the troll had moved on she searched everywhere, ignoring the battle, but could not find him. Her tears came streaming with the numbing horror of the situation. Malachi was dead, Sirion was missing, and she was alone again.

"Oh, Elohim," she cried, wishing she were not here on this battlefield. She wanted it to be over. She had nothing left. Her shoulders heaved with sobs, and her arms shook with exertion, barely having the strength left to raise her sword. All her worst nightmares were coming true. But she couldn't just give up. She didn't want to die that way. Forcing her mind to stay on Elohim and Meniah, Makilien turned to her closest foe. She didn't know how she'd survive even one more confrontation, but she had to go out fighting.

Darand gazed out across the dark sea of soldiers, his heart weeping at the loss of such an overwhelming number of good men. He did not know how many still stood, whether he had lost his son or his friends. Hope of victory had faded, he just didn't know yet when defeat would finally come. The king cast a sad glance at the walls of his beloved city, and he ached for the people inside. What horror would they witness once he and the rest of the army had fallen? Helplessness fell heavy on his shoulders. No action he could take could save them, so he did the only thing he could, look back to the battle.

He turned Antiro toward the nearest group of enemies. The horse had been a faithful companion to him these several hours. He thought for a moment of Makilien. Did she still live? What a tragedy for her and so many other young people to be slaughtered so cruelly.

Darand abandoned these thoughts when a man stepped out in front of Antiro, a long sword gleaming in one hand. Antiro reared up, thrashing his hooves, and came down snorting fiercely. Darand tried to back him up, but he was too late. In a flashing arc, the man swung his sword, and it slashed across Antiro's forelegs. Antiro shrieked in pain, stumbling. He tried to gain his footing, but his knees buckled.

The king jumped off the horse's back as Antiro fought to stand again, but fell hard to his side with a pained whinny. Darand wanted to do something to aid him, but his attention honed in on the man before him, a man who would not wait. The king's breath caught in his lungs, icy dread creeping along his spine. Zirtan stood before him, and Darand had not forgotten his enemy's promise before battle.

With slow, deliberate steps, Zirtan approached the king, his face ghostly pale in the moonlight, and his eyes like cold, glistening black pearls. He moved as a predator, stalking the animal he'd chosen as prey. Darand squeezed the hilt of his sword, carefully inching back with each of Zirtan's steps.

"I said you would die by my hand, *my lord*," Zirtan sneered.

His attack came swift and brutal. Crushing blows rained down on the king. Darand defended, but even many years of training and experience were barely enough to keep him standing. Zirtan's speed, his skill and strength, outmatched any of Eldor's finest warriors. No thoughts of retaliation entered Darand's mind, no searching for an advantage, only survival. Even then, Zirtan drove him back so quickly and so forcefully, he struggled to keep his footing.

This continued for several minutes, far longer than Darand knew it should have. Zirtan was only toying with him.

"Tiring yet, king?" A wicked grin stretched taut across Zirtan's face.

Darand did not open his mouth to reply. The end was near, and he accepted this. Gathering all the strength and skill he had left, he made one final effort to attack. But Zirtan was ready. As the king's sword came at him, he batted it to the side with contemptuous ease.

The sharp edge of Zirtan's sword flashed for an instant with moonlight. In the next, a blinding pain pierced Darand's chest. He gasped, and his vision swam. Numbing cold encased his limbs. His sword slipped from his hands. He tried to breathe, but his lungs were on fire. Slowly, he looked down. Zirtan's sword had punched deep through the center of the king's silver breastplate. Dark, glistening blood trickled down the armor from just below the blade. A thousand thoughts raced through Darand's mind in that brief moment.

But Zirtan's cold words penetrated his mind in a hiss. "I could end your life right now, but I won't. Perhaps you will survive long enough to watch me and my men enter your city."

Zirtan jerked his sword free of the king's body. Darand gasped and his mind clouded. He didn't even feel himself hit the ground. He blinked rapidly. Zirtan stood silhouetted against the sky like a creature from a nightmare. With a flourish of his cape, he turned and strode away from the dying king.

:Chapter Forty:

One Final Hope

Looming up before Makilien was the dark outline of a war machine. A ballista. With Malachi's death in mind, she approached it determinedly. Grim satisfaction grew when she found only one Shaike manning it. In the chaos of battle, the beast didn't even notice her presence until the tip of her blade came through its chest armor. The Shaike gasped and toppled to the side.

Makilien studied the giant crossbow machine, eyes landing on the thick ropes that were already pulled back and fitted with a projectile. Standing as far back as she could and still reach the rope with her sword, she turned her head away and swung down hard. The taut rope severed instantly with a loud snap. No longer did it pose a threat to any of the dragons.

Satisfied, she stepped away from the ballista. Out of the corner of her eye, she caught movement and turned. Dread knifed through her. Only a few yards away stood another Shaike. In his hand rested a loaded crossbow aimed right at her. Makilien heard the twang of the string as the creature pulled the trigger. She tried to side step, but it was too late. The bolt streaked toward her in a blink, and her chain-mail did little to lessen the impact. She cried out in pain and dropped to her knees with the bolt impaled her left shoulder. A little lower and she would have been dead.

Pain jumbled her thoughts, but when she looked up, the Shaike approached, fitting another bolt as it came. She dropped her sword and reached for her fighting axe as she pushed herself to her feet. Praying for accuracy, she drew the axe back and threw it at the Shaike. Turning end over end, the axe blade, by some miracle, embedded itself high in the Shaike's chest near its throat. With a gargled howl, it fell.

Makilien dropped to her knees again and looked down at her shoulder. The short crossbow bolt, almost a half an inch in diameter, had penetrated all the way, the metal point protruding through her chain-mail in the back. It was like a rod of fire, pain pulsing across her chest and down her arm, but she could not pull it out.

She groaned as she picked up her sword and struggled to stand. She stumbled over to the dead Shaike and retrieved her axe. She moved on, but slowly. Her vision kept blurring in and out, and at times, the ground seemed to tip. It had become difficult to immediately identify friend from foe, which discouraged her from attacking anyone.

The hesitation finally cost her. A black shape broke from the hazy mass, and by the time she determined it to be one of Zirtan's men, he had already begun his attack. Her clumsy attempt to block resulted in her sword being wrenched from her hand. She retreated, but lost her balance, landing hard on her back. She screamed as sheer agony ripped through her wounded shoulder, and she nearly blacked out. Tears rolled down her cheeks as she gasped for breath only causing more pain to shoot through the wound.

Through her blurred vision, she could see her attacker raise his sword for a final blow. More tears flowed, and she closed her eyes. This was the moment she'd dreaded, but knew would come. She braced herself, preparing as best she knew how for her death.

"Elohim," she gasped.

Her heart pounded once, twice, three times. Where was the piercing blade that would stop it?

An loud clang of metal rang out above her. She opened her eyes to see a taller man driving her attacker back. She let out a small cry of relief. Her life had been spared this time. For a moment she was too weak to move. She wanted to just stay where she was and not move again, to just close her eyes and sleep. She very nearly did give in to unconsciousness, but gritting her teeth and groaning, she managed to push to her knees. Still, she could get no farther and almost collapsed again. She felt around blindly for her sword until someone placed the hilt in her hand. Makilien looked up as the man who had defeated her attacker knelt beside her.

"Gébrale." The emotion of seeing a familiar face was almost too much. Hand shaking, she tried to wipe the tears from her face, not realizing she was swaying.

Gébrale reached out to steady her. "We have to try to get you out of here."

Makilien shook her head. "There's nowhere to go. Please, help me up. I'll be all right."

She didn't know if she truly believed her own words, but what choice was there? Gébrale took her arm and pulled her to her feet. Makilien grimaced, her joints and muscles crying out, taking her weight. But she made herself remain upright when Gébrale took his hand away. They looked at each other. He knew as well as she did that soon willpower wouldn't be enough.

"Stay close to me," he told her. "I'll protect you."

Aedan's eyes turned to the east. This night seemed never ending. He hoped for a sign of dawn, but the horizon still lay in darkness. He sighed deeply. *I'm not going to see the sun rise again.*

Snarling caught his attention. A group of goblins stood in his way. They sneered as he rushed at them, but they could not withstand his attack. A mountain wolf tried to pounce on him from the left, but he impaled it in midair. He had become less and less concerned with caution. He was just too tired to pay attention to his defense.

As he fought his way through the fray, he came upon a clearing just in time to witness one of Zirtan's men take down two soldiers, one from Eldor and the other from Beldon. His indignation burned to see two good men slaughtered so thoughtlessly by one enemy. He lifted his sword and charged forward. The man must have heard him coming, because he spun around. When Aedan saw his face, he skidded to a halt, and, for a moment, his anger and eagerness evaporated.

Zirtan stood before him, a tall, ghostly form, his long sword still glistening with the blood he'd just shed. His dark eyes bored into Aedan's, and Aedan was overcome with a cold, raw fear he had not experienced before. He took an involuntarily step back as Zirtan advanced. His sword became like lead in his hands as he tried to lift it in defense. But then, in an instant, his fury and resolve flooded back as he remembered what Lord Elnauhir had said. Kill Zirtan and his army may falter. If he could do that, there could still be hope for however few soldiers were left and the people within the city.

Blazing determination gave Aedan a burst of energy and strength he didn't realize he had left in him. He rushed forward, his sword crashing against Zirtan's with an echoing ring that pierced the night. He swung again, and yet again. Three times he was able to attack before his enemy found an opportunity to take control. And when Zirtan did, he descended on Aedan with the most fearsome force and rage Aedan had ever witnessed.

The force of Zirtan's first blow sent him stumbling two steps. Counterattack was impossible as Zirtan's sword came screaming at him from the opposite direction. Though successfully blocked, it forced him back another couple of steps.

"Fool!" Zirtan growled. "Think you can take me, boy?"

His attacks came lightning fast and from all directions, and though they continued to drive Aedan backwards, he blocked each strike. After several successive attacks, Aedan noticed a slight pause before the next attack and jabbed his sword high toward Zirtan's throat. The attack was weak and batted aside with ease, but the attempt infuriated Zirtan.

He was on Aedan again in an instant with furious attacks to make him pay, but Aedan held his own. Now and then, he found an opportunity to counterattack. Never was it successful, but frustration and rage emanated from Zirtan. This *boy* should have been dead at his feet after the first attack.

Finally, Zirtan's fury reached its height. With a monstrous roar, he delivered his most brutal attack. Aedan managed to block the first three blows, but the fourth came before he could anticipate it. He was unable to bring his blade up in time, and the tip of Zirtan's sword cut across his chest. The links of his chain-mail snapped under the force, and though they took most of the damage, he still felt steel rip into his skin. The impact took his breath away and threw him off balance, sending him to the ground.

Dazed and gasping for air, he tried to get up, but was not fast enough. Zirtan's heavy foot came down on his chest, pinning him. Aedan groaned and looked up into his enemy's pale face. Wicked triumph danced in Zirtan's eyes. He raised his sword.

The point hurtled down. Aedan cried out as it pierced his armor and speared through his shoulder.

Glaring down at him, Zirtan said, "No one challenges me and lives."

Aedan gritted his teeth. "Someday you'll face your defeat and you know Who will bring it."

Zirtan snarled and twisted his sword. Aedan groaned in agony, and Zirtan grinned with vicious pleasure at his pain. With amusement still lacing his voice, he said, "You look much like one of my captains." He paused for a moment and then chuckled in realization. "You are the son of Jaeson, aren't you?"

Aedan did not answer, but Zirtan continued with a devious grin. "He offered you the chance to join my ranks and you refused. You are very skilled for your age. I can use men like you. Though you had the gall to attack me, I will offer you a chance to redeem yourself. Swear your allegiance to me now, and I will let you live."

Aedan stared up at him and laughed coldly before declaring, "Nothing could *ever* make me swear allegiance to you."

Zirtan's expression changed to a murderous scowl, and he wrenched his sword sharply. Aedan cried out again, and darkness clouded his vision. Zirtan jerked his sword from Aedan's shoulder and raised it up, this time to kill. Aedan waited. Waited to feel its bite and for death to come. Like a silver streak of lightning, the blade descended toward his chest.

A roaring screech blasted through the air. Something dark careened into Zirtan from above, nearly taking him to the ground. Zirtan screamed as the griffon clawed at him. Aedan tried to get up, but pain left him weak, and he collapsed again. He looked around and found the hilt of his sword lying just out of reach. Biting down hard, he forced himself up again and reached for it.

Just as he wrapped his fingers around the hilt, the griffon screeched again, this time in a desperate, pained cry. Aedan turned, catching the flash of Zirtan's sword. The griffon fell to the ground. *No!* His strength flowing back, he jumped to his feet. Zirtan heard him rise and turned, but too late. With a loud cry, Aedan plunged his sword through Zirtan's chest up to the hilt.

For a moment, they stood absolutely still. Zirtan's face went slack with shock. He glanced down. Eyeing the sword dumbly at first, his expression morphed into one of burning rage. Aedan stumbled away as Zirtan let out an inhumanly loud wail that echoed across the entire battlefield and was heard by every soldier. He slowly sank to his knees and held his shaking hands up in front of his face. As Aedan watched, he disintegrated into fine, ash-like dust to be carried away by the breeze like a cloud of smoke. Soon, only his black clothing remained in a heap at Aedan's feet.

Aedan stood frozen in shock. Zirtan was gone. It had worked. A burst of joy filled his heart, but then he remembered the griffon. His eyes went to the creature, and his breath caught. He ran to him and dropped to his knees.

"Arphen!"

The griffon slowly turned his head and rested his keen eyes on Aedan.

"Aedan, you did it." He managed a weak smile. "You've defeated Zirtan."

"Only because you stopped him from killing me," Aedan said.

He looked down at the gaping wound to the griffon's chest, and his eyes filled with tears. He tried to cover the wound with his hands, but there was no stopping the flow of blood.

Choking, Arphen said, "This is my end, Aedan, but I am honored that Elohim used my life to help you achieve this victory. I pray it will be enough to save Eldor and our allies."

A tear slid down Aedan's cheek. He wanted to do something to save the griffon, but was powerless.

A moment later, two more griffon's landed nearby.

"Arphen!" Vyl cried as she and Tôr rushed to his side. The sorrow of their expressions when they saw Arphen's wound hit Aedan hard.

Looking at the two other griffons as best he could, Arphen instructed, "Spread the word that Zirtan has been defeated. Make sure the whole battlefield knows. Spread panic through his men."

"We will," Tôr promised.

Arphen sighed, and his expression was peaceful. Aedan leaned close to hear his next quiet words.

"Elohim will give you victory. I'm sure of it."

His breathing slowed, and his eyes closed. Tears ran as Aedan watched the noble griffon's life slip away. The pain of loss gripped his heart.

Tôr walked around to his side and placed his strong talons on Aedan's uninjured shoulder. "He died a noble death and is with Elohim now."

Aedan nodded and brushed the back of his hand across his face. He picked up his sword, rose to his feet, and looked at Tôr and Vyl.

"Let's end this war."

The two griffons nodded and took to the air.

Aedan turned away from Arphen's body. In doing so, he caught sight of his father again. The man stood several feet away, just staring at him. Aedan had no idea how much his father had witnessed, but he took a step toward him. At this, Jaeson turned and hurried away. Aedan called out to him, but he would not stop.

As much as Aedan wanted to go after him, stopping Zirtan's army was more important. He followed after Tôr and Vyl, and the three of them shouted the news of Zirtan's death, placing the fear and doubt they'd hoped for into the enemy. Aedan was exhausted, but hope of victory helped him push through the pain of his wounds and his body's fatigue.

Close to panic, Zirtan's men dropped by the thousands as Eldor's army surged forward. It was just as they had hoped. Knowledge that their seemingly undefeatable leader had been brought down stripped the enemy of their advantage. Though still far outnumbering Eldor's force, chaos engulfed Zirtan's army, and slowly, they began their retreat. It started with only a few, but soon, more and more turned to run.

Sirion swayed, but managed to keep his balance as he watched the men around him flee for their lives. Thankfulness flowed from his heart. Victory had come. Despite everyone's despair, Elohim had given them victory. He smiled and whispered a prayer of gratitude.

But then he clenched teeth and put his hand to his side. Blood wet his palm. He grimaced, wishing he'd noticed the Shaike coming just a moment sooner and the spear in its hand. His chain-mail had prevented it from causing any fatal damage, but loss of blood made him weak.

However, the spear wound wasn't his primary concern. After the Shaike had driven him to the ground, it had given him such a powerful kick to the chest, he'd barely been able to get up before the creature finished him off. Ribs were broken, he was sure of that, and breathing was difficult, bringing him intense pain.

He took another step to stay out of the way of the retreating men and swayed again. The ground rolled beneath him. He tried to draw in a deeper breath to clear his head, but he ended up coughing painfully. The taste of blood filled his mouth. He groaned and was chilled with the realization his body was more damaged than he had first thought. Spitting the blood from his mouth, he turned toward the city. When he tried to move, his legs buckled, and he went to his knees. All strength abandoned him. His body seemed to sense the loss of urgency to fight.

He coughed again. More blood. He made a determined effort to rise, but he did not get far before something pushed him hard from behind. He fell, rolling to his back with a groan as pain burned through his chest. Dazed, he had to blink several times before a looming, dark figure came into focus. Derrin.

Sirion tried to push himself up, but Derrin's blade pricked against his throat, and he let himself fall back. He looked to the right where his sword lay at his fingertips, but made no move to grab it. It was over, and he knew it. He had no hope of defeating Derrin in this condition. Even if he were to try, his body was shutting down.

Letting out a searing breath, Sirion stared up at Derrin. The man's face was cold. No mercy shone in his eyes though Sirion had granted it to him.

"You should have killed me," Derrin spat through clenched teeth.

Sirion didn't reply. Darkness crowded around his vision. He watched Derrin raise his sword and closed his eyes. Everything faded away. He thought for a moment of Makilien, wondering if she was alive, praying she was. His thoughts then focused on Elohim, and a deep sense of peace and joy washed over him. He knew shortly he would be in the presence of his Lord.

:Chapter Forty-one:
A Terrible Price

In a panicking, dark mass, less than a quarter of the men Zirtan had led against the city fled eastward as dawn lit the battlefield. Having no strength left to pursue them, the Eldorian army simply watched their enemy fade into the distance.

Aedan's weary eyes swept over the battlefield. He thought of the army that had gathered together before the first night of battle. Heaviness weighed on his heart. So few now stood, like lone statues among the vast sea of destruction. The carnage was unlike anything he could have imagined. Not one person left standing did not bear some wound or sign of struggle. So covered in blood and grime, they were almost unrecognizable, glassy-eyed with exhaustion and the horrors they'd witnessed.

Dazed with the overwhelming mix of emotions, Aedan couldn't move. His arms and legs felt weighed down and his head pounded. He thought of his friends and dread squeezed tight around his chest. Had anyone survived? He could hardly bear the thought of finding them dead. But what if they lay wounded and needed help? This possibility moved him to action.

Moving slowly, Aedan wiped his sword and slid it into the scabbard. With desperate hope, he looked all around, searching for a familiar face, before carefully moving on. He searched the standing and the fallen, praying every moment for the lives of his friends. His progress was slow. So many lay around him. He couldn't even see where the signs of struggle ended.

Smoke rose up from various smoldering heaps and made his eyes water, burning his lungs and making him cough. Trying not to breath in the thick air, he stepped around the still body of a fallen dragon and shook his head at the loss. When he looked ahead, his eyes settled on an approaching soldier. Gladness filled his despairing heart.

"Halandor," he said hoarsely.

"Aedan." Halandor laid his hand on Aedan's shoulder and eyed his torn and bloodstained jerkin. "Are you all right?"

Aedan gave a slow nod, though really, he wasn't sure. "Have you found anyone else?"

Sorrow and regret shadowed Halandor's weary eyes, and he shook his head. "No."

Aedan exhaled heavily, and Halandor's voice rose in encouragement. "But I've only just started searching."

Together they walked on, crisscrossing the battlefield. It seemed a near impossible task to find their friends amongst so many fallen, but they refused to give up. Edging closer to the wall, a groan caught their attention. A soldier struggled to rise, and Aedan recognized the armor immediately. He and Halandor rushed to the man's side to help him up.

"Thank you," Darian gasped.

The prince didn't appear to be badly injured, but he clutched his shoulder and gritted his teeth.

"What's wrong?" Aedan asked.

"My shoulder is out." Darian's eyes went to Halandor. "I need you to put it back in for me."

Halandor gave a quick nod and took Darian's arm at the wrist and near the elbow.

"Try to relax, all right?"

Darian drew in a couple deep breaths, and Halandor carefully maneuvered his arm. The prince bit down hard, squeezing his eyes shut. In a moment, Aedan heard a muffled pop. Darian sucked in his breath, but then blew out a sigh as he reached up to rub his shoulder.

"Thanks."

"Do you have any other injuries that need tending to?" Halandor asked.

Darian shook his head. "Nothing serious."

"My lord!"

The three of them turned. Nirgon and Gilhir moved through the bodies to reach the prince.

"Thank Elohim!" the general breathed. "It is good to see the three of you."

"Have you found anyone else?" Halandor asked.

Nirgon hung his head. "Lord Glorlad, but no others."

"We'll keep searching," Halandor said.

The five of them spread out and resumed the search. One by one, they checked the fallen for a face they would know. Aedan could stomach a lot, but the gruesome sights he encountered pushed him to his threshold. They'd paid a terrible price in this war, far greater than they had feared in the beginning. He tried to let his mind numb itself to the carnage, but he found himself overcome with the fear of coming upon a friend who had been slain.

"Elohim," he whispered, but lacked words to continue. Yet he knew Elohim could see the turmoil in his heart and mind.

The brightness of the morning sun bathed the battlefield as Aedan pushed on, one step at a time. With each minute, he struggled to hold onto hope that they would find anyone else they knew alive. Too many had fallen.

Not far from the gate, he paused and let his eyes range over the area. Through the drifting smoke from a smoldering catapult, a horse caught his eye. Its silver armor was marred and spattered. Blood ran down its forelegs, but it stood quietly, unlike the other horses moving around nervously. Squinting, Aedan realized the horse was black.

"Antiro?"

The horse's head rose, and his ears flicked forward. A weak, but responsive nicker came from the animal, and Aedan knew. He rushed toward him. But when he realized Antiro stood over someone on the ground, he froze. His gut twisted inside him. The man's silver plate-mail was exactly like Darian's. Dread squeezed his throat, but he willed himself forward. When he reached Antiro's side, all he could think of at first was the horrible sight of crimson blood trailing all down the king's breastplate. Aedan knelt next to Darand, his heart lodged in his throat. He feared the king was dead.

"My lord," he spoke with hesitation.

He gasped when the king's closed eyelids moved. Hope surged through him, and he looked desperately around the battlefield. Finally, he spotted Halandor.

"Over here!" he shouted. "It's Lord Darand!"

With as much speed as they could manage, Halandor, Darian, Nirgon, and Gilhir raced to the king's side. Darian dropped to his knees beside him.

"Father!"

Aedan moved back, his eyes shifting between the king and the prince. Darian's face had paled.

"Father," he said again, fear robbing his voice.

This time, Darand's eyes fluttered open, and he groaned. His clouded gaze settled on Darian.

"Son," his voice came out weak and labored.

Darian took his father's hand. "I'm here, Father."

The prince's voice wavered, and Aedan felt his own emotion building. Behind him, Nirgon shouted for someone to bring a stretcher.

Darand tried to draw in a breath, but a choked cough racked his body and blood trickled from the corner of his lips. His face twisted in pain, but when he looked at Darian again, his eyes were fully alert.

"My son," he murmured, squeezing the prince's hand. "This is the end for me."

Darian shook his head in desperation. "No."

But peace and acceptance had come to Darand's expression. "It is my time. Elohim has gifted me with a long life full of blessings, the greatest of which is you." The king paused, painfully drawing in a breath. "Darian, the time has now come for you to take your place as king. You are strong and wise. I know you will lead our people well through this time of both joy and sorrow, and through whatever else the future holds for this country. Elohim will always be at your side as He has been at mine. Consult Him in everything and always do what is right, no matter the consequences."

With tears filling his eyes, Darian replied, "I will."

A weak smile came to the king's face. "I love you, Son."

"I love you, Father."

Darand looked up past his son, his eyes searching for the faces of his friends.

"Do not mourn too deeply for me," he told them before his eyes returned to Darian. "You know where I am going and that we will see each other again."

Darian nodded, though his eyes reflected deep pain and sorrow.

Still smiling, Darand breathed out slowly, and his gaze settled on the sky. His eyes closed, and his grasp on his son's hand loosened. Darian bowed his head. Still holding his father's hand tightly, silent sobs shook his shoulders.

Aedan's heart ached at witnessing the passing of such a noble man and the pain of his friend. He glanced up at Halandor and Nirgon. He'd never known men of such strength, yet both shed tears for their king. Tears welled in Aedan's eyes, and he rose as men arrived with a stretcher only to find they were too late. He backed away as they lifted the king's body reverently onto the stretcher to be taken to the city.

In a daze, he turned and gazed across the large area yet to search. He dragged in a deep breath against his constricted airway and tried to block the pain inside. He had to be strong for those who had survived. But he wasn't sure how long the fragile shield would stand. He stumbled on without looking back to see if anyone followed. He had to blink to keep his vision clear as he took in the faces of one slain soldier after another, images that would forever be in his mind.

At last, Aedan looked up and stopped. Relief beat in his heart, flooding through his body. Vonawyn stood before him. Her dark hair fell in matted strands around her face and her armor was marred and filthy, but she was alive. Already, Aedan felt his shield crumble at the sight of her. With tears in her eyes, Vonawyn rushed to him and into his arms. They held each other tight. Aedan struggled to fight emotion, but tears flowed. All the pain and exhaustion crashed in.

When they finally parted, he barely had the strength to stand. Vonawyn steadied him, afraid he would collapse.

"Aedan, it looks like you've lost a lot of blood. We have to get you to the palace."

But Aedan shook his head. "I haven't found everyone yet."

He looked off across the battlefield, though it was difficult to focus, and tried to gather strength that just wasn't there. Then Vonawyn's warm hand came to his cheek, and he looked back into her eyes.

"Men will be coming from the city to help with the wounded. You can't stay out here in this condition or you'll be among those needing to be carried inside." Her voice was calm, comforting, but determined. "Come on."

She put his arm around her shoulders and turned him toward the city. Aedan gritted his teeth and walked with her, trying not to use her for support. But waves of pain and dizziness assailed him along the way, and he often realized she was bearing much of his weight. He hated being so weak. Nearing the gate, he stumbled and almost took them both down. Here, Vonawyn stopped him.

"We'll rest here a moment," she said, breathing heavily.

Aedan squeezed his eyes shut. They'd never make it to the palace like this. *Oh, Elohim, please give me a last bit of strength.* He wanted to tell Vonawyn to leave him until someone brought a stretcher, but he never got the chance.

"Tanzim!" Vonawyn called out.

Aedan raised his eyes. He never would have believed he'd be so relieved to see the face of a Shaike.

445

Halandor brushed away the remaining tears from his face, but deep sorrow riddled his heart. After witnessing the death of a man he'd served and admired for most of his life, it was a struggle to go on searching, fighting against the despair that it likely would not be the only personal loss he'd suffer that day. But he did go on—searching, hoping, praying. *Every life is in Your hands and precious to You. No one goes before the time You have set.* The words gave comfort and encouragement to him as he thought of each of his loved ones.

But it did not stop the numbing fear that seized him when his eyes landed on the motionless body of a blonde-haired Elf. Even from a few yards away, he saw the blood. More blood than most could lose and hope to live. Tears burned his eyes again, and at first, he could not move, but he willed himself forward. Shaking, he knelt next to his friend whose face was gray like death.

"Loron," he said with no hope of an answer, but he gasped when the Elf's eyes opened. However, his normal, clear blue gaze was dull. He opened his mouth, but no words came.

"Don't speak," Halandor said. "I'm going to get you to the city. You'll be all right."

But the wave of relief that had rushed through him moments ago, failed him now as his eyes dropped to the puncture in Loron's leather armor, low on his right side. Blood continued to flow, soaking everything including the trampled grass beneath him. Halandor pressed his hand down over the puncture, hoping it might in some way staunch the flow. Loron gasped, but was too weak to move. Halandor's eyes darted everywhere, searching for help. His mentally whispered prayer was answered when he found another familiar figure nearby, this one not seriously injured.

"Elmorhirian!"

The dark haired Elf spun around at his call. He crossed the distance in an instant, kneeling opposite of Halandor.

"Is he alive?" Elmorhirian asked, for Loron's eyes had closed once more.

"Yes, but we need to get him help immediately. He's bleeding out fast."

They lifted Loron between them and moved with as much haste as they could manage toward the city. Neither spoke, focusing on their task. Every moment lessened Loron's already slim chance of survival.

A few yards from the gate, two Elves of Elimar came out carrying an empty stretcher. Elmorhirian called out, and they hurried to meet them. Once Loron was laid on the stretcher, Halandor again put his hand over his friend's wound.

"We need to get him to the palace," he told the Elves.

They nodded and lifted the stretcher. Just past the gate, Loron regained consciousness again and managed to grab Halandor's wrist. This time, his eyes were clearer.

"Find the others," he gasped.

Halandor hesitated, reluctant to leave his friend in this condition. But others they knew could be just as bad off. Slowly, Halandor nodded, and fell behind. Standing still in the middle of the street, he watched them go, fingers still dripping his friend's blood. In all likelihood, Loron would be dead when he saw him again. Halandor hung his head. *Please, spare him.*

Elmorhirian put his hand to Halandor's shoulder. They looked at each other, sharing the sorrow. Hearts heavy, they turned back to the battlefield.

For a long time they searched, helping those they could, always on the lookout for friends and family. Halandor couldn't imagine how long it would take to clear the battlefield, nor how so many wounded could be cared for. There just weren't that many healers in the city, and half of them may have died in battle themselves.

Fighting despair, Halandor stopped again as he neared the far edge of the battlefield. This time he found Gébrale walking toward him. In his arms was the unconscious form of a young woman in royal blue and black.

:Chapter Forty-two:

Missing

Makilien became aware of a dull aching in almost every part of her body. She had no recollection of time or location. The faint hum of a voice echoed in her ears. She tried to remember what had happened. Memories of the battle came first, then of victory. She'd seen Zirtan's men fleeing, but then she'd become dizzy and remembered no further. She tried to open her eyes, and after great effort, they parted a slit. But all she could see was a dimly-lit blur. Yet, it wasn't the bluish-gray light of the outdoors. Instead, it was a warmer, yellowish light. Her eyes slid closed

A voice murmured again, this time clear enough for her to know it was female. It sounded familiar. She wanted to open her eyes and respond to the voice, but had no strength. For a long moment, she just laid there, her senses slowly clearing. She could distinguish more than one whispered voice now, and softness all around her. Again she tried to open her eyes. This time it came more easily. She blinked, and a familiar, loving face came into focus.

"Mother." The word barely made it through Makilien's parched throat.

Tears glimmered in Hanna's eyes, and her smile trembled. "Makilien. Don't worry, sweetheart, you're all right."

Hanna reached for a cup and gently lifted her daughter's head. Gladly, Makilien drank of the offered water. When her mother laid her head back against the pillow, Makilien scanned the room. The smiles of dearly-loved faces warmed her heart with joy and thankfulness. Gathered around the bed were her father, Leiya, Halandor, Aedan, and Vonawyn. Tears pooled in her eyes.

"You're all right."

Vonawyn smiled and squeezed her hand. "Yes, we are."

Makilien breathed in, but a stab of pain ignited in her shoulder. She winced.

"I put a painkiller in the water," Vonawyn told her. "It should start working soon."

Makilien's eyes moved between her friends again before stopping on Halandor. With dread already churning her stomach, she asked, "What of the others?"

Halandor sighed and dropped his gaze for a moment, his troubled expression telling her he had hoped she would not ask so soon. Fear slowed her heart. Finally, his eyes met hers.

"Lord Darand and Arphen are gone."

He paused to let the news sink in. The shock made Makilien dizzy, and she closed her eyes. Tears leaked past her eyelids. A couple quiet sobs broke free. Both her mother and Vonawyn held her hands with whatever comfort they could offer. When she managed to master her sorrow, she turned questioning eyes back to Halandor, and he went on.

"Lord Andron is unconscious, but we expect him to recover and wake soon." He paused again. "Torick and Elandir are still in bed, but are on their way to recovery. Loron is yet unconscious, but still alive, thanks be to Elohim. He almost didn't make it."

"And everyone else?"

"Most everyone is awake and should recover fully."

With these words, Halandor glanced across to where Hanna and Néthyn stood on the other side of the bed. They looked at him, their expressions sober, as if silently sharing something. Makilien didn't understand why, but it put a knot of growing dread in her stomach. Then she realized one person she would have expected to be at her bedside was not.

"Where is Sirion?"

The only sound for a moment was the dreadful thudding of her heart. Halandor looked at her, his expression a mix of remorse and sadness. Makilien thought she might die in that moment, waiting for an answer.

"We don't know," Halandor murmured.

Makilien couldn't comprehend that. "What do you mean?"

Halandor sighed heavily. "We can't find him. We assume he was taken with the other wounded to one of the makeshift healing houses. We've been looking for him, but so far we have not been able to locate him."

Makilien drew in a ragged breath. Intense fear and panic assaulted her, bringing with it a wave of nausea. Barely holding onto her composure, she asked in a shaking voice, "How long have you been looking?"

"It's been three days since the end of the battle."

"What if you don't find him?" Makilien asked, choking.

"There are many wounded, Makilien," Halandor said to comfort her. "It's possible we missed him. We'll keep looking."

Despite this, she realized the likelihood of finding him after three days of searching was slim, and if he was not found

451

among the wounded it meant only one thing—he was among the dead.

"No," she cried. Overcome with grief and desperation, she tried to get up, completely oblivious to the pain. But Vonawyn held her down.

"Makilien, you must lie still."

"But I have to go look for him."

Vonawyn shook her head sadly. "You are much too weak and injured. You must stay in bed and rest."

Makilien did not try to get up again, but her mournful sobbing continued despite the comfort of her parents and friends. Eventually, exhaustion won out, and she cried herself to sleep.

Everything was numb but for the suffocating pain of sorrow. Makilien opened her eyes. A couple candles glowed on the nightstand, but the room was dim. She shifted her gaze. Her mother stood in the balcony doorway, staring out into the nighttime darkness. Makilien breathed in and moved her arm a little. Her muscles had almost no strength in them.

Hanna turned. "Makilien," she murmured and came to the bed. She brushed the hair from her daughter's cheek.

Makilien searched her mother's face. "Have they found him?"

Hanna's expression fell, and she rubbed Makilien's arm. "Not yet."

Makilien swallowed hard, tears clogging her throat.

Wanting to ease her daughter's sorrow, Hanna spoke encouragingly, "Now that you are awake again, we should get some nourishment in you."

She walked over to the table and brought a bowl and spoon to the nightstand. Carefully, she situated extra pillows behind Makilien to elevate her. Sitting on the edge of the bed, she spooned warm broth into her daughter's mouth.

"Where are Father and Leiya?" Makilien asked after swallowing the first spoonful.

"They went to sleep a little bit ago."

Makilien looked into her mother's tired eyes. "You should get some sleep too."

Hanna smiled. "I will."

The two were quiet for a while after. When Makilien finished the broth, it left her feeling comfortably warm and nourished, but it did not add strength or energy to her body, and she hated being helpless.

"I need to get better," she murmured. "I need to get up . . . to go search for Sirion."

Her mother's gaze was sympathetic as she said, "You need to rest in order for your body to heal." She gave Makilien a hopeful smile. "Many are looking for him. I'm sure they will find him."

Tears filled Makilien's eyes, and her lip trembled. "What if he isn't in one of the healing houses? What if . . . what if he's gone?"

With deep sorrow in her eyes, Hanna took Makilien's hand in hers.

"Then we will be here to help you through it."

The tears trickled down Makilien's cheeks. Her voice broke as she whispered, "I love him, Mother."

"Oh, Makilien." Hanna squeezed her daughter's hand tight. "I am so sorry you have to suffer this pain. I wish somehow I could take it away."

Using her good arm, Makilien pushed herself up. She was lightheaded at first, but the broth and another night of sleep had restored some strength to her body. She glanced to the balcony door. The sun was shining, and early morning was still upon the city. Situating her pillows as best she could, she leaned back with a sigh. Everything inside her wanted to get up, but she was still too weak.

A moment later, her mother entered the room and smiled as she came to the bed.

"How do you feel?" she asked her daughter.

Makilien shrugged, then winced at the pain radiating through her shoulder.

"Better, but still weak."

"Are you hungry?"

Makilien nodded, acutely aware of the emptiness in her stomach.

"I'll go downstairs and get you something."

"Thank you," Makilien murmured.

While waiting for her mother to return, Makilien thought of her injured friends and prayed everyone would recover. She thought of Lord Darand and Arphen, and those who were already gone. Then she thought of Sirion and the last time she had seen him in battle. Memories from the fight tortured her mind. A steady stream of tears fell from her eyes. She closed them tight and tried to wish it all away.

Someone sat beside her. Makilien's eyes opened to her father's sympathetic face.

"I hate that there must be war," Makilien cried. "I've seen it twice, but it hasn't become any easier to deal with."

Néthyn put his arm around her and held her close. "I don't believe it ever does."

Makilien's tears continued to flow as she fought hard against sorrow. "I just want for everyone to be all right. I can't bear to think about going on without those who are gone."

"It will take time for the pain to subside," Néthyn replied, gently stroking her hair. "You just have to take it one day at a time."

Makilien leaned against her father and nodded, more thankful than she could ever put into words that he was not among those who were gone.

"Elohim has a plan in all this," he comforted.

Makilien gave him a weak smile and nodded again. "Thank you for reminding me." Wiping her face free of tears, she asked, "How did we win the battle? Was Zirtan killed?"

"Yes, he was."

"Do you know who did it?"

Her father smiled. "Aedan did."

Makilien's mouth dropped open. "Really?"

"Yes, that is what Halandor told me."

Makilien sat in silent wonder, pondering the incredibleness of it. It didn't escape her notice that the very people Elohim had used in bringing victory had once been captives of Zirtan. And in a large way, that alone gave her much comfort. Elohim did have a plan, just as her father said.

Makilien stared at the golden light of the afternoon sun bathing the wall near the balcony door. All was quiet. Her parents and Leiya had been gone for a while to let her rest, but she had yet to find sleep, her mind occupied by thoughts and prayers.

A gentle knock caught her attention, and she looked toward the door. It opened slightly, and Aedan looked in.

"I'm sorry. I hope I did not wake you."

Makilien shook her head. "No. Come in."

He walked inside, and Makilien pushed herself up a little higher against her pillows.

"I was just coming to check on you," Aedan said, taking a seat in the chair beside the bed. "How are you doing?"

Makilien released a sigh. "I'm all right, I guess."

That's when she noticed Aedan's arm was in a sling.

"Are you all right?"

He glanced at his arm. "I'm fine."

"What happened?"

"I was stabbed," was all he said.

They did not speak for a moment, but then Makilien said, "I heard you killed Zirtan."

Aedan nodded slowly. "Yes . . . but I couldn't have if not for Arphen. He saved me from Zirtan and gave me the opening to defeat him."

Makilien swallowed hard. "That's how Arphen died?"

Aedan gave another nod, and Makilien saw the sorrow in his expression. Both sat quiet as they mourned the loss. When she could speak again, Makilien asked, "Has anyone found any sign of Sirion?"

Catching the desperate hope in her eyes, Aedan hated to disappoint her. "No," he answered quietly. "I was out looking with Lord Glorlad and Elmorhirian before I came up here."

He watched her expression fall, almost feeling her disappointment.

"I will keep searching for him, Makilien," he promised.

:Chapter Forty-three:

A New Era

"**M**akilien, are you sure about this?"

Her knee ached, and her legs shook a little, but her determination was strong.

"Yes, I'll be fine. It's been more than two days since I woke up. I missed Lord Darand's funeral," she said softly, "I won't miss Darian's coronation."

Her mother nodded in understanding. "All right, I will help you change."

She helped Makilien out of her nightgown and into her blue ceremony dress. It was difficult and slow, and hurt Makilien's shoulder, but she tried to conceal the pain. Finally, she had on her vest and overskirt, and her mother tied her arm up in a sling. That helped ease the pain.

After brushing Makilien's hair and tying it back neatly, her mother said, "There. All finished."

Makilien stood in front of the mirror and smoothed her vest. "Thank you."

Hanna smiled, standing behind her. "I'm going to go change and help Leiya."

"Do you need my help with anything?" Makilien asked.

"No, we'll be fine. If you're sure you'll be all right, you can go on alone. I know you are anxious to see your friends."

And that she was. Since the battle, Makilien had only seen Halandor, Aedan, and Vonawyn. She left her bedroom and walked the quiet halls. By the time she made it downstairs, she was a little winded and lightheaded, but still glad to be up. Voices broke the stillness as she neared the throne room. Stepping inside, she found a large crowd already gathered. She paused in the doorway and scanned the faces. Halandor spotted her right away and left the gathering to meet her.

Smiling, he said, "It's good to see you up again."

"It feels good to be out of bed . . . though I honestly don't feel that steady on my feet," Makilien admitted. "But I couldn't miss this."

Halandor offered his arm for support and guided Makilien across the room. The first person they met was Torick. He was on crutches, his left leg splinted, and a long healing cut ran along his jaw line and down the side of his neck. Though his face was a bit pale, his eyes were as sharp as ever.

"Ah, Makilien," he said with a smile.

"Hello, Torick," she replied, her own smile coming through. "How is your leg?"

"It's busted up pretty bad, but the enemy is going to have to try harder than that to kill me."

Makilien's smile grew a little, and she looked around. Many familiar faces surrounded her. Elmorhirian and Elandir stood nearby with Loron. He was still very pale, and Makilien guessed it had taken much persuading to be allowed out of bed, but the Elf brothers seemed to be keeping a close eye on him. Excusing herself for a moment, Makilien walked over to him. All three Elves smiled at her as they said their greetings.

"It's good to see you, Loron," Makilien said. "I heard how close we came to losing you."

"And that's not an exaggeration," Elmorhirian added. "I still don't think he ought to be out of bed, but he's stubborn."

Loron chuckled softly. "And you wouldn't be?"

Elmorhirian shrugged. "Just saying."

Makilien grinned at them, and Loron's eyes turned to her. "I guess Elohim still wants me here."

"I'm thankful of that, because we certainly do," she replied.

They shared warm smiles, and after a few more words to each of them, Makilien turned back to Halandor and Torick. As she continued to scan the room, she found almost everyone closest to her. Everyone but the one she was so desperate to see. She longed to have Sirion appear in the crowd—to feel a touch on her shoulder and turn to see his smiling face. Her throat tightened as the fact hit her that if Sirion was still alive, he must be badly injured else he would never miss Darian's coronation. She swallowed hard, tears pooling in her eyes.

"Are you all right?"

Makilien looked up at Halandor and then away again, blinking quickly. She nodded. Halandor put his arm around her shoulders, and Makilien fought to keep control of her emotions.

After a time, her family joined them, and the crowd of people moved into their positions. By now, the room was nearly filled to capacity. People from every country were present. Carmine, Indiya, Emaril, and Eborin were also there with a few of the griffons. Makilien stood with Halandor and Torick and their other friends with the lords near the throne. Everything grew quiet in anticipation. The hush remained until a proud trumpet blast echoed from the main entrance.

All heads turned as the double doors swung open, and Darian entered.

The prince was dressed in the finest black jerkin, delicately embroidered and trimmed in silver, over a royal blue shirt. A dark cape lined in the same blue draped from his shoulders. Makilien noticed immediately that the prince had let a short beard grow. It gave him a more mature and kingly appearance. His expression was serious, and in his eyes was a hint of sadness. Makilien could only imagine the sorrow of having to replace his father, but his approach to the throne displayed confidence and dignity.

Once he reached the foot of the throne, Darian stopped. Nirgon stood before him, the one chosen to preside over the ceremony. In the silence, the general's eyes swept over the crowd.

"People and friends of Eldor." His strong voice carried throughout the room. "Never in our history have we and our allies gathered such as we have now. Together, we have faced a struggle unlike any generation has ever seen. Despite the fear and the despair, we fought, died, and achieved victory together. Only a couple days ago, we of Eldor mourned the loss of our king. A man noble and strong. A great leader, defender, and friend. But most of all, a man who understood where his strength and position came from."

A tear slipped down Makilien's cheek as she remembered Darand, his kind smile and how quick he had been to welcome her into his city and his life. The true care and compassion he'd shown to both her and her family.

"Lord Darand will be remembered always for his love for his people and his friends, as well as for his courage, and will go down in history as one of Eldor's most beloved kings."

Nirgon paused for a moment, the emotion building in his voice. "Now today, we gather with you, our friends, to witness the beginning of a new era in Eldor—the crowning of Lord Darand's son, Prince Darian. People of Eldor, do you accept him as your king?"

The quiet hall exploded in a resounding yes from the Eldorians. Pride for both Darian and the country swelled inside Makilien as her answer mixed with the peoples'.

With a hint of a smile, the general turned to one of Lord Darand's oldest advisors who stood at his side. An ornate pillow rested in the man's hands upon which sat the king's crown. Nirgon took it in his hands, turning back to the prince who sank to one knee. Raising the crown, Nirgon said, "In the sight of Elohim and those gathered here, I crown Lord Darian, King of Eldor. May his reign be blessed and pleasing before Elohim."

He set the crown on Darian's head, and the new king rose amidst much applause, smiles, and tears. He ascended the throne's platform and turned to face the crowd. A hush fell once more as the king's eyes took in the faces of those around him.

"My father led Eldor faithfully through times of both peace and war, earning the great love and loyalty you gave him, and even now already show to me. I pray that in all ways I will lead with the same honor and strength as my father. As said by our forefather Baltar, 'May it never be that the One who gives us life be denied in this place.' I promise before you all to lead this country with Elohim as my guide as my father did."

With those words, Darian sat upon the throne, and the room erupted in cheers. Shouts of "Hail, Lord Darian!" and "Long live the king!" echoed above the applause. A teary smile came to Makilien's face and a bittersweet feeling settled in her heart. Lord Darand would be greatly missed by all, but Darian would be a wonderful king. She wiped her moist eyes and prayed his reign would be a time of peace for the country.

After the ceremony, Darian spent a long time with the people, as each person wanted to wish him well and personally swear their loyalty. Makilien hung back with her friends until most of the people had departed from the throne room. She then took her turn to approach Eldor's new king. He smiled warmly.

"Makilien."

"My lord." She bowed her head respectfully and returned his smile.

"I am glad you were well enough to have joined us. I am thankful to have my friends close today."

"I am happy to have been here to witness this. It was a very moving ceremony." Makilien cleared her throat, hoping her next words wouldn't bring her tears back. "Your father would have loved it. He would have loved to see you here right now."

"I hope I can be everything he taught me to be," Darian replied.

A wide smile broke out on Makilien's face. "You will be. I know already you will be a great king."

Darian's eyes shown with gratitude. "Thank you for that faith in me."

"I also wanted to say," Makilien went on, "I expect my family will now call Eldor home, and you will have my loyalty always as my king."

"I am pleased to know you and your family will be here," Darian replied, heartfelt joy in his smile.

They paused for a moment, and Makilien watched his expression grow more serious.

"I'm sorry things are so difficult right now," he said. Shaking his head, he continued, "After all you've done for us, I hate to see you bear such sorrow."

Tears constricted Makilien's airway, and she waited for the moment to pass, slowly letting out her breath and clearing her throat. "Thank you . . . I am trying so hard to hold on to hope."

Darian placed his hands on her shoulders. "If there is anything you need, ever, all you need do is ask, all right? I'll do whatever I can to help."

Makilien nodded and thanked him again. She turned to let others have their opportunity to speak to him, but Darian stopped her for a moment more.

"I would like to speak to you and Aedan when I am finished. If you are not too weary, would you stay until I have had a chance to finish speaking with everyone?"

"Of course."

During the time that followed, Makilien stood off to the side, praying silently. She had so much to pray for and her heart hurt so deeply, but she wanted to be able to remain strong today. It wouldn't do to have come this far and then break down. After all, Darian was mourning the loss of both his father and some of his friends while having to be a leader to the people. She couldn't imagine it, and admired him all the more for it.

When the king had finally finished, the room cleared until only Makilien and Aedan were left standing in his presence. Together, they faced him.

"What would you like to speak with us about, my lord?" Aedan asked.

"Darian, please," he told them. "We are friends and always will be. I don't require the use of titles among friends." He came closer. "What I wanted to do is to thank you both as king. Aedan, I have not had the opportunity to thank you for your part in our victory when all hope was lost. I know neither you nor Makilien care for elaborate ceremonies or celebrations in your honor, so accept this now from me personally by way of thanks."

He held out his hand. In his palm lay a silver ring set with a blue stone just like the one Makilien had been given and Halandor, Torick, and Nirgon wore.

Aedan shook his head. "I hardly feel I deserve this."

"And that is why you do. True heroes don't go looking for glory. They are led by Elohim," Darian said, and he put the ring on Aedan's finger.

"Thank you," Aedan replied. "I am greatly honored."

Darian smiled and looked between him and Makilien. "You've both done great service to this country. I spoke to the sculptors early this morning. They are going to begin a statue of my father for the King's Hall. I've also instructed them to create one for each of you."

Makilien and Aedan's eyes widened as they looked to each other in wonder and then back to their king.

"That is far more than necessary," Makilien spoke for both of them. "We only did what we had to at the time."

"I understand your feelings, but I must insist. The Hall is to remember those who Elohim used to most influence the events of our history. He has worked extraordinary miracles through the two of you, and I don't believe that should be forgotten."

"I only have one request then," Aedan said.

"What is that?" Darian asked.

"I ask that a statue also be made for Arphen. Had he not sacrificed his life, Zirtan would have killed me. Victory would not have been possible without him."

Darian nodded. "Of course. I will inform the sculptors."

With these words, the three of them left the throne room. It was still early in the day, and a celebration meal awaited them.

:Chapter Forty-four:

A Time to Trust

"We're not going to find him, are we?" the words slipped out of Makilien's mouth before she realized she had spoken them.

She looked at her friends gathered in the throne room and held her breath. Their faces fell, and a sickening dread twisted her stomach, creeping like ice along her skin. Halandor's expression was hesitant, tears already gathering in his eyes.

He stepped closer and took hold of Makilien's shoulders. Looking her in the eyes, he spoke with the deepest regret mixed in with his own sorrow. "It's been a week. We've searched everywhere . . . Sirion is not among the wounded."

It was as if she'd been struck with a cold, cruel dagger. Numbing cold gripped her body. Her lungs wouldn't allow her to draw breath, and her knees lost strength. She would have collapsed if Halandor had not held her up.

"No!" The strangled cry broke free, and she fell into Halandor's arms, sobbing against his chest. But the more she cried, the more the crushing pain intensified. Sirion was gone. No matter how hard she cried, no matter how hard she prayed, she could not bring him back. He was *gone*.

Halandor held her tightly as she trembled against him, desperate for a way to ease her sorrow. Tears fell from his eyes, and as his gaze swept the room, he saw the pain of the others, particularly Lord Glorlad. The Elf lord wept openly. Elnauhir was there to console him, his eyes moist. Elandir and Elmorhirian stood side by side, both shedding tears, and Lorelyn and Vonawyn embraced as they cried. The rest were at various stages of grief, dealing with the sorrow in their own ways, but no one's pain hurt Halandor like Makilien's.

She cried harder than she ever had before, consumed with an emotional pain more terrible than any physical pain she could have endured. She so desperately needed comfort, but at the same time, she had to figure out how to cope with it on her own. Pulling away from Halandor, she fled the room, leaving her friends behind, stumbling through the palace with no sense of direction, vision blurred and mind too overwhelmed to give any thought to where she was. Finally, overcome, she stopped in an empty hall. Falling back against a pillar with a sob, she slid down and buried her face in her hands, her mournful cries echoing on the silent granite surrounding her.

"Oh, Elohim, why?" she cried in agony.

Her body shook with the intensity of the sorrow and the deep, unbearable pain of loss, her shoulders heaving with every wrenching sob.

"Help me, Elohim, help me," she pleaded, desperate for something to dull the anguish.

The flood of sorrow was so intense and suffocating, she thought it might consume her, and at the moment, she didn't care, the hurt was so great. She would have done anything to bring Sirion back. If only they hadn't been separated on the battlefield. She gasped for breath between sobs, crushed by the weight of loss. She could not imagine life after this.

Whether minutes or hours passed in that painful blur, Makilien didn't know nor care until someone touched her arm. With effort, she raised her head. Through her tear-blurred eyes, she recognized her best friend.

"Aedan," she whimpered, and put her arm around him.

"I am so sorry, Makilien," he said, his voice rough with emotion as he held her close.

She squeezed her eyes shut again, trying desperately to shut out everything, including the pain.

"Why did he have to die?" she gasped. "Why him and not me?"

"Because Elohim still has plans for you here." Aedan drew in a deep breath, fighting his own sorrow. It was intensely difficult to see her so devastated, but he had to remain strong for her as he always had been. "I wish I could do something to change what has happened. I'd do anything to take away your pain."

She cried quietly into his shoulder, letting herself find some comfort in her friend as she had as a child.

"I wish I could understand this," she whispered.

"I know."

For a long time they sat there as Makilien poured out her sorrow in memories and questions, Aedan offering whatever words of comfort he could manage. She had cried until there was nothing left but little hitching sobs. Finally, he helped her up and brought her upstairs to her family.

Hanna immediately embraced her daughter. Makilien clung to her mother like a lifeline, Hanna's soft voice soothing her heart. Leiya's small arms wrapped tight around her waist, and her father's hand rested on her back as they all offered her love and comfort.

Makilien stayed with them in her room for what hours remained of the day. She passed on both lunch and supper. As evening descended, her weariness overtook her, and sorrow mounted again. Soon the walls of her bedroom closed in on her, and she couldn't even find comfort in her family. Barely holding back her tears, she rose from the couch where she'd been sitting with her mother.

"I need to get out," she gasped, heading for the door.

Hanna rose with her. "Do you want one of us to go with you?"

Makilien looked back at her, eyes full of such sorrow her family thought they might never forget it. "I just need time."

Hanna bit her lip and nodded slowly.

Makilien hurried from the room. She did not know where to go, but when she came to the balcony, she ran out to it, gripping the railing so hard her knuckles whitened and gulping in the fresh air. The sky had darkened overhead, but the horizon was still a little pink. As she looked out across the city to the battlefield, the enormity of what they had suffered overcame her. The last hours had seemed like a horrible dream, but reality crashed in. This was not a dream. She would not wake up from it.

Stumbling away from the railing, she sank down on a nearby stone bench and sobbed again. Memories of Sirion flickered in her mind, fueling the sorrow and her tears. She hugged her knees up against her chest and rocked slowly, wondering if life could ever be normal again.

Her tears eventually subsided, and the moon was high in the night sky when she heard someone join her. She glanced to the door. Torick crutched toward her and eased himself down on the bench. He gave a long sigh and did not say anything at first. Makilien waited, but she didn't think anything anyone could say would help with the grief.

"I've lost a lot of friends in my time . . . but there is no pain like that of losing the person you love," Torick said at last.

Makilien tried to swallow down the lump in her throat, and new tear trails glistened in the moonlight.

"When you give a large part of your heart to someone, it feels like that part has died with them."

"Yes," Makilien choked. She turned watery eyes to Torick. "You know?"

Torick nodded with deep understanding.

"Yes, I know."

"How?"

Torick leaned back, sighing again as he glanced up at the sky. He then looked back to Makilien. "Because I lost the woman I loved . . . the woman I was going to marry."

Makilien was stunned. Torick had never shared much about his life, certainly not something so personal and painful.

"Idie," he went on, saying the name lovingly, his expression tender and longing. "The loveliest, kindest, and most gentle woman I'd ever met. I don't know what she saw in me, but she loved me, and oh how I loved her. I loved her with all my heart."

Torick paused, his voice thick. Tears glittered in his eyes. "We were going to be married in a week. She and her two younger sisters went out to the forest to gather berries and herbs as they often did." There was a tremor in his voice and it broke. "That day they came upon a bear with cubs. The bear was startled and attacked. Idie sacrificed herself to protect her sisters. By the time I got to her, it was too late. No one could do anything to save her."

Tears leaked from Makilien's eyes. "I am so sorry, Torick."

He nodded slowly. "So am I."

"What did you do?" Makilien asked, desperate for something, anything to help. "How did you deal with the pain?"

Torick stared out past the balcony for a long moment, regret in his eyes. "I became bitter. I questioned why Elohim would let something so cruel and seemingly unnecessary happen to Idie, and I soon turned my back on Him. I secluded myself away from everyone. I felt no one could understand my pain and that being near them would only make me feel worse."

Makilien too stared out into the night, an awful realization dawning that the same feelings Torick had experienced had been trying to creep into her heart. She hugged her arms around herself, unaware of any pain from her shoulder, silent tears of sadness and regret rolling down and dripping off her chin to soak into the fabric of her dress.

Finally, Torick looked at her, and Makilien met his serious, but compassionate eyes. "Don't become bitter, Makilien. You may never understand Sirion's death, but it does fit into Elohim's plans. On your own, the pain is unbearable, but Elohim will give you strength to bear it. Don't turn away from Him."

Makilien squeezed her eyes shut for a moment, saying a desperate prayer. "How did you turn back to Him?"

"Halandor finally helped me to see what I was doing was only hurting me. Don't turn away from those around you either. Your family and friends, we all want to help you and give you comfort. Don't try to bear the sorrow on your own."

Torick's words did more for Makilien than she could ever tell him. Covering her face with her hands, she cried heavily again. Torick put his arm around her and hugged her close as she let her sorrow drain.

"Does the pain ever go away?" she asked at last.

"Your heart will always bear a certain ache, but in time, you will heal and joy will return to your days. You'll be able to look back on the time you spent with Sirion and cherish it. Eventually, you'll be able to live your life without the pain affecting every day. Elohim will heal you. Take comfort in Him."

Makilien nodded. In a broken voice, she asked, "Was there ever anyone after Idie?"

Letting out a sigh, Torick shook his head. "No. She was the only one."

Makilien drew in a shaky breath. This would be her too, she decided. There could never be anyone but Sirion. It just wasn't possible.

Sensing her thoughts, Torick said gently, "You're very young, Makilien. I know you can't possibly consider it now, but don't give up on love completely. Only Elohim can see what lies ahead of us."

Makilien opened her stinging eyes and slowly pushed herself up, her body weighted down by the exhaustion of an almost sleepless night. Her head throbbed, and coldness crept along her skin despite the summer warmth. The light of dawn shown from her balcony door. A new day. The first of those she would now wake up to knowing Sirion was gone. How she prayed Torick was right and someday the pain wouldn't be so great.

She slipped out of bed, but when her feet touched the floor, she went no farther. Her tears were spent, but she cried inside. Cried over her memories and what could have been.

This was how her mother found her—just standing, red-rimmed eyes staring off at nothing. She came to her daughter's side and gently touched her shoulder. Makilien blinked and looked into her mother's concerned face.

"Will you help me get dressed?"

Tears pooled in Hanna's eyes. The emotionless words hardly sounded like Makilien. It killed her to see her daughter in such a state—utterly defeated, her fighting spirit gone.

"Of course."

She helped Makilien change into a dress and braided her hair. When she finished, Makilien turned to face her, the smallest ember of hope in her eyes fighting to survive.

"I need to go for a walk . . . outside the city."

"That is quite a ways to go," Hanna said with concern. "Will you let me go with you?"

Makilien said nothing, but nodded.

Together they left her room. They met no one except the palace guards who wordlessly let them out. Outside the palace courtyard, they passed through the quiet city. They said nothing, but to be outdoors helped Makilien, the fresh air filling her lungs and clearing her head. Along the way, they passed people here and there. Makilien looked into the faces of the women, catching the hopeless expressions of those who had suffered loss. She had never liked to imagine what it would be like to be one of them, but now she was. One of the grieving.

Finally, they arrived outside the city gate, and Makilien turned west. They walked on a ways until they came to a little hill overlooking the meadow and stopped.

"This is where Meniah tended the sheep," Makilien said, breaking the silence that had followed them from the palace. She turned to her mother. "Can I go on a little ways alone?"

Hanna nodded. "I'll wait for you here."

Makilien walked down into the meadow. The lush grass brushed against her dress and white flowers swayed before her, their beauty the opposite of the devastation just over the hill. Soon she came to one of the large stones from the mountains and knew it was where she had seen Meniah after battle and learned who he truly was. She sat down, her emotions building.

"I wish I could see You," she murmured. "I know You are here and that You can hear me, but I wish I could see You."

Tears came and rolled down her cheeks.

"I don't want to be bitter, and I don't want to question You. I just miss Sirion so much already. I wish I could understand why it was his time." Makilien paused, weeping softly. "Please help me. I don't think I can bear this. I don't want it to destroy me."

A warm, soft breeze rippled the meadow and brushed Makilien's face. With it, she could almost hear Meniah's voice, kind and gentle as she always remembered it.

Trust me.

Makilien cried a little harder.

Trust me.

Slowly, she nodded. "I do."

She wiped her hands across her face and thought of Aedan's answer when she'd asked why she was still alive and not Sirion. Drawing in a breath, she closed her eyes and said in a trembling voice, "My heart is broken, but I will trust You, and I will serve You. What is it You would now have me do?"

:Epilogue:

Stars dotted the night sky, twinkling against an almost black backdrop. The cold, silvery moon shown down, offering more light than the dying embers of the fire—just enough light to illuminate the battered body and glint in the dark eyes studying it.

"Will he live?"

The grim voice was as cold as the moon overhead and void of any true concern beyond that of his own gain.

Brushing back his long hair, the other man glanced over his shoulder, but his eyes settled again on the labored rise and fall of the wounded man's bandaged chest. Absently, he fingered the edge of his black, Elven-like vambraces.

"I don't know. Only time will tell."

Map & Guides

Northern Wilds
(Goblin Territory)

Aldûlir

Reylaun

Andin

Carel

Eldinorieth

:N:

W   E

S

Pronunciation

NAME	PRONUNCIATION
Aedan	Ay - dan
Aldûlir	Al - doo - leer
Althilion	Al - thil - ee - on
Antiro	An - teer - oh
Arphen	Ahr - fen
Baltar	Bal - tahr
Carmine	Cahr - mine
Darand	Dahr - and
Darian	Dahr - ee - an
Demera	De - mayr - a
Derrin	Dayr - in
Dolennar	Doh - len - nahr
Eborin	E - bohr - in
Elandir	E - lan - deer
Eldinorieth	El - di - nohr - ee - eth
Elimar	E - li - mahr
Elmorhirian	El - mohr - heer - ee - an
Elnauhir	El - nah - heer
Elohim	Ee - loh - heem
Emaril	E - mah - ril
Eredan	Ayr - e - dan
Falene	Fa - leen
Gébrale	Gay - brayl
Gilhir	Gil - heer
Halandor	Ha - lan - dohr
Idie	Ī - dee
Indiya	In - dee - yuh

Irrin	Ī - rin
Jorin	Johr - in
Laena	Lay - nuh
Leiya	Lee - yuh
Lokye	Loh - kī
Lorelyn	Lohr - e - lin
Loron	Lohr - on
Makilien	Ma - kil - ee - en
Malachi	Ma - luh - kī
Meniah	Me - nī - uh
Minarald	Mi - nahr - ald
Néthyn	Nay - thin
Nirgon	Neer - gon
Reylaun	Ray - lahn
Rhûnland	Roon - land
Rommia	Ro - mee - ah
Saras	Sahr - uhs
Shaike	Shayk
Sirion	Seer - ee - on
Torick	Tohr - ick
Tôr	Tohr
Vayzar	Vay - zahr
Vonawyn	Vah - nah - win
Vyl	Vil
Wythel	Wī - thel
Zirtan	Zeer - tan

Character Guide

Aedan - Makilien's best friend from Reylaun.

Andron - Young king of Beldon.

Antiro - Makilien's black horse who can understand Human language.

Arphen - A male griffon and leader of the griffons serving Eldor.

Baltar - The founder of Eldor.

Carmine - A red male dragon. The oldest surviving in Eldor.

Darand - The king of Eldor.

Darian - Son of King Darand and prince of Eldor.

Demera - Younger sister of Gébrale and daughter of the former king of Rhûnland.

Derrin - A young man from Reylaun who is in love with Makilien.

Eborin - A black male dragon. Leader of the dragons of the Irrin Mountains. Mate of Wythel.

Elandir - The oldest son of the Elf lord Elnauhir.

Elmorhirian - The youngest son of the Elf lord Elnauhir.

Elnauhir - The Elf lord of Elimar.

Emaril - A green male dragon. Mate of Indiya.

Eredan - General of Beldon's army and old friend of King Andron.

Gébrale - Captain of the people of Rhûnland and heir to the throne. Demera's older brother.

Gilhir - A high ranking Elf captain from Althilion.

Glorlad - The Elf lord of Althilion and uncle of Sirion.

Gorgon - Cruel Shaike captain.

Gornath - A spy of Zirtan who nearly killed Makilien and Darian.

Halandor - A Half-Elf man of Eldor. Close friend and mentor of Makilien.

Hanna - Mother of Makilien.

Indiya - A blue female dragon. Mate of Emaril.

Jaeson - Father of Aedan.

Jorin - Younger brother of Zendon.

Laena - Kind shopkeeper in Andin.

Leiya - Makilien's younger sister.

Lorelyn - Wife of the Elf lord Elnauhir.

Loron - An Elf of Elimar and close friend of Makilien and Halandor.

Makilien - A young woman of Reylaun who killed Zendon.

Malachi - A dark green male dragon from the Irrin Mountains. Old friend of Carmine.

Meniah - Son of Elohim who gave his life for the people.

Néthyn - Father of Makilien.

Nirgon - General of Eldor's army.

Rindal - Grouchy innkeeper of the Black Stag.

Rommia - Aedan's younger sister.

Sirion - Half-Elf from Althilion. Nephew of the Elf lord Glorlad.

Tanzim - A Shaike formerly in service to Zirtan.

Tôr - A male griffon and close friend of Arphen. Brother of Vyl.

Torick - A man of Eldor and close friend of Makilien and Halandor.

Vayzar - Zirtan's appointed governor of Reylaun and bitter enemy of Makilien.

Vonawyn - Daughter of the Elf lord Elnauhir.

Vyl - A female griffon and close friend of Arphen. Sister of Tôr.

Wythel - A white female dragon. Mate of Eborin.

Zendon - Zirtan's general who Makilien killed in battle. Older brother of Jorin.

Zirtan - Evil ruler trying to gain control of Dolennar.

BOOKS BY MOLLY EVANGELINE

Makilien Trilogy
Truth
Courage
Trust (Coming Soon)

Pirates & Faith
The Pirate Daughter's Promise
Every Tear
A Captain's Heart
Finding Faith

Made in the USA
Lexington, KY
03 December 2015